T0051417

I SAT
ALONE BY
THE GATE

a novel

I SAT ALONE BY THE GATE

MARY EFENDI

GREENLEAF
BOOK GROUP PRESS

This book is a work of fiction. Names, characters, businesses, organizations, places, events, and incidents are either a product of the author's imagination or are used fictitiously. Any resemblance to actual persons, living or dead, events, or locales is entirely coincidental.

Published by Greenleaf Book Group Press
Austin, Texas
www.gbgpress.com

Copyright © 2023 Mehriban Efendi

All rights reserved.

Thank you for purchasing an authorized edition of this book and for complying with copyright law. No part of this book may be reproduced, stored in a retrieval system, or transmitted by any means, electronic, mechanical, photocopying, recording, or otherwise, without written permission from the copyright holder.

Distributed by Greenleaf Book Group

For ordering information or special discounts for bulk purchases, please contact Greenleaf Book Group at PO Box 91869, Austin, TX 78709, 512.891.6100.

Design and composition by Greenleaf Book Group
Cover design by Greenleaf Book Group
Cover Image: Islamic door and window vector silhouette; used under license from Shutterstock.com

Publisher's Cataloging-in-Publication data is available.

Print ISBN: 979-8-88645-050-7

eBook ISBN: 979-8-88645-051-4

To offset the number of trees consumed in the printing of our books, Greenleaf donates a portion of the proceeds from each printing to the Arbor Day Foundation. Greenleaf Book Group has replaced over 50,000 trees since 2007.

Printed in the United States of America on acid-free paper

23 24 25 26 27 28 29 30   10 9 8 7 6 5 4 3 2 1

First Edition

CONTENTS

CHAPTER 1

. . . .

DANCING BAREFOOT

Years later, I would come to realize that this was one of the happiest days of my life. My parents were dealing with visas and passports, piling paperwork on the red oak desk that took up most of my grandfather's office. But all I could think of were the goodbyes I would have to bid before we moved to America.

I had just turned eighteen. The summer heat was claiming the city of Baku, and now that my final school exams were over, I could take a deep breath at least in that regard. The exam-induced stress had robbed me of my appetite and had me refusing my grandmother's *qutabs*, *dolmas*, and beef stews. But now, it was replaced with a strange, satiating nostalgia for even the vilest of my teachers at school. Take my math instructor, a one-armed, blue-eyed, forever unsmiling tyrant who would preach that happiness could be found in nothing but work. He would often stare me down, hoping I'd fail the geometry problem in front of the entire class. I found myself missing the old man and suddenly thinking of him with fondness. And my friends! How I cherished their slightest humor, took in their every word, admiring their features and finding brilliance in their most ordinary traits. Life seemed so appropriate and calm—a straight road devoid of any twists or turns, populated by my dear, imperfect friends. However, that road was coming to an abrupt end. Without warning, my highway had hit an ocean and we were left staring at it without any idea of what to do.

It was the morning of my farewell party. We had agreed to meet at the Sahil Metro station, a few minutes' walk from my grandma's place, and board the minivan that my father was supposed to arrange. Even my brother, Rufat, who usually kept to his own company, yielded to the overwhelming emotions of parting and decided to join us. The three of us arrived at the entrance to the subway at ten a.m. to find that the rest of the group had been miraculously punctual. My friend Dilara, who was habitually late to everything, showed up on time, her picture-perfect cocker spaniel puppy squirming in her arms. The morning was bright and already congested with a strange olfactory mix of traffic fumes and cooked *shawarma* that wafted up from street-food vendors that sprouted up like mushrooms around Baku Metro stations. Seymour, a tall, redheaded school mate with a sharp, green-eyed stare, was holding bags of food—sweets, freshly baked bread, a box of white feta cheese, and bottles of soda.

"We can't go to the countryside and not have lamb kabob," Seymour said.

None of us had known how to marinate a lamb, so he'd volunteered for the task himself. Now, Seymour described for us how he had spent the evening before with his father—a broad-shouldered, mustached, retired colonel—spicing and marinating the lamb before carefully packing it into the cooler. The cooler stood beside him, promising a juicy delicacy of lamb kabobs. My friend Arif tossed a small, greenish-yellow watermelon from one hand to another, killing time. The Metro station was getting crowded, so we were all eager for the minivan to arrive so we could get on with our trip. The minivan didn't show up, but I soon noticed my father approaching us, his clothes slightly disheveled, his long hair in a ponytail, and a familiar, alcohol-induced tremble in his voice. Somehow, alcohol always pulled the rug out from underneath our steady lives. Birthdays would be cancelled, and visits postponed. A minivan rented in advance would simply not arrive. *I wish I was surprised,* I thought.

Nevertheless, I felt panic rise inside of me. I was embarrassed and angry but did my best to keep it under the surface. *Just a few more days and you don't have to deal with it. Just one more party to cancel,* I thought. I didn't know much about the country we were moving to, but I knew I wouldn't have to deal with this anymore, so that was one good thing about it.

At first it seemed like calling off the farewell party altogether was the only way to avoid causing a scene. But events took an unexpected turn when Adele, Arif's mother, turned around, made a loud joke, and grabbed my father by the arm, whispering something into his ear. I've always admired Adele. I loved her tall, relaxed figure, her feminine lines, and her perfectly shaped eyebrows. She wore a loose cotton button-down shirt and light blue capris—always so stylish. I can't recall what she said or did, but fifteen minutes later, we all boarded a small minivan with our bags and Seymour's cooler of lamb kabobs, joking around and singing popular songs. Adele sat in the back row and conducted our chaotic choir. My mother chose not to join us.

"Maryam, with all the things we need to finish, do we really need this trip to Arif's summer house?" my mother had asked me shortly before the minivan departed.

I knew better than to argue with her. Mother would never give in if I begged and pleaded. With her, you had to keep quiet and weather the storm, and then if you were careful, you could do things your way. If you didn't object to what she said, Mother would move on to something else and you could get away with stuff.

We left the bustling city, and the minivan struggled to adapt to the rocky roads of Baku suburbia. Gradually, there were fewer fancy cars and grocery stores and roadside kiosks selling refreshing drinks, cigarettes, and newspapers. Once in a while, we'd see an empty field with patches of sunburnt grass and a cow or two. This rural setting was just a half-hour's drive from a crowded city of mixed architecture, rush-hour traffic, and modern hotels side-by-side with the minarets of mosques. Mickey, the puppy that Dilara had gotten for her last birthday, paced the minivan, yelping at the singing crowd before eventually giving up and curling up in her lap. A small, gold-rimmed ornament with a picture of a boy not older than four dangled from the minivan's rearview mirror. I caught a faint, kind smile from the wrinkled old man in the driver seat.

We entered Mardakan, a seaside village that Bakuvians retreated to during the summer to take a break from the city life. I recognized the familiar labyrinth of uneven asphalt streets with tall brick fences painted a phosphorus-white, with occasional blue or green gates hiding the houses, pools, and fig trees that stood behind the fences. Outside, one could see nothing but an uneven brick wall, while inside, families gathered over meals. The minivan slowed and through the window I heard the loud slapping of the stones against a backgammon board and the buzz of a radio in someone's garden. My favorite season for the summer retreat was here. If we were not planning to move away, we'd be packing for Mardakan to spend the summer with Nana.

Arif's summer house was on top of a hill, surrounded by shrub-covered cliffs and a bay hugging it from three sides. The house blended with the arid landscape, harmonious with its sparse vegetation, brown rocks, and thinning clouds almost touching the roof. We were greeted by an elderly couple who kept up the property and tended to a large garden behind the house. They carried the bags with food to the kitchen and led us to the living room to cool off after the long drive. The puppy scurried past us, scrambling over the slippery floor and scaring the plump cat lounging on a faded orange wingback armchair. The walls were a mosaic of gray and pink stones with floating shelves lined with dusty books. There were a few pill vials on the countertop. A stone fireplace stood at the center of the living room, decorated with a set of clay vases full of dry herbs and flowers. A bright red kilim rug hung above it, serving as the center-piece of this eclectic room.

"This place looks cool now, but the summers here felt like exile," said Arif. "There was literally nothing to do, no one to play with," he continued. "Except maybe for this cat."

"I'm sorry, Arif, that sounds so sad. We were very lucky to have other kids in our neighborhood," I replied. "I spent most summers with two sisters who lived in the house next door, and a boy named Emin. We'd play, quarrel, make up, and repeat it all again the next day. A few weeks into the summer, I'd get used to the hot sand of Mardakan and ditch my sandals. I'd always leave them somewhere in the yard and Mother would send Rufat to go find them."

"No wonder he hated you as a child!" Arif said. "Fetching sandals in the heat?"

"Don't pity him," I replied. "He'd get ice-cream money for it. Anyways, one of the girls was my age and we got along pretty well. In fact, she's the one who taught me Azeri. I didn't speak a word when I arrived, and she didn't understand Russian. By the end of the summer, we swapped languages like that and, guess what? She went to Russian school, and I went to Azeri school. No way I would have passed the exam if not for her."

"Oh wow, that's so cool!" Arif said.

"It was really lucky for us both that we found each other. Her younger sister was such a little brat, honestly. We both couldn't stand her. She had no one her age to play with, so her entertainment was ruining our days. She'd break our toys, tell on us, torture the cat, you name it! She told everyone I had a crush on the neighbor kid. I mean, I did have a crush on him, but she was just out of control."

"How old were you?" Arif asked.

"Old enough to have a crush." I winked. "I don't know. Twelve? Old enough to steal apricots from his yard, too."

"You stole apricots from his yard?" Arif exclaimed. "You never told me this story! I can't imagine you pulling this off. Really?"

"I did pull it off," I responded. "We didn't have much to do there. In absence of any other entertainment, I came up with a plan to steal apricots from the neighbors' yard. My friend was bigger than me, so her task was to keep an eye as I squeezed through a breach in the fence into their garden. The apricots were not ripe, and his grandpa caught me right away. I was a good planner, but a lousy thief."

"What did he do?" Seymour joined our conversation, rolling up his sleeves to get started with the lamb.

Seymour had a large steel pot and a pack of skewers with ornamented wooden grips in his hands. He began working his lamb-kabob magic as I continued.

"Nothing. He led me to the house and gave me a bowl of ripe apricots and made me introduce myself to the entire family. I didn't care so much about the damned apricots. We were after some type of adventure, that's all."

"That's the problem!" Arif said. "Time just drags during these summer retreats. No TV, no friends, nothing to do here!"

By now the kitchen was a world full of the magical clanking of pots and pans—the delicious sounds of food being prepared. The elderly lady who had greeted us walked in with freshly picked tomatoes, cucumbers, and a bunch of purple basil. Arif grabbed two glasses, filled them up from a large blue canister, and handed them to me and Seymour.

"Water from the spring!" he said. "Just kidding, there is no spring. We have to get water delivered here weekly."

Dilara's puppy made a clumsy turn around the hallways and jumped outside where Rufat, Dilara, and my cousin were gathering.

Our table was set up in the garden, under the mulberry tree spreading its branches into a generous shade, shielding us from the dry heat of the Absheron desert. A gentle breeze ruffled the leaves. I could smell the fresh aroma of chopped vegetables laid out like a mosaic on the makeshift wooden table.

Seymour, being the oldest, assumed the role of passing out the bowls of salad, fresh tomatoes and cucumbers sprinkled with oil and vinegar. While we helped ourselves to the salad, Arif took the bowl of roasted eggplants and placed it in front of himself. It wouldn't take much to notice his obsession with all things eggplant: eggplant rolls with walnut stuffing; eggplants Georgian style; eggplant caviar either warm or cold; eggplant dolmas stuffed with ground beef, fried onions, turmeric, and cinnamon. The teenage obsession with fast-food meals of crispy fries, Big Macs, or Kentucky Fried Chicken that was making its way into the post-Soviet world had left Arif unmoved. He stuck to his eggplants. No one else liked eggplants, anyway. It was the type of food you hated as a child and *might* happen to love later.

We drank tea from *armudi* glasses, ate dried fruits and preserves, and polished off the crunchy cardamom pastries that Dilara's mom had baked the night before. Dilara, the only one who didn't touch the pastries, was busy recalling the latest debate tournament, which had ended in a complete fiasco for our team.

"That debate tournament was a disaster," Dilara said. "The only success was that all the judges were cute and some of us flirted around with them. But the last debate against the team made up of nerds was the worst. I mean, they knew their stuff, but their delivery was so *lifeless*, you wondered if you were watching a mummy recite a speech. We didn't know shit, but at least we were alive! We lost anyways, but not without shocking everyone when *your grandmother*," she gestured to Rufat and me, "decided the judge was wrong and got up from her chair to object! She just gets up and starts making her case to the judge, talking right over Musa—that medical student with the curly hair and tiny glasses—who was trying his best not to cry. What a way to end the tournament!" Dilara burst into laughter.

Rufat reached for another piece of the pastry. Dilara was a good storyteller, her eyes shining, lips pursed and glistening. Her entire body, even her bouncing, light brown curls, engaged all who were listening as she started to recount another story.

When all the food was finished, we went down to the rocky beach, took pictures, and waded knee deep into the cold Caspian waters, avoiding the rocks and looking out for tiny white fish. Rufat took a dip, emerging from the water immediately, shivering and cursing the cold. He ran up the stairs to grab towels and didn't return.

Surrounded by friends and family, I felt a sadness creep upon me. So, I escaped the crowd and went to explore the ancient-looking summer house, which I knew had been built by Arif's great-grandfather, a prominent banker back in the day. The entrance of the house led to a round auditorium with a tall ceiling and a sunroof. The stone walls were decorated with faded oil paintings, as well as figurines that had been made by Adele during her seclusion after divorcing Arif's father. Her artwork was playful and elegant, predominantly shades of blue and gray with splashes of red and yellow.

I drifted into daydreaming as I studied these objects in silence but was brought back to the present by a sharp look from the plump cat, which was now lounging on the sofa among the worn red and blue cushions. She slowly rose on all fours, stretched her back, and jumped off the sofa, inviting me to follow her. I obliged, following the cat as she went down the hall and then up the stairs, where the bedrooms and private quarters were. The house was empty, and I felt brave enough to proceed, knowing I had the excuse of the cat. I walked into the first bedroom in the hallway. It had two large windows overlooking the sea, birch furniture, and a large vanity mirror with photos of the family tucked into the sides of the frame. I pulled out a photo of Adele with Arif. He must have been seven or eight in it. I was tucking the picture back into the mirror when I suddenly heard someone enter the room.

"So . . . you're leaving tomorrow?" Arif asked as he walked into the bedroom and approached the mirror.

I wanted to say something cheerful, but my mother had decided we would move to another continent with no plans to come back. No one asked me or Rufat if we wanted to go, but why would that surprise me? No one ever asked us anything. I felt no different than a trinket, to be packed into a suitcase and taken across the ocean for the hope of a better life. If anybody had asked, I'd tell them that I foresaw nothing in this move to America but a painful and instantaneous separation from everything and everyone I loved. Arif put his arm around my shoulder and pulled me closer. We stood there, the sides of our faces touching, waiting for this moment to pass, a bit startled with the sudden wave of emotions, but happy that nothing disturbed the silence.

The evening was an ordinary one, filled with familiar jokes and loud music, some dancing and singing. All the sadness associated with our leaving was covered up with hopeful plans of a reunion somewhere across the globe. There were loud laughs, but barely any smiles. At last, the party was over, and we were all back in the old minivan, tired yet still loud and lively. Arif sat next to me, looking out the window, his baseball cap pulled down, absent and quiet. He held my hand in the dark for the rest of the drive, occasionally throwing me a heavy look before looking away, into the streetlights illuminating the highway. The chatter in the minivan died down when we entered the city. I closed my eyes and imagined a perfect setting, me and Arif dancing barefoot on the rocky shores of Mardakan, silent and happy.

CHAPTER 2

. . . .

THINGS WE TAKE WITH US

A few hours before our departure, my grandmother was busy rear-ranging our suitcases, looking around in search of something special that she could still pack into our future. I sat across from her in my late grandfather's rosewood armchair and watched her swift move-ments, lifting folded sweaters and wrapping them around vases, saucers, and other crockery that I doubted we needed. Her auburn hair, woven into two braids, fell cheerfully across her broad shoul-ders. The warm, pink light of a tasseled floor lamp added color to her cheeks, a color she would often don during bouts of high blood pressure, which happened a lot lately.

I did not want to disturb her. I knew too well that busying her-self with work had been her refuge for years. My grandmother had turned to it during my father's alcohol binges and financial fiascos, and also during my mother's stints of depression that followed. She produced batches of pastries, pots of vegetable stews, and fruit pre-serves, canning them with her iron clamp and jar sealer and lining the tall built-in kitchen cabinet with them. There stood her testament, a gallery of her work, inspired by her children's deficiencies—colorful, delicious witnesses stuffed with pain and defeat. Perhaps channeling her stress into producing these canned goods was the reason why her face had been spared the wear and tear of these trying years. Her eyes still glistened with some unfounded faith that the future would hold something better for all of us.

Named after a perfume, Aida, or "Nana" as we called her, accompanied my grandfather to different countries throughout his mysterious KGB career and carried memories of each like decorations on her shoulders, recounting them as legends full of heroes, magic, and luck. She'd talk about the beauty of the Taj Mahal and the Dwarkadhish Temple, called the Monkey Temple because of carved figures of monkeys indulging in bananas on the front. She'd complain about the unbearable humidity of Bombay, melting sugar cubes into water in the summer, and the powerful rains of monsoons. She'd talk about receptions she attended in Bombay country clubs, one of them being the place where she'd first held a cigarette in a slender tube and chatted with the famous Raj Kapoor over a glass of red wine.

I knew that this goodbye would be hard on her and could foresee the blank stare she would have after seeing us off at the airport. I could almost hear that mute cry and the slow tears and the mindless cooking and cleaning she would do in search of relief.

My father did not drink on the day of our departure, but his shoulders seemed heavy with either regret or guilt, which he concealed under his exaggerated excitement over our departure, as if he planned to join us eventually.

"Think we'll settle in Chicago or move to New York," he said. "I always thought I'd end up in New York eventually. What do you guys think?" We smiled and nodded.

My parents were divorced, their conversations strictly limited to obtaining the necessary immigration documents, and even though we played along with their staged friendliness, Rufat and I both knew our father would not be joining us. I wished this knowledge didn't inspire relief in me, but it did.

When the clock struck one a.m., he loaded our suitcases into the trunk of his Mercedes, and we left for the airport. Baku resembled a fine European city at night, with the swaying of the maple leaves against the rows of intricate balcony railings, the slender coniferous trees along the boulevard, and the face of the moon reflecting on the water. I rolled down the window and felt the humid air caress my face, wondering if the sky would be as distant and the air as gentle on the other side of the world.

We made a left, and in the dark I saw my high school with the newly painted door and tall columns on each side, the windows with prehistoric air conditioners sticking out, the folds of the drapes in the window frames, and the chimney rising all the way to the triangular roof. I wanted to single out the window of our classroom, but the road was clear, and the car sped off before I could find it. I sighed at the memory of this busy but blissful year, surrounded by strict yet well-meaning teachers, with their old-fashioned spectacles, heavy handbags, familiar jokes, and cynicism in their eyes.

At the airport, waiting for us, was a group of people who had come to say goodbye. I saw a few of our neighbors encircle my mother, asking questions and not waiting for answers, their red-rimmed eyes moist and anxious. I saw my mother's maternal uncle, Eldar, a famous soccer referee nicknamed "the Elephant" because of his larger-than-life personality and, of course, his very big nose. Ever since Mother's parents had passed away, Eldar had become a father figure, someone who'd been there for Mother when things got rough, and things had kept getting rougher in the past few years, so we saw a lot of Eldar. She seemed calm now, standing next to him, but during the last week, I would often find her sitting by the open window, smoking a cigarette, looking lost.

The night before our departure, I woke up to find her sitting by my bed, looking distressed.

"Is everything okay?" I asked.

"Can you tell me that everything will be all right?" Mother asked, her slumped body surrendering to a strange weakness, leaning on me in a way that she never had.

"Yes, Mama, everything will most certainly be all right. Don't you worry about it," I repeated almost hypnotically, pronouncing the words slowly, carefully, like a spell. I did not know what to make of these moments of weakness, so I played my part, reassuring her, even though I was afraid of what was to become of us overseas.

"Mama," I began, "why do we have to leave Baku? Why can't we stay?"

"There is nothing for us here, Maryam. We sold the house to get your father out of prison. I had to sell my car. We've talked about this, haven't we?" she replied.

"But we also don't have anything there! How can you be so sure that it will be better?" I argued.

"We have a chance to build a new life there. You'll go to school. I'll learn the language—"

"I like our life here," I interrupted. "I don't want to leave."

"Maryam," she said, her tone now cold and distant, "we are leaving tomorrow. There is no point in discussing this. You should sleep."

She got up to turn off the light. It was always Mother's decision when the conversation ended, leaving no room for dialogue, creating a widening rift between us that would stretch into the future.

As our flight's departure hour came closer, the euphoria died down, replaced by last-minute concerns about passports, visas, baggage receipts, and instructions on how not to get lost in Frankfurt. Out by the entrance to the airport, I saw the silhouette of my father. His eyes were reddish and weary from lack of sleep, his whole body leaning on the wall and his hands in his pockets. He wore an off-white polo with light gray pants and blue loafers. He kept away from the crowd of loved ones surrounding us.

At last, my father took his calloused hands out of his pockets and approached Rufat and me. He kneeled down and I found myself looking at his face, his oily black hair, the nose he inherited from my grandmother, his prominent forehead, and the deep melancholy in his expression. He held us in his embrace and time stopped for a moment. I wished that I had felt something clean—the kind of feeling a child should feel when separating from a parent—but it was green and muddy, like water of a stagnant pond. Whatever I felt was flawed, corrupted by family arguments we had tried to drown out with the sound of the stereo, the ominous clanking of his whiskey glass, and my mother's quiet sobbing at night.

Still, I cherished the familiar scent of his cigarettes and cologne, the overwhelming presence of his long, wavy hair, and even the tired slump in his shoulders. He got up from his knees and walked us to our mother, and we approached the passport control. Somewhere in the distance, I could hear Nana's voice. I turned around for one final wave.

CHAPTER 3

. . . .

AIRPORT PEOPLE

The interim point between our past and future, the Frankfurt airport, greeted us with gloomy skies, light rain, and crowds of travelers rushing past. We spent five hours there, all three of us slightly cold in the chilly airport hallways, busy watching foreigners and waiting to board a flight to Chicago. A mother with three children caught my attention. She had ginger hair and wore an olive-green cashmere sweater on top of a plain white t-shirt. She was holding a toddler with almost-white hair, wearing an embroidered jacket buttoned all the way up. Her eldest son, probably seven, was pushing a cart with two gray suitcases and a bright blue backpack. Somehow, she also managed to push a stroller, where I guessed the newborn lay. The woman seemed in control of all three of her children, occasionally making sure the oldest one pushed the cart in the right direction, answering random questions from the toddler, and peeking in the stroller once in a while. The toddler with pale hair consumed all of my attention. Her skin was almost transparent, her marble-colored locks falling gracefully over her jacket, contrasting with the magenta, green, and orange of its embroidery.

I recalled seeing so many blond men and women during a two-week school trip to Bushey, a small town in the outskirts of London. I had been infatuated with the fairness of their skin, the intriguing transparency of their blue eyes, and the liquid texture of their blond hair. My sight, so unaccustomed to these features, could not get enough of them.

At the airport, the ginger-haired woman was looking for a section of the waiting area where they could all fit, but everything was taken. She looked around again and then simply sat on the bare floor. The whole family, including the toddler, was now sitting on the floor of the hall. I looked at Mother to check her reaction, but she had an absent look in her eyes and was probably upset that smoking was forbidden here. The toddler crawled closer to the glass window and climbed up a little to get a better look at the monumental airplane parked at the gate, while all this time not a word was uttered by the child's mother. She sat on the floor with her back against the wall, the newborn in her lap.

I thought of all the things my grandma would say if she learned I had ever sat on the floor in a public place. Cleanliness was the ultimate scale Nana used to rank people. In her world, there were two kinds of people: the neat people who made the world turn, and the messy people who deserved to live but who did not contribute to human progress. The realization that I belonged to this second group was a big disappointment for her. One fine afternoon, she caught me mindlessly pushing the vacuum back and forth across the floor with one hand, reading from a book I was holding in the other, which forced her to finally accept that her dear grandchild belonged to that unworthy group of messy people.

I felt cold from all the sitting but was too lazy to look for a jacket in my carry-on luggage. I was too involved in my spiderweb of thoughts, the recklessness of this young family, unaware of the danger posed by germs, and my grandmother's voice in my head. Suddenly, I felt something warm surround my shoulders. It was Mother. She had retrieved her yellow cable-knit sweater from the luggage and wrapped it around my shoulders. I let the gentle wool surround me from everywhere and sensed the warmth slowly rise inside of me, spreading all the way to my fingers and toes.

I suppose I must explain why we were headed to Chicago. My mother, tired of my father's never-ending financial and adulterous escapades, decided to marry her longtime friend Teymour. Similar to Mother, he felt completely cynical about marriage and was ready to enter it again only to rescue her from the endless cycle of hopes and disappointments. Teymour had traveled to Baku several times in the past few years, and I vaguely remembered Mother and him carefully reviewing stacks of paper and visiting relatives who held government posts with requests to expedite this and that about the immigration process.

The prospect of immigrating seemed so lengthy, not to mention legally complicated and improbable, that we hardly paid any attention to it. Teymour and Mother had been equally disappointed in unions that originated in romance. They'd seen their share of feelings that faded, wives and husbands who faded almost as quickly as the feelings. They had spent long hours on the phone confiding in each other, tending to each other's broken hearts. They'd seen depressions and rock-bottoms and still managed to float back up to the surface. While there was no love to be shared, there was a strong friendship that had been tested over a lifetime, and that was a ground much more stable to build a relationship on, they reasoned, than butterflies in the stomach.

Unlike Mother, my father had long ago moved on from the exhausting collapse of their two-decades-long union and, in fact, had encouraged her to move us out of Baku.

While Mother and Teymour struggled to get all the paperwork in order, which took two years, I never quite believed that the day of our departure would arrive. Our hypothetical move to another country was a good story to tell, a pleasant thought to entertain. I'd sit by the window at night, look at the glittery surface of the Caspian, hug my knees, and let myself sink into a fantasy of some distant future, of people much taller and louder, the kind I'd only ever seen on TV screens. I would try out basic English phrases, feel their texture on my tongue and imagine they'd be words I would one day say effortlessly, naturally, like a native.

America was a big canvas spreading in front of me, giving me full liberty to use any colors I wanted. I'd drag the heavy Zenith radio out to the balcony, wrap myself in a shawl, and look into the dark abyss of the sea as my fantasies came alive.

And here I was now, at this airport, looking into a very different sort of abyss. Was this it? Had it begun? I remembered months of preparation, waiting in lines in municipal offices, obtaining confirmations and registrations printed on poor-quality, faded paper covered with purple and brown dots, stamps smeared with someone's hasty signature in the middle, futile attempts to gather immunization records from local clinics, and mysterious sealed envelopes.

I had spent many sleepless nights imagining this moment, but now nothing felt special about it. Outside, the rain drizzled, and inside, crowds of people rushed past us, indifferent. The world blended into one foreign and empty place where we remained unnoticed.

. . . .

CHAPTER 4

LIKE AN AQUARIUM

We arrived in Chicago exhausted. Not a trace of last night's elation was left, and confusion had set in heavily in our bodies. I felt an overwhelming desire to take a shower, hoping that the water could wash away all the extra weight I had accumulated in the last twenty-two hours. As we walked towards the baggage claim, it began to hit me that the universe that nurtured me for years had shrunk down to just three people—and then I noticed Teymour rushing towards us. He wore an old t-shirt, green cargo shorts with big pockets, and flip-flops. Back home, these were the kind of clothes men only wore at home or at their summer houses. Yet somehow, he looked so natural and comfortable in this outfit.

"Hey, kiddos!" he addressed us, embracing Mother.

"Teymour! Finally!" Mother smiled back.

"How was the flight?"

"The longest I have ever been on," she replied. "It feels like it lasted a lifetime, but here we are."

I spent the flight in and out of sleep, re-reading the letters I got from my friends on the day we departed. There were seventeen of them, little windows into a large and colorful life that was now reduced to blue ink on a lined sheet. Each time I read a letter, the wave of feelings that came with it weakened. I realized that their magic was not infinite. The juice would run out someday and something else would take its place. My entire universe had ceased to exist, replaced by a foreign city and a man in shabby shorts and a faded t-shirt who had restless hands and tired eyes.

"Let's not stand here," Teymour said, motioning to the parking garage sign. "Give me those suitcases."

I had known Teymour since I was a child, yet he remained alien to me. No matter how hard I tried to get to know him during his frequent visits, I could never grasp what kind of person he was. I had tried and failed to reach that level of comfort with him when a person becomes familiar and predictable. He remained strange to me. His movements were abrupt, his thoughts unorganized, his humor sharp and stinging, but I sensed a comforting kindness in his eyes. Eager to get a closer look at it, I would strike up conversations with him during his visits, but his answers remained clumsy and dry, his jokes were not funny, and his knowledge of Russian was slowly deteriorating. I soon learned how to ignore the jokes and stick to basic conversations, but I grew fond of his silent kind-heartedness.

The moment we stepped outside the airport we noticed a huge, bright blue sky hanging above our heads. The phosphorus-white clouds shone brightly and moved quickly across the sky. They looked much bigger than the clouds in Baku. I wondered if it was just my imagination, but then I noticed both my brother and mother staring at them as well. It was refreshing to feel the windy air as the rays of the sun warmed our bodies after being encapsulated in an airplane for eight hours.

Teymour loaded our suitcases into his black Mercedes-Benz coupe and moments later we were on a highway headed towards the shiny cluster of skyscrapers that made up Chicago's downtown. I found the plastic resin smell of the car oddly pleasant. The seats were uncomfortably warm, but the heat emanating from the leather contrasted with the heavy blowing of the air conditioner. Apart from Teymour's occasional gestures and sudden lane changes, the drive was incredibly smooth, even soothing, and I was even able to relieve some of the anxiety brought on by the feeling of landing on a different planet.

Teymour tapped the wheel of his Benz and turned on the stereo to play Dire Straits, a British rock band famous for songs with lengthy, experimental passages. I came to love this band years later, vaguely remembering Teymour's monologues about the depth of the lyrics and the rich sound of the guitar. At the time, I had longed for a familiar Middle Eastern tune to remind me that, somewhere across the ocean, the sun was rising high above the sea and the teahouses were filling up with regulars who would be playing backgammon as the radio played another love song by one of those plump Azeri singers still clinging to their status as superstars.

As we got closer to the city, the grandiose view of Lake Shore Drive exploded like a firework in my mind. The winding six-lane highway flowed like a river into a cluster of mid- and high-rise buildings reflecting the blue sky. As I gazed at this colorful foreign world, the Dire Straits song came to an end. Then came the unexpected—the vintage sounds of a '70s violin recording with a subtle Turkish drum tapping in the background and the beautiful voice of Sezen Aksu and her famous "Lost Years." As her voice rose in the pleasant, air-conditioned salon of the car, I pictured Nana sitting on the balcony, facing the sea, finishing up her tea as the evening fell. I realized I did not even know what time it was back home. Something heavy, almost metallic, placed a heavy grip around my neck and made breathing difficult.

"Hey, Rufat, you like basketball?" Teymour asked.

"Yeah, I am a Bulls fan." Rufat grinned.

"Well, then you are in the right city," Teymour replied, entering the ramp to the garage.

I had never seen such a massive indoor garage! Another car was about to exit as Teymour slammed the brakes, stuck his hand out the window in a gesture to let him pass, and we heard a loud beep from the car. The blonde woman in the driver seat frowned and raised her hands in protest. He flipped his open hand and showed her his middle finger before driving on.

"Sorry, guys!" Teymour said, not looking sorry at all.

This was quite a start to the day.

Teymour lived in a luxurious one-bedroom apartment. The lobby had high vaulted ceilings in a warm peach color, a low-hanging chandelier with six terracotta lights, black marble floors, a tufted sofa, and a large leafy plant. I wondered if the plant was real. Even the nicest apartment buildings in Baku had dark unheated entrances with flickering lights, electric wires covering the walls, and spray-painted elevator doors. This was a different world. Teymour said hello to the concierge, and we walked through the open doors to the elevator area. But when Teymour opened the door of his apartment, we all gasped. None of us had ever seen an apartment in such a state of filth and disorder.

The coffee table had dirty dishes and glasses with leftover drinks and an empty pizza box that smelled awful when I got close to it. The floor was strewn with colorful pieces of cereal. There was a large mattress with a gray blanket on top of it by the window. There were all kinds of random things on the floor—several unwrapped packages of some sort, unopened letters and ads, crumpled papers, magazines, a mountain of clean laundry, CDs, plush pillows, and half-empty bottles of lotion. Out of all these items, the *Playboy* magazines surprised me the most, but then I remembered that Teymour worked for *Playboy* as a programmer, which got him a free subscription.

"Welcome!" Teymour said. "This place is a bit of a mess, sorry about that. I only had time to do grocery shopping. Been working a lot lately. And I do need to go back to work, but I should be back soon."

"It's not a problem, Teymour," Mother replied. "We'll manage."

"Let me show you around first," he said. "Here's the kitchen. It's a bit small and there is no table. I eat at that coffee table over there." He gestured.

"No, it is perfect. Do you happen to have loose-leaf tea?" Mother asked.

"I didn't until yesterday." He smiled. "Tea is in this cabinet. After twenty years in America, I finally switched to coffee, but I still remember how much tea we used to drink back home. Tea all day!"

"Tea all day!" Mother smiled back.

I was wondering if Teymour would change before he headed to work, but he just grabbed his keys and cell phone and headed for the door in the same faded shorts, worn t-shirt, and flip-flops. *What a strange person*, I kept thinking. The absurdity of his outfit blended well with his odd personality while his random, disorganized thoughts kept you wondering who he really was.

For the next two hours, all three of us frantically attempted to clean up and organize the apartment. Mother concentrated on cleaning the kitchen, which was the toughest part. She took a large bowl, filled it up with hot water, and poured out just a little of the dishwashing liquid before realizing that there was no sponge. She looked around, searching for a small piece of cloth that could be used instead of the real thing, and couldn't find anything. Rufat finally found it underneath the sofa. The soapy liquid in the bowl trick was a way to economize water use in an Azeri household. This way, you didn't have to keep the water running; instead you concentrated on soaping and scrubbing the dishes and then rinsing them all at once. My grandmother enforced this practice in our summer house in Mardakan (she was in the *enforcing* business), where we relied on a limited supply from the water tank for all of our consumption.

I picked up all the random objects from the floor and brought all the dirty dishes to the kitchen. Rufat organized the CDs and unopened mail under the coffee table. I swept up all the cereal from the floor and tried a piece of one. It was sweet. I bet Nana would kill me for eating something from the floor. Oh well, no one was there to scold me now.

The rigorous cleaning exercise brought a feeling of unity as we realized that it was just the three of us from now on; our entourage of empathizing supporters and advisors would no longer accompany us. A few hours later the apartment was cleaned, tea was made, and Mother was in her usual place—puffing her cigarette by the open door of the balcony. I approached the floor-to-ceiling windows, looked down, and felt dizzy. *No drapes, no nothing. Like an aquarium,* I thought.

I went into the kitchen, grabbed a handful of cereal, and asked Mother to pour me some tea. And just like many times in the coming weeks, I cozied up on the ugly but comfortable brown sofa and hugged my knees. I don't remember falling asleep, but when I woke up, the place was suspiciously quiet, and the sky was dark and buzzing with evening traffic. I moved closer to the window and looked outside.

The streetlights painted the evening sky into an unnatural and unsettling color of orange. There was something very unnatural and disturbing about this lit-up sky. Something felt wrong about the bright orange, like a key element of the planet was missing on this side of the world. This new sky played a part in this buzzing evening traffic, with cars rushing by and pedestrians coming in and out of a subway station, like aliens on another planet going about their evening, unaware that somewhere across the ocean one colorful life has ended and another one has begun, blank and formless like loneliness. The tight grip around my neck intensified, solitude surrounding me from all sides, the silence of the living room louder than ever and the breathtaking view of Chicago so foreign and cold, with its shining buildings and aircraft lights on top of skyscrapers. I peeked into the bedroom and saw that both Mother and Rufat were sleeping. Teymour must have gone out. I had no desire to sleep, and a long night was ahead of me. I felt alone with nothing but my anxiety for company.

That was the beginning of summer 2003, when our lives changed forever.

CHAPTER 5

A BOW TO GOD

My days would begin the same, but somewhere between washing my face and my mother's call to have breakfast, I would feel the familiar iron grip around my neck. It would start in my stomach, climb up my chest, and clench the middle of my throat, making it difficult to speak and even breathe, a sort of strange, subtle torture. My attempts to distract myself did not work.

Sometimes I was able to concentrate on the savory smells coming from the kitchen. I would close my eyes and envision the hot and buttery Azeri breakfast made up of eggs, onion, and fresh tomatoes and feel a faint anticipation of my once-favorite meal. But as soon as Mother served it on the coffee table in the living room, my silent torturer would intensify his grip and I'd feel nauseous. My heartbeat picked up and Mother would have to fix me valerian-root extract to bring down my pulse.

My refuge in sleep in the afternoons led to insomnia as I filled the nights with random Internet browsing and sobbing by the large window that looked out over the sparkling lights of Chicago, all while trying to get my silent torturer to answer at least the simplest questions in my head. Why was this experience so physical? What exactly was collapsing inside of me with such force?

This internal battle was followed by periods of apathy. I felt pain that centered in my neck and extended into my thinning arms and stomach and then down to my knees. I missed the familiarity of my grandmother's house. I missed my father and Nana and the loud chatter of my family, which had been replaced with hollow silence. Since our arrival, we had spoken with Father and Nana only once.

The phone call home had been more difficult than I ever could have imagined. Tears gathered in my eyes, but my voice did not quiver. I spoke of the park across the street and the pristine hallways of the apartment building and how we had fast Internet here. The questions that followed from my grandmother were so full of excitement that I could not disappoint her, so I babbled on and on about the hot water and fast Internet and the greenery outside.

"Tell me, my child, do they sell dill in the stores?" Nana asked.

This obsession with herbs that ruled over Nana's culinary world was stronger than her curiosity about America. She solved her life's problems with local dill, mountain parsley, curcumin, and turmeric, and their absence at our grocery stores seemed to be the only thing she could not survive.

"They do sell it, but in these small plastic containers. That wouldn't be enough for one spoonful of your dill rice, Nana."

"What kind of a country is that, Maryam?" she said. "Unless you are making fun of me."

"I wish I was making fun of you, Nana, but it is true," I answered.

I wondered how it was possible that I'd crossed an ocean and still found myself talking about herbs with this woman.

"What do you eat there?" she asked.

"Whatever Mother cooks—chicken stew, potatoes in tomato sauce, saffron rice." I was getting impatient but restrained myself. "She made chicken stew today."

"Did you make friends already?" Nana tried to change the subject.

"I haven't really met anyone yet," I said and fell quiet, out of energy.

Silent tears rolled down my cheeks, but I kept the smile on, hoping it would help conceal my sadness. I avoided all phone calls after that and resorted to emails. It was easier to pretend that way.

At night, I would bite harder into my nails and brush my hair for hours in hopes of finding peace. The grip around my neck intensified even more at night, and at times I found it necessary to use the last possible resort and talk to God.

"Dear God," I would begin, "I wish I could explain the reason for my suffering to you. I wish I could describe it. If I did, I would know what to ask for in my prayers, but all I know is that emptiness consumes me. The world is still a place with a blue sky and sun, but there is no meaning in it, no feeling in it, no color, and no taste in it. Instead, there is this tight grip right here," I would wrap my hand around my neck, "and it squeezes so bad. Please make that go away. And help me not give myself away to my father or Nana. Let them think we are good."

I soon found two things that eased the iron grip around my neck. One was a mindless reading of Dale Carnegie's famous *How to Stop Worrying and Start Living*, the only book in Russian that I found in Teymour's flat. It gave me hope to read how Carnegie once considered himself one of the unhappiest people in New York, and now he promised to cure all your worries if you read his book. I was skeptical of his arguments but reading stories of men and women who overcame their stress provided temporary relief.

Exhausted from nerve-wracking analysis of my state, I would lock myself up in the small half-bathroom by the bedroom and carefully examine my face, as if searching for any possible clues. My nose seemed slightly slimmer as a result of all the nausea-related weight loss. My skin seemed slightly transparent and grayish. My long hair framed my skinny face and fell heavily on my shoulders. These intense stare-downs with my own reflection almost always ended in an outburst of tears that made my face look lifeless and ugly. I would slowly descend to the bathroom floor, clutching my hairbrush and nervously running it through my hair.

Days when Carnegie wouldn't help me, I would turn to a channel that broadcasted a church mass throughout the day. I stumbled upon it when mindlessly flipping through the cable channels and something on the screen made me stop. My inexplicable misery made me indifferent to the specific religion that offered refuge. I longed for the presence of God in any shape or form, so I watched the Sunday Mass, often not understanding the true meaning of the priest's words— trying instead to focus on the presence of God in the movements of his hands, the enlightened expression of his face, and in those seated in the grand hallways of a large, well-lit auditorium adorned with intricate and colorful mosaics of biblical scenes. In those moments, I felt calm, and the grip was gone for a few minutes. But these rare times of sanity were always followed by another wave of anguish.

While mother drowned her worries and anxiety in excessive smoking and I battled with my newly found demons, Rufat escaped into the virtual world of video games. Or maybe it was not an escape after all, because Rufat did not experience anything close to the despair I felt. He seemed just fine, even *happy* to be here. His step was light and cool, and his mood did not swing from bad to worse, like mine. Sometimes, afraid of the devastating effect of loneliness, I'd come and sit on the unmade bed where all three of us slept and watch him push the buttons on the joystick over and over. I sensed that my presence was making him feel uneasy, as if my anxiety spilled into his world. I'd watch the strange images on the computer monitor, follow the movement of his hands, hoping I could take in some of the comfort it was giving him. He smiled at me once in a while, reaching out into the deep well where I sat in the dreadful company of my silent torturer.

CHAPTER 6

. . . .

HAPPINESS IS
BITING INTO A PEACH

One afternoon, Mother decided we needed to get groceries from the store around the corner and asked us to get dressed. I went through my things and chose a yellow button-up shirt that I got as a present from my aunt. I was convinced it would look very *American* with a pair of wide-leg jeans that Mother bought in our semi-annual shopping trip last winter. Rufat decided he was not going to change.

"You're going to go like this?" I asked.

"Yes, what's wrong with that?" he said and gave me a look. "This is America!" Unlike me, Rufat lacked the disoriented fogginess that dominated most of my day. He found refuge in downloading Azeri pop music, the stuff we listened to in the summer, upbeat and careless songs with simple lyrics and easy tunes, and no sadness crept under his skin. Under his skin it was still summer. When I saw the look on my mother's face, I realized we both looked rather ridiculous, but she was too worried about our venture into the unknown to say anything and so off we went into the long carpeted hallway with identical doors and mirrors. We passed the friendly concierge and gave him our rehearsed smiles, which he returned with a look of curiosity.

Down on the street level, we patiently waited for the "WALK" sign to turn green, crossed the street, and approached a large signboard reading "Potash Brothers." We opened the large glass doors and walked inside. None of us had ever seen a grocery store this big.

"Oh my . . . " Mother said, her voice filled with awe. "You better not wander around or we will lose each other here."

As she said this, Rufat was already gone in one of the aisles. I noticed that Mother brought the leather case with our legal documents with her. For the next few months, she would carry it absolutely everywhere and almost lost it once.

The store had high wooden ceilings with wide metal pipes running across the perimeter, suspended lighting fixtures, and several large columns in the middle. The store was organized in rows with large rectangular posters showing a list of items that could be found in each row. I later found out that these were called "aisles." There were seventeen aisles in this store, with products that encompassed the needs of all stages of human life, starting from baby formula and diapers and millions of baby trinkets of incomprehensible use to incontinence solutions and arthritis creams for the elderly.

The only store back in Baku that had come close in size and grandeur to Potash Brothers was Ramstore, an expat grocery store that opened in Baku after the first wave of oil and gas expats arrived, which created demand for a Western-style pristine shopping environment without the need to bargain or question the hygiene standards of traditional Azeri outdoor bazaars. Ramstore was mostly a place for the expats, but it still entertained us with its oversized logo—a large green kangaroo with a bowtie—during our weekend drives to the summer house in Mardakan. I imagined that if we had ever ventured into that Ramstore for a tour, it would have had similar lighting to this Potash Brothers store. The products would be organized just like this, and the whole place would smell like a ham and cheese sandwich fresh from the fridge.

Right by the door I noticed a whole aisle filled with boxes of breakfast cereal, a food item that separated you out as a child of the well-off in the '90s. We craved the infamous Corn Flakes so much that back home, Father used to buy our affection back with that sacred Kellogg's box with a green rooster on it after each time he disappeared from the house for a week. Mother got mad that we sold her out for a box of cereal, but it was one of those rare cases when we didn't care, because nothing would stand between us and the crispy, lightly sweet corn flakes that melted so quickly in our mouths.

While Mother was busy looking for the fresh produce section, I wandered into the cereal aisle and looked at the wall covered in brightly colored boxes. There were so many of them and they all sounded so delicious! I thought of picking one and trying to convince Mother to buy it. The variety of products left me uncertain, yet I was happy to sense a sudden awakening inside as the grip around my neck loosened. After few minutes of wandering, I chose Rice Krispies—a bright blue box with three Disney-type characters swimming in a bowl full of creamy milk, rice puffs, and strawberries. Just as I reached out to grab it, I heard my mother's voice.

"Maryam, come here!" she called.

My confidence was suddenly gone. I placed the blue box back on the shelf and hurried in the direction of my mother's echoing voice. I passed by the dairy section, with all its brightly colored milk and yogurt containers, pictures of fruit, flowers, and pastures on them. I passed the household and kitchenware section and found myself in the fresh produce area, which looked like a carnival of fruits and vegetables! Pyramids of apples, lemons, oranges, peaches, and other fruits were lined up one next to another. I noticed a longing sense of hunger come back to me, grab me somewhere below my chest, and pull really hard.

"Oh, here you are, Maryam," Mother said. "Go get some peaches and let's head back. I want to have dinner ready by the time Teymour gets home."

I grabbed a plastic bag and filled it up with peaches and followed Mother and Rufat to the cashier.

The world looked different when we left Potash Brothers. The wide open, cloudless sky had transformed into pale saffron, the hue it acquired when nearing a sunset, I had learned. The pedestrians had slowed their tempo, and large blue and red CTA buses were lined up at a busy intersection, waiting for passengers to come up. We walked silently back to our building, gave another rehearsed, thick-accented "Hello! How are you?" to the concierge, and proceeded to the elevator area.

I found myself impatient to try a peach, so I grabbed a plate and a knife from the cupboard and stepped onto the wide balcony. A wooden folding chair was the only seating here. It looked quite out of place compared to the upscale outdoor furniture and potted plants arranged on the neighboring balconies. I sat down with the peach on the plate and a knife in my hands and looked at the city, inhaling its humid air, enjoying my favorite time of the day: sunset. The loud clanking of pots and pans coming from the kitchen made me feel at home for a moment. If I closed my eyes and listened to these sounds, I could almost convince myself that I was back in Baku, killing time on the balcony as Nana prepared dinner.

Right across 33 Sutton Place stood an old rectangular building with tall semicircular windows and a red brick roof, which turned out to be a library established by Walter Newberry in 1887. According to a blurb that I found online that same night (the things I googled out of desperation!), Newberry died at sea while on a trip to France. His will included a provision for the creation of a free public library if his daughters were to die without heirs. I found it pleasant to watch people walk in and out of that building, some with large backpacks and others with just one book in their hands or tucked under an arm.

After a few minutes of people-watching, I finally cut the peach and bit into its flesh and found myself in utter disappointment. Despite an appetizing appearance, it tasted of paper and sugar-free sweetener. I gave it another bite only to confirm it lacked the bouquet of flavor present in the peaches I'd eaten back home. A mere bite of a ripe peach would result in a flow of juices down your chin, its soft flesh producing a saturated, sweet and sour taste. I remembered how we would gather in the large living room of our summer house, watching a Disney movie on a cassette as Nana brought in a bowl with cherries, plums, apricots, and peaches. We were already at the age when fighting over fruit was too embarrassing, so we resorted to indirectly snatching the most coveted ones. For me, that was always the peach. On days when I was lucky enough to grab it first, I'd climb back into the old brown armchair and enjoy *Aladdin* for the hundredth time.

As I walked back inside to rinse the plate and knife and toss the remainder of the peach in the trash, the magic of this early evening slowly evaporated into the air and the familiar grip around my neck was back. I saw Rufat lying on the couch, watching another basketball game, looking careless and happy. He nodded at the uneaten peach.

"I know. The food here tastes like paper," he said. "But I am still glad we are here."

I did not answer. Another long, sleepless night was approaching.

. . . .

CHAPTER 7

PRACTICAL ARRANGEMENT

Within a few days of our arrival, I realized that things were not going according to the plan. In the evenings, Teymour and Mother would retreat to the balcony to smoke and speak alone. They did not realize that I could hear them from my spot by the window. At first, I hadn't been interested in their conversations, but now, as the tension slowly grew between them, I started listening to understand what was going on. Since our arrival, Teymour looked troubled, easily distracted, and more restless than usual.

"I met her about a year ago," he began. "I did not plan on it, but you know how that goes. You make your plans, and he makes his own." He pointed to the sky and pulled on his cigarette. "I've accepted the blissful existence of a single guy. No romance, no nothing. But then I found myself spending more and more time with her.

"I never met anyone like her. She's different, but in a good way, you know? She doesn't mind my crazy ways. You know I can't sit in one place, how I must comment on everything. She just smiles, sometimes in a kind way and sometimes with cynicism. She lets me do my own thing. I like that."

"I understand, Teymour." Mother looked down. Teymour's hands were all over the place when he spoke, his cigarette shedding ashes on the tiled balcony floor. I wondered how Mother made any sense of what he was saying.

"If I don't marry her, she will leave me for good. And I don't want her to leave, Leyla." He rubbed his forehead nervously.

"So, you want a divorce . . ." Mother said bitterly. "I don't have a life back there, but it looks like I'm nothing but an obstacle here as well."

They both stayed quiet for a while.

"It's not like that," he said after a pause. "It's not like that and you know it. I looked forward to this just as much as you did. I am just stuck in a difficult spot, and I am afraid of making a wrong decision, that's all. I've lost sleep over this, lost my appetite, too, and the pills are not helping much. Either way, you don't have to listen to all this. These are my problems to handle."

I kept my gaze on the window not to give myself away and tried to process what I heard. Teymour was speaking from a place of truth. I believed him when he said he lost sleep over this. I could see he feared losing someone who, despite his cynicism and sarcasm, had managed to crawl deep under Teymour's skin and resurrect in him a dormant hope for many long, happy years together. I thought for a moment that maybe we could all go back and undo this terrible mistake, but something whispered to me that Mother would rather jump out of this building than do that.

I met Sarah, Teymour's American girlfriend, a few months later. I remember studying the fine lines on her face, the gentle curl of her lips, her caramel-colored eyes with permanent crow's feet that some-how added more sophistication and dreaminess to her look. The tip of her pointy nose accentuated the pronounced V-shaped contour of her upper lip. Somehow, Sarah married cynicism and sincere love of life in the tone of her voice and in that elaborate smile. Her opinions only peeked through carefully phrased, occasional comments.

The next morning Teymour told Mother that he had made a decision. He wanted to file for divorce as soon as possible.

"I know this is shocking, but you and the kids will need to go back," he said.

They were certain that both Rufat and I were asleep in the bedroom, but I was awake and witnessed the scene through the reflection of a mirror. Mother maintained a blank expression on her face, while her hands were constantly rubbing one another, giving away her true feelings. The idea of going back was what frightened her. She watched him pace around the room, looking for his anti-depressant pills, opening all the drawers, glancing back at her, hoping to read some impossible solution that neither of them had considered.

"Do you know where my pills are?" Teymour asked. "It's a small orange container with a white top and a label. They were somewhere here." He pointed at the kitchen counter. "Did you clean this place up?"

"Sit down, I'll get them." Mother got up. "And calm down, please!"

She took out the small container from the cabinet, poured water into a glass, and handed it to Teymour. I noticed that her hands were shaking.

"I can't go back, Teymour," she started. "We will talk to a lawyer—"

"Already did. I spoke with several," Teymour interrupted. "There is no way to keep all of you here. Someone has to go."

Mother fell silent for a minute and then resumed her plea in a shaking voice, recounting the hardest moments of our last year in Baku, with Father in prison and our closest friends gradually turning away from our crumbling family. Her broken monologue brought tears to my eyes because it suddenly revealed how weak she had become, despite the stoic posture she had maintained while receiving blow after blow from life. The heat in their conversation subsided and they spoke like friends again. Teymour reached out and held her trembling hands in his.

"Okay. Give me a few days," he said.

However, things got worse quickly.

CHAPTER 8

DEATH IS ALWAYS AN OPTION

As days passed by, the confrontations between Mother and Teymour did not subside. In fact, they became more frequent. Both refused to give in to the other's exit plan. Teymour wanted an immediate divorce and a subsequent return to Baku, and Mother stood firm that it was not an option. She kept asking to speak to another lawyer, and he kept insisting that the situation doesn't change when you change whom you consult. As Mother's stance grew stronger, Teymour's mental health seemed to deteriorate. There was still a huge gap between us, yet I felt sorry for him. He looked just as lost inside of himself as I was with my somber thoughts. I observed him gulping down several pills at once and randomly running out to the balcony to take calls. Despite a vague understanding of what was going on, both Rufat and I tried to stay out of it. We were too young to have a say but too old to pretend we didn't understand what was going on.

One afternoon, their argument got out of control.

We were both in the bedroom, watching *Notting Hill* with Julia

Roberts and Hugh Grant, remembering that we had last seen it on the 1st of November, 2001, when Baku had been hit with a powerful earthquake with an epicenter in the Caspian, which was followed by weeks of aftershocks. At one point during the movie, Teymour began yelling at Mother more intensely than he had in the past and we both ran into the living room. Mother was sitting in an armchair, her face pale and palms pressing into the wide armrests. She looked frightened.

We walked over and stood by her side, barring Teymour from coming closer. He paced the room, saying something in English that we could not understand. Then he grabbed his keys and cell phone and started opening all the kitchen drawers, searching for his pills. I could tell that our presence made Teymour feel slightly embarrassed about his loud and aggravated tone. I felt like we had to somehow intervene and not leave Mother alone but being so far removed from the logistics of this practical arrangement, we hardly had an opinion on it. I could tell that Mother's blood pressure was rising and that she would be needing the usual cocktail of hypertonic medications. Teymour felt uncomfortable continuing now that we were there and headed for the door, but before he closed the door, he dealt all of us quite a powerful emotional blow, which haunted us long after he left.

"I'm not going to sign anything," Mother said, looking down. I wished she would stay silent and not pour oil into the fire.

"If you don't sign it, I'll bring a sheriff in here," Teymour shot back. "I'll get that divorce whether you cooperate or not."

Right after he said those words, I saw a drop of regret in Teymour's eyes, as if he couldn't recognize himself, but it was too late. I had never seen Teymour like this. I noticed my brother's fist tightening in anger.

"I can't stay here. I'm going for a walk," Teymour said.

We both sighed with relief when he closed the door behind him, but then we noticed the despair in Mother's eyes. I recognized the symptoms—her face was covered with tiny red patches and her lips were dry. She placed one hand at her neck while the other one supported her forehead. Unlike my grandma's hypertensive attacks, my mother's were always accompanied by vision problems, which scared her to death. Her vision would blur, and a strange white patch would show up in the upper-left corner of her vision.

Mother was laying down on the couch with her face against the wall. I gently called her and told her she needed to place her feet in the hot water that I brought in a small basin. I remembered that Grandma felt much better after this. She looked at me with her green eyes, red-rimmed because of the inflammation, and swallowed down two heavy sobs.

"Mama, come on . . . Try to sit down," I whispered.

"Don't worry so much. I am all right. It's the usual thing," she said with a faint smile on her lips.

Mother's condition could be monitored by the birthmark on her forehead, which only became visible in moments of rage or high blood pressure and was usually concealed by a thick layer of makeup. Her aching forehead wore the inflamed red mark as a sign of danger. I sat by her and tried to remember when I'd last seen my mother smile. Not just a polite smile of courtesy, but a real, genuine one filled with joy. It must have been in the company of her co-workers at the Academy of Sciences. I recalled the weeks leading up to her Ph.D. dissertation defense: her practicing in our carpeted living room, light filtering through the sheer curtains, a thick scientific text in her hands, her focusing on a spot on the wall and gesturing with her hands as she spoke of partial wave analysis. I then recalled the dining table full of flowers that were brought by those who attended—her co-workers, senior physicists, secretaries of the academy, and gray-haired mentors that supervised the research. In those rare moments,

Mother looked free from her sorrows and disappointments. She did not look happy or sad, but completely and wonderfully captivated by the subject at hand. All other times, sorrow followed her, adding a strangely attractive mysteriousness and gentleness to her persona, like the train of a medieval gown or a rising trail of cigarette smoke. Now her face lacked any emotion. There was no bittersweet mystery, just plain pain.

The wet towel on her back cooled off, so I ran to the kitchen, opened the faucet, turned the knob all the way down to let the water heat up, and then soaked the wet towel again. I returned the hot towel to her neck and went to check on Rufat.

I walked into the bedroom and found him sitting at the edge of the bed, his hands clasped in prayer and eyes raised to the ceiling. His lips were slightly open, and he dug his bare feet into the carpet by the bed. I held my breath and left the room to be with Mother.

It took God about twenty minutes to act. Mother's state stabilized and she was no longer in pain. That was encouraging, but it also gave us a chance to stop and think how alone we were in this glossy and unknown city. We were alone and scared and could hardly allow ourselves the thought that this string of events would ever bring us to a better tomorrow. But they did.

CHAPTER 9

. . . .

BIT BY BIT

When I woke up the next morning, Mother had fully recovered and looked as fresh as ever. I noticed that the furniture in the living room looked a few shades lighter under the bright rays of the sun pouring in from the windows. Mother placed a woven basket with bread on the coffee table, which already featured warm breakfast, and went back to the balcony to finish her cigarette. Somehow, the dreadful events of last night seemed so far away in the morning light. As I sat comfortably on the couch and watched Mother inhale the cigarette, I felt a pleasant realization that I did feel better and had even developed an appetite.

Until last night, I had not considered that losing my mother was a possibility, and even the slight hint of that outcome I had experienced had proven to me that, no matter how desperate I felt in my complete loneliness, things *could* get worse. Death was always an option. Mother finished the cigarette and walked back into the living room. As it happens sometimes, the turmoil of last night did not frighten her, but helped her summon all the strength and will she had left to put together a plan of action. She no longer looked lost. She looked determined, even confident.

"I am going to speak with a lawyer myself, today," she said.

Her English wasn't so good, so I assumed that I was coming with her. I couldn't decide how I felt about this. The walls of the apartment provided a bubble of security that contained my torture and eased the iron grip around my neck. I had grown accustomed to my new state and knew how to deal with it better enclosed by these walls, so every endeavor into the unknown was a painful experience.

Somehow, Mother sensed that I wasn't thrilled to accompany her on this day and mentioned that Anna, Teymour's family friend, had volunteered to go with her. Rufat preferred to get out of the house and would be joining them, too. I was relieved. She then sat in the armchair and took a small piece of bread, spread some butter over it, cut a thin slice of feta cheese, and ate it. *After darkest night comes a shining day. And a breakfast*, I thought. Mother's appetite suffered first when something even distantly troubling happened in her life. She'd stop eating and smoke instead. So, to see her enjoying the bread and cheese felt good, reassuring.

Mother and Rufat left around noon, and I took my usual place by the window, looking down at the Saturday scene of downtown Chicago, the glass wall and thirteen floors separating me from the picture-perfect panorama of city dwellers roaming the streets on their bikes, walking their dogs, and drinking mysterious beverages in paper cups. The view from above offered a line of bright red umbrellas from the breakfast café on the corner of Sutton and State Street. The row of cars parked by the sidewalks looked like a string of shiny toys and went well with the cheerful mood of this sunny afternoon. The silence of the empty apartment felt healing.

My daydreaming was interrupted by a call. I hesitated to pick up the home phone, but then remembered that Mother said she'd be calling. It turned out to be Anna, Teymour's friend.

"Good morning, Maryam!" she said. Then, without waiting for an answer, she continued, "Do you have anything against Assyrians?"

Anna had a high-pitched, almost exclamatory tone. She spoke with a strange mix of Russian and Jewish accents. Her question jolted me out of my melancholic stupor because I was absolutely sure that Assyrians only existed in my history textbooks.

"What do you mean?" I asked. "Assyrians still exist?"

She probably thought my question was sarcastic and went on.

"You know, in the Middle East, you always have a problem with one another!" she explained. "Ashur, this Iraqi guy, he owns a small public-aid optical not too far from Devon Avenue. My cousin who is also an optometrist sees patients there on Tuesdays and Fridays. They need someone who speaks Russian. It is a perfect first-time job, dear! You Azeris are not particularly hostile towards Assyrians, is that right?"

"No, we are not," I assured her. "Not at all!"

The salary would be one hundred dollars per week, and I would have to work on Saturdays too. I politely answered "yes" to all her questions to make sure I got the job, but my mind was consumed with the ancient Assyrians and the bits and pieces of my knowledge about them.

The Assyrian empire, once the mightiest in all of Mesopotamia, remained undefeated for centuries. Its capital, Nineveh, was located in modern-day Iraq and, at its political and military peak, Assyria stretched from Cyprus to Iran. Eventually, the empire was defeated by the joined forces of Media and Babylon in the famous battle for Nineveh and never regained its independence. That was all I could remember from my ancient history class, so I assumed that Assyrians ceased to exist as a nation. However, according to Anna, they were alive and well and even operating an optical in the Devon neighborhood!

I calculated that my monthly salary would be four hundred dollars, which was incredibly good for an eighteen-year-old from Baku who'd never worked a day in her life. Of course, this was by Baku standards. Back then, I did not know to calculate whether that was above or below minimum wage. Anna said that I could start as early as tomorrow and promised she'd explain how to get to the optical by the train.

In the evening, Mother sat us both down at the coffee table and announced that we would be moving to a different place by the end of the week. She had spoken with the lawyer, and they somehow figured out a way we could stay in the country legally. Teymour was on board with this and said he'd help in any way he could. She had a rather official tone that made me believe good things were going to happen soon.

"Teymour will help us move to another apartment soon. We'll stay there for few months," Mother began.

"We saw it today!" interrupted Rufat. "It's the second floor of a house. It's as big as our summer house!"

"The lawyer promised to fix our paperwork," she went on. "But it may take up to a year."

"What are we going to do all this time?" I asked.

"We will do what all others do," she responded. "We will work and build our lives here, bit by bit."

Soon we would move to another place, a place that would be our own, even if only temporarily. At the time, none of us, not even Mother, understood that to work and build our life, we needed *permits*—small laminated cards that magically opened doors to jobs, schools, medical offices, and other places. Unaware of this obstacle, Mother sounded confident, even optimistic, and I got some energy back from the sparkle in her eyes. I did not say anything but felt grateful to see the excited grin on my brother's face.

. . . .

CHAPTER 10

COFFEE AND SANDWICHES

The aftertaste of that unpleasant night before, when Teymour and my mother had fought so fiercely, was still fresh in our memories. This made it hard to be around Teymour, but we were just as stuck with him as he was with us. It must have been unpleasant for him as well. The evening turned into a game of trying to avoid looking at him, but other than the balcony, there were no escape routes in this glass box.

"Come on, guys! Let's go visit my friends Philip and Anna in Deerfield. We'll drive around, you guys can play with their cat. It'll be nice!" Teymour said.

Mother must have noticed the pleading look on our faces and gave him a positive nod. When we finally got out of the building's garage, the red disc of the sun hung above the subway bridge, painting the smooth metal surface of the train red. Minutes later, with Teymour behind the wheel, we took a ramp to I-94 and headed north, leaving the city skyline at our backs.

"Can you please open the glove compartment and take out the Beethoven CD, Leyla?" Teymour asked Mother.

Mother clicked the black handle and the compartment opened. I knew that Teymour detested driving in silence, especially now since the unpleasant memory of that night hung in the air. Every time we got into his car, he would pick a song from his collection, tell us all he knew about this piece—something about the origin of the song, what inspired it, or when he had first listened to it. I liked hearing these stories and he did a good job telling them. They made the music come alive in such a vivid manner that I could see it in front of my eyes. He spoke of these songs while looking ahead, never turning around to look at us, as if he were addressing no one. Now, given the tension between us, I expected him to skip the story, but he didn't.

"They say when Beethoven died, he left everything he had to a secret lover, to whom he addressed a letter. 'Immortal Beloved,' he called her. His friend tried to figure out who she was because he apparently had so many." He gestured with his right hand. "Anyways, she turned out to be his brother's wife. It's a strange story, but this piece was used in a movie about the whole thing. It's my favorite. In the scene where this piece is used, his carriage is stuck in the mud, and he pushes it forward to get to his Immortal Beloved. He ends up getting there too late. It was sad and brilliant!" He inserted the CD and pressed play, turning up the volume.

The music began slowly, with the ominous sound of the violin as distant tapping on the door. Then along with the tapping, a group of violins started with a simple melody. Then another layer of violins was added, then another, and, in few moments, a magical choir erupted into a strange blend of bottomless, hopeless tragedy of unrequited love. The music coupled with the speed of Teymour's car on the empty highway pushed me into an abyss of memories.

I was back in Mardakan again. At first, my visions were careless and happy ones, picking figs and mulberries from the trees, but then I saw the summer we moved there while Father was in prison. I remembered how Nana howled and shrieked like a wounded animal imagining him in a cramped cell. She came out of her stupor once a week to buy groceries and cook meals to deliver to prison. I remembered the guilt I felt when I once stole a peach from the heavy sack she carried from the bazaar, wobbling side to side on her swollen legs. My dreamy escape turned into a grim prison cell. I opened my eyes to rid myself of these images.

I looked outside the window and accepted that lately, our lives had turned into an endless string of unfairness that we had tried to escape by moving to the States. But what had we found here? We were all stuck in limbo, far away from those we loved, unsure about tomorrow, living a life where nights dragged on forever and tomorrows brought only nothingness.

Teymour parked the car in front of a house and turned off the engine. I looked around. Evening had fallen upon the neighborhood and since the suburbs were not dotted with tall streetlight poles, a bright blue shade covered the shingled roofs of the houses. Anna and Philip's house resembled a glass box supported by wide caramel-colored wooden logs, with a small patio on the second floor enclosed by a glass fence and five flights of stairs leading up to a glass entrance door. Just like in Teymour's apartment, there was no trace of curtains or rugs, showcasing the house to all the passersby. At a closer look, I realized there wasn't much to hide. The place was as sterile as a hotel room, with cream-colored walls and a white dining table with four chairs and a large red lamp hanging low above it. Philip opened the front door holding a huge black cat in his arms.

"Teymour, Leyla, Rufat, and Maryam!" he exclaimed with a thick Russian accent. "Welcome to the Goldberg house! This is Gizmo," he said and pointed at the black cat. "He runs this place."

We stepped inside a brightly lit living room and started taking off our shoes.

"What are you doing, Leyla?" Anna said to Mother. "Are you crazy? Put . . . put those back on."

What? How can they permit guests to soil their home with shoes like that? In Nana's universe, this was a sign of utter disrespect to the hostess, who presumably spent hours vacuuming and cleaning the floor in anticipation of the guests. Nana's universe had turned out to be a small place. No matter how controversial, Anna's comment had come out, and I honestly could not picture her wiping the floor with a rag in her bare hands and her knees pressed to the floor like Nana did. She was too polished for that, with her lean, muscular physique, her face flatteringly accented by a cute pixie cut, stylish red glasses, and a pale gloss on her lips. The only instance in which I could imagine her in the kitchen was on the cover of a magazine!

I let myself wander in the house. Everything about it was different. There were no framed pictures on top of the fireplace mantel, no elaborate pieces of decor on the coffee table, and no fruits or nuts on three-tiered trays that you would find in all Azeri households. In fact, there was no trace of food anywhere. Philip and Anna didn't lead us to a lavish table covered with fruits and desserts, saucers with red and white cherry preserves, and steaming cups of tea. Yet, despite their non-traditional reception, I liked them and their place a lot. In this house, you didn't have to follow the strict rules of Azeri etiquette. You didn't need to refuse the food several times before you yielded because they didn't try to stuff you as soon as you walked in. It felt odd, but in a way, liberating.

I watched Anna and Philip chat with Mother in the kitchen. It was impossible not to notice how Philip admired his wife. He'd touch her shoulder every time he passed near, or make her the object of a funny joke, or rush to respond to a question posed to her by

Teymour or Mother. Every topic was an excuse to engage each other in some way. Unlike all other adults that I'd met before this day, Anna and Philip were more interested in me and Rufat than Mother, asking our opinion about things and then discussing it between each other, as if we were their peers. The grip around my neck loosened.

"I'll make coffee!" Philip announced.

So, no food, I thought, beginning to feel hungry. He took out a round silver barrel from one of the shelves and the aroma of freshly ground coffee filled the space, intensifying our hunger.

"Mmmm . . . that smells good!" Rufat said.

Philip poured the ground coffee into the shiny espresso machine and pressed a button. The machine made a loud buzzing sound and a black creamy liquid poured from the dispenser. Anna took out tall double-walled cups and poured milk into five of the six cups.

"Philip likes his black. Otherwise, he calls it a milkshake," she said with a smile.

Philip handed me a glass. "Maryam, would you like to take a walk in the neighborhood?" he asked. "It's nice and cool."

I nodded my head in a shy "yes" and we took the stairs down to the front of the house. On the way out he handed me a hoodie in case the weather got chilly. The neighborhood looked serene, with rows of beautiful houses adorned with small and large pots and beds of flowers and bushes cut in a perfect round shape. Some of the homes were completely dark, while in others I could see a pale evening light in the kitchen and a shining silhouette of a large TV. I heard a few dogs bark in a nearby park and from somewhere in the distance came a familiar rhythmic sound that I recognized immediately. It was the sound of waves hitting the shore. Astonished, I stopped and looked at Philip.

"I didn't know you had . . ." I hesitated to find the right word.

"We do. It's not the Caspian, but Lake Michigan is also nice.

Anna and the girls go there a lot." He lit up a cigarette. "I heard you got a job."

"Yes. Anna got it for me," I answered.

"And tomorrow is your first day?" he asked.

"Uh-huh," I responded shyly, wondering why someone his age would speak with a child like me.

"You don't look so happy. Tell me, how do you feel here?" he asked.

I was shocked by his question, because I lived in a society where feelings were to be kept to yourself and never discussed with even the closest family members. I never questioned if I liked or disliked this harsh rule. I simply followed it. I wondered where in my body I should look for feelings and how I would tell the difference between feelings and the large gray cloud that possessed my mind most of the time. I was certain that feelings resided somewhere in me, like wild creatures roaming in a cave, filling the walls with strange shadows and never approaching the tiny opening that led outside. He noticed my confused face and rushed to help.

"It must not be easy to be around Teymour all the time. I love the guy, but he's a bit crazy, and I kind of want to kill him sometimes. *That* kind of love." He lit up a second cigarette. "Do you miss your hometown?" he asked.

"The thing is," I started, "I liked back home. I liked my life there. Some things were bothering me, like my cousin's constant desire to control me, my father's drinking, my mother's depression . . . but there were good things too."

"Okay, now we're getting somewhere," he said, encouraging me. "Tell me what was good about it." He turned to look at me for a moment, catching me off guard with his determined stare.

I studied Philip's face, noticing his long, chiseled nose, the aristocratic flair of his curly hair, carefully combed back, his large intelligent forehead.

"It's as if someone made this year the best year of my life on purpose, to make me suffer even more, thousands of miles away from home, away from friends. I went to a public school by my grandmother's house. It had a small yard and security and all. They'd only let us out to buy sandwiches for lunch from the corner bakery. A driver brought me at nine a.m. and picked me up at four. It was a tiny world. Nothing in it was strange or unfamiliar. Nothing ever changed in it, not even the teachers. I liked it. I had friends who felt like family. I had a whole summer of activities planned. Instead, I got on a plane and came here because my mother didn't want to live there anymore. But I do! I want to live there. I was wrong about my dreams of coming to the U.S. All I do is sit by the window, talk to myself, and run to the bathroom to cry so that Mother doesn't notice. Nights are even worse. I look at the clock and wait in pain when it will hit four, then five, then six, then Mother will get out of her bed and go smoke her cigarette in this foreign city that I hate."

At some point I had begun to cry and when I was done with my monologue, my face and neck were drenched in tears. We sat on stone steps leading up to a small community park. My temples throbbed with a pulsating pain and my body shivered. I looked around, a little embarrassed for letting out so much in front of a complete stranger and crying on top of that. *How could I have said all these things? I barely know this man!* I kept repeating in my head. Philip stayed silent for a moment, allowing me to regain myself, and then spoke with an understanding smile.

"I know your friends, your family, your hometown . . . all of this means the entire world to you. It is all you know, but if you look up you will see the sky. Do you see all those stars?" He raised his hand to the sky. "Baku is a beautiful city, but it is just one star out of so many. You have a whole life to discover them, Maryam. And soon you will smile again. You will be eager to discover new cities, new possibilities, new people. This new life that you hate so much, it will get better soon." He was looking at me while he spoke. "But I do think I know what we both need right now."

"What?" I asked.

"A nice toasted bagel with cream cheese and lox!" he responded "Eat! We need to eat! Let's go! I was worried about you, but now I can see that you don't need my help! What you need is good food. Anna is horrible at cooking, but it's hard to ruin a salmon cream cheese bagel—although I should never underestimate the powers of that crazy Jewish woman!"

I took a deep breath, smiled, and followed Philip back to the house. As promised, he cut the bagels, toasted them, and spread a generous pat of cream cheese on each before topping them with smoked salmon. That meal was the first one that I truly enjoyed in America. I bit into it, chewing the salty, creamy mix of ingredients and downing two glasses of hot black tea with sugar, happy that the cells of my tongue had gotten some of their feeling back.

Now that all the mess of my thoughts, the regrets mixed with doubts and grudges, had been lost somewhere by the steps of a suburban community park, I felt relaxed and allowed my thoughts to wander. I kept thinking about the ancient Assyrians—the rise and fall of their empire and how trivial my problems were compared to those of an empire. I imagined how the sun set upon the ancient Nineveh with its grandiose temples and the surrounding river and how the warriors and politicians would rush home to their wives and kids and enjoyed supper with their loved ones. It seemed as if history played a joke on humanity by covering everything in the past with a blanket of mystery that seemed to imply a deeper meaning to existence, while the truth was that real modern-day life, with its mundane routine, was just as ancient as this world!

CHAPTER 11

. . . .

STEPPING OUTSIDE IS DANGEROUS BUSINESS

Anna called around nine on Monday morning and gave Teymour the address of the optical store. He jotted it down on a piece of paper in his illegible handwriting and went into the bedroom to check something on his computer. A few minutes later, he came back with directions on how to get there. Now that the drama was behind us, he smiled more often, stopped rubbing his forehead, and didn't gulp down as many pills.

"It's all very simple. One train ride and then a bus," he explained. "You'll get off at Sheridan on the Red Line and then take CTA bus 155 to Rockwell. From there you walk south on Rockwell until you reach the shop. You got my cell phone number written down?"

"I memorized it," I said.

"My first job here was a pizza delivery guy," he said. "I got lost all the time, wasted a lot of money on gas, and didn't really make much. This is a nice, clean job, Maryam."

I wasn't sure what he meant by clean, but I nodded in agreement and took the paper from his hands.

Mother looked concerned. "Are you sure you understood everything?"

"Yes, Mama," I lied. "Remember I took the subway on my school trip to London? I know how it works."

Teymour gulped down the tea, took a bite of his sandwich, and headed to the door.

"I'm out!" he said. "Good luck, Maryam! Leyla, relax, she is a smart girl. She'll be fine!"

"Wait, Teymour!" Rufat stepped into the hallway. "I'm coming with you guys!"

"Where are you going?" Mother protested. "You didn't even finish your breakfast."

"Oh, just to check out the neighborhood. I checked the map on the Internet. If I stay on Lake Shore Drive, I'll be able to walk back, no problem."

"Cool, man!" Teymour said, grabbing his sunglasses.

Mother tried to protest, but Rufat acted quicker than she could react and, in a minute, all three of us left her alone at the flat. We stepped into the elevator, and I realized this was the first time we had been alone with Teymour. The air was cool and full of pleasant anticipation that comes with sudden changes. We said goodbye in the hallway and parted ways.

I was finally among all the ordinary Chicagoans I had observed from the window. Until now, I'd greeted them in the morning, followed them with my eyes as they made their way to the train station, and parted with them as they entered the revolving doors of high-rise buildings. I watched them as they walked their dogs in the park and fed the pigeons by the fountain, marveling at the bright choices of colors in their clothes, which contrasted so much with the black and brown that we primarily wore. They seemed unafraid to mix bold colors like blue and yellow, red and green, purple and orange, while we chose various shades of blue, gray, and brown. Obviously, there were outliers even where I came from, but wearing screaming colors like these would often be taken as an act of defiance, a challenge to society, and would have elicited intimidating glares from passersby.

Besides the colorful clothing, there was something else I found very peculiar about Americans. They appeared to be comfortable with their imperfections. Azeri women spent so much time concealing features that they thought were unpretty. Legs that were too thin meant you could not wear a skirt. A waist too thick meant you'd stick to baggy clothes and always choose the color black to avoid adding more pounds to your figure. Nose jobs were not so surprising anymore, an entire city of similar noses chiseled by the same plastic surgeon visiting from Turkey. It seemed as if your body and your face were more public than private, and your appearance had to conform to some unspoken rules.

I sat on the other side of the balcony glass and studied their clothes, bags, pets, and morning beverages and could not help but notice how different they were. Watching them from above was one thing, but descending into the crowd was completely different. It made me anxious. Would I fit in with the usual Monday morning scene? Would I be able to cross the road? Would I board the right bus and get off on the right stop? And if I did get lost, how would I find the way back home? I took a deep breath and walked on.

The fear of not belonging was still there, but my desire to try was stronger.

CHAPTER 12

. . . .

MARISKI

The streets were buzzing with traffic and the morning folk were all hurrying somewhere. The string of breakfast places I had first seen from above looked like a postcard from some tourist city in Europe, with beds of roses hanging from the rail fences and cups of coffee and croissants served on white saucers. I noticed an elderly man wearing beige shorts and what I would later find out was called a "polo" shirt. He was half-reclining in his chair with his legs crossed and a large newspaper in his lap. I wondered how he could read with the loud buzz of the cars, the music of the radio coming out of the speakers, and the occasional barking of the tiny dog at his side. As I walked on, this scenery was followed by the large windows of a bank building with an oversized blue logo. There were seven or eight employees standing behind the teller windows and staring at computers. They wore navy suits with light blue shirts, identical and fully consumed by what they saw on the blue screens. I picked up my pace and crossed another street, finally making it to the subway entrance.

I took the stairs down and found myself in a long, dirty corridor with vaulted ceilings, symmetrical columns on each side, a few bare light fixtures hanging in the middle casting a pale light, and a monitor that estimated the time until the arrival of the next train. There were large dark stains of dirt or mold on the vaulted ceiling that made the place look like a crime scene. I noticed that while I was examining the station, looking around at passengers, the grip around my neck softened. I could still feel it, but it bothered me less.

The train arrived a few minutes later. The cars turned out to be well-lit, clean enough, and they didn't smell like sweat. They had large windows and there were plenty of seats available. I took a seat by the window, pressed Mother's monumental bag to my chest, and started looking around.

I assumed that all stations on the Red Line were underground and prepared myself for forty-five minutes' worth of the loud tapping of the tracks echoing off concrete tunnels, but twenty minutes later, the train emerged above ground, revealing a green park with a small pond and several weeping willows dipping their heavy branches in the water. The park turned out to be a cemetery. This came as a surprise as cemeteries back home looked rather creepy, with barren ground and no greenery, except for wild bushes that reached your knees, and rows of black gravestones with faded portraits. This cemetery, which I would later learn was called Graceland Cemetery, had a broad, manicured lawn, bouquets of flowers at each grave, and several large trees. It was peaceful, the kind of place where you'd like to lean against a tree and read a book.

Most of the younger passengers were bobbing their heads to the inaudible music coming from their headphones, while the older ones looked around in search of some interaction. They all smiled. *What a strange habit—to smile for no reason,* I thought.

"A nice break from humidity is what we need," said a lady sitting near to me on the train. She had on a white linen dress and held a cane on her lap. "No rain for weeks and no winds either." She leaned over to look out the window.

"So much for the 'Windy City,'" responded a man nearby, wearing a baseball cap and reading a newspaper.

"Well, you must know the story. That name's got nothing to do with the *weather*," the lady said. He nodded in silence and flipped to the next page.

What a coincidence! I thought. My hometown of Baku was short for *Badu Kube*, which translates as "the City of Winds" from Persian. I recalled seeing a "Windy City" postcard in one of the stores on State Street when we went grocery shopping and did not make the connection, which didn't surprise me. Most of the time, I walked around completely submerged into my own world of gloom. The thought of having ended up in another Windy City after crossing the ocean put a faint smile on my face.

I got off at Sheridan station and walked over to the CTA bus stop, where I hopped on the 151 bus headed north. I had learned from the complicated bus route map at the station that this bus would only take me as far as Devon and Lakewood, where I got off and picked up the 155, the bus line that traversed nearly all of West Devon Avenue. As I rode, I observed that the street was a never-ending string of grocery stores, electronics shops, cafés, restaurants, pharmacies, and bookstores. Most were of Indian or Pakistani origin. Every light pole had a banner advertising some Indian skin-whitening cream with a famous Bollywood star, or an insurance company, or some cultural event. I noticed a group of young Indian girls with long braided hair wearing colorful saris.

Devon was so busy and crowded that, for the first time during my adventurous commute, I grew worried that I'd miss my stop. I got up from my seat and approached the bus driver. I held on to the pole by his seat and asked, "Did we pass Rockwell?"

"No! Approaching in fiiiiive!" he responded.

Five what? Minutes or seconds?

"Okay. This is my first time taking the bus," I said. "Would you be so kind to tell me when we get to Rockwell?"

The driver eyed me from top to bottom and nodded with a chuckle. I felt embarrassed for a second, but anything was better than getting lost on your first day at work. A few minutes later, I heard him announce the stop in an almost theatrical manner.

"Aprooooooaching Dee-voooon and Rooooock-weeell!" he spoke with a voice that reminded me of American commercials that I saw on television.

I hopped off the bus and got my bearings, determining which way was south on Rockwell, as Teymour had said. But before turning my back on Devon Avenue, I spied a Russian bookstore called Balalaika with a poster of Alla Pugacheva—a Russian pop diva, a favorite of my grandparents' and parents' generation—glued to the front window and a pile of books propping up a loudspeaker that was playing one of her songs. Walking briskly down Rockwell now, I looked for the address plates on the rows of offices that lined the street. I passed a café with a small Turkish flag on the window, selling coffee, Turkish delights, and *simit*. I later found out that it was one of the three Turkish spots in the whole city, and it happened to lie on my route to work. But what I saw next was truly a pleasant surprise: a tiny Georgian bakery selling *khachapuri* and other traditional Georgian pastries. I peeked in the window to check out the pastries and saw a tall man in his fifties wearing white clothes with an apron over them.

The next building was the optical shop. The sign out front read "Vision Express Optical." The place looked old, with dusty carpeting and a row of old visitor chairs by the window. There were two cabinets with plastic and metal frames, and several faded pamphlets were laying around on the shelves. A tall counter stood in the back of the room with a glass divider behind it. I noticed some movement in the back and then saw a man come out. He was tall and lanky, with legs too long for his body and a small bulging belly. His shoulders were narrow, but he somehow managed to look slim despite his protruding stomach. He was blessed with a head full of curly hair that was dyed black and combed back with gel. Unlike all the optometrists I would meet later in life, he did not wear any glasses. His nose was unusually long and thin but suited his face quite well.

"Hello, my name is Maryam," I began. "Anna said you had a job for me." I wasn't sure what else to add and was hoping that was enough to refresh his memory.

"Anna?" he looked puzzled.

"Oh, Anna said that the doctor who works here," I stumbled, "that the doctor is her cousin, and I don't know his name. He said you needed someone who speaks Russian." I could tell by his reaction that he'd finally managed to connect the dots.

"Oh, yes!" He touched his forehead and flared his nostrils. "Yes, yes, yes!" he repeated and gestured for me to follow him. "Come, come!" he said. "W-w-what was your name?" He stuttered when he spoke, but it hardly seemed to bother him. Besides, stuttering didn't stop him from speaking too fast. I was hardly able to follow along with what he was saying.

"Maryam," I answered.

"And you speak Russian?" It sounded more like "Rashy-ann," but I figured that's what he meant.

"Yes," I answered.

"Okay, Maryam. C-c-come meet everyone else. I am Ashur. You call me Ashur, okay?" he said, raising his bushy eyebrows.

I nodded in agreement and followed Ashur into a small back room behind the glass divider. The room had a coffee table in the middle and tall counters across the perimeter of the room and looked even shabbier than the storefront. There were two older men sitting by the coffee table and watching television. They were in their fifties, or maybe sixties, I couldn't tell. One of them was wearing a cream-colored polo shirt, khaki shorts, and flip-flops. His hair was white, unlike the other one, who also had a lot of hair like Ashur, and just like Ashur's it was dyed black. He leaned on the coffee table with his whole body, and I could tell he was shaking his knees nervously under the table.

I noticed that all of the counters were peppered with dark brown cigarette burns, and this made the place look even more unappealing. The side desk was covered in random papers, letters, old calendars, pamphlets, and old business cards. The air was filled with a mix of cigarette and coffee smell, reminding me of my father's dark basement office where we sometimes played computer games after school. Besides coffee and cigarettes, there was also a scent of something else, some kind of a spice that filled up this place. It was quite strong, but it did not bother me.

Ashur introduced me to the tall guy, whose name was Shammoun. He had a kind smile and spoke in a low voice. I noticed a heavy gold chain on his neck with a large cross, which reminded me that Assyrians were Christian. The other one's name was Youel. He seemed too busy to notice me. Ashur gestured to him and said, "This is Maryam, the girl Anna sent. She speaks Rushhy-ann!"

"Hi, Maryam!" he almost shouted and immediately got up from the table, disappearing into the back of the office. *What a character*, I thought.

"Don't pay attention. Youel is a little c-c-crazy." Ashur waved, rotating his finger in circles by his temple.

I had no idea how to respond and just smiled politely. Ashur showed me to the tiny desk by the back wall, covered in white and pink slips, boxes containing glasses and written prescriptions, pens scattered everywhere, a heavy stapler, and piles of unopened mail.

"D-d-d-don't look at this," he said, pointing at the table and laughing. "Come here first! I will show you where the c-c-coffee is. Then we can come and look at this paperwork. Come! Come! Are you always so slow?" he called as I followed him to the coffee machine in the back. For someone who stuttered, he spoke *fast*.

"Can I c-c-call you Mariski?" Ashur asked.

"Mariski?" I asked surprised. "Who is that?"

"Isn't that a Russian name? You the Russian here, so we c-c-call you Mariski," he said and laughed.

I figured he was referring to "Marusya," the nickname for Maryam. I wasn't particularly happy with Marusya, but Mariski sounded different, and I wasn't going to argue about anything on my first day, so I smiled, nodded, and followed him to the back of the office. By the end of the day, all three men were referring to me as Mariski.

Ashur appeared to be in a constant hurry, stuttering and repeating everything twice on purpose, gesturing with his hands, walking fast, and producing a pleasant clap as his shiny shoes hit the stone floor.

What a hole in a wall! I thought.

CHAPTER 13

. . . .

THE FEELING THAT
PRECEDES HAPPINESS

I spent the first day trying to tidy up the messy desk where I was supposed to work. While I was organizing it, Ashur kept looking at me impatiently, wondering if I was messing up his order of things on the table. When I was done, he pulled up a chair and explained what my job really entailed. I had to answer phone calls with a polished "Vision Express Optical, how can I help you?" a line that I carefully wrote on a piece of paper and attached to the white wall facing my desk, along with a hundred other random Post-Its that made the wall look like a mosaic of modern art.

"See these slips?" He pointed at an old plastic container. "F-f-first name, last name, d-d-date of birth. You fill out this p-p-pink slip, but with g-g-good handwriting. You have g-g-good handwriting?" he asked, suddenly turning towards me.

"Yes," I stuttered.

"You know t-t-typing?" he asked. "You need to type, Mariski, so they can read it. And then you s-s-staple these two together and you p-p-put it into *this* box, not that other b-b-box. *This* box!" he pointed to a different box. "Then at the end of the week, we mail it to Kaitlin."

"Who is Kaitlin?" I asked.

"Kaitlin, the woman in p-p-public aid office. You got a p-p-problem, you call Kaitlin. D-d-don't worry, Mariski. I handle it," he said and raised his hand.

I could tell that Ashur was simplifying his language to make it easier for me, speaking in sort of a child's language. I did nothing to indicate that he didn't need to explain things to me that way. I just nodded. Ashur explained that a government agency would receive the forms and then manufacture the glasses for all of his public aid patients and ship them back within thirty days.

Ashur didn't really have to lure in his customers with a clean office, fancy frames, or good customer service. Most of them were immigrants who were not looking for polished customer service, gleaming-clean medical facilities, or friendly staff. They were here to receive free glasses for themselves and their children, paid for by the government.

That afternoon, I got busy with all the paperwork that had to be organized at my desk, cleaned out all the drawers, and collected all the pens around the messy office and put them into a plastic glass on my desk. I found a place for the heavy black stapler, which looked more like a weapon than an office supply object, and found a tape dispenser. At around four p.m. the desk looked tidy and the three men sitting by the coffee table were pointing at it and saying something in their language. I couldn't tell if they were happy or annoyed with my fervent organization of their old, rusty, smoke-filled establishment.

At around five p.m., Ashur pronounced the phrase that I would hear him say every single day for the next ten months.

"Yalla, guys! Let's go!" He'd slap his knees and get up. "Tomorrow is another day!"

I picked up my bag and headed for the front door, excited to hop on the bus and take the same route back home. I was fascinated with Devon Avenue, with its busy intersections, crazy traffic, pedestrians crossing the streets in places where they shouldn't. Its lively nature occupied my brain so much that my silent torturer would loosen his grip and I could breathe. As the bus drove me through the streets, my eyes followed men and women dressed in traditional Indian clothes walking in groups, appearing jubilant and cheerful. It was contagious. How wonderful, that one could cross the ocean and find themselves looking at mothers and children walking the streets, peering into store windows, and catching buses to get home in time for dinner.

I got off the bus at Lakewood, took the 151 to Sheridan, and boarded the train. I watched how small shops and crowded intersections gave way to the greenery of neighborhoods adjacent to downtown and eventually found myself underground, a few stations away from home.

Exiting the train onto State Street felt like magically emerging in another country. How different could parts of one city be? Gone were the small shops, groceries, kiosks, and pharmacies. I was back in a world of skyscrapers, nicely trimmed boxwood bushes, and buzzing traffic. This part of town was inhabited by men and women in formal suits and business skirts, carefully eyeing the intersections and continuing to talk on their phones even as they crossed the street.

We had chicken stew with tomatoes and turmeric, the dish Mother made when she didn't know what to cook—her safe bet. I realized I was slowly getting used to how chicken tasted here, big chunks of meat that were soft and plump, but lacked flavor, scent, and taste, just like the peach.

"So, I went to see the John Hancock building today," Rufat began. "It didn't take me much to get there."

"Where and what is John Hancock building?" Mother asked, turning to Teymour.

"Oh, it is not far at all, don't worry," Teymour answered. "Nice! Impressive, huh? What else did you do?"

"Then I went to Lake Shore Park." Rufat took a bite of the chicken. "Like you suggested. Played soccer there with some guys that took me in."

"Played soccer with who?" I asked, surprised.

"With the kids on the beach, why?" Rufat answered.

"Some kids you didn't know? You just started playing with them?" Mother asked.

I was amazed how my brother lived in a parallel universe, full of excitement about this new country and its people, comfortable to just go and play soccer with some people he didn't know and I, in the meantime, lived entirely in my head, fighting invisible demons and afraid of any interaction with people. Even his appetite seemed better than mine. Didn't we come from the same place and go through the same damn thing? He found energy to play video games, polish off his dinner, and play soccer with strangers on the beach, while I limited myself to observing people from the height of the thirteenth floor, engaging in never-ending self-talk, while listening to the monotonous songs of Diana Krall.

"That's cool, Rufat. I like this! No need to be afraid of people. Soccer is soccer, that's what you do on the beach! Chicago is famous for how friendly people are here. It's a midwestern thing. If you go up north to New York or Washington, you won't get such treatment," Teymour said.

"That's right! They were very chill. They had some spare balls on the side, and I busied myself with them while they finished the game, and then one of them invited me to join, so I joined. Like you said, super laid back and friendly people," Rufat confirmed. "Nothing to worry about, Mama! Hey, Teymour, since you're in a good mood," Rufat said, then paused. "I got some not-so-great news. I think I infected your computer with some virus by downloading music," he said. "From questionable Russian websites."

"Oh, God," Teymour cringed. "Of course you did. Look, it better be easy to fix." He did not appear angry or upset.

"Just some Russian virus—should be no problem," Rufat said, picking up the joke.

"Don't worry about it this time, but we need to talk about the websites you use," Teymour said.

Mother was still puzzled about Rufat's adventures at Lake Shore Park, but she went on eating her dinner, occasionally glancing at him with a mix of pride and concern. After dinner, she took her usual place on the balcony and enjoyed her cigarette. Rufat was playing games on Teymour's computer, and Teymour, now unable to do any work, decided to take another "walk around the neighborhood."

I had nothing else to do but to sit by the boombox and listen to Dire Straits' "Your Latest Trick" again. The setting sun painted an orange backdrop for the evening skyline. The glass buildings reflected the orange of the setting sun. I'd spent so many evenings sitting by this window, watching this scene, but only truly noticed its majestic beauty today. I felt a pleasant tiredness in my shoulders and a sense of relief.

I thought of Mardakan again. I closed my eyes and saw the faded green gates and the old mulberry tree, then the rows of grape vines, then the miniature apple trees in a small, fenced area, and, eventually, the winding stone pathway that led to the two-story house.

I saw Nana in one of her loose floral dresses that reached her knees, with her hair parted in the middle and the two braids touching her shoulders. Her henna-colored hair glistened in the golden light of the setting sun as she watered the yellow and maroon flowers that only bloom after sunset. Their name escaped my memory, but I tried to remember.

I saw my grandfather reading his newspaper on the balcony, giving Nana instructions on how to water some of the trees as she smiled serenely and ignored everything he said.

"You think he knows better than me?" she asked, fixing the few stubborn strands that fell on my forehead, a habit she refused to give up.

When the sun finally descended behind the horizon, the imaginary world I built dissolved before my eyes. I regretted not having a pen and a paper to jot it down. It would have made another escape to this place much easier next time. All I would have to do is close my eyes and recognize everything just as I pictured it this evening. But it was too late. The sun disappeared and a gigantic shade swallowed the city. In search of the sort of peace one longs for at a day's end, I still turned to my past.

. . . .

CHAPTER 14

"WE ALL HUMAN BEINGS"

My journey to the colorful world of Devon Avenue soon became the highlight of my days. The red and blue CTA buses I boarded after the train passed by numerous Indian-Pakistani stores with colorful saris and *lehengas* covered in pleats of rich embroidery showcased on tall, glossy, faceless mannequins. Until then, I'd only seen saris in Bollywood classics that, for some unknown reason, were so popular in post-Soviet countries. The heroes of these films were always fighting windmills. They were unfortunate lovers separated by fate or some incurable disease, destined to reunite not for a happy end, but to die in each other's arms. They were elephants that rescued children from poisonous snakes. They were twin sisters, Zita and Gita, separated at birth only to recognize each other from an identical mark on their shoulders decades later. Fantastic stuff, far from the ordinary. The heroes of these films would sing and dance as they wished, converse with animals, inhabit beautiful mansions, and were always on the verge of something larger than life. Nobody knew why these films were so popular during my childhood, but the vibrant, melodic world of Indian actresses with their waist-long hair, pointy eyeliner, and flowy outfits was forever stamped in my memory. I imagined that the world around you adjusted as soon as you put on these magical dresses. I wondered if I could walk in and try on one of the elegant embroidered saris, like trying on another life. Of course, I had neither the money nor the occasion to wear a sari, so I stuck to daydreaming and window-shopping.

On my fifth day at work, I visited Argo's, the Georgian bakery next door. This tiny place was filled with the fragrant smell of freshly baked *tandir* bread, a smell that would haunt me in my sleep. Since we had arrived in America, all three of us craved the famous crusty *tandir* bread, baked in a vertical clay oven. We looked for it in the bread section of Potash Brothers but did not find anything even close to it. It turned out this place sold fresh *tandir* daily, so every evening on my way home, I stopped by to pick up a loaf.

The wall on the right was covered with Georgian miniatures in elaborate frames, a large culinary map of Georgia, and a clipping from a local newspaper praising the egg and cheese pastry that Argo's Georgian Bakery was famous for. There was a glass-top refrigerator by the counter with frozen dough products for sale. A tall, wide-shouldered man with graying hair and blue eyes stood by the kneading table. He rested his flour-covered hands on the table and looked out into the busy street. He had an unlit cigarette between his lips. The white of his apron, his white t-shirt, and his powdered hands strangely complemented his spotless, almost doctor-like outfit.

"Georgian?" he asked with a thick Georgian accent.

"Azerbaijani," I replied. "I work at the optical nearby."

"Close!" he replied. "Did you just come?" he asked, tilting his head to the left and lighting up his cigarette.

"Twenty days ago," I answered.

"I am Irakli." He finally smiled, taking a drag. "Don't worry, it will get better soon."

How did he know? I flushed. My face must have betrayed my insomnia, the nights of aimless searching for something that faintly, distantly reminded me of home or for something like home, something that had roots. Something that did not feel ripped out of a warm place. There was no use in hiding it, but bursting into tears in front of a stranger was more than I could take. From then on, I stopped by to get the bread, said my polite goodbye half-aloud, and rushed out of the store.

We worked late on Tuesdays and Fridays, as Eugene, Anna's cousin who'd just gotten his optometrist license, would see patients from three to seven. The room would quickly fill up with families of five or six, usually newly arrived in the U.S. and barely speaking any English. Just like the rest of the locals from the Devon community, our patients came from all over the world. The vast majority of them were Indian or Pakistani, but our patients reflected the vibrant international community of the neighborhood. I had never seen so many nationalities walking on the same sidewalk, leisurely speaking their language, existing in parallel worlds—all of them frequenting the same opticians, dentists, libraries, and bus stops. It was hard to believe that somewhere in the world, Pakistanis were in conflict with Indians, and Arabs and Jews could not share a land.

On Tuesdays and Fridays, the small reception area of the optical shop would fill up with Ukrainians, Russians, Koreans, Greeks, Assyrians, Arabs, Orthodox Jews, Africans, and others from countries I had only vaguely heard of. I spoke Russian with anyone who came from post-Soviet countries and Turkish with Turks, proud to share that I was from Azerbaijan, a brotherly state with a similar language. When neither of the languages worked, I resorted to my hands to explain myself. This method never failed. *What a strange thing*, I thought, *to come to the United States all the way from Azerbaijan and work in a store where you can learn any language except English.*

The three men spent their day glued to the television, watching CNN as the U.S. Army hunted Saddam Hussein and his sons in abandoned caves somewhere in the desert. Occasionally, one of them would get up from his chair, exclaim something in Assyrian, point at the rest, and light up another cigarette. I later learned from Anna that Saddam persecuted many Assyrians in Iraq, that it was one of the reasons there were so many of them here in Chicago, and that they were anxious to see him captured.

Youel apparently came from Australia, which had a sizable Iraqi-Assyrian community too. He was a man of little patience and no plans in life, but he made the place a little less dull. He would often get up to throw away the stale morning coffee and brew another pot.

"W-w-why you wasting coffee?" Ashur would ask.

"I have to get up and do something. If I don't, you go crazy," he'd respond. "You know that. We all go crazy! Besides," he would point at me, "she wants coffee!"

Of course, no one would take him seriously, but we all smiled.

"Fine!" Ashur would roll his eyes.

He would throw out the garbage and walk to the nearest pharmacy to buy snacks, all the while humming Assyrian folk songs and enlivening the place with some activity. When the clock hit four p.m., he'd slap his knees and get up from his chair to light up a thin incense stick that emanated that familiar strong smell that I noticed on my first day. It was called *bissma* and Assyrians used it to ward off the evil eye. The smell was too dominant, but I kept smiling when Youel would bring the smoky thin stick and hover it above my head, mumbling something in Assyrian. He mentioned that one of his old flames recently told him that he had a son, a son he knew nothing about for years. I couldn't tell if Youel bought that story. I thought that for someone whose life revolved around the coffee machine and the pharmacy across the street, jobless and bored, the idea of a son somewhere out there was a warm one to cling to, especially at this past-fifty age. He said he was saving money to travel to Australia and meet his son, but there were no definite plans and the words sounded more like an echo in the wind. On some days, this was believable, but on others I could tell it was a good, teary-eyed story to pull and given that neither Shammoun nor Ashur showed any reaction to this, it was probably nothing but a tall tale.

Unlike Shammoun and Youel who never married, Ashur was divorced and had no children, but served as a father figure to his nephew, a blue-eyed six-year-old with cherubim-like curls and unending energy to destroy things. Ashur, unlike the child's mother, let him get away with anything and spoiled the kid, but once in a while he'd be fed up with never-ending requests and fall into a mood to discipline the brat. That usually lasted a day. I never found out the name of the child, as Ashur addressed him only as Babi. Babi called every afternoon right before we closed to ask for some junk food or a computer game.

"What you want, Babi?" Ashur would ask. "Okay," he'd repeat several times.

"D-d-did you do your homework?" Then immediately, "G-g-give me your mother." Ashur would do his questioning, but I never saw him decline the requests. It reminded me of how I'd pester my father with the most ridiculous requests when I had the flu. I'd ask for canned pineapple, bananas, a video cassette with Disney movies, or a Spice Girls poster. He'd always give in no matter how ridiculous I got with my wishes, so flu became a special coveted time for me.

The third Iraqi man, Shammoun, was the strangest of the three, both in appearance and in character. He was very short and bulky, with a bald head, a long nose, and sad eyes. Unlike the other two, he always wore shorts, a t-shirt, and flip-flops. Despite his bulky figure, his movements were fragile and clumsy, and he'd complain about his heart, shaking his head and repeating the same phrase over and over.

"My heart, Mariski. No good, no good!" he would repeat. "My heart, you know? It's no good!"

"Then don't smoke!" I'd say, trying to imitate their accent. Shammoun would shake his head again, followed by another "My heart, Maryam! No good! No good!"

Youel never missed an opportunity to join in. "You see, Maryam?" he'd begin. "My mother told me to stop smoking. And what did I do? I quit! I don't smoke no more!" He'd raise his palms to his head. "I quit means I quit." He grinned and repeated his victorious "I quit" two more times. Ashur would glance at Youel, shake his head, and take out another cigarette. The place was drenched in cynicism and sarcasm.

I wondered what was it about Iraqis that made them repeat everything twice? A simple phrase like "Do you want to have lunch?" was always modified to "Do you want lunch? Lunch?" or asking if you want coffee was always "Coffee? Coffee?" Soon I adopted the habit, unsure if I did it to fit in or because I liked it. Strangely, I did want to fit in. I even shared the little bits of my knowledge about Babylonian and Assyrian kings, hoping to impress them, but with little result. The battles and cities that I mentioned were vaguely familiar to them. They didn't seem the least bit interested in my cultural background, aside from one question that Ashur asked on my second day working there.

"Are you Muslim?" He sat with his arms folded, only turning his head to ask the question.

"Yes," I answered, realizing that this was the first time someone had asked a question about religion.

"Shia or Sunni?" he went on. Now this was a difficult question, because I didn't know.

"I don't know. I'll have to ask my mother," I answered.

"You don't know?" he repeated.

"No, I don't. We're not very religious in Azerbaijan. We had that whole period of communism during the Soviet times, so religion was banned," I explained.

I could see that Ashur remained indifferent to this tidbit of history.

"We all human beings," he said, turning to the television and lighting up a cigarette.

As time passed, I realized that all three of them somewhat disliked Muslims, which was strange because their traditions, rituals, and cultural celebrations were so similar to that of Muslim cultures in the Middle East, and yet they found a world of difference between themselves and others. Later in life, I witnessed a similar phenomenon in other neighboring communities that had a keen eye for differences but would ignore things they had in common.

The strongest anti-Muslim voice was Shammoun. He always had some creepy story about a nine-year-old child bride who had been killed by her forty-year-old Muslim husband, or a woman executed for stealing bread to feed her hungry children.

"Mariski, you tell me," he'd begin, "what was the fault of that poor woman?" He'd go on, looking at me, "She no want *nothing*! She want bread! She want food for her children. You tell me, Mariski!" He'd bump his knees against one another and wipe the side of his lip.

"Those bastards! What you have to do with God? *Nothing* you have to do with God, I say," he'd answer himself. I'd be relieved to see he was not actually waiting for me to say something. However, with time I realized that this was not a blanket feeling towards all Muslims out there. Shammoun was concerned with religious fundamentalists who used the religion to get away with stuff that should never be allowed.

"I live with Muslims side-by-side in Baghdad for thirty years! We cut bread together, we dance at weddings together, we sick together, we get better together. I play soccer with them. Those are normal Muslims, Mariski, but these," he'd point at the TV, tuned to CNN showing scenes from the American war in Afghanistan, "these are animals, Mariski. Not humans. They have no mother, no father! They no respect the bread they cut with another person. No God in their heart, Mariski!"

I'd look at the TV and see images of men dressed in baggy clothes, dusty rags wrapped around their heads, rifles hanging at their sides, and a strange desperation in their eyes. Men whose like I've never seen back home or anywhere else, except these daily images from Afghanistan or Iraq on television. In their eyes I did not see a thirst for anyone's blood or the perversity that Shammoun described. I saw nothing but fear and the broken emptiness of a world that was destroyed with nothing to replace the rubble. In a strange way, I recognized both their emptiness and fear, even though back then I knew nothing about these wars and the people who were left orphaned for decades. But you don't need to know that to recognize the signs and scent of despair. *What do you even know, that you could answer him?* I thought, and kept quiet.

The truth is that these stories exhausted me, but I kept shaking my head, speechless, to assure him I despised all these terrible acts as much as they did. These occasional bursts of anti-Muslim sentiment were complicating my feelings for the Iraqis as I would go through waves of affection followed by wariness. However, weeks passed and all four of us morphed into one big, loud, and contradictory family that ate, laughed, worked, and argued with each other. I'd laugh at their jokes, serve them coffee or tea, listen to the songs they hummed during monotonous afternoons, and complain half-heartedly about the cigarette stains on the counters.

CHAPTER 15

. . . .

EATING ALONE IN SILENCE

That weekend Teymour helped us move to a second-floor apartment of a large house that his friend owned. He and his family occupied the first floor. They had converted the second floor into a stand-alone apartment with its own entrance, kitchen, and bathrooms. It was a nice, light-filled place that stretched like a long, wide hall from kitchen to the living room, with tall leafy trees peeking from all the windows. The honey-colored hardwood floors reflected the light pouring in and contrasted with the lush greenery, and the place had a pleasant, fresh vibe. It reminded me of our summer house, although lately, I looked for things that were even a distant reminder of our wooden hut in Mardakan—a flower bed with marigolds, the way the wind ruffled the branches, the dry scent of the summer in the twilight.

Teymour called up his friends ahead of our move, looking for spare household items. By the end of the week, he had found a large couch, a couple of mattresses, some silverware, and even an old

TV. We had nothing but a few suitcases, so the move was smooth. Teymour's friend and his wife were waiting for us on the terrace when we arrived. They took us to the second floor and showed us around. All the while, his young wife bombarded Mother with questions in that typical too-direct, almost uncomfortable back-home way, trying to understand how we ended up in America with little money, no documents, and not much of a plan for the future. Teymour tried to fend off question after question, but she must have known him long enough to dodge his sarcastic remarks and press on. If she had known how difficult it was to get a word out of Mother when she didn't care to share, she wouldn't have wasted her time. We watched Mother dodge question after question in her second-nature way, and soon the woman chatted away about her own life, complaining about traffic, Chicago heat, and her husband.

Soon they were gone and Mother, armed with cleaning supplies she bought at Potash Brothers, started her rigorous cleaning routine. The floors were vacuumed and then wiped twice. The windows, the insides of cupboards (and in some cases the walls, too) were wiped and lined with paper towels. Mother washed all the clean dishes and silverware again, refusing to load it into the dishwashing machine (it would take her a year to finally trust the damn thing). Finally, when the practically empty apartment was scrubbed clean, she sank onto the brown, weathered couch and sighed, exhausted and happy. If there was one thing that never failed to lift Mother's spirits, it was physical exhaustion through cleaning. Cleaning was her religion and her therapy, one of the few things she shared with Nana. She'd jump out of her deepest depression at the sight of a messy house, put all her force into scrubbing it clean, and then indulge in the happiness that followed. Unfortunately, it didn't last long. It was not a permanent solution, just a quick fix that faded by the end of the day.

That evening after we ate our turkey and cheese sandwiches and drank sweet tea from the chipped cups Teymour had gotten from a friend, the family downstairs invited us to join them on the terrace for evening tea. I was sure mother would turn down the invitation, but surprisingly she agreed and even changed into new clothes. The terrace was wide and empty, nothing but a round table and a swinging couch and a few white plastic chairs that I'd seen in teahouses back home. There were cups and saucers and a stack of dessert plates on a saffron-colored tablecloth. The chatty wife of our landlord, whose name was Narmina, brought out a powdered walnut cake on a round Madonna plate, a dowry staple for all Azeri women.

"Please, come, help yourselves," she said. "Amina will bring out the tea in a moment. Amina is my niece," she explained. "She's been with us for a few years now. She works in the city, at a dental practice, but comes to visit us. She looked after my son since he was a baby, practically raised him. We're one big family."

Mother smiled politely, but Narmina was in no need of encouragement. She went on with her story as Amina brought out a tray with a teapot and strawberry preserves in a jar.

"Come, Amina! Be careful with that teapot, will you?" Narmina said. "Oh, this girl!" she exclaimed and touched Amina's shoulder. "She arrived here not knowing anything about running a house. You'd ask her to pour tea and she'd bring it out in one of those huge mugs, the ones that look like a bucket. People here drink coffee in the morning in those. I can't stand them! There is something wrong with drinking tea from anything but crystal glasses, don't you agree?" she went on, obviously not expecting an answer.

Amina was not pleased with this clumsy introduction but did not look surprised either. She slumped her shoulders and nodded until Narmina was done with her tirade. Mother listened, sipped her tea, and took a bite of the cake, pausing before chewing it. I kept quiet and observed Amina. She had a delicate shape. Her collarbone glowed with a light summer tan and her hands were covered with protruding veins. She traced them with her fingers and rubbed the back of her neck once in a while. One of her eyes was sort of half-closed. It must have been a birth defect, but it looked as if she'd just had it with this world and was permanently sad and bitter about it. We finished our tea and the conversation died down. Mother must have been exhausted after all the cleaning, so she did nothing to keep up her end, and soon we went upstairs to get ready for bed. It was already pretty late when we heard a knock on the door. All three of us came out, surprised and not expecting a guest this late. Mother opened the door and found Amina standing there with a plate of leftover cake.

"Good evening. Oh, are you guys ready to go to bed already?" she said in a relaxed manner. "I thought I'd chat with Maryam if she was free," she explained. "Here, this is for you," she said, handing the cake to Mother.

"Sure, Amina. Thank you." Mother took the cake but did not seem too happy about the visit.

"I didn't get to chat with you downstairs," Amina addressed me now. "Narmina did all the talking. Do you want to have some tea and chat?"

I didn't know how I felt about a late-night chat with a stranger, but there was nothing else to do. Mother had already let her. Amina's straightforward, unapologetic directness was both jarring and refreshing.

"Sure," I said. "I'll make some tea."

"Good," Mother replied. "Well, you two enjoy! Rufat, you got no business here. Brush your teeth and off to bed."

"Yeah, I don't care much about girl talk anyways," Rufat said and disappeared into the back of the apartment.

"I like your brother. Does he always say stuff to your face like that?" Amina asked. "It's better that way, you know?"

"Don't listen to him," I said.

"Narmina is my cousin, but she's much older, so she calls me her niece," Amina said.

"You do look like her. A little," I replied.

"You mean the looks? I guess. I hope that's where it ends, really," Amina said.

That is not where it ended, though. Just like Narmina, Amina could keep up a one-sided conversation for a while. During that late-night tea, I learned all about her without asking a single question. I sipped my tea, munched on the dry walnut cake, and yawned once in a while. It seemed as if she'd been waiting for a stranger to unleash all her untold stories on ever since her arrival in the U.S. She wasn't all that interested in me, so I kept nodding and letting her talk. It turned out Amina came to America to learn English but had spent most of her time babysitting an infant of a neighboring family and taking the free ESL classes at the nearby church. Once in a while she'd quarrel with Narmina and at the point when things had gotten too rough, she'd been lucky enough to snag a job as a dental assistant in the city and move out. She now lived in a small studio by Lake Shore Park and biked to work every day. Her English was impeccable now. She hardly had any accent.

"It's a nice clean job," she said. *There's that phrase again,* I thought but said nothing. "It's easy to learn, comes with good pay, and if you mess things up, there is always another place that needs a dental assistant. You've got to be okay with blood though. Can't pass out on a patient. Half the time you're in their mouth with a suction tip, sucking away their saliva mixed with blood."

"Wow, how do you get used to *that*?" I asked.

"That's peaches, Maryam. You get used to that and other things," she said and looked away. "Try getting used to spending New Year's Eve on your own. Away from your mom and dad and annoying sisters. You're lucky your mom and brother are here. I've been alone all this time. When I saw you, I thought you could be my sister. You kinda look like her, too. Long hair, big eyes, smart as hell."

Amina's thoughts raced with such speed that I gave up trying to keep up with them. She tilted her head to the side and spoke, looking at the full moon outside, throwing a knowing glance at me once in a while, not asking any questions, and making a bunch of incorrect assumptions. I sat there, hugging my knees and listening as she spilled out story after story—patients with bloody mouths, a studio where she lived alone, a bike that she rode to work every day, Saturdays spent lounging on the grass in the park, going to the zoo sometimes, a security guard who kept asking her out for coffee. In my last year back home, I had barely learned how to take a bus from my grandmother's place to school. The whole ride had taken less than ten minutes and I would still get nervous as I'd climbed inside every morning. I had lived such a shielded, protected, bubble-like life, centered around my grandmother's apartment, our small yard, and the school, always surrounded by people who assisted me with this or that. Here was a girl, only a few years my senior, who lived a solitary, independent life working at a dental office, biking to work, and spending evenings in her small place eating dinner she cooked herself.

"I better get going," she said, looking at the clock. "It takes a while to get to work from here and you need to go to bed. I'm glad we met though. You're not the talkative type, are you?" she asked.

As if I could have squeezed a word in, I thought. "I get better with time," I said instead, smiling back. "Thanks for popping in."

"All right, I'll come again if you promise to do more of the talking next time."

"I'll try," I replied.

Amina gave me a long, tight hug and promised to take me to Lincoln Park one of these days.

"Here's my number," she said and handed me a piece of paper. "Don't be a stranger."

"I don't have a number yet, but I'll give you a call from work," I replied.

I closed the door after her, checked on Mother and Rufat, and then settled in on the mattress Mother had laid out for me. I folded my arms behind my head, watched the still branches of the tree outside, and thought of the loneliness that was stamped in Amina's half-closed eyes. I imagined her studio in the city, the bike parked by the entrance, the evenings in front of the television, eating alone in silence, heaviness settling on her slumped shoulders. Then, slowly, I drifted off to sleep.

. . . .

CHAPTER 16

PHENOMENON OF
A STOPPED CLOCK

The family and friends of the Iraqis never called in advance. They just showed up in hordes on a daily basis. There was no way to tell who was a friend and who was actually a family member because almost all of them were introduced under the vague all-encompassing concept of "a cousin" or "an uncle." They simply walked into the store from the back and joined the three usuals at the coffee table, whispering a serious and barely audible "*Assalamu alaikum.*" Very quickly, I stopped paying any attention to them and concentrated on my work.

The regulars wouldn't even say hello and would proceed to fix themselves some coffee with cream in one of those thick Styrofoam cups that Youel bought in large packs from the pharmacy across the street. Most of the time, they didn't acknowledge my presence, even though they passed by my desk when entering, which didn't bother me.

On days when we had several visitors for lunch, I would come up with some excuse to buy this or that and would set out to discover Devon Avenue. I would walk around, fascinated with the mosaic of store signs, billboards, posters, and people in bright clothes roaming the sidewalks. On one of these walks, I finally made it to Balalaika, the Russian store that sold books and CDs.

The place was dark and cool inside, with rows of books and a wall full of CDs. I picked up one of the classics that I recognized, opened it, and inhaled the delicious woody fragrance of a book that has never been read before. I placed the book back down and approached the wall of CDs. Most of them were stuck in a certain period of time, probably the late '90s. Perhaps that was the period when the store owner had immigrated to the U.S. I checked out the wall from end to end and confirmed I was right. It had the late '90s written all over it, with popular Soyuz compilations, bands that were at the peak of their popularity around 1998, and then time seemed to suddenly stop. There wasn't a hint of the alternative rock bands or rappers who'd gotten popular in the past ten years. The shop owner was a short, plump woman with curly brown hair, round glasses, deeply planted eyes, and cheeks covered with rosacea. She leaned on the counter, clasped her hands, and followed me with her eyes.

"We have new stuff coming soon," she said, reading my mind.

"Super," I mumbled.

"Although people gravitate to songs and books of their period. Time stops once you cross the ocean," she added. "Did you just arrive?"

Is there an inscription on my forehead that all of them can read? I thought. *First Irakli, now this woman.*

"Yes. We just moved. Me, my brother, and my mother," I answered. "We are from Baku."

"Baku!" she exclaimed. "I once took a train to Baku. It was beautiful back then."

"It still is," I said quietly.

"Take your time," she said and disappeared in the back.

I could tell she knew I was not here to make a purchase but to cling on to some memories of a past we somehow shared—a popular song, a classic we studied in Russian literature class in high school, a postcard with a familiar view. All post-Soviet countries were still connected through a common language, but, more than that, they were connected by common virtues and pains, by a common past, by a history that was sometimes glorious and often tragic.

I realized that I would also lose touch with the city I grew up in and abandon everything that was dear to my heart. It was a dreadful thought, a chance for my silent torturer to stop time and tighten his grip around my neck. I felt another panic attack approaching. I had to get out of there fast, so I stepped into the busy street as I felt my heart pound faster, but the city buzz wasn't enough to drown out the loud and disturbing voice in my head, and the grip around my neck made breathing hard. I no longer remember what triggered it but I felt weak and defeated as I recognized the unpleasant pressure mounting in my throat. I walked back to the optical and entered through the back door and rushed to the bathroom before anyone saw me. I opened the faucet, hoping the sound of the water would be loud enough to conceal my sobbing.

I leaned against the wall and counted to one hundred, waiting for my heart rate to go down. Then I washed my face with ice-cold water several times. My eyes were slightly red, and all the makeup was gone, but I was calm and ready to go back to my desk. I slowly opened the door to avoid the usual screeching and, as it opened, I came face to face with a man. He was right in front of me. This sudden movie-like incident was so startling that we both took a step back and couldn't utter a word.

"I am sorry," he said. "I scared you." He opened the door the rest of the way and stepped aside to let me out. I bolted out of the bathroom and took my seat at the desk. The image of the man's face under the bright bathroom light was still in front of my eyes. He was a little taller than me, with a wide, athletic figure, dark skin, and black eyes. The rest of the men were consumed by another *Cops* episode. Youel was dusting off the old cassette player in the corner to put some music on. Shammoun quietly sat on the stool by the wall and kept bumping his knees together as he always did when he was bored. Ashur was on the phone with Babi.

"What do you mean you f-f-forgot to walk the dog?" he yelled. "You're the one who wanted this d-d-damned dog! Now the dog pisses in the living room and your mother is mad at *me*." His kindness had a tendency to backfire. "Go! Listen! Go and clean that mess and forget this number!" He hung up.

Such dialogues occurred daily so no one took them seriously. I knew Ashur wasn't even mad but had to keep up appearances with the kid.

"All animals except cats are filthy," Shammoun announced.

"I hate cats, too," Youel added.

"Lazy, spoiled kid," Ashur said, taking out a cigarette from his pack.

"You spoil the kid, then you yell at the kid. Then you spoil him, then you yell at him, Ashur. Poor thing is confused. With kids you need discipline. You cannot just say yes to everything. Then they come and sit on top of your head," Youel said rapidly. "They sit right here." He gestured to the spot where his hair receded.

"S-s-says the father of-f the year," Ashur exclaimed. Youel shot back a wounded look and his lips trembled. The exchange was unpleasant but did not continue.

There were two more middle-aged men sitting by the coffee table and occasionally talking to Youel. I saw them for the first time and didn't know their names. I was grateful for the noise and the afternoon chaos in full swing because no one noticed how shaken up I was. I wish I knew that what I had experienced in those early months were classic panic attacks. Perhaps they wouldn't have frightened me so much and I could have eased back into my daily routine more quickly. I sat at my desk with my hand on my pulse and kept counting. Breath in, breath out. Suddenly, I heard someone's steps behind me. This must have been the man I had just seen by the restroom. He passed by my desk and approached those sitting at the coffee table.

"Assalamu alaikum!" he said.

"Hey Eric!" Youel and Shammoun replied.

In an instant, the room was filled with laughter and loud chatting as the men hugged and exchanged salutes. I figured Eric was not Assyrian since the group switched to Arabic as soon as he entered. Eric shook hands with everyone and took a seat by the coffee table next to Ashur. Youel brought him a cup of stale coffee with cream. It was astonishing how he made such a splash in the shop with his appearance. A few names of the cities in the U.S. were mentioned, then a few cigarette brands followed by what seemed to be a dispute involving two brands of tequila. *What does this man do?* I wondered.

Eric was wearing a blue polo shirt that darkened his complexion further and suited him. There was a shiny silver watch on his right hand, and I could see a thin white gold chain on his neck. Unlike the others, he wasn't wearing a cross on it. His forehead had a few fine wrinkles that hinted he was probably in his forties. Despite the older age and the wrinkles, there was an air of youthfulness about him. This love of life and charisma defined him more than his age. It was the first thing you noticed about him.

"Eric is not his real name," Youel said to me in a low voice.

"That makes sense. You all have at least three," I joked.

"You learning, Mariski!" he said, bursting out laughing. "You learning!"

"What does he do?" I asked.

"Oh, he is strange," Youel began. "First, he study political science at University of Chicago. What do you study that for? Politics is dirty games, that's all. No need four years to learn that, Mariski. Then he move to California because he like the weather there. So beautiful and nice, of course. But!" He paused dramatically. "Too expensive, Mariski. So, he is back here, working as . . . how you say it? Journalist."

"I see," I replied.

"He is forty-seven and he won't get married," Youel continued. "Like me! My poor mother told me if you don't marry before thirty-five, you will never find a woman good enough. After that, you look at a woman, you find something wrong with her. You think you young. You careless. You fly like a bird! You don't want to spoil. Then you get old. Then you don't have anyone to take care of you." He sighed. "Look at me! Look at Shammoun!"

I propped my chin with my palm and listened to Youel. He spoke English, but this half-hearted, melancholic monologue was so typical of men of his age back home. Even when they spoke of their regrets or life lessons, they did it with a smile and no sign of remorse. You knew that, if given another chance, they'd do it all over again.

Ashur suggested closing down the store early that day. It was a chance to spend some time wandering on Devon Avenue, but I decided that the day was already packed with adventures and that I would really enjoy a quiet ride on "the L," as I had learned to call the train by then.

The bus arrived quickly and was full of passengers, so I found a standing spot by the window and allowed the usual scenery of Devon Avenue to occupy my thoughts. I read the familiar names of the stores. The Sari Palace appeared to be closed. The short, mustached owner of Local Teahouse was fixing the tablecloth for the few outside tables, and a samovar was steaming with freshly brewed tea ready to be served for evening regulars. There were still a few customers in the famous India Book House on Devon and Maplewood, which reminded me to stop by this place one of these days. The bus passed by Noor Meat Market, Gandhi Electronics, the famous Indian restaurant with a tall "Viceroy of India" sign that featured a half-lit crown at the top, Sukhadia's sweets shop, Patel Brothers grocery store, and a cute little place called Sabri Nihari, which looked like a bakery.

I longed for the familiar feeling of home. I imagined the entrance of my grandmother's apartment and her cheerful look as she greeted me, the savory, mouth-watering smell of her food filling up the air, and the lazy yawn of our cat as she circled around hoping for a snack. I remembered the entrance in tiniest detail—the old, broken-down wardrobe where Nana kept slippers, old shoes, some blankets, and boxes of random items that should have been thrown out long ago, the old kilim rug in front of the door, and the intricate wooden coat-hangers carved as elephant heads with their trunks forming a U-shape. I missed watching the glistening waves of the Caspian from her balcony, the flocks of seagulls hovering in the air, and the trees swaying with the evening breeze.

On most days, my present seemed bleak and devoid of any emotions compared to my past, but somehow my strange encounter with Eric had awakened my long-forgotten curiosity about the world around me.

. . . .

CHAPTER 17

HOW TO DRINK A CAPPUCCINO

When I arrived to Vision Express Optical the next day, I found Eric sitting in my chair with his hands clasped behind his head, his back arched against the chair, and one foot on top of the other. Youel was singing a tune from an old Assyrian song and lighting up another bissma, and Shammoun was wandering around the room, looking for his glasses.

"I didn't really introduce myself yesterday. I'm Eric," he said in a quiet voice. "A friend of Ashur." He pointed at Ashur.

I suddenly became aware of my plain clothes and lack of makeup.

"Very nice to meet you," I said, sounding more polite than I intended, like a schoolgirl.

"And very nice meeting you as well," he said and smiled. "I think I heard your name is Maryam. Is that right? Do they call you Mariski all the time? A very silly nickname, but it sticks."

I told him Mariski was the nickname of a Russian girl who had worked at Vision Express Optical years ago, but he knew the story already. It turned out he knew the original Mariski as well. Her black-and-white picture was still pinned to the wall along with Ashur's family photos and a few cards featuring Assyrian patron saints. In the picture, Mariski was standing next to a church altar, her black t-shirt tucked into navy jeans with a wide leather belt. All three men smiled whenever they spoke of her. I disliked the nickname, but they repeated it all day long and before long it was too late to get rid of it.

"That is what they call me. I've given up," I said, turning my chair to face him. "But I like Maryam better."

"Tell me about it!" Eric said.

I felt strangely comfortable speaking to him. He took off his rimless glasses and smiled at me, preparing to say something else to continue the conversation, but Ashur had already hung up the phone, picked up the large leather-bound checkbook, pulled up a chair to my desk, and sat down. Eric stepped aside and went to go join the rest by the coffee table.

"Mariski!" Ashur called. "T-t-take that black pen. Take it and write here. Write my n-n-name. Like it is written on this check."

Ashur hastily explained my task and asked me to finish all fifteen checks before he headed to the bank this afternoon. He didn't seem pleased to see me talking to Eric. He paced about the room, picking a silly fight with Youel and then Shammoun, which always led to the choir of all three men talking at the same time, but soon all four of them got up, yelled, "Yalla yalla, guys" and headed for the door discussing something in Arabic. They got into Ashur's old, faded blue Ford and drove off. I walked around the empty office, trying out some of the modern frames, checking out the newly arrived flyers about Gucci and Versace frames, styles I'd imagined I would see only in glamorous magazines. A tall older gentleman in a button-up shirt walked inside and asked if he could get an exam and a free set of glasses here.

We'd get three or four visits like this a day, a fresh immigrant on a hunt for free stuff. They'd ask for free glasses, free eye exams, and even get disappointed with their twenty-twenty vision. The obsession with getting things for free was rooted in one simple fact: Back in their countries, including mine, nothing—absolutely nothing—was free and *nothing* came easy. Our customers, three or four a day, enjoyed their little daily victories when they got this or that for free. I gave him my usual line about getting his public aid card and calling back to get an appointment first.

"Fridays are best, but if that doesn't work, we have limited hours on Monday and Wednesday too. No walk-ins!" I warned. "Here, take this card and call this number when you're ready."

"Okay, okay," the man said and headed for the door.

I was going to fix myself some coffee when I noticed a thick book lying on top of the pink and white public aid forms. I picked up the book with curiosity. It was called *Palace Walk* by Naguib Mahfouz. I couldn't figure out if he was an Assyrian or Arabic author. The cover depicted a narrow street lined with two-story buildings, with cafés and shops on the first level and small rectangular balconies looking out to the street. It looked identical to the narrow streets of the Icheri Sheher, the Old Town cradled in the heart of Baku, a little oasis preserved from the fifteenth century with fortress walls and narrow streets. It depicted the same small grocery stalls and tiny teahouses and the same tiny balconies overlooking the busy street scene. Next to the book, I saw a small cigarette case with an intricate design and a large trident in the middle. I remembered Eric taking cigarettes from the case the previous day, so the book must have been his. Besides, the three men didn't look like they were into reading. I flipped through the publisher's note, the copyright notice, the acknowledgments, and on to the first chapter of the book:

She woke at midnight. She always woke up then without having to rely on an alarm clock. A wish that had taken root in her awoke her with great accuracy. For a few moments she was not sure she was awake. Images from her dreams and perceptions mixed together in her mind. She was troubled by anxiety before opening her eyes, afraid sleep had deceived her. Shaking her head gently, she gazed at the total darkness of the room. There was no clue by which to judge the time.

"It's a good book," said Eric, unexpectedly behind me. "It might be a little too early for you, although you must have read the Russian classics by now, haven't you? If you have, this will be a piece of cake, I'm sure."

For the first time in the past month, I really wanted to say something meaningful, but my mind was blank. I was a little embarrassed that he caught me reading his book.

"I did read some of the classics. I've never heard of Naguib Mahfouz, though," I said.

"How do you like it?" he asked.

"It is captivating," I replied. "Definitely hooks you from the first page."

"It's my third time rereading this book. They say when you reread books, you end up finding new things each time. I can't say that about this one. In fact, I like it for its familiarity, for its simple storyline. I like it because when I read it, I feel exactly the same way, I notice the same emotions each time."

"I have yet to read the same book twice," I confessed. "There are so many of them, it always feels like cheating to pick up a book that I've read before. Do you read a lot?"

"I do read a lot. Helps to escape the world when it gets boring, and that happens . . ." he paused, "well, a lot. How about you,

Maryam?" he asked. "Don't worry, they won't be back for a while. We can chat a little."

"So far, I mostly read whatever was in the school program and there was always so much of it that I never had time for leisurely reading. I did read Mario Puzo's *The Godfather* last summer."

"It probably felt like a children's tale after Dostoyevsky."

"Not really, I found it both deep and simple. It was a refreshing read after *Crime and Punishment*, which I had to finish first. *The Godfather* made sense, the story line was straightforward and easy to follow. *Crime and Punishment* was torture."

"Well, now that I know about your literary tastes, can you tell me about yourself? Where are you from, again?" he asked.

"Azerbaijan. I'm from Baku," I answered.

"How long have you been in the U.S.?" he asked.

"About a month."

"But your English is spectacular!" he protested. "Are you here with your parents?"

"My mother and my brother. My father is back home," I answered. "All of my family is back home."

"I noticed you have a CD player." He pointed. "What are you listening to?"

"Yes, it looks like one but it's actually a radio," I explained.

"You listen to the radio on your way to work?" he guessed.

"I do, but I can't get used to the music here. Too much hip-hop," I answered honestly.

"Do you ever listen to Joe Cocker?" he asked suddenly.

"'You Are So Beautiful' is the only song I know," I replied. I was glad I knew one.

"Yes, that song is a masterpiece. It's one of his best, but it's not my favorite. I will bring you my favorite of his CDs next time I come in here. I went to his concert, and it was incredible." He fell quiet for a moment before he continued. "I could see the guy is on drugs, but you can really tell that he feels every word and every note of the song."

I realized he didn't remember that the round thing on the table was not a CD player, and that I could not play his Joe Cocker CD, but I did not want to interrupt Eric's monologue about the intense feelings of a drug-addicted singer. *What a strange man*, I thought.

Eric appeared so taken up by the same world that I dreaded each morning, so emotional about music and history, and even though I knew I was just an outlet for this waterfall of impressions, a canvas where he could paint these things, I was happy to be that for him. As he spoke, parts of me that had lain dormant under the rubble of my former life slowly started to move again. It was an almost physical experience and I wanted to stay close to this miracle. I felt the familiar inspiration that surrounds you when you watch a film in a movie theatre or hear a song in a live concert. The words and sounds gain a new elevated meaning and your whole body tries to absorb as much of it as it can.

"Coffee?" He suddenly broke the silence.

I still wasn't familiar with his informal language, so I didn't realize that this was an invitation, not a question.

"Yes, we have coffee." I rushed to get him some. "It's all the way in the back, over here."

"No, no . . . Maryam, that coffee isn't good." He shook his head. "I'll go get it from the coffee shop close by."

"Oh no, thank you very much, I'm fine with the coffee here," I replied.

Eric recognized this instinct to refuse all offers of food or drinks, a typical gesture that has nothing to do with actual desire and is a mere show of politeness you'd expect from any well-mannered Azeri. He didn't bother with a second request and just said, "I'm getting you a cappuccino!"

I had no idea what that was. My best guess was some kind of an Italian pastry and since I had a terrible sweet tooth, I got excited. He picked up his keys and cell phone from the desk and left the store, coming back ten minutes later with two cups and a brown paper bag.

"Your cappuccino, my dear," he said.

"Oh, *that* is a cappuccino!" I inhaled the rich smell from the cup. "What is inside of it?"

"You've never had a cappuccino?" he asked, bursting into a light-hearted laugh.

"No! I was sure that it was some kind of Italian pastry," I confessed.

"Well, I got that, too," he said and smiled with his eyes.

Eric took out an almond and pistachio biscotti and placed it on a napkin in front of me.

"Well, since you've never had a cappuccino, I have to teach you how to drink it like an Italian. I had this Italian friend in California, who said 'all coffee in America is crap, especially Starbucks.'" I did not want to interrupt him, but I wondered what Starbucks was. "Anyways, this guy, he said that you should only drink cappuccino in the mornings and then, throughout the day, you can have espresso shots, but having milk-infused espresso drinks throughout the day is just disgusting."

Again, I had no idea what espresso was, but I kept quiet. I didn't want to distract him from the cappuccino topic, because of how easily Eric got distracted. This quality had a dual nature. Sometimes, it made him charming and dreamy and sometimes it was difficult to keep up with the trajectory of his thoughts.

"So how do you drink a cappuccino like an Italian?" I asked.

"All right! So! Let's take off the cover." He removed the cover of the cup. "Do you have brown sugar?" he asked. I stared at him. "Never mind. Do you have *any* sugar here?"

"Yes, of course." I rushed to the back and grabbed the tall white sugar container and a small plastic spoon.

"Here!" I said, excited to see what followed.

"We take a spoon of sugar, sprinkle it evenly on top of the foam . . . yes . . . Just like that. . ."

The foam was of an off-white color with a few light brown lines swirling around in the middle. It looked delicious. I sprinkled the sugar on top.

"It's actually much better with brown sugar," he said. "But you guys don't have it and you don't even seem to know what it is! That's okay, that's okay. I'll bring it later."

"Okay, and what do I do next?" I asked.

"You mix it up with the spoon so that some of the coffee at the bottom mixes with the foam. That will add a little flavor to the foam. Then you take the spoon and dip it inside and eat it!"

I picked up the fluffy mixture with the spoon and put it in my mouth. Eric was looking at me attentively, not to miss the first and truest impression on my face.

"Mmm . . . Very tasty!" I said.

The taste was exactly how Eric had described it—sweet, milky foam laced with the richness of coffee. It was both delicious and practical as the foam sprinkled with sugar could pass as a dessert and the rest as a drink! Eric thought this idea of mine was quite creative and we both laughed as we ate the almond and pistachio biscotti.

Very soon after we finished the coffee, Ashur and the rest showed up. They were in a high-spirited, cheerful mood as always, pulling the same old jokes on one another and laughing with a fresh enthusiasm. I finished the day filling out forms and confirming appointments for the next day. When others were present, Eric switched to Arabic and spend most of his time speaking with Shammoun.

My evening ride back to the city was consumed with thoughts about Eric and our afternoon together. I wondered about the coffee shop where he bought the cappuccino and whether this drink was available at other places. It seemed funny to me that he called it a "coffee shop." I had never heard of that before and was curious to see what it looked like. But there must have been lots of coffee shops around, because men and women on the bus and the train carried those paper cups everywhere. I saw abandoned paper cups on benches at the bus stop and L stations, and with time I could differentiate between the large ones used for soda drinks and the smaller ones used for coffee and tea. The soda cups were usually plastic, as big as a bucket with contrasting colors, and often had the name of the drink on the outside. The coffee cups were smaller and made of paper, with an intricate design and a cardboard sleeve that protected you from the hot contents of the cup. Not having a paper cup probably gave me away as a "fresh-off-the-boat" immigrant in this country. I thought of getting coffee on the way to work one of these days.

"Not coffee—cappuccino!" I whispered.

CHAPTER 18

LIFE IN SKOKIE

Teymour visited us a few times a week. He'd show up with a bag of groceries or a fresh-from-the-oven pizza and then proceed to smoke his cigarettes outside. His conversations with Mother still took place on the balcony, with the heat and humidity underpinning evening traffic buzz and cigarette smoke. All they talked about now were "suburbs with good schools and transportation." Naturally, as Rufat was still school-aged, he got all the attention as the school year approached and it became clear we'd need to settle down in a neighborhood with a "good school." I heard bits and pieces of their discussion and felt jealous about the school year that was about to begin for him—about the books he'd need to get, classes he would need to enroll in, the hours he'd spend sitting behind a desk and looking out the window, and the hallways full of other students bothered by nothing but upcoming exams. Then, one evening Teymour announced that they'd found an apartment in Skokie, and we'd be moving there this coming weekend. Skokie was what Teymour called a "small village up north." Now, in my head at that time, a village implied lack of streets, lots of cattle, miles of open land, and a barter-like system that would get you fresh milk, yogurt, or butter. That is how I pictured a village, but Teymour described something entirely different.

"Good neighborhood. Lots of Russians. Buses operating on schedule, and there's even a train nearby," Teymour said. "Rufat will go to Niles North, which ranks better than Niles West. Plus, it's on my way to work, so I'll stop by a lot," he added. I was a bit relieved to hear that a village in this place was different than a village back home.

"Does that village . . ." I began, searching for the word Teymour had said. "Skokie. Does it have a beach like Philip's village?"

"Philip's is actually a *town*," Teymour corrected me.

Who cares? I thought but nodded. I still had no idea how to differentiate between villages, towns, and cities. It was all one big city of Chicago to me.

"No, unfortunately, it doesn't have a beach," Teymour said. "But Wilmette does and it's nearby. All you have to do is get a girlfriend with a car that can drive you around," he joked to Rufat. "Hey Maryam, if you're nice, they can take you too!"

"No, thanks," I said and laughed. "I'll take the bus."

That weekend, Teymour signed a one-year lease with a Bulgarian landlady who had a heavy accent. Teymour impatiently wrote his and Mother's names on documents that the landlady kept producing from a never-ending stack of paper. Then, the preparations began. We had not really accumulated anything since our arrival, so the move was quick. Teymour showed up that afternoon with somebody's truck, loaded our few suitcases and boxes into the back, and we drove away. It occurred to me that, before coming to the U.S., I had only lived in two tiny flats in my entire life. One was Nana's apartment by Seaside Boulevard, and the second had been my parents' newly remodeled, fashionable-yet-unhappy home on Azadlig Prospect. I had only been living in this country for three months, yet it felt like a lifetime. And now we were headed to our third residence in such a short time. I sat in the back seat and looked at the tall windows of the building reflecting the sun, the neatly trimmed trees surrounding the entrance, the closed umbrella of the breakfast café, and caught myself feeling nothing.

Teymour took the highway, and somewhere in the distance we saw the clustered downtown skyline. It had been just a few weeks since we'd first moved out of his apartment, but it already felt like an eternity. We reached the village of Skokie thirty minutes later. Teymour took a detour route to drive through the main streets—the intersection of Lincoln Avenue and Oakton Boulevard. The streets were tidy and not overcrowded with shops. We drove by a jewelry and watch repair, a dry cleaner with a faded neon sign, an antique shop showcasing old leather furniture and a few lamps, a kosher bakery, and a small Christian church with a "We Prayed for You Today" sign. There were hardly any pedestrians and the village looked almost deserted. Our two-story duplex was on a cozy, tree-lined street not too far from the village center.

"Your apartment is on the first floor," Teymour said, parking his car by the mailbox. "The one on the right."

We climbed out of the truck and stood in the shade of the trees, slightly sweaty from the drive, enjoying the cool afternoon breeze. I could tell Mother was impatient to call this place home. She went inside, and we followed. We barely had any time to look around before she plunged us into a rigorous cleaning campaign. Rufat and I didn't even have a chance to do our usual fighting over who gets which room. Instead, we found ourselves dividing housecleaning chores among the three of us. Mother took on the toughest—the bathrooms and the kitchen—while we were told to vacuum and dust the bedrooms and the living room, including the closets with mirrored sliding doors that we discovered doubled the size of the room, visually.

"Leyla, you know, they clean these apartments before someone moves in," Teymour said, attempting to reassure her. He gave up after Mother flashed him her signature "don't even go there" look.

"I shouldn't bother," Teymour said.

"Yeah," Rufat and I confirmed in unison. "How they say it?" Rufat asked. "Pick your battles."

Mother was on fire. She insisted on thoroughly washing all the windows—once with a moist cloth and once with a dry cotton one to polish the glass. We both hated the task, but Mother was adamant about the windows, so we knew it was pointless to protest.

Fifteen minutes into our task, I heard the sound of a popular radio station blasting "Where Is the Love?" by the Black Eyed Peas and Justin Timberlake. I'd hear this song quite often on the radio during my bus rides. At first, I was sure it was Rufat, but the sound was coming from the kitchen, and he'd been in his room all the while. Still, it was hard to believe that Mother would simply turn on the radio. It's just something she never did.

I picked up the bucket filled with soapy water and entered the kitchen to rinse and refill the bucket and add a few drops of liquid soap, but it was just an excuse to check if my suspicions were true, and Mother really *was* in a mood for some music. I saw her with a wet piece of cloth, moving from one shelf to another, her hips moving along to the rhythm a little. I hadn't seen my mother like this in a long while—joyful, happy, and carefree. She turned around and came to take the bucket from me without a word. The expression she always wore these days—worry with a hint of cynicism mixed with bottomless sadness—was suddenly gone from her face. Now, Mother appeared free, liberated from her past, from her sticky, predetermined reputation of the good wife who'd been abandoned by an ungrateful husband. A thin strand of golden hair fell on her perspiring forehead, illuminated by the bright light that poured out of the two small windows above the sink.

I watched Mother as she emptied the bucket into the sink, turned on the faucet, filled it up with hot water, and poured out a small amount of the soapy liquid. She always seemed excited during household chores, and, when she was done, she'd always throw the now-clean rooms one final victorious glance, confirming she'd done everything right. Then, Mother would pour herself ruby-red tea served in a small pear-shaped armudi glass and enjoy a cigarette.

I stared at her back as she refilled the bucket and mixed up the pale blue liquid until it rose up in tiny white bubbles. I was happy to see her so elevated and optimistic about our future, ready to leave the past behind.

She gave me the bucket, a half-smile lighting up her beautiful face. "Let's finish and we can have some bread with cheese and kielbasa!" she said. "Would you like that?"

"Mm-hmm." I nodded, afraid to say something wrong and spoil the moment.

She turned around, picked up the sponge, poured a handful of baking soda into the sink, and began scrubbing it with the thick side down, her whole body moving forcefully. I stood for a moment longer, looking around at Mother's new domain and thinking of the countless meals we'd share around the wooden table, which stood, conveniently, right next to the refrigerator. I took the bucket and went back to my new room.

Having a separate room that I could decorate to my liking—a place where I could rearrange the furniture as I wished and plaster the walls with photographs of friends, where I could pile my personal treasure trove of books and CDs on the desk in the corner—that was the first luxury I'd experienced so far during my life in the U.S. Even back home, I'd never had a room to call my own.

By the time Teymour returned, we had somehow managed to vacuum all the rooms, clean the refrigerator, and dust and wipe the windows, and we were now folding our clothes on the built-in shelves of our walk-in closet. This arduous cleaning exercise unlocked a new hidden source of energy in my mother. She swept and scrubbed and wiped everything several times, drops of sweat covering her forehead and the area above her upper lip. Teymour was astonished with our progress and amused by Mother's infatuation with cleaning.

"Leyla, I think we can take a little break to eat," he said. "Kids look like they need a break."

Mother ignored him and continued scrubbing the sink.

"All right, woman! Enough with the scrubbing. We're all hungry," he said in a humorous tone.

"Can't you just order pizza?" she asked.

"I can, but I want to get out of this place for a bit. Come on, you got all weekend to scrub!"

"It's not looking good outside," Rufat said.

We all came closer to the window and noticed there was no sign of the smoldering sun in the sky. Now it was covered with thick and fast-moving greenish clouds. Something about their faded green color was alarming, yet amazing. The wind picked up and the sky grew darker. Then, suddenly, I saw small icicles hit the ground, each making a thumping sound.

"What is *that*?" Rufat asked.

"That is hail!" Teymour answered.

Hail, I found out, were quite large pieces of ice, a sort of frozen rain. It fell on the ground and I thought it looked like a special effect from a Hollywood movie, something unreal, that is. But here it was, enormous round rain droplets, frozen into balls and hitting the ground angrily. They piled up by the mailbox and pounded the trees that had buzzed with cicadas just a moment ago. *Maybe they'll take a break now*, I thought.

Whatever this wonder of nature was, it looked like the apocalypse to the three of us. Only Teymour was unimpressed.

"Give it ten minutes and we go," he said, lounging on the couch. "Hey Leyla, you got another ten minutes to scrub! A bonus!"

"This will end in ten minutes? Yeah, right!" she said and went back to the kitchen.

"I hope it doesn't damage my car," Teymour said.

Just like he predicted, ten minutes later, not only was the hail gone, but the greenish-looking clouds that had swirled into a dark, ugly face also disappeared from the sky. The sun was shining brightly again. The cicadas must still have been recovering from the assault because they were quiet for the time being. A few minutes later, we were in Teymour's car, all washed up and ready to eat.

"Well, now that we've survived *that*, how about a French onion soup?" Teymour asked.

None of us knew what a French onion soup was, but it didn't sound so good, so we kept quiet.

"It's better than it sounds. It's not just onion. It's a lot of cheese and croutons," he tried to convince us.

"I'm getting fries. You get the soup," Rufat joked.

Teymour parked the car and we walked into a small café at the Old Orchard Mall. I sat at the table and looked outside, noticing a neighboring parking lot full of teenagers sitting on the bare ground, clutching books in their hands. Some of them wore long capes and many had a black lightning shape scrawled on their foreheads. Others held brown wizard wands. Despite the heat, many of the kids were wearing yellow and red woven scarves around their necks.

"Harry Potter fans!" Teymour exclaimed, noticing my curious look.

"But why are they all here?" I asked.

"The next book will be released in six hours, at midnight," he said. "Which reminds me . . . I need to get it for my daughter."

I remembered how my friends from school obsessed over everything Harry Potter during ninth and tenth grade, rereading the books, quoting their favorite characters, proudly sporting house scarves to school. I started reading the books to keep up with my friends' obsession about everything Harry Potter, but the world of secret spells and monsters didn't appeal to me, so I quit. I was more intrigued by romance books about the kinship of French and Spanish kings, the intrigues that took place in their majestic castles, the wars they waged around the world, and their unhappy marriages filled with deceit and betrayal.

That evening, as I lay in my new bed and watched the tendrils of the fern cast strange shadows on the ceiling, I thought about the kids in front of the bookstore. Knowing that they were still in front of the tall, brightly lit bookstore with their magic wands and scarves and capes made me happy. I looked at the wall clock to see what time it was. In just ten minutes, the doors to the bookstore would open and a happy, excited crowd of fans would pour into the bookstore, form a winding line, and patiently wait to receive their tickets to a magic world. The exhaustion brought on by the hour and the summer heat would evaporate into the air and they'd dive into the book on their way home in the pale light of the back seat. Some of them would gulp down the book immediately, delving into the secret world of Harry Potter and his friends and emerging finally satiated and ready to wait for another book, for however long it took.

The teenagers in front of the bookstore were still fully immersed in childhood, where nothing was ridiculous, not even showing up to a bookstore with a magic wand and a cape. No matter how I tried, I could never picture myself doing any of it. At first, I blamed it all on our sudden move to the United States, the abrupt manner in which I'd been taken away from everything that was dear to me. But then I realized that it wasn't true. I couldn't remember that period of childhood in my life at all. I had distant memories of years I'd spent at my grandmother's house, my afternoons usually filled with watercolor drawings and watching cartoons. I remember feeling happy then. When I was twelve, right around the time when my mother lost all hope of repairing her marriage, I'd moved back in with my parents because she thought my presence would help bring Father back.

My memories turn bleak in that period, filled with Mother's quiet sobbing in the evenings, the picture of my father sitting in the brown leather recliner in the living room, sipping his whiskey and watching movies, the frequent visits of two elderly ladies, our neighbors, and the occasional candlelit evenings that we'd spent gathered in the kitchen during the blackouts that had been so common in the late '90s. The contrast was startling. In my grandmother's household, everything had revolved around me. At home with my parents, I seemed to play a supporting role in my parents' conflict, constantly pulled from one side to the other, used as a bargaining chip, and eventually, when I was inevitably unable to remedy their issues, I was sent back to my bedroom. It is there that I developed a habit of sitting on the floor for hours, my arms around my knees, listening to songs on the radio until the early hours of the morning. I found comfort in the dead of the night when my parents and their never-ending problems were asleep. The silence of those nights excited me, but then the morning would come, and I'd be thrown back into the thorny reality.

CHAPTER 19

. . . .

UNCHAIN MY HEART

When I walked into the optical building on Monday, I have to admit I was delighted to hear Eric's voice in the background. I slowed down my pace to throw a glance in the mirror, happy I had taken my time to put on some makeup that morning. It had been a few weeks now that I'd been more mindful of what I wore again. Back in Baku, I paid attention to my clothing. We all did, but here I couldn't have cared less if my skirt matched my shoes or if I wore any jewelry. Here, nobody made up their mind about you looking at your clothes. Nobody really seemed to take notice of anybody else. You could walk around in the most bizarre outfit and hardly attract any looks. The need to look a certain way was not there anymore, but, lately, I caught myself paying attention to my outfits, lining my eyes with a pencil, and putting some gloss on my lips sometimes. Today was one of those days. My hair was up in a ponytail, and I was wearing eyeliner.

When Eric saw me come to my desk, he was a little surprised.

He got up from the chair and leaned on the dark blue file cabinet behind me.

"Good morning," he said with curiosity.

"Hello," I replied.

He wore a washed-out gray t-shirt with a round logo that I didn't recognize, khaki pants, and brown moccasins with a blue velvet strap on top. His graying hair was combed back, glistening with the styling gel that all Iraqis seemed to consume by the ton. I grabbed the double-walled coffee cup that I had bought from the Turkish store and went to the back office to fix myself some coffee. With all the dressing and makeup in the morning, I hadn't had a chance to make breakfast and had just wrapped a leftover muffin in a napkin and stuffed it into my bag. I took out a small paper plate from the shelf and unwrapped the muffin. It was still crunchy at the top with bits of brownish walnuts. I poured fresh coffee into the glass, added a little powdered creamer, and leaned against the wall. A long corridor separated the coffee area from the back office, so I could safely study Eric without worrying that he would notice. I held on to the glass with both hands, my right hip, shoulder, and head resting on the cold wall.

Eric was still leaning against the file cabinet, his left leg crossed over his right, his arms crossed at the elbow, and his head turned towards the television, unaware of my secret stare. I noticed that the skin on his hands was slightly darker than the rest of his body. Even though his hands were smaller than mine, they were strong and wide and covered with protruding veins. The casual outfit he wore made him look so much younger than the other three men sitting over at the coffee table. Eric was so much livelier, more present, and in-step with current fashion. Most of Ashur's friends had lived in America for decades—working immigrant jobs, buying houses, and operating small businesses—but they still looked and acted as if they'd never left Baghdad.

My coffee cooled down and I put a large piece of the crunchy muffin top into my mouth and washed it down. I returned to my desk and grabbed the blue box with new prescription slips, starting to fill out the public-aid order forms with patients' first and last names and dates of birth, followed by their prescriptions at the bottom. The whole time, I was very aware that Eric was right behind me. I wondered if he was still watching television. For a few minutes, the room was quiet. All four men were watching another episode of *Married . . .With Children*, a comedy about a suburban family that constantly teased each other with sarcastic jokes and laughed at their own imperfections. The show was annoying, but Youel loved this kind of slapstick humor, so whenever he'd stumble upon it when flipping through the channels, he'd leave it on despite loud objections from both Ashur and Shammoun.

"What? What? You don't get enough of Saddam Hussein?" Youel would ask. "No more of that bullshit. At least they joke here!"

I tried to concentrate on the forms in front of me, but that was hard to do with Eric standing right behind me. He walked across the room and leaned against the wall separating the inner office from the patient waiting area. I realized that all three times I had seen Eric, he had refused to sit down at the coffee table, always choosing to lean against this or that wall, as if sitting down would drag him into their world and domesticate him somehow. This way he remained an active spectator, engaging them in small talk and discussing the news, but never fully descending into their world. When his arms were not clasped at his elbows, he'd casually put them into the pockets of his jeans or grab his left shoulder with his right hand and just leave it like that. He held his coffee cup with two fingers— the thumb and the index one—leaving the rest up in the air. It was truly remarkable how I could spend weeks with these men and hardly register what they wore and how they stood and what habits they had, but I easily and gladly absorbed any and all insignificant movements, details, gestures, and remarks Eric made. I found out from Youel that Eric was a journalist at the *Chicago Tribune* covering the Middle East, so he'd often be out of town, mostly on business, but sometimes for pleasure.

This morning, Eric looked more cheerful than before, jumping on the bandwagon and making fun of George Sako, a family man with three sons and a beautiful wife who kept trying to convince Ashur to open a restaurant with him. Ashur kept rejecting the idea as financially risky, but he was getting bored with the shop and the stable income that didn't require much of an effort. He no longer wanted to be a frequent client of the late-night establishments, but rather a proud owner of one, a person of connections who inspires reverence. So, when George called, Ashur would light up a cigarette, listen to him talk, and chuckle once in a while, his eyes smiling and dreamy. Eventually, Ashur gave in, and the project was on. Only George didn't seem to know much about running an Arabic night club. Frequenting such places was one thing, but running one was another.

Ashur listened to George with patience, repeating the same sentences over and over in English and then in Assyrian, shaking his head at how little Sako knew about restaurants and how he was ready to invest all his money into it.

"I ask him simple q-q-questions and he says, 'Don't worry; God will take care of it,'" Ashur said. "As if we're building a ch-ch-church!" he'd yell.

This morning Youel and Shammoun were having fun reciting the most recent stories about George to Eric. He held on to his stomach, letting out a guffaw as they interrupted each other in their enthusiasm, their loud voices filling up the room. Then the phone rang.

"Vision Express, how can I help you?" I answered.

"Hi! Can I talk to Ashur?" It was George.

I placed the call on hold and motioned for Ashur to pick up the receiver on the other side.

"Who is it?" he asked

"Sako," I said, giggling.

As soon as I pronounced the name both Youel and Shammoun gave out a loud laugh.

"All right, all right, g-g-guys! Enough, okay? Let me t-t-talk to him!" he protested.

Ashur picked up the receiver and walked out of the coffee area to make sure George didn't accidently overhear some stupid remark in the background. In the meantime, Eric picked up his empty paper cup and headed towards the coffee station. He refilled his cup with coffee and returned, stopping by my desk.

"Long time no see," he said.

"How are you doing?" I asked.

"Good, good," he said, looking as if he wanted to add something to his answer, but deciding against it.

"So, this restaurant thing is happening?" Eric asked.

"It looks like it is," I said. "But when it comes to the restaurant, they always switch to Assyrian, so I can't really tell."

"Yeah, they go back and forth a lot. I've picked up some Assyrian, but it's pretty limited. Besides, Arabic is native to them too. Come to think of it, among the five of us in this room we got six languages. Three for this group and another three for you."

"How did you know I speak three?" I asked.

"Aren't you from Azerbaijan? Your native language is pretty close to Turkish. Then there's the Russian, which you studied in, and your English is getting better."

"How did you know I studied in Russian?" I asked.

"I'm a journalist, Maryam. All I do is read and write and constantly fail to make sense of the Middle East—the birthplace of contradictions!" he answered. I sensed a barely palpable pride in his voice as he uttered these words. I wondered what a *Chicago Tribune* journalist who made a living through reading and writing was doing in this hole in the wall on the outskirts of the city, but then journalists were strange fellows, looking for answers in odd places.

"I brought you something," Eric said suddenly.

Eric took out a CD with Joe Cocker on the cover wearing a black leather motorcycle jacket, peeking out from behind dark sunglasses, his eyes curious and his forehead wrinkled, his unshaven chin dotted with silver hair. The title read *Unchain My Heart*. Eric looked around to confirm no one was watching.

"It's my favorite. You can listen to this on your way home on the bus," he said.

"Thank you . . . thank you. I will," I responded.

"He said that you moved to Skokie?" Eric asked, pointing at Ashur.

"Yes, a few weeks ago," I answered.

"Where in Skokie do you live?" he asked.

"We live on Bronx Street, close to Gross Point Park."

"Is that close to the large fitness center on Church?"

"Yes, we've passed by that place a few times on our way to the Old Orchard Mall," I replied.

"Yes, that's the one," he replied. "There's an indoor track on the third floor there. I go sometimes in the evening for a walk. Do you know that place?"

"Yes, I go there with Mother sometimes, too," I answered.

He hesitated for a moment. "I'll be there today around seven p.m. Come if you can."

His gesture and proposal were both so unexpected and confusing that for a few moments I just looked blankly at his face. It must have been obvious that I was at a loss for words, so Eric changed the topic quickly and started asking questions about my family.

"So how is everyone back home?" he asked. "Did you register your brother at the high school? Niles West?"

"He's going to Niles North," I corrected him.

"Yes, that's right," he agreed. "A friend who is a real estate agent sold a few homes in Skokie last fall. He said that school ranked pretty well."

I had no idea what he was talking about. At this time, I did not realize schools were ranked in America and that these rankings could affect the price of a house. To keep the conversation going I nodded enthusiastically, my mind consumed with the CD on the desk and with what sounded like a proposal to meet.

A minute later, Ashur walked back into the area. He noticed the CD on my desk and threw a disapproving glance at Eric. Soon after that, Eric said goodbye to the group and left. I made up an excuse that I needed to buy something from Three Sisters Delicatessen, a Russian grocery store nearby, and left the optical shop hoping that once I made it up to Devon Avenue, the bustle and continuous traffic noise would help me get my thoughts in order.

It had been weeks since I'd taken an afternoon stroll on Devon. Now that I commuted from Skokie, I no longer took the Devon bus that had driven me past the string of colorful shops, grocery stores, and sidewalks full of pedestrians from every corner of the world. I resorted to frequent, not-so-random trips to the grocery store with the excuse of picking up something for my mother as a way to stay connected with this vibrant world. I passed by a row of familiar shops, waving to a Pakistani shop owner sitting at his usual side table and bathing in the warm light of the summer sun.

I thought about the Joe Cocker album Eric had brought me and wondered if he ever thought of me. I imagined him picking the CD off a shelf and choosing to put it in his car so he could give it to me. Or maybe the CD was already in the car, and it had been a last-minute whim to bring it to the shop? Did he find me interesting too, even if just a little? What I felt towards him wasn't just a friendly feeling and I knew it. This was a fascination of some sort, the kind you feel towards eccentric, charismatic personalities. My sudden feelings for him would remain in my head and become a mental escape, like the summer house in Mardakan, or a crush on a movie star who didn't even know I existed.

On the way back, I stopped by Three Sisters and bought Russian-style cottage cheese, even though we still had some left at home. When I walked back to the optical shop, I saw Ashur with several patients who'd come in to pick up their glasses. I left the cottage cheese in the fridge and rushed to his side. I noticed a sudden coldness in his voice and a brashness in his manners. *Maybe because I was gone for so long*, I thought. But deep down, I knew it had to do with Eric. The CD was now in the middle of the desk instead of the shelf where I left it, so he must have looked at it.

Ashur had recently started giving me rides home and had taken to adding an extra twenty dollars to my weekly hundred-dollar paycheck. He would buy me a loaf of bread and some pickled cucumbers when he went grocery shopping for himself. I had started to regard him as an uncle who took care of me even though he didn't have to, and it troubled me when he was upset with me. This had happened a few times in the past for reasons I still couldn't quite understand, and I had blamed it on his moodiness. Hours later, he'd revert back to his old self, cracking jokes with Youel and Shammoun and asking me to make a fresh pot of coffee.

But today was different. No matter what I did, he remained cold and, when closing time approached, he said he wouldn't be able to give me a ride home this evening. I packed my stuff into my bag along with the Joe Cocker CD and took a bus home, arriving well after dinner.

I spent the evening collaging photos from my last school year and my farewell party on a piece of large cardstock that I was planning to hang on the wall opposite my bed. Mother peeked in once in a while, asking if I wanted anything to eat. I promised to join her and Rufat in the kitchen in fifteen minutes. I glanced at the clock and noticed that in fifteen minutes Eric would be walking at the third level of the fitness center at the intersection of Gross Point Drive and Church Street.

I couldn't decide if I should go to the fitness center. On the surface, there wasn't anything wrong with the idea of going. After all, so far all of the acquaintances we'd made since our arrival to Chicago were all over the age of forty. Besides, Mother didn't seem to object when I'd spent the whole evening speaking with a thirty-seven-year-old car dealer at Teymour's friend's house a few weeks ago. In fact, she had loosened up her grip on me a lot in the last few months, either because I was now the main breadwinner in the family or because it was virtually impossible to control someone in a city so large and unknown to her. But then again, I knew full well that things were different with Eric. It wasn't pure curiosity about chatting with a foreigner that kept me glued to the clock and biting my nails. I could sense my interest in him could easily unfold into a feeling that was just . . . wrong.

When the clock hit exactly seven p.m., I picked up the cut-out photos laying around on the floor, swept them up, and left them on the cardstock sitting on my desk. Mother was busy filling up the kettle with water in preparation for her usual daily teatime in front of the television. I stood in the middle of the kitchen and waited to catch her attention. When she turned around, it was with a startled expression on her face.

"I'm going to walk a little in the fitness center."

"Alone?" she asked, surprised.

This was my last chance to save myself from an outright lie and still have Mother to blame for the fact that I chickened out on taking Eric up on his offer to meet. But it was too late.

"Yes," I lied.

"Okay, take this," she said and handed me a ten-dollar bill. "And on your way back stop by Walgreens and buy me some nail polish remover."

I slid the money into the pocket of my jeans and left the apartment. The streets were filled with a loud buzz produced by the once-every-seventeen-years emergence of cicadas that northern Illinois is famous for. The trees were fully occupied by large armies of these insects. They produced an almost frightening buzz that could not be drowned out by evening traffic or by shutting the windows. I quickened my pace, worried that one of the cicadas would drop onto my head. For a few minutes, I was able to distract my mind from the purpose of my adventure, but the Weber Leisure Center already towered in the distance. It was a large, four-story building with several wings, housing group-exercise rooms, a cycling studio, a yoga studio, a swimming pool, and several basketball courts. The indoor track ran around the perimeter of the building, every three laps equating to one mile. The lanes of the track were always filled with elderly Chinese couples in white sneakers, young families busy trying to control their kids, and a few runners. I walked into a brightly lit entrance, passed the lobby, and took the stairs to the third floor.

I stepped onto the track and looked into the incoming crowd. Eric was not there. The thought liberated me. Suddenly, the weight of my lie and the boldness of my move was lifted from my shoulders, and I felt a strange pride for having had the guts to come in the first place. Now I felt safe from the turmoil that would've been brought upon me if Eric had been there and realized how unready I was to allow my feelings to go any further. I passed by the Monday-night regulars at a relaxed pace, taking out the CD player that I had recently picked up from a garage sale on our street. I had grabbed it at the last minute, with the vague hope that Eric wouldn't be there after all, and I might find myself in need of a soundtrack for my evening walk. The CD was already inside, so I inserted the headphones into my ears and pressed play.

The first song was "Unchain My Heart." It started with the singer's cigarette-infused, coarse, but strangely melodic voice, enhanced by piano and saxophone accompaniment that paved the way for an energetic entrance on the drums. I adjusted my pace to the beat and let my mind get lost in the music until the whole world became a music video for the song.

Soon the beat of the song and Joe Cocker's voice made me forget why I was there. Instead, I thought of the last few months and felt proud of how we'd gotten through them. I recalled the sight of Teymour's cramped and messy apartment, the busy tableau of State Street, and the colorful world of Devon Avenue. They all swirled interchangeably to the beat of the song. It was the first time I had thought of our adventures in the U.S. without an overwhelming sense of regret and nostalgia for Baku.

But even in this uplifted mood, there were clearly cracks in my happiness. I looked at people around me with envy, realizing that, for us, happiness would never be effortless again. One day, we'd get jobs and houses and brand-new cars like all of Ashur's friends did, but we would do so against the wind, with both happy and sad memories of Baku springing to mind at the most unexpected moments. I wondered if we would ever be unchained from our nostalgia.

I decided only time would tell.

I took out the headphones, put them in my bag, and took the stairs down. Suddenly, the liberating feeling I'd experienced was now gone and I realized that I'd just spent an hour waiting around for someone who'd been the one to suggest we meet up here and then simply hadn't shown up. It wasn't a pleasant feeling. I stopped by Walgreens to pick up nail polish remover for Mother. The irritating buzz of the cicadas had died down a little. I crossed Church Street and looked up at the windows of the large apartment complex across the street, imagining the evening family dinner scenes of the Americans living there before I continued on.

I was tired from the walk and my stomach was already growling from skipping dinner. When I arrived at home, Mother was sitting on the couch watching television with a large plate of fruit on her lap. I handed her the nail polish remover and went into the kitchen to fix myself a sandwich.

"There is still warm bread in the oven," she said. "I left it for you."

It felt good to be home and far away from the crazy idea of meeting up with Eric. Now I was glad he hadn't shown up. I took out the slightly crunchy bread from the oven, cut it in half, and topped it with a spoonful of spinach-and-shallots sauté that Mother had made for dinner. I added a piece of thin-sliced Havarti cheese that Teymour had brought the other day, then sprinkled it with a little salt and joined Mother on the couch with my plate.

"There is fresh-made tea in the kitchen. I'll bring you a glass," she said with a smile on her face. She sprang to her feet and came back a few minutes later with a large, faceted glass filled with steaming tea.

"Sugar?" she said, stopping in the doorway.

"Yes, three spoonfuls," I answered.

We spent the next two hours eating sandwiches, drinking tea, and recalling the hardest moments of our lives both here and in Baku.

"That last year in Baku felt like a bad movie," she said, suddenly seeming so relaxed and open to sharing her thoughts. She spoke to me like I was a close friend.

"You know what was the toughest for me?" she asked.

"It must be the time Dad was in prison," I said, guessing.

"I had to go to one of your father's friends' house and ask for money. He was one of his closest ones. We hosted them so many times in our home. Took them to restaurants and resorts," Mother recalled. "I knocked on the door. You were standing next to me. I saw the tiny opening in the door go dark. It was either him or his wife peeking through the door hole. One of them saw us and stepped away from the door," she said and sighed. "He did not even open it."

"I never liked him," I confessed. "I did not like any of Dad's friends." The truth is I had not liked my father either during that period of wealth and depravity culminating with his imprisonment. I did not like remembering that time, but that is where Mother's mind landed when she relaxed, in the rubble my father had left her in.

"As angry as I was at your grandmother for keeping her silence while your father squandered his fortune and destroyed his own family, I could not leave her alone when he was in jail. She would have died of sorrow," Mother said.

"Do you have anything left after selling your jewelry? Did you save anything?" I asked.

"Well, I did not have much to begin with," Mother said. "Most of it had been stolen two years before at our summer house. Whatever was left I sold, but it didn't yield much. We spent most of it on your father's weekly food parcel."

That is how Mother was—easily frightened by life but doing wonders under pressure. I recalled how she had maintained her composure during a powerful earthquake that struck Baku on a chilly November night. Her voice was strong and confident when the walls began to shake. She pushed us out of the apartment and motioned to the stairs. She did not panic or scream or lose her composure. She held herself upright, much better than some of the men who lived in our high-rise, giving directions to tenants, making phone calls, and somehow finding a pair of shoes for me and Rufat. However, for this miracle of force to occur, the pressure had to be swift and immediate, with no time afforded to pondering. Here, our future was still uncertain, yet weeks passed, and we got by. The world did not end. Immediate danger was averted. So Mother was back at her reminiscing game. In the comfort of an old couch, the past could be dissected. It could be up for debate.

"It feels like it was a hundred years ago. On another planet," I said with relief.

"I don't mind that." She smiled.

"Same," I said quietly.

"I brought you and your brother here hoping our life would get better, but just look at the mess I dragged you into," Mother said, dipping a cotton pad into the nail polish remover bottle. "Those first few weeks at Teymour's house were so rough. I cannot forgive myself for putting both of you through this, Maryam."

"Don't think about it, Mama." I had wanted to say something better—something good, something kind, but I couldn't find the words. The air was still. The buzzing of cicadas was barely audible now, a temporary ceasefire.

"I promise you it will get better, Maryam," she said, placing her hand on mine.

"It already is. A little," I answered, hoping what I said was true.

Our existence here in the U.S. was taking shape, but sometimes it seemed that instead of growing together, the three of us were leading separate lives. We experienced separate realities. Mother was still preoccupied with the rubble of her past, with occasional glimpses of cautious optimism in her eyes. It must have been the distance between her past life, filled with heartbreak and regrets and unfairness, and the hypnotizing allure of getting a blank page in life. Once in a while, I stopped by the public library on my way to the optical shop to check my email. There was always a message from Arif, Dilara, and Seymour. My friends tried to cheer me up with these letters, but it felt as if they only emphasized the distance between us. Everything they wrote was familiar, yet with each passing day, I could feel it become a blurry image, a distant memory, something that almost had never happened. They spoke of school, complained about teachers and parents, and talked about their holiday plans. They were curious about my new life and asked many questions, but I barely had the energy to process what was happening, let alone write about it. Our days were repetitive, our future uncertain, and better days were hard to make out. I took longer and longer pauses before emailing my friends back, and took refuge in the silence, pushing them away.

. . . .

CHAPTER 20

LONELINESS CAN BE A CHOICE

When I made it to work the following day Eric was already sitting in my chair in his usual relaxed manner with his arms behind his head and one leg on top of the other. I noticed that he raised his head to confirm it was me as I entered the store. I felt myself bristling, a heat coming to my face, but then I remembered I had done nothing to acknowledge that I had accepted his offer to meet. The idea had seemed outrageous at the time, and I still wondered how just a few hours later I had found myself on the third floor of Weber Leisure Center with Joe Cocker pounding in my ears. I bit my lip for remembering that.

Eric looked at me with a strange hope in his eyes, following my every move until I reached the desk, took the headphones out of my ears, and put them back into my bag. He looked fresh this morning, a few graying strands falling onto his wide forehead. His face was clean-shaven, and he was wearing the same dark-blue polo shirt that he'd been wearing on the day we met.

"Did you listen to it?" he asked abruptly, rising from his chair.

I was taken aback by his sudden question. The absence of his usual formal greeting made it clear he'd been thinking about it. I had been listening to the CD before I fell asleep last night and all of the morning today. I took my time studying the lyrics of each song, feeling the mood of the piece, and guessing at the emotions that inspired it. I wondered if Eric also lived in a world so influenced by the emotions of music, and if it had as tight of a grip on him as it did on me.

"I listened to it in the evening and all of the morning," I said. I found myself confessing much more than I planned. "His voice is so *tough*." I bit my lip because I did not know the word that described Joe Cocker's signature screechy, cigarette-coarse voice.

Eric looked puzzled. "What do you mean by tough?" he asked.

"It's like . . . when you smoke a lot of cigarettes. You know, like Ashur's!" I said.

Ashur turned around when he heard his name and threw a surprised look at us.

"What is it, Mariski?" he said, expecting some form of explanation.

"She is describing Cocker's voice," Eric said with a childish smile.

"Who? Who?" Ashur did not look pleased.

Now that Ashur was involved in the conversation, Shammoun and Youel felt like they had to be included as well. All three men looked away from the television and straight at us, trying to assess if the conversation was worthy of joining. Shammoun and Youel were still sleepy from yesterday's outing and preferred to turn back to the television, but both Eric and I noticed an angry look from Ashur. It was so bitter that it made me look away and prompted an unpleasant wave of emotion inside of me. A troubling suspicion about his strange bursts of anger lingered in my mind, but a minute later I brushed it aside as a product of my imagination.

"Sometimes his voice is kind of breaking," I said, trying to elaborate. "It's like he is struggling through every note. It is not smooth. How do I say this? His voice is constantly breaking, but after you listen to him for a while, you get used to this strange quality. It stops bothering your ear and you almost expect it." I was surprised how easily the words flowed this time.

Eric's face lit up with a smile. He seemed pleased that I had taken my time in listening to and describing the music, registering each emotion very carefully and sharing it with him.

"Yes, that is a very true description. Do you already have a favorite?"

"Not yet," I answered. "I must listen to the album several times. There are a few songs I didn't like, though."

"Which ones?" I could hear the impatience in his voice.

"'With a Little Help from My Friends,'" I answered, seeing a surprise on his face. "Yes, I didn't like that one. It is too loud, and I didn't like the melody. Also, I didn't really understand what the song is about. I even looked up the lyrics in the library but couldn't make sense of it."

"This song is about a lonely person that gets by finding a refuge in his friends, surrounding himself with them, spending time with them," he said. "You know, accepting their help once in a while."

He seemed a bit disappointed I had discarded the song so quickly without really reading into the lyrics. Perhaps he was suddenly becoming aware of the age difference between us, blaming it on the fact that I couldn't understand how loneliness could be a choice.

It was difficult for us to speak when Ashur was around. By now it was obvious that he disliked how friendly we were with each other. I was convinced he noticed my secret affection towards Eric and disapproved of it because of our age difference. As a result, Eric and I both seemed to wait for an opportunity when Ashur went to run errands or was busy speaking on the phone with his restaurant partner, who called more often these days. At all other times, Eric would stand by the counter, his one leg over the other, watching television or stepping out to the front office to take a call. Sometimes, I would catch him looking at my profile as I raised my head from the public aid forms to answer the phone.

Eric came to the office every day that week and we continued to steal a few minutes here and there to chat about history, literature, music, and countries that he had visited or was planning to visit. Eric spoke of his time as a student in a very affectionate and excited manner, recounting the political science and American government classes that he'd taken, remembering the personalities and appearance of his professors and political events of the time that stirred heated debates in the classroom. He spoke of his previous girlfriends at the time—the Lebanese, the Argentine, the Russian—meticulously describing their personalities, the sounds and words they couldn't pronounce, and how he was fascinated with their accents. I tried to detect any remnants of romantic feeling he might still be harboring somewhere deep inside, but Eric seemed to treat them as anthropological studies, remembering the tiniest details of their personality, but not how they made him feel.

It occurred to me that he was collecting these lovers of the past like souvenirs, admiring their intricacies, remembering when and how he acquired them, but he no longer had any feeling towards them, leaving them idle on the shelves of his aging mind. For a moment, I imagined myself in their place, trying to think of the words he'd choose to describe my mixed culture, the number of languages I spoke, the mole on my right jawline, the slight angle of my eyes hinting at my Eastern roots, and, of course, my favorite Joe Cocker song.

I didn't have many memories to offer him, but he listened to me attentively and later remembered the details of our conversations. When I told him a few stories from school, his face lit up with a forgiving smile, making me feel suddenly too young, so I avoided any subject that would remind us of the age difference, ultimately resorting to simply listening to him. He didn't seem to mind.

I liked listening to him. I liked how he moved his hands when he spoke, as if grasping an apple with his fingers. I liked the pitch of his voice—a little coarse but gentle, almost whispering, so that I had to read from his lips sometimes. I liked that he always showed up with a book in his hands, even if he continued to get alienating looks from all of the inhabitants of Vision Express except me. I liked that his clothes and accessories were stylish, yet not overbearing.

When he spoke, his face leaned forward, drawing attention to his dark and intelligent eyes framed by rimless glasses with thin wires tucked behind his ears.

That whole week, I spent my bus rides home reliving the short but meaningful conversations afforded to us that day. I noticed that, when I was with Eric, I stopped comparing every minute of my present with my past. I willfully accepted that I now lived in the U.S., had a job, and had formed my first friendship with a man more than twenty years my senior. I enjoyed coming up with creative ways to draw parallels between American and Azeri culture. The deeper I analyzed, the more hidden parallels I encountered. When I shared them with Eric, he'd light up a new cigarette, his eyebrows drawing together as he inhaled and his mouth letting out a puff of the smoke as he nodded.

"You are curious girl, Maryam!" he would say. "I never thought about this, but you're right!"

No matter how the conversations captivated us, Eric never mentioned meeting up at Weber Leisure Center again, and the next Monday he didn't show up in the office. He didn't show up the next day either, or the day after. I wondered if Ashur had spoken to him, but something told me that he had nothing to do with his disappearance. It was Eric's prerogative to enter and exit the lives of people as he wished, and he wanted to keep it that way. It didn't upset me, as I was confident that sooner or later, he'd come back, ready to receive a new share of my stories and bring me more of his favorite music, telling me about some movie he recently watched or a book he was reading.

During Eric's absence, Ashur would revert back to his old friendly self and start random conversations with me.

"Mariski, your handwriting . . ." he'd begin.

"Yeah," I replied. "What about it?"

"It's t-t-too neat!"

"And what's the problem with that, Ashur?"

"Well, the b-b-bank don't think my signature is my signature. You get it?"

"I have no clue what you mean." I was puzzled. "What do you mean they don't accept it?"

"I send my ch-ch-check. I sign it. They come b-b-back and say it's not you. You get it now, Mariski?" he explained. "I can't c-c-carry you around in my pocket to sign all my ch-ch-ch-checks, you know?"

"Why not?" Youel joined in. "She is tiny, tiny! Put her in your pocket and anytime you need a check, pull her out! Ha, ha!" Youel would not pass up an opportunity to jump on a joke like that.

"Mariski, I'm kidding, I'm kidding," he said, having caught my annoyed stare. "I burn some bissma for you now. We don't want no evil eye. No evil eye on our angel Mariski!"

"Hey Ashur, why you complaining?" Shammoun decided it was time he joined in. "Write your checks yourself. Thirty years in this country, you make Mariski write your checks. You lazy!"

"Me? L-l-lazy? Shammo, Youel, I am the only one that works here. You b-b-bump your knees all day and *this one*," he pointed at Youel, "c-c-can't keep a job for a month. Father of the year!"

Since the comment was so spot-on, it wasn't so funny anymore, and both Youel and Shammoun turned to watch the episode of *Cops* on television.

Now that we both lived in Skokie, Ashur would often give me rides home. Even though I refused several times out of politeness, he'd shake his head and point me to his car, and so we'd drive home together on days when he didn't have to attend to restaurant-related business. Usually, we'd both be silent during the drive. Ashur would drum a familiar tune with the insides of his palms on the wheel and look around impatiently, occasionally cursing the drivers who didn't yield the right of way.

"Ashur, can I change the radio channel?" I asked.

"Sure, g-g-go ahead! You like this stuff?" he asked but didn't look like he needed an answer. "No good music in America, Mariski!" he sighed and tapped on the wheel.

I tuned the radio to the only channel I knew that played the same set of familiar songs every day. Sitting in Ashur's old Ford, enjoying the pleasant air-conditioning inside of the car, I remembered being in Baku during the glory days of my father's banking career, when I would spend several hours in a car daily as my dad's chauffeur drove me to and from school and the numerous after-school activities that didn't end until eight p.m.

I remembered the days of not having to think where the car was going because there was someone else whose job was to remember instead of me. I now realized that had been a perk of being a banker's daughter, but at the time it hadn't seemed like a luxury at all. My father's bank prospered when I started school and so, for as long as I could remember, our life was filled with all kinds of helpers—drivers, cooks, cleaning ladies, tutors of all kinds.

We led a life removed from so many of the realities of Azerbaijan, unaware of the long lines at the grocery store. Our clothes were imported from Europe, our fridge always full of delicacies such as black caviar and Dutch cheese. When the headmaster of the private gymnasium I attended had issues with the municipal officials or needed a truckful of bricks or help in obtaining some license, it was my father she called. Once when I was a third-grade student, one of the teachers spoke roughly to me outside of class and I, the sensitive, overprotected flowerchild, living life inside a crystal bubble, cried the whole rest of the evening. My father stormed the school and threatened to pull me out.

"She's been crying for hours. I don't want to hear anything!" he yelled. "I'll find another school with teachers who have better manners!"

I stood by my father, still upset and slightly embarrassed to cause so much commotion, because despite my father's affluence, I was a quiet, shy child. Speaking up, being bold, talking back to teachers—these were things that remained foreign to me, so it was quite uncomfortable to stir up so much trouble in our small private gymnasium of hardly one hundred students.

"Your daughter does not need to look for a different school," the headmaster assured. "I will fire this teacher for such disrespectful conduct, and let's close this matter."

That response satisfied my father and we left, but the incident remained the talk of the entire school for months to come. From then on, there was caution in the voices of all of my teachers, which I hated. Even the ones who had always been quite attentive and nice to me before the incident were wary of me afterwards. Such was the power of money and connections. One only realizes its magical effect when it's no longer there. All of this ended gradually when things started going downhill and my father descended from his oligarch's throne to the life of a regular tax-evasion criminal.

I felt a lingering memory of the security and isolation we had felt back then during these evening rides with Ashur now. Just like so many of our chauffeurs, Ashur never spoke to me and delivered me home without any instructions, patiently waiting for me to enter through the swinging doors of our two-story building before raising his hand in a goodbye.

Then, one day, Ashur started a conversation about my family. He asked me how my grandmother's health was and if I had called her recently. I answered with surprise, not providing too much information as I thought of these questions as mere politeness on his behalf, rather than sincere interest. But one question followed another and, in a few minutes, family stories about my grandmother and her four siblings spilled out of me like rice from a sack.

At some point, when we entered the village of Skokie, I suddenly felt Ashur's warm hand over mine. This felt strange and alarming, but I froze in place, unsure what to do. I noticed that despite his thin frame, his hands were square and smooth, covered by scant black hair and darker than the skin on his face. Ashur's hands resembled that of a laborer. They were covered with tiny patches and slivers of white paste that he used when working on the ancient framing machine that roared like a broken fridge. The tips of his fingernails were covered with the same white paste, and it wouldn't come off despite his frantic attempts. We were both silent for a moment. He raised and tilted his head to the right to see how bad the traffic had gotten and looked away in frustration.

I wanted to get away. I wanted to signal that I didn't like this, that it was not okay, but I was afraid of something I could not define. What if this was just an innocent gesture? What if I got it all wrong? I looked out the window, furrowing my brows in discomfort, but how would he notice if I didn't have the courage to turn my face towards him? Could it be that I was completely mistaken? I remembered how fatherly he always treated me, buying me bread to take home, giving me a ride, and slipping extra twenties into my modest weekly salary.

We continued like that for few more minutes, until we reached another busy intersection and Ashur raised his hand to yell at a white Lincoln that cut him off. I seized the moment and quickly removed my hand. He noticed it but didn't say anything and so we continued through the quieter streets of downtown Skokie until we reached Bronx Street.

"All right, Mariski! See you tomorrow," he said. I tried to read this new, strange expression on his face.

"Goodbye," I answered quietly and left.

I tried to distract myself from what just happened. After a few hours of mindlessly tidying my closet, I sank heavily into my bed and cried. I wasn't sure what I was crying about. The tears came down slowly and in silence, disturbed by an occasional sob. I was mourning my careless existence in Baku, for I no longer lived in a capsule protected by my father and his army of servants. For the past few months, I had been thinking of Vision Express Optical as an extension of my life in Baku, with elderly men who watched television, smoked cigarettes, munched on nuts, and were fully consumed by things they could complain about. Ashur was the heart of that universe. His silent care and protection were familiar to me, putting my mind at ease that someone is always on a lookout. His unpleasant looks when I spoke to Eric only confirmed his fatherly feelings towards me, or so I had thought. But were they actually fatherly? Deep inside, I knew I should not brush off this incident as trivial, but I did not find the strength in me to see it as it was, so I worked to convince myself that all was still good.

I took a quick shower before bed to wipe off the bitter aftertaste of the day, changed into my pajamas, and climbed into bed, holding a family photo of my grandparents. The picture must have been taken at a birthday party, as my grandfather wore his vested suit and the table was covered with plates filled with saffron rice with spade-shaped *qazmagh* and lamb stew, a dish my grandmother prepared on special occasions. I recognized the familiar dreaminess in my grandfather's gaze that meant he was tipsy. He wrapped his arm around my grandmother, and she leaned her head towards his. She was wearing a polka dot dress with a boatneck top. Her arms were adorned with three golden bracelets that she'd worn since their return from India.

"Nana, what was it like in India?" I asked her once.

"Very humid," she began. "We'd spend days at the club, drinking lemonade and fanning ourselves."

"What club?"

"The club was the place with a pool and a café. That is where all the embassy staff spent their time. Your father loved going there and so we would go. *Memsaab, memsaab*, the servant would call me."

"You had a servant, Nana?"

"I did. During the three years we spent there, I did very little housework. Can you believe it?"

"Hardly!" I laughed. "You're still making up for it! What about that picture of you holding a cigarette?"

"Not a cigarette," she corrected me. "Cigarette holder! Is that the one where I am standing next to Raj Kapoor?"

"The man with thick black hair soaked in gel?" I asked. "Yes, I guess that is the one."

"I had to attend functions with your grandfather. All the wives of diplomats drank wine and smoked, and so did I," she explained. "All right, it was a marvelous time. Of course, you wouldn't know, but Raj Kapoor was like, let me think, like the Leonardo DiCaprio of the time. Very famous and very handsome!"

"You look like a celebrity too!" I confessed.

"He was an actor, a celebrity, starring in Bollywood movies and I . . ." she paused. "I was the wife of a spy. An actress, too, but in a far more dangerous industry."

My grandfather's "dangerous industry" remained foreign to me, as he'd taken whatever secrets he'd had to his grave years ago. These bits and pieces of their adventures slipped from Nana's tongue once in a while, but they were too vague, too ambiguous to put the puzzle together. Besides, back then I was too preoccupied being a child and cared little for these gems. Despite a childhood spent in the shade of a world war, and later, despite her husband's difficult career, Nana's look remained soft and young, unblemished by the difficulties of life. There was an undying fire of optimism in her eyes. I thought that she would know how to make sense of what happened today. She'd tell me what to do. She'd run her fingers through my hair, smooth my eyebrows and pinch the tip of my chin, and all would be good.

I closed my eyes, hoping that sleep would end the troubled string of thoughts that tired both my brain and my body, and very soon it did.

CHAPTER 21

. . . .

SOMETHING LIKE A FAMILY

The summer months passed, paving the way for a beautiful fall, and ending the overwhelming chorus of the cicadas. We met up with Teymour and Sarah quite often, arranging picnics at Lake Shore Park with mother's homemade sausage-and-cheese sandwiches, bowls of fruit, and a thermos full of home-brewed bergamot tea that smelled heavenly. Teymour would lay on the thin woven blanket we'd bring with us and chat with other strangers passing by in the park. I could tell he was relieved the drama was behind us and it turned out that there was enough space for both Sarah and our family in America. Mother and Teymour reverted to their humorous exchanges that always centered around their time at Moscow State University. As for me, the snapshots from those early days in his glass-box apartment were too fresh and I wasn't ready to warm up to him. That window, the tiny people descending into and emerging from subway stations, the haunting orange of the nightly sky, the tasteless fruits, and mirror images of mother and Teymour on the verge of a fight were still all too real in my head. Nevertheless, the unpleasant after-taste was fading, and I found myself liking his presence, though I did not participate in conversation so much.

"What are you thinking, Leyla?" Teymour asked one day. "Think you can live here?"

"I see more of a path here for us than there, I can say that for sure," Mother replied.

"Nothing left there . . ." Teymour said. "And I am glad you are here," he added with unusual caution in his voice. I caught him glancing at Rufat and me, checking for reaction.

Mother smiled back gratefully but did not utter a word. I looked away at the calm surface of Lake Michigan to avoid giving myself away. A group of children and parents gathered by the blue ice-cream truck that jingled a playful tune to announce itself. The afternoon was warm. The sun fell on Mother's suddenly younger, happier face and I held my gaze to take it in.

"That dorm on the main campus of MSU," Teymour began, refer-ring to their alma mater, Moscow State University, "I have such vivid recollections from our days there. Small, crowded rooms, the beds with metal railings. A window looking at the main square, the lac-quered desk with that heavy table lamp."

"And that tiny round table, barely big enough for two people," Mother picked up. "Yet, you're right. The best years of our lives, weren't they?"

"What was so special about it?" I asked.

"Lack of real problems," Mother began. "A great city that unfolded in front of you in all its glory. Company of intelligent, ambitious, yet adventurous people from different countries. It was the Harvard of USSR! Plus, we were students, and everything is different when you're a student." She was mainly addressing Sarah, who also appeared interested. Mother never indulged in such a relaxed tone with us. No, with us she was always serious, cautious, calculating, ensuring, but with others her stories had an elegant, easy flow and were quite captivating. I was grateful for Sarah's presence, and I let myself listen closely. I had yet to find out if life indeed was different when you are a student, but the sparkle in her eyes was convincing.

"Plus, I was there with their dad," she said and pointed to us. "And both sets of parents sent us money that was enough to enjoy ourselves. We could get in trouble all right and there would always be a way out of it. We laughed a lot."

"You know what I'm thinking, right?" Teymour said, and we all got curious.

"Oh, not again, that old story about Tatiana!"

"Yes!" Teymour exclaimed. "Listen, children. We were all living at the dorm. Your father introduced us to Tatiana, a family friend from his years in India, who bored us for hours with her whining. Your mother had the patience of an Egyptian mummy to listen to her never-ending whining about the soloist of a band that she happened to love," he began. "I don't even remember the name of the band. Anyways, me and your dad would openly tell her to cut it out, just be done with these stories. But not your mother. No! She'd nod and listen, encouraging the whining even more, driving us all mad. So, Tatiana kept coming and, once she started, there was no way to stop her. We'd lose hours listening to this stuff."

"She had these big, almost scary eyes and her hair was always a mess," Mother picked up the story. "Very smart, but completely obsessed with this guy who was pretty much a rock star. But she didn't care. She kept complaining that he ignored her. I mean, he ignored most of us, let alone Tatiana. Anyways, Teymour was helping me get shoes from this tall wardrobe when she knocked."

"Why did I even come over?" Teymour scratched his head.

"To eat. I spent half the time at Moscow State making you sandwiches," Mother shot back.

"Riiight," Teymour agreed. "So, I'm standing on top of the table with shoes in my hands, all right? She," he pointed at Mother, "is literally inside of the wardrobe, handing me another pair, and your father is lying on the bed. And suddenly, she begins to knock and call for your mother. And we freeze in place!"

We all pictured this hilarious scene: Mother inside the wardrobe, Teymour on a table, and our father lounging on a bed. I struggled to picture them as students, to imagine a time when my parents were in love, just two students studying physics, escaping annoying neighbors, and hanging out with Teymour, a few years younger than them, always hungry and as clumsy as now.

"How long did she knock?" Rufat asked.

"Fifteen minutes! That woman would not give up easily!" Teymour exclaimed.

"If she had stayed any longer, we'd have suffocated from inaudible laughing," Mother said.

I munched on grapes and watched their eyes fill up with a strange kind of communal joy, as they grabbed each other by the wrists, correcting the tiniest details in these dorm stories and bursting into laughter all the while. The stories were truly surreal, with interesting characters from countries I had never visited and intellectual debates fueled by dark, strong tea infused with industrial spirits stolen from the chemical lab.

Soon the weather got cooler and our picnics in the park were no longer comfortably warm, so we'd stay in, ordering Chicago's famous deep-dish pizza with mozzarella and green peppers covered with a thick layer of tomato sauce, enclosed in crispy crust.

"Fruits suck here, but they make it all up with deep-dish pizza!" Rufat would say.

We'd watch those cookie-cutter action movies with aliens invading the world, ruining half of the planet, only to be destroyed by some guy with superpowers he didn't know he had.

"How about another Tom Cruise action movie?" Teymour would ask, getting some pushback from Mother and Sarah.

"I'm fine with the usual very bad movies, but no spoilers, please," Rufat would say.

"Yes, no spoilers!" Teymour would repeat.

"When I said no spoilers, Teymour, I was talking about you," Rufat would say, turning to him.

"I never do it," Teymour said. "Maybe once. Fine! I did it once."

Rufat would shake his head and hand out the paper plates and napkins. As I sat on the side of the couch by the window, chewing on my Giordano's pizza and observing Mother, Sarah, Teymour, and Rufat form something like a family, I felt snug. *Boy, have I missed this feeling*, I thought.

CHAPTER 22

. . . .

RUSSIAN CLASSICS

Since our move to Skokie, I had experimented with my work commute to finally get back on a bus that took me through Devon. Eventually, I discovered a new route to work, which involved a fifteen-minute train ride to Howard—a connection point for several CTA lines that was also a departure point for buses that would take me back to Devon Avenue. This route took an additional fifteen minutes but had two advantages. First, the express train took me through a thick forest with trees painted by the mighty Chicago fall in hues of yellow, orange, green, and red. Its beauty was so overwhelming and fresh that it fascinated me without fail every morning. The intensity of the colors increased with each day. I boarded the train in the mornings, cutting through this enchanted forest with incredible speed, the scenery morphing into a continuous ribbon of yellow, orange, green, and purple.

The second advantage to my new commute was, of course, getting back to Devon. I liked to sit occupying the last seat, propping

my elbow on the window-frame, greeting the numerous shop owners, marveling at the store fronts of the sari palaces, and watching
Orthodox Jews, Indians, and Arabs pass by in clusters. I would get
off the bus one station early to pass by the Turkish, Russian, and
Georgian stores on foot and greet the store owners with a smile.
Their relaxed and happy faces set the mood for the rest of the day
and made me feel closer to home. Hadn't we Azeris, in fact, been
surrounded by Turks, Georgians, and Russians since the beginning of time?

If I managed to see all three of the store owners in the morning,
I'd walk into the optical shop with a sense of pride for my culture
and the history it carried on its shoulders. *It's a shame*, I thought, *that
the Iraqis at Vision Express Optical don't share my love of history.* They
didn't know much about political ambitions or the victories of their
legendary ancestors and only knew vaguely that they'd been around
for a while.

With time, I'd walk into the optical shop with familiarity and
ease, no longer shy and hesitant before uttering a word. I picked up
a few conversational phrases in Assyrian and used them throughout
the day to prompt a laugh from Youel and Shammoun and surprise the visitors. Though my knowledge of the language was scarce,
I caught myself being able to decode Ashur's short phone conversations, picking up words like "bread," "home," and "car," among others.
Pretty soon all three of them figured out that I was quite fluent for
a conversational speaker and started paying attention to things they
would say around me and warning all newcomers, "Mariski speaks
fluent Assyrian."

Fortunately, the incident with the hand didn't repeat again. I felt I
had sent a clear enough message by refusing rides from Ashur several
times afterward. He insisted the first time that I join him, but then
stopped pushing. Besides, I had gotten used to my evening stroll

along Devon Avenue with a daily stop at Three Sisters to pick up cottage cheese, sauerkraut, pickled cucumbers, and cubed seasoning for chicken soup, or some other thing that Mother requested every day. As time passed, I tried to forget about the incident altogether, loosening up on my alertness around Ashur and reverting back to our previous friendliness, like that of an old uncle and a niece. The afternoons would pass in silence, disturbed occasionally by visitors who came to talk business with Ashur, drink a cup of coffee, curse Saddam, or simply pass time before dinner.

After listening to my endless stories and fascination with Devon, Mother and Rufat took a bus trip and visited me on one sunny Saturday in September. They showed up around one p.m., an hour before Ashur closed the shop for the weekend.

"Shammoun, didn't your sister send cookies yesterday with lunch?" Youel scrambled to find something he could put on the table. "Mariski, your parents don't teach you to tell people when someone come over? Ahead of time! Huh, Mariski?"

"Please, don't worry about it," Mother said, not ready for such grand gestures. But, of course, she caused quite a stir with her entrance. This was no Jewish household in a posh suburb—we were back in the Middle East, where tables were covered with food and guests were force-fed. This was familiar territory.

"No worries! We have cookies from Dina." Youel smiled. "Mariski, go get some coffee for your mother. Come on!"

"Youel r-r-runs this place," Ashur joked. "Me, Mariski, and Shammoun—we all work for him. We do what he says. Youel, can we g-g-go home early today, what do you say?" Ashur yelled to be heard at the back of the store.

Mother and Rufat sipped their coffee, ate the cookies, and weren't sure what to talk about with the men. We left when Ashur closed the shop and spent the rest of the day wandering from one trinket shop to another, exploring old records at Balalaika and finishing up the day in a Turkish bakery, drinking glass after glass of tea and munching on *kurabiye*.

Now that I had gotten very efficient at completing my work in the morning hours of the day, I had free time and started paying more attention to the conversations among the three men. Soon, I noticed something that astounded me. Both young and older visitors of Vision Express Optical would salute Ashur and Youel, but then to Shammoun they would bend in something like a bow. Some of them would go as far as lowering their forehead to touch the large agate ring on his right hand and whisper something inaudible. Shammoun met their acts of reverence with a solemn face that was gentle but stopped shy of a smile.

One morning, Youel noticed the look of surprise on my face and smiled.

"Tell her, Shammo!" he said. "Tell her so she knows the truth."

"Mariski, you see all these people that come here? Some day in the long ago, in the past, I give them jobs. Shammo is an old man, but when young I was troublemaker. Then troublemaker of Chicago become godfather. You watch the movie, Mariski? Hey Youel, think she knows?"

"I read the book too," I said.

"You bookworm, you, of course you read the book," Shammo said and laughed. "Do you know the street nearby intersection of Devon and Clinton? I rename that street 'Sargon Drive!' In the name of our king, Sargon! The great king of Assyria he was, Mariski." He sighed. "That's why, all the old people you see, they come here . . . they kiss my ring! I give them jobs . . . them and their kids, they come to me. But it's in the past! Because why? Because my heart no good, Mariski! When you are young, you drink, you smoke. *No problemo!*" He raised both of his palms up. "But when you are old, you have to take pills! Why I need a life like that? I don't need it! I smoke . . . Ha, ha, ha!" he said, his chuckles slowly morphing into a coarse cough and his smile replaced with a painful grimace.

"Shammoun, what is wrong with you?" exclaimed Youel. "Who you got except that poor woman, your sister? Poor woman, cook for you every day. She come here every day with food and soup! Shame on you! Shame! You need to get married! I will go back to Australia and marry." Youel's problems were solved either by bissma, the Assyrian incense stick, or marriage.

"You go, my friend," responded Shammoun. "You go! Good luck to you! May God give you patience and health. Woman will make a hole in your brain. Big one! No marry for me, thank you very much!"

Until then, a godfather had been a fictional creature in Mario Puzo's book that the neighboring boy had lent me years ago. I could never imagine that the aging gentleman with sad eyes, furrowed eyebrows, and a sick heart who greeted me with a kind smile every morning was once a mighty godfather who could solve conflicts, give jobs to people, or rename streets. I simply could not picture him angry or hostile, so I made a note to ask Eric when he finally returned if Shammoun had been bluffing about all this.

The painful grip around my neck that had taken hold of me since my first day in the States subsided gradually and was eventually replaced by a numb nostalgia for my life in Baku. I would take pleasure in recounting the tiniest details of the most routine activities, like walking across the street to buy bread in the morning or the last few nerve-wracking all-nighters I had pulled in preparation for my high-school exit exams. My mind drifted away from all the celebrations and farewell parties and focused on lazy afternoons spent by the tall window with a large wooden frame that offered a grand view of Seaside Boulevard and a busy five-lane road constantly jammed with cars. Despite the irritating traffic buzz and air polluted by exhaust, I liked looking out of the window and plotting destinations for the families that passed in the cars. Some were headed for a family celebration or a wedding, I'd imagine. And others had filled up their car with bags full of basic household items and produce and were headed to Mardakan, the seaside village that served as a summer refuge for city-dwellers.

In Skokie, I still went to the public library around the corner to use the computer, but I no longer rejoiced at the sight of my email with unread messages from Dilara, Arif, and Seymour. They now served as a reminder that despite our absence, life in Baku still went on at its usual pace. My days were dull in contrast to my classmates' weeklong debate camps or getaways to the seaside. In the first few weeks, I had remained in a state of disbelief that we had, in fact, permanently moved to a country across the ocean. But now as the dreaded fact sank into my consciousness, messages from home produced nothing but nostalgia. If I avoided any reminders about the sweetness of my past life, I managed to stay calm and collected and find some pleasure during the day, but my mind desperately looked for the slightest hint of Baku and these memories attacked me unexpectedly, some prompted by weird things such as the smell of burnt resin or even trash! Who knew the smell of burnt resin could bring back memories?

Despite a full-time job and long list of errands that Mother supplied me with on a daily basis, I continued living the life of a spectator, observing the pedestrians on the streets during my bus rides, then watching the Assyrians at the optical shop, and finishing the day glued to the television. I was free of the constant anxiety that drained my energy, robbed me of appetite, made me lose track of time, and consumed me in a dark slumber. A vacuum seemed to have replaced the turmoil that had reigned inside of me for the past few months. Both my heart and my mind were blank—a space unobstructed by any emotions, devoid of any dreams.

As the time passed, more and more random bits and pieces of my brief encounters with Eric came back to me. This would usually happen during the peak load time at work, when I rushed quickly between the visitor area full of families that came to get their eyes checked and the back office to pick up the phone. Suddenly, the expression of surprise he'd worn in response to something I had said once would appear in my mind's eye. At times, the image was so clear and vivid it would prompt a smile on my face. I'd spend hours trying to remember the exact color of his shirt, the book he'd been carrying, the dark green cigarette box he'd put on my desk, and other things that were captured at the obscure corners of my memory.

"Maryam, tell me, is it true that you guys had to read *War and Peace* in tenth grade?" he asked one day. "That and *Crime and Punishment* by Dostoyevsky. It baffles me that anyone would think a tenth grader could understand those heavyweight Russians at that age. Or, perhaps, I'm making an assumption," he said and hesitated. "Well, tell me, did you read it?"

"I skipped the war parts," I confessed.

"I guess that makes sense. But, besides the war passages, what do you recall? I don't mean the events. What did you grasp from that book?" he asked.

"When I think of that book, and, in fact, all the other books I read in that school year, the memory comingles, blurs together with the memory of my teacher. Short, white-haired Svetlana Savelievna. She had a fragile frame, a hump on her back, long, wrinkled fingers, almost transparent skin, and long, colorless nails.

"There is a moment in the book when Graf Bolkonsky sees an old, lifeless oak tree and compares his life to it, devoid of love and hope or any meaning. Then he meets Natasha, falls in love, and notices that spring has arrived, and the oak is now covered with tiny branches and leaves. It's a famous passage, not something I alone noticed, but

I liked it. I remembered it." I got a little uncomfortable, afraid of giving myself away.

"Go on, Maryam," Eric said. "What did you think of it?"

"I thought it was a monstrous book. Too long, but it had bits and pieces that I understood even back then."

"What were they?" he kept insisting.

"That love can turn things around. That there is a season to be stark naked, unarmed amid cold and emptiness, but spring always comes. Trees come back to life; grass grows back. It didn't last much for Bolkonsky, though."

"We're not talking about Bolkonsky, Maryam." He looked at me.

I didn't have the courage to say another word and smiled back. And just like all the other ones, this moment was now just a memory, something that might or might not have happened. I filed it back in the library of my memories and went on with the day.

. . . .

CHAPTER 23

YALLA, GUYS! LET'S GO!

September came and left, paving the way for a chilly October. The leaves on the trees, still colorful and bright, had been swept off the branches and now covered the ground like a fine Persian carpet. Aside from the chilly morning air, October welcomed us with winds that made my morning stroll to the Skokie Express train station even more pleasant. The summer heat had hung above us for months, rarely disturbed by a light summer rain or a breeze that came sweeping from Lake Michigan. Thus, we greeted the frequent October winds as you greet a relative that has been away for a while.

Along with the winds, October brought new developments. The sleepy and slow pace of life at Vision Express Optical picked up in preparation for the long-awaited grand opening of Ashur's restaurant, Arabesque, a lifelong dream. We had visitors who came to talk restaurant business every day now. They'd speak in Assyrian, but I picked up on the myriad topics they discussed—the licenses one had to obtain when opening a restaurant, menus, chefs, belly dancers, musicians from the Middle East including a drummer, a guitar player, and, of course, a singer. Ashur paced in the narrow space of the optical shop in a new, impatient manner, like students do in the hallways of school, eager to break free and never return.

"In B-B-Baghdad, you open a restaurant? No problemo! You go pay a bribe and you're done," Ashur complained. "Then you open the restaurant. Everybody happy. Your customer happy, you happy, your wallet happy! In America, by the time you get all the d-d-damn licenses, you're done! You don't want no restaurant, Mariski! You thank God for this optical store, this h-h-hole in the wall, and kiss goodbye all your dreams. I got the b-b-business occupancy permit, I got the liquor permit, food-handler permit, this permit, that permit, shit permit!" he went on and on as Shammoun and Youel nodded their heads in agreement. "The last permit will be a permit from this damn city to die. They will stick it on m-m-my grave!"

"All right, Ashur! Relax, man!" Youel said.

"Relax? It's easy for you to s-s-say! I put all my money into this business. If I d-d-don't open it in a month, I'll start losing money. And not just my money, that dummy Sako invested all he has too. If we lose it, he'll never leave m-m-me alone!" Ashur continued.

"Ashur, I said relax! Don't say bad stuff! Say good thing and good thing happen!" Youel replied.

"Yeah," Shammoun said in his sleepy voice. "Youel, burn some bissma."

"Oh God, no bissma, please!" I said.

All three men turned around and looked at me, but I couldn't care less. I felt the onslaught of a migraine attack and knew the strong fumes of the incense would finish me off.

"Look at Mariski!" Youel started.

"Leave her," Ashur said suddenly. "I can t-t-tell her migraine is about to begin."

I was grateful to Ashur and felt bad for all the roadblocks he encountered before the grand opening. I wanted to say something to cheer him up, but I was just as frustrated by all the official documents one was required to obtain for life's most basic procedures in America. He was right. You could expedite so much in life with a simple bribe back home. This was such a normal thing that the concept of a bribe, a thing that was illegal, a thing that signified the breaking of a law, was a muddy one. It was stripped of a negative context and symbolized the amount of money you needed to make life easy for yourself. Law was a liquid matter, fees varied based on your connections, and punishment for breaking a law was distant and remediable if you had the money.

Every day, Ashur was consumed more and more by the licenses that stood like hurdles on his way to his restaurant's grand opening, and I was left with the lion's share of all the work in the shop. There wasn't much else happening in his life besides frequent calls from Babi nagging for another toy or some junk food. He'd spend his evenings at the restaurant talking to electricians, maintenance guys, meeting with contractors, chefs, and musicians. He did most of the work because he could not trust Sako. Besides, Sako lived in an extended family clan, always busy with his sons, catering to this or that uncle, and generally unable to concentrate, but he had much more money invested, so in a way this arrangement worked for both men.

"The guy who s-s-sold me this place taught me this line of work," Ashur told me once while giving me a ride home. "He said, 'Ashur, you can go f-f-find something b-b-better to do in life, but if you screw it up, this b-b-business will put bread on your table. So, in the evening, when your k-k-kid calls and asks for a chocolate bar, you don't think about it.' And he was right. Thirty years in this country, this piece of shit optical store fed the whole family—all my brothers and sisters and even the family of my ex-wife. Otherwise, I would have gone off and become a journalist, like your friend Eric." He shot me a glance.

Ashur had never referred to Eric like this before and it alarmed me, so I kept quiet and didn't say a word. Ashur's nostalgic mood suddenly turned dark, and he went on again about the licenses.

I'd spend my days shuffling between the front and back office, answering phones, filling out the paperwork, and attending to customers. The pace of work had a healing effect on me. The busier I got, the less time I had to recall how careless my life had been just a few months ago. My sheltered life as a high school student began to feel like a myth, a thing that had never happened.

By the end of October, Ashur had obtained all the licenses and hired a young, enthusiastic chef who designed an innovative Mediterranean menu, full of saffron, cinnamon, basil, and other spices, creating chef-signature items that blended Mediterranean with Persian cuisines.

"I got chef B-B-Binyamin. I got all the d-d-damn licenses lined up, but this tiny Lebanese wo-wo-woman won't say yes to me," Ashur complained, slapping his palms on his knees.

Reem, the Lebanese belly dancer, was one of the most famous in the city of Chicago. She would show up once in a while with her now-seven-month-old baby daughter in a car seat, sleeping peacefully. She'd sit between Youel and Ashur and speak in her melodic voice as all three men switched to Arabic. Watching them, you'd never think they were talking business, but after her departure, Ashur would make phone calls to find out how much she was really making at Chicago's number one Arabic night club, called Souq. That is where she performed on Fridays.

"She come, she laugh and joke, and I telling you, Ashur," Youel would say, "she going to get her way. She is good!"

"I hope she d-d-dances as good as she negotiates!" Ashur would snap back.

In the end, Reem did get her way. She would switch from Souq to Arabesque and promised to do her famous "Egyptian Goddess" act as the opener. I kept wondering how she could remain so slender, so untouched by motherhood, her stomach flat, her skin so smooth, and no sign of tiredness on her face.

"I don't eat!" she once confessed to Shammoun when he asked the question.

"I am lucky like that. This baby is an angel. She loves sleep more than her mother. When she sleep, I sleep," Reem offered.

"Say *Mashallah*. A baby that sleeps is born once in hundred years!" he said as if he had any clue what he was talking about, but such was the effect Reem had on the men. They smiled and agreed with everything she said, caught in the magic spell of her silky black hair, slender waist, and cherry-shaped eyes.

At last, the long list of obstacles on the way to the grand opening of Arabesque was crossed off, done, completed! The men walked around the shop with a victorious bounce, tapping familiar tunes on the coffee table, running their fingers through their dyed hair, and poring over the guest list. The word got around that Ashur would be opening the new it-place in the Middle Eastern nightclub scene of Chicagoland, and, as expected, he was suddenly a popular man, which meant we'd get more important people casually dropping by the shop for a cup of coffee. One of them was Ralf Eldaoud, a patent attorney that specialized in intellectual property matters. Unlike the other regulars at the shop, he looked like an attorney and definitely dressed the part. He was also living proof that you could come to America, work hard, enter the sought-after club of big-shot lawyers, and still find yourself craving late-night establishments where they play loud music you'd heard as a child, music you found utterly annoying yet you somehow didn't mind now. A place where water pipes were found by each table, inhaled by both men and women, a place that transported you to a place you vaguely missed.

"Hey, Maryam, the g-g-grand opening is next weekend. You come with your mother, okay?" said Ashur one afternoon. "You think she'll want to c-c-come?" he asked. "What do you think?" Ashur had a habit of first stating his opinion and only then asking if he had assumed correctly. This meant you didn't need to bother with an answer. He'd made up his mind already.

"Yes, I think so," I answered, pretty sure Mother would appreciate an opportunity to dress up like she had back home and attend a fancy event.

"I want to invite her. She is a very nice lady," Ashur said. "Ralf, have you met her mother?"

Ashur knew Ralf had never met my mother. This is what the Iraqis did quite often. They would ask a question as a statement and then follow with a suggestion or a favor. I had become so used to these verbal tricks, almost expecting them, and played along.

"No? Whose mother?" Ralf was caught off guard.

"Mariski's."

"Mariski?" Ralf asked. This was another trick. Ralf knew they'd been calling me Mariski, but he did not like the nickname, so he'd pretend he was surprised every time he heard it. What a curious bunch they were!

"Who is Mariski?" Ralf said, even more puzzled. He had been watching television when Ashur had pulled him into our conversation.

"That's what we call her," Youel replied.

Ralf Eldaoud turned towards me with his whole body. His green eyes enveloped me with his usual wise and merciful smile, as if admiring me for enduring the ongoing circus of ignorance.

"Youel, her name is Maryam. Why would you call her Mariski? What is Mariski, anyways?"

"So, what of it? Ha! You know how many names *I* have? I have Jimmy, I have Ashur, I have Youel . . . I think it's nice to have many names," Youel said, raising his hands with his palms out.

None of this offended me. In fact, having multiple names gave me a strange feeling of shelter, as if accommodating the constant desire to fit in. At Vision Express Optical I was Mariski, which meant I spoke Russian and had some relation to Maria, the Russian girl who stood witness from the faded photograph to all that happened in the shop. Ralf gave out a deep sigh and turned back to me.

"What is your mother's name?" he asked.

"Leyla," I replied.

"What a beautiful name! And is she the reason behind your beauty?" he asked.

"No, actually. I take more after my father's side. My mother has fair skin, blonde hair, and green eyes," I answered. "Her family comes from Garabagh, it is a—"

"I know," he interrupted, "it's a mountainous area in Azerbaijan, isn't it?"

"Yes," I replied, astounded with the precision of his answer, for this was no common knowledge. "Wow! How do you know all this?"

"I read, my dear," he said with a sarcasm meant to pinch the others in the room. "So!" he continued. "Do you have a picture of your mother?"

Ashur, still seated at the coffee table with his arms crossed over his chest and his one leg over the other, turned around to look at Ralf's expression. He knew that I carried a passport picture of my mother in my wallet. Ralf looked at the picture for a moment, not uttering a word, and then looked up at me, as if looking for a trace of her on my face.

"What a beauty!" he exclaimed.

"She is," I whispered.

Mother's picture never failed. It always produced the same reaction in people—an impressed smile, a moment of silence, and then a long praise. In those moments, I truly wondered how the allure of my mother's beauty could expire as it had for my father. Day in, day out, I witnessed how Mother applied makeup, did her hair, and put on her impeccably ironed clothes. Her final look always left the same incredible impact on me, because she looked nothing short of spectacular. Her almost-transparent skin lent a pink glow to her face and made her look European, while her features were unmistakably Eastern. The color of her almond-shaped eyes was green most of the time, but tinged yellow with certain lighting, and her golden hair, though she did color it, wasn't too far from natural.

In those early days of our time in the U.S., when I'd lock myself in the bathroom, opening the faucet to the fullest and losing myself in tears, I'd look at my reflection in the mirror, studying my red nose, moist eyelashes, and inflamed lips. Soon I realized that I *did* look like her. Our face shape was almost identical. I had the same short, snub nose, and my mouth, though smaller, was a replica of hers, but this only became apparent after careful examination.

Ralf Eldaoud looked at the photo a bit longer and then returned it to me.

"She is truly beautiful, dear Maryam," he said. "Ashur, have you invited this beautiful lady to the grand opening?"

"Of course!" Ashur smiled.

I suddenly felt protective of my mother, for it was one thing to marvel at her beauty and completely another to recognize a man was interested in her. I had taken out the clipboard that Ashur used to jot down names and contact info of patients and was picking up the phone to confirm the appointments for tomorrow, when I noticed a pamphlet with a fragment of a blue angular glass building on my desk. The title read "Smart Choice. Start Here." There was something hopeful, inspiring, and forward-looking in this building, as if one could transport themselves into a different life if they were only to step inside. It turned out to be the newly built campus of Oakton College, a local community college with a location in Skokie. Ashur noticed that I was examining the pamphlet with dreamy fascination.

"Eric s-s-stopped by earlier. He left this for you," he explained. "He said you call this woman. Here, I g-g-give you her number." He handed me a ripped piece of paper with his illegible scribbling. The woman's name was Varda. Surprisingly, I deciphered the number easily.

"Thank you, Ashur!" I said. "I wonder if they'll let me enroll in classes in January even if I don't have a Social Security card yet?"

"No idea, Mariski." He shrugged.

I spent the next thirty minutes studying the pamphlet. Inside, there was a picture of a large metal structure that reflected the sunlight and was big enough to provide shelter from sun to several students lounging on the grass, their heads buried in colorful textbooks and their backpacks lying flat on the ground.

On the inside of the pamphlet, I found a letter from the college president that started with, "Dear Student—What is the secret to achieving your dreams? I believe you can find it in our motto: Start Here!" The president had a round face, with a long, pointy nose, deep-set eyes, and a pleasant smile. Her short dark hair framed her face, softening her features and adding a stylish and modern air to her persona. There was a soft light emanating from her small yet expressive eyes, and her smile displayed two rows of perfect white teeth.

I jotted down Varda's number in the top right corner, put the pamphlet into my bag, and picked up the phone to confirm the appointments for tomorrow. Soon the calls were made, the files for tomorrow's patients were pulled out from the tall metal file cabinet that Eric always leaned on, the coffee pot was washed clean, the trash was taken out by Youel, and we set out on our way home.

"I have to stop by A-A-Arabesque, so I won't be able to give you a ride," Ashur said.

"I have to stop by the store anyways," I explained. "Ashur, you think I can call this woman tonight?"

"Of course, Mariski!" He tapped on my shoulder. "I know Varda, she is a f-f-friend of mine too. Yeah, call her—she's home after six." He turned around and started walking towards his car. "If a guy picks up the phone, don't be shy. It's her son." He chuckled.

"You know me too well!" I said and wondered if I should have kept that to myself.

On my way home, I put on the headphones, leaned my head against the cool glass of the window, and allowed my mind to wander. I caught myself thinking that, for the past few months, time had been cut into distinct pieces of past and present, with the uncertain future hanging over us like a huge grayish cloud. The idea of becoming a student changed everything. I imagined myself strolling through the newly renovated hallways of Oakton College, feeling the weight of my backpack and clutching a few textbooks in my arms. The vision exhilarated me. Could the promise of college justify all the sleepless nights I had sat by the window and wondered why we'd abandoned our comfortable lives back home and moved across the ocean? Maybe my loneliness would find an end in this shiny building.

I remembered the long winter days in our tiny classroom on the third floor of my high school. I remembered sitting in our coats, trying to distract our minds from the shivering cold as we listened to the one-armed Nikolai Mikhailovich write out a geometric equation on the scratched-up blackboard. *They don't have chalk here,* I thought. *They have markers and whiteboards.* Surely, there would be heat in this building!

CHAPTER 24

. . . .

TWO DOLLARS

I saw Mother's silhouette sitting by the living room window when I approached our building, her hand supporting her chin and her eyes searching for someone. Back in Baku, I'd grown accustomed to seeing two sides of my mother. One was pensive and silent, disappointed in men and comfortable in her somber solitude. This was her private side, the one only a very few saw. To the rest of the world, she was bold and brave. Her hair was platinum blonde, her lipstick the color of a dark plum, and her driving style aggressive. She was one of the first women drivers in the '90s and proud of it. But she was a different person now. She worried a lot and without her native city as the backdrop, the vigor, the courage that she wore so proudly vanished. Something about bus trips and trains terrified her. She'd whisper a little prayer in Arabic every time I left for work and when I returned, she greeted me with such relief—as if she hardly believed I had made it back safe and sound. Her mornings were occupied with house cleaning, tidying, and cooking. I realized she spent the rest of her time sitting idly by the window, awaiting our return, with terrifying images of us being kidnapped or some other nightmare invading her consciousness. I wondered if she had any idea what to do with her life now that she'd moved continents in search of a better life. She had seemed to run out of the initial steam. Her early energy, her hopes of starting anew had withered away and were replaced by the dangerous helplessness of a woman who needs a man to make the move for them both. I recognized that state of hers, but this time, there was no man to move mountains. I had to do something about her.

As I opened the swing doors that led into the hallway of the building, I remembered an ad I had seen at the library earlier in the week. It was an advertisement for English and computer classes for newly arrived, Russian-speaking immigrants. The classes were held in the branch office of a Jewish community center I passed by on my way to work. It was always full of people from all over the world. A plan was brewing in my head. I needed to get Mother out of the house by any means.

"Mama, have you been sitting by the window again?" I asked.

"Yes," she said, caught off guard with my sudden question.

I took off my shoes and my jacket and took a deep breath. There was a slim chance my plan would work.

"Okay, from next week I am signing you up for English and computer classes. I saw an ad at the library branch close to work. It's at the Jewish community center and the classes are in Russian."

"No, Maryam," she objected, as expected. "Besides, we don't have any money for classes."

"Yes, you will go!" I snapped back. "And the classes are free."

"Watch your language," she said. "I said I don't need classes."

Her tone reverted to cold and serious, one that I knew too well. Insisting felt like insanity, but I was not ready to give up. In fact, I felt a strange desire to keep pushing.

"Yes, you do," I said, the words forming on my tongue before I could even think them up. "Go once and if you don't like it, don't go again! If you ever want to get a job in this country, you'll need to learn the language." I left the room.

Somehow, I had a feeling that I had won this argument and that Mother would go, because deep down she knew it was the right thing to do. She had gotten in a habit of consulting me on all matters now, suddenly interested in my opinion about random topics ranging from our neighbors to Teymour's friends to the color-coordination of her clothes to what to cook for dinner and a whole array of other topics. I answered her questions with patience, but they left me feeling uneasy as I knew the root cause of this dramatic change— Mother was beginning to feel lost in this world. She was in constant need of guidance and reassurance, this time from me.

Just as I had started harnessing hope for a better future and planning a path that could take me into the light, Mother had succumbed to uncertainty. The initial euphoria that liberated her was subsiding, and though she could see clearly that both I and Rufat would find our way in this new country, she couldn't help but wonder what was to become of her. I couldn't solve this puzzle for her, but something told me that getting her out of the house was the first step, so during dinner that evening I brought up the subject again.

"So how about those English classes, Mama?" I asked. "You'll learn English, make some friends, maybe even find some kind of a job that way."

"I do need to find a job," Mother agreed.

"You won't find a job sitting by this window," I said, getting a sharp look from her.

"Show me the place tomorrow," she finally said. "I'll give it a try. I guess you are right. I have nothing better to do during the day. All this thinking by the window is leaving me restless."

"Good deal. It's few minutes from the Russian store too. You can stop by on your way back and pick out the cottage cheese yourself. I always seem to get it wrong."

"Very funny, Maryam," she said, "very funny!"

After dinner, Rufat ran back to Gross Point Park to play soccer with his classmates, I retreated to my bedroom, and Mother washed a bowl of fruit and took a seat on the couch to watch television. I pulled the Oakton Community College pamphlet out of my bag and looked at it again, staring at Varda's number scribbled in the top right corner.

It turned out Varda was expecting my call. She explained the admissions process and I jotted down the list of documents that would make me eligible for in-state tuition. The difference between in-state and out-of-state was so significant that I quickly realized the only way I could afford to take classes was if I proved I was a resident of Illinois. Otherwise, I couldn't afford to step foot in that building. I came back into the living room and recounted my conversation with Varda to Mother. She listened without uttering a word, then suddenly got up and disappeared in the kitchen, returning with a large orange shoe box that she used to collect mail. She sifted through the letters and found electric and gas bills, but they were both in Teymour's name.

"Don't worry! I remember when we were signing up, he said that we could change it to my name. So, if it's possible to change it to mine, it should be possible to change it to yours as well, right?" Mother asked.

A few days later, Teymour showed up at our house with a triumphant expression on his face. In his hands, he held two white envelopes, both with my name and address inked in the tiny opening covered with plastic film. I jumped to my feet and gave him a big hug, then took the envelopes and put them in a yellow manila folder, where I gathered our newly received tax IDs, a translation of my high school diploma and my final grade report, and the copies of our visas, pleased that I now had the whole arsenal to make the trip to Oakton College. The next day, I announced to Ashur that I was going to try to enroll in college that Friday.

"Aaaa Mariski! Look at you-uuu-uuu!" exclaimed Youel. "You are finally going to school! Great future! Great future I see for you! And good you won't be like me! You know, I was good in calculus in high school. Wassouf, my teacher, he said, 'You are smart! Don't waste your head, Youel.' Ha, ha, ha! He was soooo ugly, Mariski . . . sooooooo ugly!"

"Mariski, don't listen to him," said Shammoun. "He talk too much! You smart! You will be a doctor, yes? Look how you write! Your writing is so pretty! Not like this one," he said, pointing to Ashur.

I felt contentment wash over me, like the warm rays of a setting sun. I went to the front office and took a seat by the window. The sun was shining, but it didn't offer any warmth. I thought of Eric. Here, separated from the three Assyrians by a thin plastic window, I felt hidden, free to remember the words he had uttered during our short conversations, the look in his eyes, magnified by the rimless glasses that he wore. It felt so good to know that it was he who'd found the pamphlet and spoken with Varda about me.

It had been close to two months since I'd seen him, and I no longer looked for him in the crowd when sitting in the last row of the bus that took me to the Howard L station every day. Memories of him no longer inflicted pain or suffering. With time, I learned how to think of him as an oasis, appearing and disappearing at random. I saved these thoughts for times when I was alone, and the perfect circumstances presented themselves. And, while more and more details vanished from my memory with each day, the faint hope of seeing him at the grand opening warmed my heart. As I carefully wiped the dust from the shelves, I imagined how rich and eventful his life must be in comparison with mine. I tried to remember the title of the novel he once forgot on my desk, recalling only the palace on the cover.

I had taken the cleaning cloth and carefully wiped the mirror and the shelves. I was rearranging the boxes with newly delivered glasses in the corner, when a plump Russian lady walked in. Her white hair showed remnants of her pale blonde natural color and was up in a bun with a bright pink hairband around it. The skin on her face was pale and wrinkly, her thin lips covered with a thick, buttery lipstick.

"Can I help you?" I said, not ready to switch to Russian.

"I want Ashur!" she said.

"You heard that? She want Ashur!" said Youel's voice from the back.

Ashur got up from the coffee table to greet the lady.

"Yes, my dear, how c-c-can I help you?" he asked.

The lady took out a pair of crooked glasses and handed them to Ashur. One handle was missing a screw and was hanging loosely. Ashur placed the glasses on top of the counter and bent his head to examine them, his palms pressed against the counter. He began to explain that he would need to replace a screw when she suddenly exclaimed:

"Ashur! Can you," she appeared to be searching for the right word, "screw me?"

Ashur looked at her with a smirk on his face, trying hard not to explode into laughter, but our patient was completely unaware of what she'd just said. A few weeks ago, I wouldn't have understood the humor of it either, but I'd heard the phrase in one of the movies we watched with Teymour and Sarah. A moment later, when Ashur was able to subdue his instinct to laugh, he raised two fingers and said:

"T-t-two dollars!"

At this point, it was impossible for Shammoun and Youel to

control themselves. They burst into a roaring laughter. Youel turned up the volume of the television to drown out their laughter, but the Russian patron connected the dots. Ashur took the glasses and walked into the back office, throwing me a glance, wondering if I got the humor and smiled approvingly when he saw me laughing.

"What a dummy! She t-t-tell me 'Can you screw me?' Ha, ha! Of course, ma'am," he said once out of the lady's earshot. "No problemo! Always welcome!"

Shammoun and Youel laughed louder than the television. The lady bent her head to the right in an attempt to see what was happening inside. She probably thought she could be the reason for our laughter but couldn't guess what she did to cause all this. While Ashur was screwing a tiny bolt into her glasses and securing the arm with his pliers, she examined herself in the mirror, pursing her lips and adjusting the linen bag that hung on her shoulder.

"Two dollars! Two dollars! He says, 'two dollars, ma'am!'" repeated Youel, unable to stop laughing. "It's too funny. I cannot, I cannot . . . I go get another coffee. Who wants coffee? You? You? You?" He pointed at all three of us.

The incident lifted our moods and we all agreed to have another cup of coffee, even though we knew it was probably too dark and bitter at this point. Ashur had brought a tall carton of whole milk to use instead of the powdered cream that, in my humble opinion, ruined the already-bad coffee.

"Here, Mariski, give it to her!" He handed me the glasses.

I took the glasses, wiped them off with the microfiber cloth, and stepped out into the front office.

"Here you go, ma'am. Ashur fixed your glasses for you," I said, feeling a little embarrassed for laughing at her a few minutes ago.

"Senk you," she said, looking as if she forgot something. "Where is Ashur?"

I turned around and gestured to Ashur to step into the front office. He came out with a happy smile on his face and tapped the lady on the shoulder in a friendly manner.

"Thank you, mai frend!" she said and smiled.

"You welcome, you welcome! Anytime you have a p-p-problem—you c-c-come to me, okay? You come and I fix it for you," he said in a playful tone and winked at her.

"You the best, Ashur! You the best! I thank you for everything. Now I go home!"

Youel brought back three cups of steaming coffee with milk, and we all sat at the coffee table and laughed a little more at the episode as we chewed on pieces of apricot-walnut cake that Shammoun's sister had brought that afternoon. As soon as the clock hit five, Ashur slapped his knees with his palms, turned off the television, switched off the light in the front and back offices, and said the phrase that signaled the end of every working day at Vision Express Optical:

"Yalla, guys! Let's go!"

. . . .

CHAPTER 25

IN FRONT OF
A CLOSED DOOR

The registrar's office opened at eight a.m., but I'd been up since six, reviewing the list that I had printed at the library a few days ago and arranging the documents in the folder.

The building was enormous. The suspended glass structure reflected the blue cloudless sky and shone like a spaceship. The entrance was preceded by steps that ran the perimeter of the building, separated by three metal banisters. In the distance, I could see a small pond surrounded by tall grass, with several weeping willows rooted very close to the waterline.

I took the stairs up and walked through the two sliding doors, remembering Varda's instructions. I made a right and kept going, soon recognizing the wide-open area that Varda described as the admissions office. There were four employees at the front. Each was seated behind a wide desk with a bright blue lamp suspended above. Each leaned forward in front of their computers, reading something with concentration, none of them noticing me. I saw a sign reading "Admissions and Financial Aid" hanging above the first counter and approached the lady standing there. Her curly red hair was pinned in a bun above her head and thick glasses kept sliding down her nose. She refused to acknowledge me until I had cleared my throat several times.

"Good morning," she finally said. "How can I help you?"

"I would like to take classes here. Here, I've filled out the application and brought all the necessary documents. I got them in this folder."

The redhead quickly sifted through the contents of my folder.

"What about your Social Security card? And your ID?"

"I don't have it," I replied.

"Well, that will pose a problem," she said.

"I did bring two bills with me," I argued, though I was already losing hope.

"We can take the utility bills, but only if you have a Social Security card. I cannot accept just this. Did you read our website?"

I had and I knew that this might not work. Varda had warned me that sometimes it all came down to who was working at the counter. Technically, I could not study until I had a Social Security card, but a utility bill could potentially work as proof-of-residence. Even though I had prepared myself for the possibility that I might not have any luck today, the entire exchange had come and gone too quickly—my defeat had been too effortless, and I could not keep my composure. Her words struck me, and I suddenly could not control the tears rolling down my cheeks. I felt embarrassed to cry in public, to show such weakness. The lady at the counter maintained her blank stare and had no discernable reaction to my tears. I wanted to scream. I wanted to tell her about the day I found the pamphlet lying on my desk and how it brought faith into my life, filling me with hopes and aspirations to become a part of this place. Yet, I stood in front of her, unable to utter a word, and simply collected all the papers from her desk, pitifully arranging them in their folder and putting them back into my bag.

"Are you okay, ma'am?" she finally asked.

I didn't bother to answer. Instead, I walked away from her desk, defeated and embarrassed. Tears continued to roll down my face. I turned right and started walking aimlessly in the corridors, lost in a crowd of students rushing to classes, joking around with each other as they sipped their teas and coffees from tumblers, until I reached a large cafeteria. I stood at the entrance, aware that I only had money for the bus ride to work and home, and watched clusters of students sitting at tables, munching on muffins and sipping coffee, and occasionally looking at their open textbooks.

I felt a deep and impassable valley separating me from the happy scenery in the cafeteria. The students that I saw appeared careless and free, burdened only by their student responsibilities, exams and papers and deadlines. While I knew that they probably stressed about all these things, there was nothing more I wanted at that moment: to have an exam to study for, a deadline to anticipate, a paper to write, a textbook to lend, a professor to fear . . . The realization that my teenage problems—paying for groceries, looking after my mother and brother, befriending three elderly men at Vision Express Optical, dreaming about a man twenty years my senior—were highly unconventional made me feel even more excluded. Perhaps I was forever banished from entering a world where normalcy, and the pursuit of an education, would be available to me.

I dug the nails of my right hand into my palm, leaving four imprints that ached the rest of the day. If I could have set the place ablaze with the force of my mind, it would've burned down in minutes. My fascination with the students quickly turned into spite, their idyllic laughs, friendly faces, and lax mannerisms infuriating me. All doors in this country appeared closed to us and I felt like such a fool for feeling hopeful. I needed to get away from this place, so I quickly turned around and started walking away.

I was in the midst of this furious departure when, on the other side of the hallway, I noticed a tall, dark guy with curly hair pushing a library cart full of books. By the strange, knowing expression in his eyes, I figured he had witnessed the entire thing and followed me to the cafeteria. For that alone, I wanted him to disappear, so my foolish hopes and their ridiculous demise wouldn't have to be seen by anyone. I blamed myself for betting all the positivity I could muster on the magic of this shiny, light-filled, futuristic building, as if it could somehow give meaning to our hop across the continents. No such meaning existed and the man across the hall would not change this cold and hard fact. The sooner I got back to Devon, the better, so I squeezed the few dollars in my pocket, put the manila folder back in my bag, and marched on.

I lowered my head and walked towards the entrance, past the dark-haired guy with his library cart, aware he was following my every step. I hoped he'd choose to ignore me and continue organizing the books on the cart. But when I heard his voice, I was startled but not surprised.

"I am Arash," he said and set his books down on the floor, extending his hand in greeting. "I saw you at the registrar's," he added.

I hope you enjoyed the show then, I thought. I wondered if he had also figured out that I'd stood in front of the cafeteria with no money to buy anything. Did he pity me like I pitied myself? I was so angry with myself for nurturing the false hope that I could just walk in here and become a student so quickly, for believing that things can happen easily, without a struggle. I bit my lip and thought of something to say, but there was nothing to say and nothing to do, except to catch my bus and get back to the optical shop and forget these silly dreams.

I started to walk away. Arash left the library cart in the hallway and rushed after me.

"Wait! Wait!" he said in a rush. "Do you speak English?"

"Yes!" I replied. *Why am I responding to this guy? Do I want him to follow me?*

"Why are you running, then? Baba, wait! Are you Iranian?" he continued on.

I felt embarrassed for behaving so strangely in front of him. After all, I'd simply come to sign up for classes and hadn't had the documents they needed. What did he or the admissions lady know about the string of events that had rocked my world in the past few months? What did he know of the knot in my throat, the tears in the bathroom, the ten pounds I'd lost along with my appetite, or the friends whose emails I no longer read because they only reminded me of how far and unreachable my dear world had become? I must have looked insane, but I did not care. I had no desire to explain myself, yet something stopped me from running. He kept looking at me without the slightest surprise on his face, as if he'd read my mind, as if he knew how I felt.

"Azerbaijan. I am from Baku," I said, feeling the fury die down.

"Neighbors, then! What is your name?" he asked, smiling as if in recognition that I had chosen to stay and talk with him after all.

"Maryam," I answered.

He had a handsome face with a round chin and upturned eyes that shone brightly. His thick eyebrows accentuated his gaze. He wore a brown cardigan on top of a gray t-shirt tucked into his dark-blue jeans with a fancy leather belt adding some color and making him look quite fashionable. There was something familiar and charming in his presence that eased the tension inside me. Everything, from his thick accent to his choice of words to the features on his face to the contagious light in his eyes, reminded me of the one thing I missed and needed the most: back home.

"Come with me," he said and turned towards another hallway. I found myself silently following him. We climbed the stairs and ended up in a hallway that was a series of tall, windowed islands, warm with natural light, each a gathering of low tufted couches and a minimalist coffee table, larger than our living room. One of them was occupied by students working on some group project. They didn't seem to notice anyone. We took an island at the very end of the hall and sat down. Arash disappeared for a few minutes and came back with a thermos and two slender tea glasses. The sweet aroma of cardamom filled the air.

"All right, since you didn't disappear while I was getting the tea, let me seize the moment and introduce myself," he said. "You *must* drink tea, it's in your blood." He looked at me trying to gage any reaction. I smiled.

"Did I say my name already? I am Arash. I do some work here during the week and I take classes too. I need another few semesters before I can transfer to U of Chicago. It's just cheaper here and, plus, I get some pocket money out of the library job."

I was strangely comfortable not saying a word and letting him do all the talking. I sipped my tea and listened as he told me about the classes he was taking this spring, where he lived, how long it took him to get to campus, and how the winters here were unbearable, but not much better than in Tehran, the city where he grew up.

"So, what happened at the registrar?" he said with caution. "Or you don't want to talk about it?"

"I was trying to sign up for classes and . . . " I began. "And I got all these documents. I've been gathering them for weeks now and, apparently, it was not enough. So, no group projects for me." I pointed at the group of students with jealousy.

"How long have you been here?" he asked.

I told him I'd been here since early June, but I didn't stop there.

I ended up telling him my whole life story, sharing the details of my parents' broken marriage and how my father's banking career had landed him behind bars with no money and no friends, and then how we had escaped to the U.S. only to go through another ordeal, trapped in Teymour's luxurious and messy apartment. Somehow, the story spilled from my lips, fleshed out down to the tiniest details, coherent and powerful, leaving an awestruck look on his face.

"Now that I speak of all these things, they sound so surreal," I confessed. "That whole period when my dad was a wealthy banker, when I had tutors, chauffeurs, swimming coaches, birthday parties in fancy restaurants, trips to London to study English. All that, followed by this plunge into nowhere, his imprisonment, and the whole thing being picked up by the news. It all sounds like some bad movie, packed with too much action. Only it's not a bad movie," I said and paused. "It's the story of how I got here."

I think it was the first time that I had told the story in such an impartial tone, as if I were a narrator who had nothing to do with the characters in the story, never judging them or feeling anything towards them. I thought of my grandmother's house, of its walls that witnessed the rise and fall of our family, taking in all its glory and sadness and suffering and regret, yet still standing, supporting whatever was left of us.

Arash had listened to me in silence, occasionally refilling my glass with tea and watching me cup it with both hands, hoping to warm up in the heavily air-conditioned hallway of Oakton College. When I was finally done, he just sat there with a deep and calm understanding lighting up his face. I looked outside at the rippling surface of the pond, where a few ducks peacefully moved over the water, circling around the heart-shaped leaves of the lilies. I knew I'd gone overboard with my life story, yet I felt no awkwardness. Instead, I was certain that from now on, nothing would turn him away from me.

His devotion to me would grow stronger with the coming months, but it had been apparent from the moment I saw him.

"Wow, now that I think of it, I've got quite a lot of baggage," I said.

"That you do." Arash smiled.

"After going through all that, you'd think I'd do better at the registrar's this morning," I said. "After all, there are rules and, in this country, rules don't bend." I took a sip of tea, now cold.

"Well, lucky for me you speak English," he said. "I wouldn't want to miss out on this story. KGB colonels, physicists turned into bankers—you're a Pandora's box!"

"I don't know what a Pandora's box is," I said and smiled.

"I just learned this expression. It means someone or something full of surprises," Arash said.

"I got plenty of that," I replied, smiling again.

"Maryam," he said, a serious expression on his face, "you're right, rules here don't bend. Well, not as easily as where we come from, but there is a way. Trust me!" he said. "We'll find it."

A week later, we were back at the registrar's office with the same manila folder, now filled with several printouts from Oakton's admissions website. This time we were luckier to see a different admission officer, as she turned out to be Arash's friend and was also from Iran. He told me later her nickname was Tanny, and she had come to the U.S. on a student visa a few years ago and was hoping to stay here. Perhaps because of that, she recognized the pleading expression on my face and finally placed the sacred "Accepted" stamp on my application—at her own risk.

CHAPTER 26

THE GRAND OPENING

If October gently eased into the lives of Chicagoans with a masquerade of colorful leaves and refreshing winds, then November kicked in the door with a thick rubber boot, sweeping out the faded bushes, baring the trees, and filling the sky with V-shaped flocks of cranes headed south in search of better weather. The change was so drastic that we spent one full day at a strip mall, shopping for warm boots, cardigans, sweaters, scarves, coats, and hats since we relied entirely on public transportation and could not afford to dress lightly.

The store was warm and spacious, a sea of clothes to drift among with Christmas carols playing the background. Oversized posters of teenagers sporting fashionable khaki jeans, cable sweaters, and fingerless gloves surrounded us, their eyes shining and mouths gaping in wide, happy smiles. Mother was pushing a large blue cart, into which each one of us threw whatever we wanted to try on in the fitting room.

We were on a mission to buy warm clothes, but all three of us also threw in a couple of fancy items that were both impractical and expensive. My eyes stopped on a tall black mannequin wearing a short satin dress with a strapless heart-shaped bust decorated in sequined embroidery that sparkled and glowed. It would have been an ordinary short dress if not for the satin train that fell to the floor in elegant creases. I grabbed my size from the rack and ran to the fitting room. The short Indian lady at the counter pointed to an empty compartment. I got in, carefully took off my turtleneck, pulled off my boots and jeans. I unzipped the dress and slipped it on, realizing I would need help zipping it up. Luckily, the Indian lady was still there and when I peeked out of the compartment, she understood me without words and made her way over to help.

When the dress was on, I saw the content smile on her face as she shook her head from side to side, signing her approval. I felt confident to step out of the fitting room and approached the large three-way mirror. There, in the mirror, I saw a graceful silhouette with a thin waist and feminine shoulders. I looked around and noticed the flattering look on the Indian woman's face as she clasped her hands at her chest. Then behind her, I saw my mother. She was standing by the entrance, leaning against the door of a fitting room, looking at me with a dreamy fascination on her face.

"I just wanted to try it," I said in my defense.

Mother smiled and approached me.

"Let me look at it a little." She came closer. "The front looks perfect, but the back is a little loose, I think. I mean, maybe not loose, just not as perfect as the front. Nothing that I cannot fix. Can you let your hair down?" she asked. I followed her suggestion.

I stood there, my arms raised at the level of my head as Mother inspected me from head to toe, checking how well the dress fit me and assessing if she'd be able to fix the almost unnoticeable unevenness in the back. Then I noticed her pick up the white price tag hanging loose from the side of the dress and smile with triumph.

"It's fifty percent off and the price is seventy dollars, which means it is only thirty-five," she calculated. "We're taking it!"

"Don't forget the tax," I reminded her. We were still getting used to the change in price at the counter as the cashier would add the purchase tax. We'd had no such thing back home.

On our way back from the store, we stopped by a small café located at the entrance of Old Orchard Mall that served paninis with a tomato sauce that Rufat liked so much. After, our arms were heavy with bags, our stomachs were finally full, and we returned home like victors from the battle, laying out all of our shopping trophies on the sofa and trying them on one by one, letting each other comment on them all over again while drinking the freshly brewed tea Mother had brought in on a tray. There was an unfamiliar sense of unity among us, the kind that appears among members of a ship, cast away on some deserted island. All three of us agreed that the crown jewel of our shopping expedition was the satin dress with the train. I slipped into it one last time, making a grand entrance into our living room, now wearing heels and letting my hair down. I bathed in a kind of flattery I had never heard or seen from Mother or Rufat.

After my application was accepted at Oakton Community College, I entered a new phase of life. Nothing changed about my daily routine, except that I was now wrapped in multiple layers of clothing to avoid freezing, and the thought of Oakton College warmed my heart like a distant light.

The grand opening of Arabesque was set for November fifteenth, ten days before America would go on a "four-day gluttony feast," which was how Ralf Eldaoud had referred to the Thanksgiving holiday one day back at the optical shop.

In the days leading up to the grand opening, Ashur was mostly gone from the store, leaving me one-on-one with bad-tempered patients and a phone that was ringing off the hook. Youel shared the load and helped out with looking up box numbers for those who came to pick up their glasses. Shammoun would wear a guilty look on his face when he saw me pace back and forth between the waiting area and the phone, but we both knew there wasn't much he could do except say hello and put people on hold. I smiled at him kindly, assuring him I could manage on my own. Secretly, I hoped he'd stop answering the phone altogether—instead of putting people on hold, Shammoun mostly just hung up on them.

During the short periods of silence that usually occurred around three p.m., I'd pick a chair in the waiting area and stare out the window, flipping through the Oakton College catalog and reading the course descriptions circled by Arash. I took pleasure in imagining myself walking in the crowd of students, dressed in wide jeans and a hoodie, clutching a few books in my arms. I imagined myself and Arash studying outside, where the weeping willows touched the still surface of the pond or sipping tea and talking about back home for hours.

The prospect of becoming a student sliced my world into two parts. Here at work, surrounded by the three old men who cared about me in their own way, I found a safe refuge from the world, making me want to stay here forever, yet I felt like part of me was already gone from this place as I ended each day by the window, over-taken not by doubts and fears, but by hopes and dreams of the future. My mood improved, which had a positive impact on my appetite.

"I cooked the stew that Nana used to make," Mother said one weekend. "I thought you'd like it, Maryam." The tone of her voice was calm, free of past resentment towards my grandmother. The gesture was kind and thoughtful.

"You did?" I asked, surprised. "The one with chicken, prunes, and potatoes?"

"Isn't that your favorite?" Mother asked. "Now that you're eating something other than cereal, I thought I'd cook your favorite meal. You are so pale, Maryam. You really ought to gain a few pounds."

"Thank you, Mother. I love that stew," I said with gratitude.

"She's trying to fatten you up," Rufat said, flipping through the channels. "Like a sheep."

With Mother's help, I managed to gain a few pounds before the grand opening, which made her incredibly happy, as the dress now fit me perfectly. I started secretly regarding the grand opening of Arabesque as my own personal celebration for a new chapter of my life.

Sometimes the changes coming at me ignited a panic attack, and I longed to slow down the future. I'd dig out printouts of Arif's early letters, reading into every word, as if testing whether my consciousness would react, but my mind would not let itself be tricked. Even the all-encompassing guilt that had gripped me for weeks was completely gone, and no number of letters, photographs, souvenirs, or phone calls would bring it back.

CHAPTER 27

. . . .

LIKE A SWAN

November fifteenth fell on a rainy Saturday that began with our weekly trip to the grocery store. In the interest of time, I'd split up the grocery list between the three of us, sending Mother to choose meat and poultry, Rufat to grab snacks, and leaving the fruits and veggies for myself because, frankly, those were my favorite. That morning was not a pleasant shopping morning. Our clothes got wet in the rain and we were running late getting out of the store.

Just when we had paid the cashier and contemplated stepping out into the rain, Mother's cell phone rang. It turned out Teymour was on his way to Skokie. A few minutes later, his black Mercedes pulled up outside the store and he stepped out in his usual hasty manner, wearing summer shorts, a sweater, and worn-out flip-flops, defying all possible dress codes in a way that only he could. He opened the trunk and loaded it with groceries, pushing us aside and motioning for us to get in the car. Teymour was amusing to watch, with his random hand gestures, constant shrugging, nodding, and the way he was always running his palms through his black hair. Teymour's unfinished sentences amused me, as did his rhetorical questions that hung in the air, never requiring an answer, surrounded him with a strange childish charm.

"Oh, so you will be going to this grand opening?" he asked Mother. "Who knew the old Assyrians were so party-party?" he said with a smile. "Well, that just means basketball and pizza for me and Rufat. Bulls are playing tonight!"

"NBA and deep-dish pizza!" Rufat announced.

"Seriously though, Rufat, Bulls are pretty bad these days. Want to watch baseball instead?"

"Bulls are bad, but baseball is worse," Rufat responded.

"It gets better," Teymour insisted as Rufat shrugged. I found it amusing to watch them, so much more natural and sincere than they had been in those early weeks. I did not establish such friendly terms with Teymour, but his warm relationship with Rufat made all of us feel more at ease.

Once we had arrived at home, Mother noticed that, along with our grocery bags, Teymour had brought in four additional paper bags from his trunk.

"What is this?" she asked.

"This? This is the meat for . . . what is it called? That dish with potatoes and meat and chickpeas? Can you cook it for us?" Teymour rubbed his forehead.

"*Bozbash*? How you can forget the word 'bozbash,' I don't understand," she said, looking through the paper bag.

"When do you want it?" she asked without lifting her head.

"Any day is fine, Leyla." Teymour made himself comfortable on the couch.

"Does this meat have fat on it? I hope this isn't as lean as the piece that you brought last time. It was useless!"

This conversation made me think of Nana and her endless quest for a fatty piece of meat.

"No, no! I brought the proper one this time. It has enough cholesterol to kill all of us."

Besides the large paper-wrapped piece of lamb, Mother took out plums, strawberries, quinces, apples, feta cheese, and a large ciabatta from the bag.

"Thank you, Teymour!" Mother said raising her head, gratitude on her face.

She opened the fridge to reorganize the contents so that she could fit everything we had just bought. Then she boiled the kettle, brewed cardamom tea, and made sandwiches with bologna for all of us. The four of us sat on the couch and chewed our sandwiches, gulping down tea from the steaming glasses. Teymour found the sports channel that was showing a baseball game and sat down to watch it with Rufat. Mother was busy cutting up the meat for bozbash, and I retreated to my room.

I spent the next few hours working on the collage of pictures from my farewell party, cutting out colorful frames from cardboard paper and inserting pictures from Arif's summer house into them, then plastering them to the large board on the wall. I remembered Teymour had brought in several pictures taken at one of our park gatherings over the summer, and I decided to add those to the collage. Next were the pictures with my friends, all taken in Baku.

One picture in particular stuck out, of Mother, Rufat, Teymour, Sarah, and me, all of us lying down on a plaid blanket under a tree, surrounded by containers with sandwiches, fruits, crackers, and cheese. While just a few months had passed between the two sets of pictures, I couldn't help but notice the different expressions on our faces. Our smiles, while content, seemed somewhat reserved and tense in those pictures we'd taken at Lake Shore Park. The realization of this stark difference in our faces left me heavy-hearted, but I decided to keep the photograph in the collage regardless.

I glanced up at the clock and realized it was time to get ready for the grand opening. I slipped into the kitchen, where Mother was busy stirring a large pot with lamb broth, and I told her that I'd be taking a shower.

"Okay, and I'll go next," she said without turning around.

The hot stream of the shower poured over my face, erasing the lingering thoughts about back home. The water passed over my body, leaving me unattached to the past, yet without anything to replace it except for a tiny, repetitive world. No matter how small and predictable it seemed, I had to attach to this new world to keep going.

Soon after Mother was done with her shower, she peeked into my room, telling me that Anna and Philip would pick us up, as they were invited, too. I had to be ready in half an hour.

"Put some makeup on, if you want," she said glancing at the satin dress on the hanger.

I nodded and returned a grateful smile. I put my hair up in a high ponytail and applied a little kohl around my eyes. Then I slipped into the dress, stepped into my high heels, and walked out of my room.

"Wow! Leyla, where are you two going like that?" Teymour said, sitting upright on the couch, looking surprised. I knew Teymour was clumsy with compliments, but in his eyes, I saw the same admiration for my Mother that she'd had for me back in the fitting room of the store. Suddenly, he turned and saw me, adding, "Wow—that dress! It looks nice on you because you have a long neck, like a swan!"

Like a swan, I repeated to myself. His usual unforgiving candor and the sarcastic nature of his remarks, all a part of the package, intensified the positive effect of his unexpectedly generous comment and made me smile. I held on to his phrase for the rest of the evening, occasionally whispering it to myself to keep my posture straight and show off my long neck. Mother joined all of us in the living room, looking stunning in her black cocktail dress, stiletto heels, and a fur throw on her shoulders. Just as we all convened in the sitting room, we heard a honk outside—Philip and Anna were waiting.

We arrived at Arabesque a little past nine. A short valet in a long black coat opened the front door of the car, took the car keys from Philip, and showed us to the double doors under a canopy with bunches of balloons tied to the sides in celebration of the grand opening. Ashur was standing right at the door, waving to someone in the crowd, when he saw us enter. His posture was tall and proud, his curly hair combed back, and his engagement finger featured an onyx ring. He was by far the tallest person there. I thought he looked just like a club owner.

"Mariski! What is this? Are you to be the most b-b-beautiful girl in here tonight?" he exclaimed. "Do I need to find another two b-b-bodyguards just to stand by your side?" He turned to the rest of the group. "Leyla, Philip, Anna! Welcome to Arabesque! Your table is n-n-number thirty-two. It's right there, by that lamp." Ashur pointed at a hanging lantern covered with mosaic tiles. "Yes, that one, that one! Let's go, let's go! I will sh-sh-show you."

The place was dark, and a round disco ball left the walls awash in twinkling lights, filling the room with lurking silhouettes of men and women in sparkling evening gowns and expensive suits. Assyrians loved bling. A tall man with graying hair and a low voice sang an Assyrian song while half-hugging his plump female companion with beautiful red-brown hair and dreamy eyes. Several middle-aged couples swayed to the song in a relaxed manner, along with the singer and his girlfriend.

At a closer look, I recognized the singer. It was Jimmy Oshana, a regular at the optical store and a close friend of Ralf Eldaoud. While I found all the Assyrian songs that Youel played on an old tape recorder annoying, repetitive, and lacking any melody, they sounded just right for this setting, and I soon found myself swaying from side to side and trying to imitate the lyrics with random Assyrian words that came to mind. A thick bunch of pearly white balloons decorated the pedestal where the members of the live band played their keys and drums and flutes, ancient boredom stamped on their sweaty faces.

I scanned the crowd hoping to see familiar faces and found that the place was full of men and women who had visited the optical in the last few months. Here was George Sako, Ashur's infamous business partner, with his three sons and his beautiful wife in a large crowd of relatives and friends. He took up three adjacent tables to fit all of his guests. Here was Ralf Eldaoud, the patent attorney, in his usual tailored suit, his receding shiny hair combed back, his thin brown lips forming a subtle smile, and his pensive eyes unaffected by the loud madness of the nightclub. I saw Ashur's sister, Hanna, in her thin glasses, sipping wine from a glass and whispering something to Babi, looking too academic for this place.

Her beauty was subtle. It did not overwhelm you with big, kohl-lined eyes, or the thick arched eyebrows that framed the face. It did not arrest you on the spot. She had the kind of looks that captivated you slowly with her high and prominent cheekbones, a snub nose, and piercing eyes. Her shoulder-length hair shined with soft highlights that suited her angular face. Unlike other Assyrian women sitting at neighboring tables with their swollen bodies and faces covered with a thick layer of makeup, Hanna maintained a cold, regal look, holding an impeccable posture and keeping her head up high, looking utterly indifferent to the busy dynamics of this place. Cloaked by the intimate darkness of the room, I studied her with fascination and couldn't help but compare her with Reem, the belly dancer, with her contagious laugh and her flirty ways with men.

In this very moment, the tall singer with graying hair threw a quick gesture at the band, signaling them to stop and prepare for the entrance of the belly dancer. Then the drums rattled, the bright lights softened to yellow and pink, and Reem entered the scene to the magic sound of the flute, two huge, golden wings attached to her arms. This was the dance of the Egyptian goddess Isis. Reem's grand entrance captivated the audience, ending hundreds of loud conversations and drawing men and women closer to the stage. Her skin glowed in a beautiful black costume, baring her flat, toned stomach and flaunting her full breasts and curvy hips. Her golden wings were attached to sticks that extended past her wrists, elongating her arms into fluid wings. She truly looked like a goddess. The dark waterfall of her silky black hair, with a few strands of strawberry blonde here and there, made her look enigmatic, mysterious, and irresistible. Like a goddess, she commanded the audience with the swing of her wings and the rhythm of her hips.

For the first few minutes of the dance, we all sat in awe and tried to take in as much as possible of this magical performance. The only person looking distracted, perhaps even annoyed with the performance, was Hanna. Who knew how many of these dances she'd seen in her life? Could it be that she just disliked Reem? She kept glancing at her watch and saying something to her son. Soon the belly dancer took off her golden wings and switched to a playful kind of dance, cruising around tables with her choreographed steps, embracing the guests with her charming smile and inviting them to dance with her. She looked like a glittering ornament in the sea of black dresses and black suits. Then, suddenly she approached our table, grabbed me by the hand, and invited me to dance with her, sending my heart rate through the roof and painting me red with an instant blush.

"Mariski!" I read from her lips. "Come, girl! Yalla!"

In a moment I found myself with Reem on the stage, dying of

embarrassment but unable to retreat. Reem held my hand until we reached the dance floor and then circled around me in her flirty manner, inviting me to dance. Even though I didn't know how to belly dance, my body recognized and adjusted to the playful rhythm of the drum, and I started moving with the melody. I noticed hundreds of eyes examining my dress, wondering who I was, some of them recognizing me and whispering something to the person next to them. I then saw Youel and Shammoun standing in the corner and clapping dramatically as I danced. I noticed Ralf Eldaoud watching me with a confused expression on his face, perhaps wondering what had happened to the teenager that he'd seen at the optical shop. I escaped the dance floor as soon as I sensed a pause in the music, telling myself that was enough limelight for one night.

"Maariiiski!" Youel said, grabbing my shoulders. "Amazing! Amazing!" he exclaimed. "I like it, this dress and how you dance and how you look. Just look at her!" he turned, looking for Shammoun.

"Thank you, Youel!" I laughed. "Oh, that was so . . ." I did not want to say "embarrassing," but struggled to find the right word. "Unexpected," I finally said, happy to see both of them.

"Now all these people will come to the optical to talk to you. I know what I am going to do, Mariski. On Monday when you come to work, I will burn lots of bissma! Lots of it! So that you don't catch evil eye, eh?"

"You burn so much bissma, nothing will happen to me for years," I said and laughed.

Just as he was done with his monologue, Shammoun approached us.

"What kind of beauty is that? All these fat Assyrian ladies are so jealous of you, Mariski! You look one hundred percent today! No, two hundred percent!" He held up his hand connecting his thumb with pointing finger.

"Thank you, Youel. Thank you, Shammoun. You guys also look fancy, too. I have never seen you in suits."

"No ties! I told Ashur I will wear suit but not that butterfly thing. It's too much for me. Too formal! I am already enough handsome, Mariski," Youel said.

Youel had said it as a joke, but you never knew when these two were being serious.

"Aha, so handsome, there is a line of these fat women—" Shammoun said and pointed at the dance floor. "They all want to dance with you," he said, bursting into roaring laughter.

"God save me from Assyrian women. The most stubborn and angry women in the world. I ran away all the way from Australia only to find out they are all over Chicago. No escape!" Youel said.

Then I saw Youel peek above my head. "Is that Eric?" he asked.

It had to be him, I thought to myself and suddenly heard a familiar voice coming from behind me.

"Maryam!" Eric said and came to stand next to me.

He wore a gray suit with a light blue striped shirt, which singled him out in a sea of men dressed in black and white. His graying hair was combed back, and, for a change, his face was cleanly shaven, which made him look younger. His eyes sparkled with the usual enthusiasm. He looked natural in this world of night entertainment, belly dancers, and loud music. It all seemed like second nature to him. My mind was racing through all those afternoon hours that I'd spent looking at the swaying back door of the optical shop, hoping he'd appear with a book, cigarette case, and car keys in his hands.

I looked at him for a few moments, hoping that my inner monologue remained concealed by the darkness of the room, as he engaged in small talk with Shammoun and Youel, stealing a few glances at me. Reem was now gone, and Jimmy Oshana reclaimed the podium and filled the restaurant with his romantic voice. Ashur must have adjusted the lights a bit, as the place was not as dark. Finally, Youel and Shammoun moved on to the next crowd of familiar faces and we were left alone.

"Long time, no see. So how have you been, Maryam?" he asked.

"Very good! I wanted to thank you for leaving the pamphlet on my desk. I was going to call to say thank you, but I didn't have your number. Varda helped me sign up for college. I'll be taking math and English in January," I said.

"You will make an excellent student," he said politely. "And how is the shop? I haven't been there for a long time."

"Well, it's just the way you left it," I said and smiled. The bitterness was beginning to subside. "We come, we make coffee, then patients show up, so we tend to them, then we eat bean soup with rice in the afternoon . . . Although, the last few months have been busier because of Arabesque."

"Is that so?" Eric asked.

"Reem's been coming around more often. Jimmy Oshana came several times last month," I recounted. "I never knew he was a singer!"

"He was a pretty big deal in Baghdad," he explained. "Before he moved."

"How have you been?" I said.

"Out of town a lot, so I haven't had a chance to visit. I was working on a piece about Lebanon and was in and out of the U.S." he said. "I'll drop off the piece when it's ready at the optical. Maybe you'd like to read it."

"I would love to read it." I smiled. "I looked up your book in the library, the one by the Egyptian author," I said.

"Mahfouz?" Eric asked with a curious smile on his face. He looked like he didn't expect this.

"Yes! *The Palace Walk* by Naguib Mahfouz. I haven't read in English until now, so it will be my first read."

"That is a difficult one to start with, but you can handle it," he said with a wink. "Hell, you can handle anything after the Russians!" he added.

I wanted to say something else to keep the conversation going, but I felt shy, and an awkward silence hung in the air.

"Well, you look wonderful tonight, Maryam! Quite stunning! I didn't recognize you at first. This dress looks beautiful on you."

"Thank you," I almost whispered, hoping my instant blush would not spoil this moment.

"And look, you are already blushing! Maryam, Maryam! Tell me, did you ever pick a favorite song from that album I brought you?"

Of course I did, I wanted to tell him. I had picked a song and even gotten too tired of it, since the CD had served as a soundtrack for my daily commute.

"I did. I chose 'Feels Like Forever,'" I responded, flattered that he still remembered.

This time my heart didn't race, and my palms were not sweaty. I felt a strange confidence that helped me maintain my posture as I whispered to myself, *Like a swan*. Eric did not comment on the song, but his silent smile felt like an approval. Then we walked back to our table, and I introduced him to Mother, Anna, and Philip. He welcomed them to the restaurant, asked a few questions, and then politely excused himself.

The table was now covered with appetizers, a basket of fresh-baked bread, and a large plate with lamb, beef, and chicken kabobs and a side of saffron rice. I could sense that those at the table, including Mother, had noticed my dreamy face around Eric but didn't say anything. I tried to engage Philip and Anna in a conversation about the restaurant, but my ears were still filled with Eric's low-key voice, my mind quickly recording the tiniest details of his appearance—the color of his suit, the stripes on his shirt, the light scent of his cologne, and the image of his cleanly shaven face. The more I thought of him, the clearer it seemed that I was falling deep into this hole, with no way of getting out. The thought scared me, but I felt helpless in front of this rapid avalanche of feelings that buried me. Who knew when and where I would see him next time? I tried to push away those thoughts and enjoy this intoxicating feeling, catching his glances in the distance as I replayed his words in my mind.

By the time we left the restaurant, Chicago was covered with an enormous rain cloud that poured over it incessantly. Anna, Philip, and Mother continued talking about random topics, occasionally trying to pull me into their conversation. I answered in short phrases, hoping they'd continue without me as I watched the way large drops of water burst on the window surface and streamed down the glass.

. . . .

CHAPTER 28

LIKE A CROISSANT

I spent the weekend in front of the television, reliving the excitement of the grand opening, recalling the lights of the restaurant at night, the loud music, the sparkling wings of the belly dancer, and the heaps of compliments that had rained down on me all night. I hadn't known what to make of my short encounter with Eric, so I tried not to think of him. Monday came and Youel and Shammoun did not disappoint, showering me with compliments all over again, filling the space with overwhelming amounts of burnt bissma as promised, and generally not letting me get any work done.

"She was the best! The best one! Did you see how she danced?" Shammoun said. "All the men, they were looking at you. I want to give them a kick, Mariski. Go look at your fat wife, stupid guy!"

"Yalla, yalla, guys, stop!" Youel protested. "You will give her the evil eye, Shammoun! Mariski, don't worry, here I come! What did I promise you? Here it is, come, lower your head." Youel circled the smoking incense stick around my head several times. By

the afternoon, I had a throbbing headache from the mix of cigarettes and bissma.

"Youel, I think that's enough of this thing, what's it called? I'm
good now," I said, pointing at the circling fumes of the bissma stick
mixing with the usual cigarette fog in the room.

Now that he wasn't wearing his expensive suit and onyx ring,
Ashur looked like a tall, thin optician again. His shoulders drooped
and he had the same half-bored, half-absent expression on his face.
Maybe he was upset to find himself back at the shop after such an
eventful, glamorous weekend. Maybe things didn't go so well after
we left. Maybe he had some issue with Sako after the grand opening.
I couldn't tell what went on in his head. Ashur didn't join the others
in complimenting me, but once both were done, he closed the checkbook with a clap and said, "You were s-s-stunning, Maryam."

His tone was different from the exaggerated praise that I'd always
get from Youel and Shammoun. He sounded serious, not in the mood
for jokes. It made me slightly uncomfortable, his voice so firm and
his eyes piercing through me.

The rest of that afternoon was glum, as the rain had never stopped
after the grand opening. The usual visitors to the optical shop showed
up randomly to discuss how the grand opening had gone. Although
a bit tired from the sudden influx of guests, Ashur patiently retold
everything that had taken place that evening, criticizing most and
praising a few, choosing the exact same words with each newly arrived
visitor. Thankfully the parade of guests had stopped by around four,
because our schedule was double-booked with eye exams that evening.
By five p.m., the waiting area had filled with families of five or more,
all waiting for an eye exam and hoping to snatch as many freebies as
they could from Ashur. This never got old for them.

"Are these cases free?" one woman asked. "No? What about these
lenses? No?"

They stood around, looking disappointed. "Sir, can you tell us what is free?" asked one elderly gentleman.

"Mr. Khan, listen," Ashur explained. "Nothing here is f-f-free. There is no such thing as a free lunch, you heard that s-s-saying?" *I must look up this phrase at the library,* I thought to myself.

The customers just shook their heads in disappointment and went back to the waiting area. Eugene was late, and he had left me in a difficult position. I was face-to-face with an army of far- and nearsighted people who demanded their right to be seen by a doctor, worried that they wouldn't be able to be seen today, considering all these patients crowding the waiting area.

"Sir, the doctor is on her way, I promise," I tried to explain. "She has some problem with the car. You know—it happens to everyone! Please take a seat, we'll be right with you."

We all sighed with relief when the optometrist showed up, grabbed the file of the first patient, and led him into the dark cabinet with the massive machine equipped with hundreds of lenses and other tools that she used during the exam.

"Did you see his last name, Mariski?" the optometrist asked. "Faulkner! I wonder if he is related." My voracious reading days were still in the future, so even though I smiled, I had no idea who Faulkner was. There was nothing special about this Monday evening—the crowds of patients, the scent of bissma, and the gentle rain outside. Until they showed up.

I was pulling the files of the patients who had scheduled exams that Monday when I saw Eric walk into the store with a woman and a little girl. They entered through the front door, looking cheerful despite being wet from the evening rain. She was short and thin, with light brown hair, transparent skin, and clothes that were painfully simple. Beside her stood a tiny girl with an astonishing resemblance to her mother.

They approached the counter as I stood there, frozen, unable to utter a word.

"Madeleine, this is Maryam," Eric said with a smile. "She works here at this optical. Very talented! Even speaks a bit of French."

"Ah!" Madeleine said. "*Enchantée!* Pleased to meet you."

"Madeleine is my girlfriend, and this is her beautiful daughter, Genevieve," he said, erasing all doubt from my mind. "We stopped by to get her eyes checked. I should have called."

"The doctor is running late," I said biting my tongue. "But I am sure we can figure something out."

"Excellent," Eric said.

Little Genevieve held on to her mother's coat and looked around with curiosity. To my own surprise, I managed to hide even the slightest sign of my misery and showed our guests to the back office. I even brought Eric and Madeline cups of coffee, offering a cookie to the child.

As for Madeleine, her appearance, while painfully plain, still possessed a subtle charm that was difficult to describe. I discovered I had nothing but fondness for her and her tiny daughter, except, of course, for the crisp breaking of my heart. *Like a croissant*, I thought. Her pixie cut and wide, plastic-frame glasses had a sophistication that conquered you gradually, making you notice her liberty from mainstream fashion and loyalty to a personal style that, perhaps, hardly changed with the seasons. Eric showed that familiar childish excitement about his newly found gem and was too taken up by her to notice any sadness in my eyes. I spoke politely to Madeleine, occasionally switching to my poor, limited French. I watched how her soothing sentences made Eric's face light up, the spark of a child entertained by a shiny, new toy.

Eric and Madeleine waited for all the patients to be gone. This time, there were no secret glances in my direction, no conversations about books and songs, no excursions to the history of ancient Middle East, and no stories about Eric's beloved California.

At around eight-thirty p.m., we were finally done. I collected a batch of prescriptions, slipped them into a large blue box on my desk, packed my bag, and got into Ashur's car, since he refused to let me take the bus in the dark. As I looked out the window, I thought of all the things I would need to forget—Eric's witty sense of humor, the intelligent manner of his speech, the semi-permanent faint smile on his face, the attractive glow in his eyes magnified by his rimless glasses . . . and all the other memories of him I had religiously collected over time. Ashur must have sensed something, as he remained silent on the way back that evening, tuning the radio to my favorite channel and turning up the volume before I even had a chance to ask.

Later that night, when I revisited the whole thing alone in my bedroom, I regretted hiding my sadness from Eric, not showing at least a bit of my frustration. It occurred to me that he would go on with life completely unaware of my infatuation with him and how it had brightened my depression-stricken first year in the U.S.

I remained in a melancholic daze for the next few days, constantly replaying Monday night's events in my head, mixing with scenes from my conversations with Eric and our short encounter at Arabesque. The whole thing was like a film that ran on repeat in my mind, sad and exhausting. I no longer wondered if he thought of me and slowly accepted the fact that he probably never did. His life was overflowing with social interaction with all kinds of people. It was rich with emotions and all I was, was an interesting artifact. His presence, on the other hand, consumed my dreams and enchanted me. Either way, it was all over before it had begun, and I needed to come to terms with that. I took longer lunch breaks, wandering aimlessly along the streets of Devon, finding refuge in the world of sari shops, bakeries, and crammed groceries, and observing people flooding the streets surrounded by honking cars.

At night, I would sit on the floor of my bedroom and listen to Joe Cocker's "Feels Like Forever" until I got sick of it. The trees, once covered with a mosaic of leaves, were now naked and lifeless, swaying with the harsh winds of December. Walking on the street turned into a continuous struggle, wind seeping through the thick layers of our sweaters and stinging our faces. Since the buses in Skokie were often late, we'd hop from one leg to the other at the bus station, freezing and praying to see the red and blue silhouette of the CTA bus appear from afar. Soon, I'd feel a throbbing sting inside of my shoes, as remaining warmth seeped away from my toes and locked them in a painful freeze.

This freezing cold had only one advantage: It numbed the heartache. As I stood at the bus station, freezing, taking a hit from nature's forces, the longing that concentrated in my throat disappeared. In those moments of cold, I truly believed that a warm bus and a hot cup of coffee or tea were sufficient for happiness. But as soon as I was given what I'd asked for, the heartache would come back, making me lose balance again and thrusting me deeper into my freefall.

I hoped that once I fully descended into the bottom of the pit, the feeling would run out and I'd be free. Surprisingly, it worked, and a few weeks before the end of the longest and most eventful year of my life, the numb pain that had kept me hostage for weeks started to subside. At first, it only happened for brief periods when I, extremely hungry, attacked a delicious stew or omelet my mother had perfected over the years, or when the winter sun poured into my pink-walled room, warming it up and sending a wave of sudden unexpected happiness through my body. I noticed that the episodes in my head were fading. They failed to haunt me as they did in the beginning. Soon the sorrow expired, and my heart began to heal.

CHAPTER 29

. . . .

LIFE AS WE KNOW IT

Once Mother started attending the English classes at the Jewish community center, she got her confidence back. She had gotten back in the game of making friends at the speed of light. In a funny sort of way, she even stopped referring to these classes as something I had suggested to her. It was as if she had found the place herself and signed up for classes, just as she had planned to. I was amused, but I understood that it felt good to believe she had gotten herself out of her own trap without anyone's help. *Fine by me,* I thought. There was no harm in going along with that story. The Jewish center, with its humble, two-story building, well-lit rooms, and immigrants who came from all over the world, became her domain, a place where everyone knew her, and she knew everyone.

"Yasha, from my English class, keeps copying my homework assignments. Can you imagine?" she said. "The teacher knows it, his wife knows it, but he won't care. The man is pathologically afraid of a bad grade. I mean, we are all there to learn English—who is keeping score, you think? It is truly funny," Mother said.

"I hope you're not one of those that will refuse him out of spite," Rufat said.

"I don't mind, but there are no cheat-sheets out there. What is he thinking? I hope he doesn't end up in my computer class with Sonya. I have no time to lend him my notebook for that homework."

"You're taking a computer class?" Rufat asked.

"Sonya says that any job you get requires some knowledge of the computer. Teymour says the same thing," Mother replied.

"Who is this Sonya?" Rufat asked.

"Yasha's wife," Mother replied. "They are from Odessa. Maryam, I told them they can come and get new glasses in your optical. They have those public aid cards that you guys accept."

"Sure, Mother," I replied. "Send them our way. I am so glad you're learning so much at this place." I gave Rufat a wink and he smiled back.

"Yes, I mean, I need to know the language. Surely, the Indian tutor back in Baku helped, the one your grandmother found for me," she went on. "But he taught British English, and we are in America."

"You're right, you're so right," I said and smiled.

New life meant new beginnings, but a blank page was a blank page, after all, and unless you took a brush and started painting things, it would remain an empty field devoid of trees and bushes. These conversational English and computer classes added much-needed structure to my mother's life. Now that her time was split between trips to the city and time at home, she had sprung back to her energetic self and there was less and less destructive apathy in her mood. A few weeks later Mother did find a dental assistant job through one of her friends at the Jewish community center. She rearranged her class schedule to complete training at the dental office and soon began to work full time, leaving early in the morning and coming home past six. Her hours were long, so the pay was more than enough to cover bills, and she was surrounded by Russian speakers, many of them natives of Baku. Mother loved the place and did not mind that the job was physically exhausting. She came home spent but in good spirits. Naturally, she befriended everyone at this place within weeks and soon we'd be invited to birthdays of people we barely knew and received gifts from people who never saw us. Such was the charm of Mother when she was in the right state of mind.

It was also around this time that Rufat found a weekend job at a Russian restaurant nearby. Without work permits, we all depended on low-paying cash jobs and there wasn't much of a choice, so we didn't complain. Anything that paid the bills was good enough. We didn't mind the physical labor, the lower-than-minimum-wage pay, or the odd hours. We'd been in America long enough and had met enough immigrants to know that in these first few years, you simply didn't get to choose. But this restaurant job was a stretch even for us fresh-off-the-boat immigrants.

"I'll go in on Friday night, around seven p.m., and work until they close," Rufat said. "I can't handle alcohol because of my age, so I'll be greeting the guests and helping with the set-up. The owner said I may need to stay over to help reset the place for Saturday brunches. It's a bit of a work-around-the-clock job, but it'll pay well."

It turned out to be worse than that. Rufat started the job at the end of November and soon, he no longer looked forward to the weekend. He'd be gone on Friday, often catching a few hours of sleep on a couch in the back office and then getting up to do the dishes and get the place ready for bridal showers, wedding brunches, and bar and bat mitzvas that took place almost every weekend. Rufat would come home exhausted, often bearing leftover food in containers—skewered shrimps, pork chops, fried potatoes, a soggy Napoleon cake from a banquet the night before. He'd leave the money on the table and sink into a deep sleep that stretched into Sunday afternoon. His room had always been on the messy side, but it got out of control around this time. Mother tried to get him to quit, but he refused to talk about it and just brushed her aside.

"Money is good, and we don't have the luxury to choose, right?" he said, his face suddenly so mature and stern. "Plus, if I do well, they'll send me to private parties at some houses. Those are easy to manage. It's not much work and really good pay. I just got to hang on for a little while," he said. "Until I get used to it."

Mother kept pushing, but we both knew that she could no longer veto things like she had back home. It was a whole different life out here. Soon we both gave up and realized that Rufat was no longer a kid Mother could boss around. She even tried to get Teymour to speak to him, but this time Teymour did not agree.

"Look, Leyla. You've got to do what you've got to do here. I worked nights and studied for a computer test on my lap while I taxied around Chicago. Ate *rolton*, shopped in cheap groceries, and wore the same pants for a year."

"You still wear the same pants for a whole year," Mother said.

"Look, he's becoming a man, all right? Looking out for his family, trying to make a few bucks with the sweat of his brow. Would you leave him alone, please?" Teymour insisted. "I'll have a little heart-to-heart with him over the weekend, but I'm sticking to my thoughts on this. Leave the boy alone."

"A little heart-to-heart would be nice," Mother said. "Thank you, Teymour."

The next weekend, Teymour showed up with a large desktop computer in the trunk of his coupe. He dragged it inside and he and Rufat spent a good hour installing it on a shaky corner desk in Rufat's messy room.

"Who lives here?" Teymour said.

"You don't get to comment," Rufat joked back.

We left them alone to set up the computer and connect the Internet. When they joined us in the kitchen for fruit and tea, they both looked relaxed and content. It must have been the heart-to-heart. Mother and I mostly kept out of Rufat's room to avoid the messiness there, which almost rivaled with the disarray of Teymour's apartment on that first June morning in Chicago. No threats or pleas for decency worked with Rufat and, eventually, Mother gave up. But before she stopped her attacks, she brought in a small plant of some sort and left it on the desk.

"What is *that*?" Rufat asked.

"This is the symbol of my resistance," she said, half-joking. "I am not done with you. This plant better live!" She left the room.

Rufat shook his head but watered the plant diligently.

Now that he worked so much, we saw very little of Rufat. He'd spend his days sleeping or downloading music and movies from websites, emerging once in a while to get food and, maybe, water for the plant. In passing he might tell us stories from his high school that sounded unreal. He was not as talkative as before, no longer a radio-box that imitated all the silly commercials on TV, no longer picked on Mother and me. Something in his gaze became silent and heavy, like he was on a mission. Now that his giggly teenagerhood was over, we both missed it badly. So, on those rare occasions when he sprang back into his old self, we relished it.

One day, Rufat showed up in the kitchen, picked up a washcloth, and started wiping down all the door handles.

"Did you know that most of the germs are concentrated on the door handles, Mother?" he asked.

Mother and I looked at each other, took a sip of the tea, and tilted our heads, at a loss for words, surprised and unsure of what would follow.

"Are you all right?" I asked sardonically.

"I am telling you. Instead of bothering me about the dust in my room, you should focus on these. Most of the germs come from these guys, not the dust in my room," Rufat explained.

"What else is going on at school?" I asked, biting into my sandwich. I was eager to get bits and pieces of information about this magical place: an American high school, with its wide hallways and lockers for students, theatre and art clubs, debate tournaments, and enough after-school activities to fill up your week entirely.

"I broke up a fight last week," he said.

"You got in a fight?" Mother asked, alarmed.

"I *broke up* a fight, Mother," Rufat repeated. "These two Afghan girls, they've been trouble since day one. For some reason, they've been hating on this Turkish girl, Elif, and they finally circled her in the cafeteria, punches and all. It got pretty messy, so I got in between them and pulled them apart. Eventually, I broke up the fight, but we all had to explain it to the officers."

"Officers? What kind of officers?" I asked.

"Police officers, I told you it got pretty messy, so police had to come in. Still want to go to high school, big sister?"

"That is crazy, Rufat!" Mother said. "I want you to be extra careful at school. What's with this cleaning of yours, leave those door handles alone," Mother said, laughed, and took the cloth from his hands.

"So ungrateful!" Rufat said. He grabbed a sandwich from the kitchen table and disappeared into the hallway.

"Wash your hands!" Mother yelled, but he'd already left.

Our life in America resembled a quilt made up of tiny pieces that didn't always match one another, but that surely amounted to a blanket that would keep you warm at night. Our life in Baku still served as a backdrop to this new, simple way of things. We remembered the loud family parties leading up to the New Year, the festivities that took place within the walls of the ancient Old

City, the millions of lights on the main city square, the evening traffic, and a city loud enough to take over your life. When Mother, Rufat, and I ran out of stories to tell about the stubborn Assyrians, the brawls in the high school cafeteria, and the new members of her English-language class, we'd still turn to the stories of the past, so distant, so unattainable now and therefore almost enigmatic. There was everything in it—family celebrations and gatherings, entertaining and sometimes hurtful family drama, lifelong friendships, excess food and the force-feeding of our aunts and uncles, long summer nights by the Caspian, nosy neighbors and the gossip that came with them, a life still colorful, still vibrant, even under the tight grip of public opinion. Name an adventure to spice up an ordinary life and you found it in Baku, like in those absurd telenovelas I watched on Telemundo. We each remembered Baku differently, often arguing about people and events, but there was one thing we agreed on: Despite the countless blessings and comforts afforded to us in America, we all desperately missed it.

CHAPTER 30

. . . .

REFLECTIONS

A day before the last day of the year, Mother announced we'd be spending New Year's Eve with an Azeri Jewish family that she met through Teymour. Teymour and Sarah were attending some kind of gala event downtown, so we would not join them as we had for all other holidays. While we were not thrilled to greet the coming year in a house full of strangers, we agreed, because nothing seemed worse than staying alone at home.

Ashur closed the optical shop for a whole week to prepare for Arabesque's first New Year's event, so I spent it at home, finishing up the collage of photos in my bedroom, watching Mexican soap operas—those that don't require you to speak Spanish to understand what is going on—and exploring our snow-covered neighborhood with Rufat.

The morning of December thirty-first was calm and festive, with snowflakes landing gently on tree branches, catching winter sunlight, and sparkling like tiny jewels. The house was clean and full of light. Mother sat in the kitchen, listened to a song on the radio, and smoked her cigarette by the open window. She looked almost happy, such a rare sight.

That morning, to end the year on a good note, I washed and dried my hair and chose an outfit for the evening. It was nothing fancy—leather shorts and a satin top with tights, all black again. It had been almost six months since we had moved, yet I still hesitated to wear anything colorful even on special occasions. I would open my closet, my hand moving towards the yellow and the blue, then hesitating and going for the safe bet again: black on black. By five p.m., all three of us were dressed and ready to go.

I sat on the couch and looked outside, taken up with the tiny snowflakes circling towards the ground in their elegant dance. Suddenly, I noticed Arash's car pulling into our driveway.

"Mama, that guy from college is here!" I said. "I am going to say hi to him," I told her, grabbing Rufat's jacket and running outside.

"Salam, Arash!" I said. "How did you remember where I live?"

"Salam *khanoum*! Well, didn't I drop you off here once?" he asked.

"You did, but I did not think you'd remember." I blushed. "Happy New Year to you!" I did not expect to feel so happy to see him.

"Thank you, Maryam! Same to you! And I see your mother is at the window. Please say hello to her from me." Mother and Rufat were both by the window and returned his wave with a smile. She motioned him to come in.

Arash was wearing a brown coat on top of a gray suit with a tie. His black hair was peppered with the melting snowflakes and the powerful whiff of his cologne filled my nostrils despite the piercing cold. He opened the back door of his car and took out two textbooks.

"I asked around and found a guy, Iranian . . . he also just took these classes. He gave me the books for free. So, you owe me!" He laughed.

"Oh, wow! This is so nice of you. How much do I owe you?" I asked, wondering if I could run inside and grab cash quickly.

"That was a joke, Maryam," he said. "You don't owe me money, but I do have a favor to ask."

"I knew it was coming," I joked.

"I am in that class, too, and you are going to help me get through it. There is nothing I hate more than calculus."

Then why do you take it? I thought.

"Please?" he asked with an exaggerated sad face.

"I don't think I have a choice. Of course I will! Hopefully, I actually know this stuff. You think too highly of my math skills, Arash." I flipped through the thick book.

"Didn't you go to a Russian school? Isn't math like native language for you all?"

"Oh God, I'll need to help you with the geography too," I said absently. Then, "Wait, who is *you all?*"

"All right, I think you're about to freeze." He grimaced and touched my shoulder. "And I am, too. Run home and take the books."

"Can you let me pay for these?" I pleaded, noticing the books did not look used at all.

"What do *you* think?" he smirked. "I am not taking your money. And your lips are slowly turning blue." I noticed his gaze stop at my lips and almost blushed. "Go! I'll pick you up on Monday at eight a.m."

"No, you really don't need to do that, Arash," I said. "You see that sign? There is a bus that goes to Oakton Street and, from there, I walk."

Arash shook his head and got in the car. "See you on Monday," he said and drove off without giving me a chance to object.

At around six p.m., another car pulled into our driveway to pick us up on the way to the party. Behind the wheel was an old man with kind eyes, a noble forehead, and hair as white as the snow that now covered the ground like a thick blanket. His name was Eduard and as far as I knew, he was the husband of the nice lady who had kindly invited us over to their house to celebrate New Year's Eve.

As we drove through the frozen streets of Skokie, I thought about my friends in Baku. Freed from any homework and reading assignments in the days leading up to the New Year, we'd feel the excitement in the air and spend hours on the phone with each other. I remembered the brief phone conversation I'd had with Arif that morning. His voice trembled as he spoke and at first his sentences were short and clumsy. I sensed a familiar awkwardness and mixed feelings in his voice, like two pieces of a broken vase coming closer to fitting together but failing every time. I thought about him and our interrupted romance without despair for the first time, thinking of it as a mere consequence of my family's move to the States. I accepted that time and distance had drawn the two of us apart and there was no one to blame.

The radio was tuned to soft jazz. I kept looking out the window, lost in reflections of the past, thoughts about the present, and hopes for the future. Despite the overwhelming nature of events in this past year, I felt hopeful. As the gentle sound of saxophone spilled into me, I saw a myriad of animated snapshots from the last year come alive in front of my eyes. Here was my grandmother's apartment packed with an army of well-wishers who'd come to bid us farewell, here was the endless night I spent sitting next to my hypertonic mother, wiping her forehead with a warm towel and praying she'd feel better soon, here was the first sandwich that brought me back to a healthy appetite, here was the magical world of Devon with its colorful blocks, busy traffic, and groups of cheerful immigrants, here were lazy afternoons spent in the park with Teymour and Sarah, munching on sandwiches and sipping tea.

These moments weren't all happy, but I didn't regret living through any of them. Somewhere on the outskirts of my consciousness, I was aware of all the transformations that they had prompted and felt curious about what would become of me in the future.

. . . .

CHAPTER 31

DIFFERENT LIVES

On January twenty-first, ten days before my nineteenth birthday, I would begin taking classes at Oakton Community College. I first had to take a test to determine my math and English language level, which turned out to be better than I expected. The past few months at the optical shop did nothing for my language skills, apart from picking up a few Assyrian words and conversing in Russian with our post-Soviet clients.

"You got placed in English 101. That's pretty good!" Arash nudged me on my shoulder. He could have been just saying that to cheer me up, so I wasn't sure if my results were as good as he made them out to be.

"Well, we knew you're a math genius, so your math level is Calc two," he added, flipping through the papers.

"You're wrong, and soon you'll find out the hard way!" I objected.

I signed up for English, Psychology, and Calculus I, a class that I attended with Arash. Classes started on the third week of January, so I still had a few weeks to soak in the joy of becoming a student without actually having to stress out about grades, picky professors, and deadlines. In those weeks, I walked around the building, admiring the tall ceilings, wide sunlit hallways, the greenery of the campus, and the crowds of students dressed in colorful clothes. Unlike my classmates back home, students didn't shy away from wearing bright yellow and pink, and this added to the vibrant and futuristic atmosphere of the place. Those bright colors were almost missing in my past life. As we grew up, the gray and brown and black prevailed. The time I first began to care about clothing had also coincided with the sudden decline of my father's banking career.

In Baku, there was little money and shopping was quite a rare and unpleasant activity focused on your basic needs, not something we looked forward to. I'd get a pair of jeans, black dress pants, and waterproof boots to get me through the winter. These colors resembled the gloom of the perestroika years, but soon we not only embraced the black and the blue and the dark purple, but felt like those other bright colors were simply not for our world. Here in America, months passed, and I was still caught off guard by bright colors, even though I saw teenagers wearing them everywhere. *How brave of them*, I thought.

Having spent eleven years of my life before leaving for the U.S. fully preoccupied with schoolwork, I realized that the last eight months had left me hungry for learning. So, I threw myself into obsessive studying, reading my psychology textbook during my bus ride, highlighting sections that might come up on the midterm exam. I took my time scribbling reminders on yellow Post-It notes and sticking them in between pages with such satisfaction. I was unaccustomed to such fancy and spotless facilities—public schools back home were cold and often unclean—and I was infatuated with the pristine world of Oakton Community College.

Arash showed up in front of our two-story building every Tuesday and Thursday, filling the air with the pleasant scent of his morning cologne, his eyes shining with a glorious love of life, and his clothes neatly ironed and color-coordinated to perfection. Until I met him, I always thought of love at first sight as a myth, something that didn't exist. I thought it was nothing more than a cheap marketing trick in those cheesy commercials on Turkish channels, but he proved me wrong. There was nothing romantic in that first moment when we locked eyes, but I saw something gentle and permanent solidify in his whole being, take root in his eyes—something special for me. Something that would not fade easily. I recalled the moment when he put down the books on his library cart and extended his hand for a greeting. From that instant, all he wanted was to be near me. At first, he tried to act neutral and friendly. He'd tell me about a girl he'd seen at one of his family gatherings that seemed to happen every weekend. Maybe this was true, maybe there was a girl he liked before I showed up, but I sensed that he shared these stories to gauge my reaction, to make me jealous. I felt nothing of that sort because at first I did not reciprocate Arash's feelings. With time, I grew accustomed to his presence, to the scent of his cologne, to the way he'd call me *khanoum,* and to how he was always there to play down any mishap and exaggerate any good fortune.

On one of the magical evenings in February when the ground was covered with a white blanket and snowflakes of enormous size fell from the sky, Arash and I sat in the deserted cafeteria to study for the upcoming calculus exam. By that time, I had figured that math would remain a terra incognita for him, no matter how he tried to tame the trigonometric equations that Mr. McAllister so carefully wrote out with a blue marker on the whiteboard. However, the untiring teacher in me did not consider retreat for a moment. For hours, I tried simplifying the concepts, rewording them into plain language, scribbling examples over and over to the point that I'd doubt my own knowledge, only to hear Arash's long awaited, "Aaaah! Now I get it! You see? I am not hopeless after all."

But he was. The simplest concepts of calculus and especially trigonometry would send him into a confused frenzy, and a few minutes later he would ask the same questions I had answered only moments ago. Yet there was a strange charm in his refusal to give up. There was something attractive in the way he was ready to study for hours to justify the time that we spent together.

That evening, we chose a corner table by the window so we could glance at the beauty outside once in a while. We took our heavy books and notepads out of our backpacks and started to work on a set of practice equations. Arash was wearing a brown turtleneck, worn-out jeans, and wool coat on top. He didn't chat as much today, so we sat in silence, and I found myself studying him. I noticed two tiny moles just below his left eye that added charm to his smile. I noticed his sensitive nature surfacing, as his loud personality and cheerfulness subsided under the magical lulling of snowfall and silence of the deserted cafeteria.

A few minutes into the practice test, I was back at my habit of nail-biting, forgetting all the scolding that my grandmother had done throughout the years. "If a man sees you biting your nails like that, he will never marry you!" Nana had said. *And?* I thought back then, squeezing out a promise that I would never do it again, only to break my vow a few hours later. This time, though, there was no scolding. Instead, I felt Arash's warm hands cover my left hand, both of them wrapping around mine. I raised my head from the book.

"If you don't stop doing that, I will stop you," he said. "Like this," he added and wrapped his hands around mine.

A silent smile appeared on our faces. If he had added a word or two, we would both have burst into laughter and the moment would have been gone, but he remained silent, and I recognized the beginning of *us*. I returned a similar understanding smile—one of those smiles that makes words unnecessary—and bit the end of my pencil before returning to trigonometric equations. Some unmasked feeling was now present whenever he looked at me, always accompanied by silence, too heavy for words.

We spent those winter evenings studying for Calculus, sharing childhood stories, and patiently waiting for spring. It was during these evenings that I learned things about Arash that astonished me. He worked seven days a week. He held two part-time jobs at Oakton and put in about fifteen hours a week at Carson Pirie Scott as a sales consultant in the men's clothing department. He moved to Chicago with his mother and sister from Tehran a few years ago, leaving behind his elder sister and father back home. Though I hadn't met his mother, I felt sort of indebted to her from the beginning, as it was her food that I shared with Arash twice a week. He must have told her about me, because she added more rice and lamb stew and pickles to Arash's lunch containers and brewed enough tea for two.

A few years earlier, his mother had fallen ill and had to be operated on for six long hours, with a medium-to-good chance that she would survive.

"She wasn't good, and the doctors did not sound so hopeful," he began. "They said we either bite the bullet and go with surgery or things will deteriorate. Her back was no good. She was in pain all the time, so we decided to do it. I thought six-hour-long surgeries only happened in movies."

"I thought so, too," I said. "Is that how long it took?"

"Yes."

"These must have been the longest six hours of your life." I looked down.

"Nope. I slept."

"No, you did not!" I slapped his knee.

"Maryam, things that you cannot control are better left alone. I knew I could not help her at that moment. I had to let it go. So, I slept, and I slept well, too."

He had a point, but it was one thing to recognize this wisdom and another to live by it.

"Is that how it is for you?" I asked. "If you can't change it, you snap your fingers and let it go?"

"Easy with the sarcasm, Maryam," he said without the usual smile. "It's the hardest thing to let life do its thing with things and people you love, but there is no point in fighting."

"Surrender is what you say," I said.

"Surrender, but not to defeat," he answered. "Surrender to Kismet."

"I've tried to surrender in the past months, but I still don't get why we're here," I said. "I don't understand what was wrong with our life back home to just leave everything and come here. My mother has been doing better lately. She appeared to be lost in the beginning, but she got some of her confidence back, it seems. With all the hardships and uncertainties, I think she still prefers this life to that. And me? I was tossed into the suitcase like all the other things," I said.

"You know, it's been weeks since I've responded to my friends' emails," I confessed. "These are friends with whom I spent entire summers, mornings at the beach, evenings at the café, eating street food, and wandering along the same beaten path in the city center. We'd tell each other secrets. Gosh, it's crazy that secrets were a thing in my life. I feel so far from all that. And I can't really talk to them."

"Why not?" he asked.

"I don't know. It feels like someone cut the cord between us," I tried to explain. "We don't speak the same language. Do you understand?" I asked.

"I think I do," Arash said.

"They talk about debate camp, school, how their parents are arranging some bullshit summer jobs to keep them occupied. And I barely got my mother to take some classes and look for a job so we can keep paying for groceries. I can't help it. On one hand, I feel jealous that they still get to live a life where the hardest thing is to choose where you'll spend your weekend, while my entertainment is watching people on Devon Avenue from the bus. They all are so nice, they want to know all about my new life, but there is nothing exciting to tell. In fact, I'd rather not talk about it at all. It's one of those things that you just can't explain with words, you know? I can hardly comprehend it myself. Our life seems to get into a certain shape, there is some distant hope on the horizon, but it still feels strange and wrong. It feels, what's the word? Foreign! We are on different sides of life now."

"Different lives," he said.

I nodded. "Different problems."

CHAPTER 32

. . . .

AMINA

At the end of March, winter finally eased its five-month-long, paralyzing grip on Chicago and spring peeked out from the heavy clouds, gifting us with occasional sunrays. Unaccustomed to such a cold climate, all three of us expected that March would be a warm month, but spring was torturously slow in her entrance. We all grew tired of the cold. Every morning, we opened the living room window to check if the warm winds of spring had arrived, but day after day, the weather remained sunny but cold.

Youel, impatient for the summer to arrive, and in a silly attempt to speed it up, turned down the heat at Vision Express Optical.

"Mariski, come on! What this sweater you are wearing! Look, it is March!" He pointed at the sunlit windows. "Soon it will be April and May and June and then August! Do you know how hot it was when we lived in Baghdad? This Chicago heat is nothing compared to Baghdad!

"Baghdad was hell! Yes, yes, it was hell," he went on. "You shower five times, six times a day! You sweat aaa-llll the time!" He must have been in a mood to talk because his monologue wouldn't die down.

I nodded, wrapping another shawl around my shoulders.

"You know why I don't have winter clothes?" he went on. "Because I don't like winter."

"That makes perfect sense, Youel!" I said, sipping my coffee.

"You bring all this cold here with your sweaters and shawls," he laughed.

"Of course!" I said.

Ashur was getting tired of this monologue, so he took out a twenty-dollar bill from his wallet, handed it to Youel, and asked him if he could get cigarettes, paper towels, and Windex from the pharmacy across the street.

"You're welcome," Ashur said to me with a laugh. "I'll turn up the heat. You can close the back door."

As usual, Ashur and Shammoun munched on nuts and smoked their cigarettes, enjoying the silence. Since the opening of Arabesque, Ashur always came into the office preoccupied with this or that problem at the restaurant. He'd spend hours on the phone consulting Ralf Eldaoud about licenses and then spend twice the time explaining his opinion to George Sako, who turned out to be even more of a nightmare to deal with than expected.

Now that Arabesque stole all the limelight, I realized that the optical store had always been simply a gathering place for the Iraqis. It was a place that afforded them the freedom to spend their days smoking and drinking coffee, watching TV, bickering about taxes and life in the U.S. in a passive, lazy manner, rarely disturbed by the commercial passion of running a business. The public-aid program secured a steady flow of patients without a need for customer service, clean facilities, or friendly faces. None of the patients ever complained about the clouds of cigarette smoke that rose to the ceiling, the torn pieces of paper that Ashur handed them instead of receipts, or the double-booked appointments that resulted in long waiting times.

The cigarette smoke was beginning to bother me. I had developed increasingly intense headaches from it. As soon as a whiff of smoke would enter my nostrils, my temples would throb. By the afternoon, my every move triggered a wave of pain through my body, leaving me nauseated and dizzy.

During these headaches, I'd put away my work, place my head on the desk, and wrap my arms around my head. The Assyrians would take turns approaching me with a glass of water or a cup of coffee or a plate of fruit, but I simply waved my head from side to side, unable to even lift it off the desk.

For a month, I refused medications and fought with my headaches as if the affliction was an army that could be defeated, but in the end I lost. Once I got the taste of small green Advil Liqui-Gel capsules, I gulped them down as soon as the headache would start and, an hour later, I could open my eyes again. I never again hesitated before throwing another green pill into my mouth when the headache peeked its head somewhere inside of me. Soon a bottle of Advil sat permanently on my desk among pink and white slips, unopened mail, staplers, the tape dispenser, and cups filled with old pens.

I realized that my almost daily usage of pills was alarming. Sometimes I took the pills even if I didn't have a headache, telling myself I was doing it to *prevent* a headache, but that was not true. I often took the pills to calm my nerves and it worked like magic. My muscles relaxed, my heartbeat normalized, and I could feel the world around me slow down a little. Whether it was a placebo effect or if the pills truly calmed my nerves, it worked. So, when my anxiety got the best of me, I'd take a pill.

It was a sunny afternoon at the end of March. We had just finished seeing Anna's patients and sat down to eat lunch at the round table when the phone rang. I answered.

"Vision Express Optical, how can I help you?"

"Hey girl! It's me, Amina. What's up?"

I'd seen Amina just a few times at our second-floor apartment in Jefferson Park, but since we'd moved to Skokie, we had only spoken on the phone a few times. She once invited us over to her place in Lincoln Park, but we were too busy settling down, and the idea of venturing out in the cold was not so appealing. "Let the spring come!" I'd told her and never called back.

"Why don't you come over on Saturday and sleep over? I'll cook for you, we'll ride a bicycle in the park, we'll eat ice cream, we can go see a movie . . . Huh? What do you say, workaholic?" she prodded.

"I don't know how to ride a bicycle," I responded.

"Fine, who cares! Don't you want to get out for a bit?" Amina pressed.

"I would love that, but I don't know if my mother would be okay with it."

"No problem, girl! I understand. I'll call and talk to her. Trust me—I can talk her into it."

Amina did as she said. She called Mother in the evening and magically talked her into letting me escape to the city for the entire weekend.

That Saturday, I awoke to the ringing sound of a fire truck leaving the station—an occurrence that regularly spoiled the morning for all inhabitants of our block. I sprang to my feet, jumped into the shower, and turned on the hot water. Having lived in a house where hot water was limited to a few hours a day, I felt like I was living the life every time I turned the water knob all the way down and felt the hot water touch my skin. Back in Baku, I had to be done with all the scrubbing and washing up in ten minutes because we only had running water for two hours a day. There was always someone knocking on the door, telling you to get on with it and not waste precious water. Nobody knocked on the bathroom door here in America and that felt like pure luxury every time.

That morning, the sun shone brighter, the breakfast felt tastier, and even the cold wind that swung the tall trees around our building didn't discourage me. I toasted the bread, spread a thick layer of butter and apricot jam, and bit into it. After breakfast, I threw a few items into my backpack and gave Mother a kiss. She smiled back and handed me her cell phone.

"So, I can keep in touch with you all the time," she explained. "I'll use the neighbor's phone to call, so keep the phone close and check for messages."

"But Amina also has a phone," I objected.

"That's *her* phone! She may lose it, she may forget it, she may not have reception . . . Who knows? If you're going to stay there, I need a way to get in touch with you. Deal?"

"Yep!" I replied, amazed at how quickly she'd come up with a list of things that could go wrong.

In the past year, Mother had gradually loosened up her old ways of controlling our movements around the city. Back home, the knowledge of where we went and what we did was always available to her. She could phone our driver or call the school. Besides, there were no surprises there. Most of the time, we'd come home from school and hang out with the neighboring kids in the yard. People did not move around back home, so she knew all of those kids and their parents and probably their grandparents, too. Our entire life, with all the play dates, birthday parties, tutors, piano lessons, and weekend outings, nicely fit into a radius of five miles. She'd finally gotten used to things here, but I could see she was a bit nervous about my trip to the city.

"I'll be back tomorrow, safe and sound! Don't worry about stuff and don't sit by that window, Mama," I said as I left.

Amina and I agreed to meet at the Fullerton Red Line station. My train ride would take about forty-five minutes, so I had plenty of time to cozy up in one of the back seats of the Skokie Express and daydream. As we neared the city, I recalled the hot days in June when I had boarded the train on State and Sutton, slowly moving away from the hectic hustle of downtown. I recalled how the knot in my throat had poisoned every moment of the day and hadn't let me enjoy the trip. I remembered the struggle to keep the tears from falling, a time when every word ignited pain somewhere deep inside me. It was hard to believe that one day I would put all of it behind me, but things were so different now, so much better.

When my mind got tired of playing dreadful images of last summer, I propped my elbow on the armrest and looked outside. There was something magical, cinematic about the speed of objects passing by me coupled with the music in my ears.

Amina was waiting for me across the street from the Fullerton L station. She wore a bright red jacket with a cable-knit scarf and matching beanie. Her eyes lit up with a familiar teenage excitement that reminded me of the days when I skipped the dreaded physical education class and went window-shopping with my classmates.

"What's up, girl? Did you get here all right? You look like you're cold," she said.

Despite the cold, the sky was painted in a bright blue with a few elongated off-white clouds that covered it in a soft, layered fashion. The two-way North Sheridan Road was dotted with tall light poles. Parked cars formed a colorful row by the sidewalks. The tiny domes of three-story townhomes contrasted with the blue of the sky and added an air of magic to this neighborhood. The townhomes were clustered close to one another, and each was painted in a rich red or purple or yellow. Unlike the Devon neighborhood, where the cultural chaos reigned, Lincoln Park appeared polished. It had a prescribed atmosphere to it, with random music stores, hip cafés, bars, and quite a number of bicyclists. Its inhabitants differed from those I saw both downtown and in Devon. They appeared relaxed, and an air of freedom hovered around them. I could judge that from their bizarre clothes, messy hair, and from the dreamy look in their eyes and the peculiar, knowing smiles on their faces.

Amina was always in a rush to get somewhere, unable to sit in one place for a long time. Just as we would make ourselves comfortable at a bookstore, she'd tap her fingers on the table and ask, "Ready to go?" As a result of her haste to show me around, we completed our tour around noon and headed to her studio on West Belden Avenue to have lunch.

Her apartment was located on the first floor of a five-story building. Its entrance was covered with a narrow green canopy and a rubber mat that led up to glass double-doors. On both sides of the narrow passage grew large green bushes with long oval leaves. We entered into a well-lit hallway and took the stairs down to the lower level, where Amina's apartment was. The hallway turned out to be very warm, so we both took off our coats and scarves.

Once we were inside, Amina became quiet, and I simply followed her to the mailbox area to pick up the mail. She opened the mailbox with her name inscribed on it, removed two letters from it, and put them inside her bag with a worried look on her face. Now that the mail was picked up, we took a right and found ourselves in another dark, labyrinthine hallway with gray doors on each side. Unlike the hallways of Baku apartment buildings, this place was warm and didn't smell, but its uniform nature was so lonely. I did not hear a noise suggesting that behind these walls there were families gathering around a dinner table, kids fighting over the remote control, or cats meowing in the kitchen in hopes of some snacks. This place looked like a dormant hospital hallway to me.

In that moment, our whole life in the U.S. felt, to me, much like this walk in a hallway—it was well-directed, comfortable, but devoid of the familiar emotions that saturated our lives. As we walked on, Amina kept looking ahead, unaware of the strange impact that this hallway was having on me. Her hair was now falling freely on her shoulders in soft, golden-brown curls and her shoulders were slightly hunched forward. When she finally did turn around, I forced a smile to conceal the melancholic nature of my thoughts. It had been months now that I, in the absence of a tight-knit circle of friends, had engaged in internal monologues about things, exploring America on my own, as if it were another planet, often drawing parallels and, other times, realizing the differences between the world that I had left and the one I now inhabited.

I had imagined her apartment in a minimalist European style with bright furniture, white jalousie blinds, bare floor, and eclectic decor. Instead, I found myself in a room inspired by the East. The walls were a warm, peachy color, and the wide blue curtain added a purple hue to the sunlight that seeped into the room. Two copper Moroccan lanterns with green and blue stones hung from the ceiling. The queen bed that took up much of the studio was covered with a silk coverlet and two rows of kilim cushions of bright maroon and blue.

I noticed a low desk in the right corner that was covered with papers and pencils of different sizes. Paintings featuring Eastern motifs, mosaics, and female and male silhouettes were pinned to the wall above the desk. Amina's artwork was drenched in a lethargic melancholy for a lost love and sadness. It seemed as if she no longer opposed its intrusion into her life and instead welcomed it whole-heartedly. The men and women in her pictures were separated by enormous mountains, rivers, or canyons, or some other impossible obstacle. A small sitar, decorated with intricate ornaments and delicate strings, was penciled in the corner of all the drawings.

When Amina came out of the bathroom, I was standing by the desk with two small paintings in my hands. She came closer and took one of them from me.

"That's all I do on the weekends," she said, pointing at the pencils.

She placed the drawing back, headed to the kitchen, and opened the fridge.

"You okay with lemon juice and olive oil, or do you want something else with your salad?"

"Whatever you put on it is fine with me," I replied.

I was not used to getting questions from the hostess about food. Back home, we'd simply eat whatever was cooked. Picking food, sharing your preferences, refusing an ingredient—those were the things I could only afford with Nana. With anyone else, it would be considered bad manners. I realized how deep-seated these unspoken rules were, since I still followed them blindly, even though no one was watching anymore.

There were no chairs in her studio, so I took off my shoes and sat on the floor by the bed. Amina cut up the cucumbers, tomatoes, radish, and cilantro and then put them in a large salad bowl. She added crushed mint and sprinkled the salad with lemon juice. As I watched her, I realized how comfortable we both felt in silence. I pictured her going through the same motions every day without uttering a word. Slowly, I realized that this apartment was a sanctuary, and that Amina lived her life alone.

When the food was ready, Amina spread a round tablecloth in front of the television and we sat down to eat. She had made a tomato stew with meatballs and potatoes. While we ate, Amina spoke about her family.

"My father was always kind to me, but he agreed with Mother on everything," she said. "And Mother, Mother was just harsh. It was the way she was brought up, you know? And she brought us up the same way. Can't blame her. They just wanted us to get married fast, but then . . . you know . . . they won't let you thread your eyebrows before you graduate! Weird rules, weird people. I never felt like I fit in, so even though things didn't turn out as I planned here in the U.S., I cannot imagine going back there."

"So, you are happy you live here?" I asked.

"I am, and I'm not," she began. "I'm kind of lonely, but I have my freedom."

I wondered what she meant by freedom. It was a term that Arash threw around a lot. They all seemed to mean something abstract by this word, a nuanced concept that meant something important, but I could not grasp it yet.

"I bike to work. I wear what I want. I eat what I want," Amina elaborated. "But I do a lot of these things by myself, which isn't so much fun. Anyways, I am glad you are here. You remind me of my younger sister, always thinking about something, not really talking, watching the world with those big, thoughtful eyes of yours."

"I'm not always quiet because I am thinking. Sometimes, I keep quiet because I don't know what to say," I said. I was a little annoyed that Amina kept prescribing some qualities to me that just vaguely reminded her of her sister. "This food is great! I mean, it is very good, full of flavor and not dry. Last time I enjoyed food so much was at Anna's house, when she made bagel and salmon sandwiches."

"*Nush!*" Amina said. "Thank God you're a better eater than a talker. I hate people that leave food in their plate. Plus, you know the story, right? If you want your husband to be handsome, you can't leave food on the plate."

"Amina, you haven't been back home for too long. That joke is so old, even my Nana forgot about it. Can't your sister share some of the fresh stuff?" I said and Amina giggled.

After we were done eating, Amina brought out a large copper tray, picked up all the dishes and silverware, and headed to the kitchen to make tea, refusing to let me do the dishes. As she filled up the teapot with water and poured loose tea leaves into it, my temples tightened, and a strong headache covered me like a landslide.

"Do you happen to have Advil?" I asked.

"What is it? Headache?" she responded.

"Yeah, I get these headaches almost every day. It's the cigarette smoke at the office . . . it gives me this excruciating headache that won't go away on its own—even when I am not there it comes. I live off of Advil."

"Cigarette smoke? Don't you work in a medical office? They smoke inside?" she asked.

"Yeah, they do, all day long, and the patients don't ever say anything."

"What a hole in the wall! Seriously?" she asked, handing me a glass of water and two orange pills.

I swallowed the pills and took a seat on the chair behind the desk, laying my head flat on the desk and wrapping my hands around it, and fell into a deep sleep. When I awoke, I found myself lying on her bed in my clothes. The headache was finally gone. Amina was sitting on the floor and flipping through the channels. She turned around and smiled.

"Good morning, sunshine!" she said.

"Is it morning already?" I jumped up on the bed, suddenly alert.

"No, it's evening," she said, a grave expression on her face. "Hey, we need to get you a different job. I'm not going to let you ruin your health in that hole. Listen. Tomorrow morning, I'll talk to Farah, the dentist I work for, and see if I can get you a part-time job on Wednesdays. You need to get out of that optical store. We have another doctor who comes in on Wednesdays, so we need help. And it's easy—I'll teach you. Nothing to worry about! Dr. Shafaei can be tough, but inside she is a nice person. Plus, you're smarter than me, so you'll learn faster. I'm the wood-head." She tapped her head.

Amina brought the copper tray with tea, slivered lemons, and baklava, and we shared it while watching a movie. I noticed that Amina sat on the floor, hugging her knees, just like I did all those days and nights when my silent torturer wouldn't ease his grip around my neck. I liked her sincere and contagious laugh, and her unapologetic directness.

I could not fall asleep that night. In the still darkness of Amina's studio, I watched the shadows of trees move across the ceiling, letting my thoughts wander. I missed the familiarity of my room, its pinkish walls and the hundreds of eyes staring at me from the picture collage I'd finally hung up on the wall. I missed the quiet presence of my mother and Rufat in the adjacent rooms and the awareness that I would wake up in the same apartment with them. Having survived the separation from those I loved in Baku, I could never imagine that life would ever push me even further away from my immediate family.

What would it feel like to walk on the streets knowing that no one waits for you at home? I thought. *How does one measure the meaning of life without people in it?* The gap that had grown inside me since our departure had shrunk only a little after nine long months in the U.S. These thoughts of life in solitude frightened me.

No way, I thought. *Whatever I do, I must stick with Mother and Rufat.* A few minutes later, my troubled thoughts were interrupted by slumber, and eventually I gave in to sleep.

CHAPTER 33

. . . .

SEASONS A-CHANGING

I woke up to a high-pitched whistle of the teapot and found Amina fixing breakfast, her face serious. I pulled on my baggy jeans and fixed my messy hair. Since the studio was tiny, the heat of all the cooking made it hot inside. I walked up to the window and tried to open it but couldn't figure out how to work the window lock. I wrestled with it for a few minutes until it finally gave in.

"We have the same stubborn locks at Oakton," I said. "Mmmm, it smells so good, Amina! What are you cooking there?"

Now that the cold air poured into Amina's artful studio, the smell of melted butter and eggs intensified. I heard my stomach growl.

"Eggs, Azeri style!" she exclaimed. "With real butter, tomatoes, onions, and peppers!"

"Well, that makes it Turkish style," I noted.

"Sure, you smart ass!" she said.

When the food was ready, Amina laid out the same round tablecloth on the floor and brought a large copper tray with tiny round plates with typical Turkish breakfast appetizers—pitted black olives, heavy cream mixed with honey, almond and cashew butter, an assortment of string cheese and feta, and a large copper pan with *menemen*—tomato and pepper scramble. Amina carefully split the contents of the pan in half, poured the steamy omelet mixture onto my plate, and handed me the fresh *tandir* bread. We attacked the scramble with ferocity, tearing off small pieces of bread, dipping them into the hot mixture, and picking up chunks with these pieces, just the same way we'd enjoy this buttery meal at roadside breakfast places miles away from Baku, on our way to some family wedding in the mountains.

We spent the next thirty minutes munching on olives, drinking hot cardamom tea, and nibbling on nut butters, honey, and cream. Even though I enjoyed my time with Amina, I was anxious and impatient to leave Lincoln Park with its clusters of houses, coffee shops, and vintage decor, and get back to my little town of Skokie with its streets that all looked like one another. I wondered why the idea of living on your own, so appealing initially, turned out to be so melancholic and cold in real life. I looked around, desperately search-ing for hints, convinced that the answer to this question was the lost key to regaining happiness in this new life. It seemed as if the answer must be nearby, hovering around my head, hidden in piles of Amina's love-infused artwork lying abandoned on the desk in the corner.

It suddenly hit me! The answer was lying in front of me all along: people! This world was devoid of the faces that we took for granted back home. People who were too loud, too nosy, too opinionated, too involved with your love life, people who knew no boundaries. You never felt fully understood in the company of these people, but you also never felt lonely, because they simply did not leave you alone. Amina's place was a picture-perfect world full of color-coordinated objects that only suggested emotions, while our mess of a world never spared enough time for color-coordination or design and was made to accommodate the feelings of hundreds of people. And these were people of all kinds—sellers of fruits and vegetables at the entrance into each courtyard, owners of tiny beauty parlors, neighbors, distant relatives inherited from parents and acquired through marriages, friends from childhood, their children, and the children of their children.

When you were with all these people, you felt overwhelmed because every aspect of your life was constantly invaded by their unsolicited opinions. It was *suffocation by love*. You often dreamed of getting away from them, but as it turns out their absence was not as liberating as you would expect. It was a beautiful but often lonely place.

Amina stepped out of her apartment to call the doctor and returned in a few minutes. I braided my hair and checked my cell phone for any missed calls from Mother. Since this was the only phone we had and she was going to call from the neighbor's phone, I had nowhere to call or text her.

"She said you can stop by on Wednesday to meet her and Dr. Goodman," Amina said, closing the door behind her.

"What? Really, Amina? Oh wow . . . This *coming* Wednesday?"

"Yeah, what's the issue? Just tell your Assyrians you have something to do that day. She wants to interview you first," she said calmly. "Do you have school on Wednesdays?"

"No, it's only on Tuesdays and Thursdays, but what will I tell them?" I asked. "I don't want to lie."

"Say you have a dental appointment," she laughed.

When it came time for me to leave, I thanked Amina for a great weekend, took my bag, and headed back to the train station. It was a good feeling to get back home to Mother and Rufat, to my pink-walled room, to the sticky notes on my desk and my heavy textbooks, to a place I called my own. An hour later, I got out of the warm Skokie Express train and took the stairs down to the parking lot, passing by a large Starbucks coffee shop that resembled a hunter's cabin with its seven large columns and large terrace, and made a right. The long-awaited spring was advancing on Illinois soil. My cheeks were warm from the rays of the sun and the air was filled with a pleasant chirping of birds. Seasons were a-changing.

CHAPTER 34

. . . .

THE NECESSARY LIE

For the next two days, I tried to push away the stubborn anxiety about my interview with Dr. Shafaei, but thoughts would ambush me unexpectedly while I filled out forms or flipped through old dusty prescription records at the optical. The parallels between the outdated world of the Iraqis and my life in Baku served as a safety cushion, a midway world that was stuck between the shiny, polished, yet cold reality of America and the faded, laid back, familiar charm of the Orient. I couldn't understand why leaving this place, even for just a day, felt so much worse than just getting a part-time job. It felt more like a betrayal, like a kid who decided to abandon his family and run away. It was easier to deal with the headaches and smoke and that bissma, than to take a leap and look for another job. *Why can't life just slow down a bit?* I wondered. *Enough with the wild ride!*

Switching to Amina's dental office meant working in a clean medical office with spotless facilities, staffed by people who had polished manners and a doctor with sky-high expectations. It also meant daily interaction with Americans, the necessity of speaking in a language that didn't seem awkward and foreign—but how could I erase the cultural baggage that I had accumulated in the tone of my voice, or the noticeable accent that made my English coarse and clumsy? How could I learn to put on that perfect smile and conceal the hundreds of tiny alarms that went off inside my head every time I spoke?

The morning before the interview, after class was over, Arash proposed getting some fresh air by the weeping willows pond and "talking about it." I felt apathetic but unable to object. We spent the first fifteen minutes walking around the pond and watching the brown ducks flapping their wings and preening their pretty necks by the water. The air was still cold.

"What if she is an old, grumpy woman that will yell at me all the time?" I said, taking the little Advil bottle out of my backpack and swallowing two pills.

"You have a headache?"

"Yes," I lied. I was beginning to feel anxious again.

"If she's ugly and mean," he said, smiling, "then you can quit and go back to the old grumpy Iraqis who yell at each other all the time. Look, you will progress at the dental office—so far, you haven't learned much in that optical store besides a few phrases in Assyrian. And you're ruining your health!"

I sat by the weeping willows and watched the rippling circles adorn the surface of the pond and rehearsed the lie I had to tell Ashur about the dental appointment on Wednesday. I kept repeating the words in my head all throughout my bus ride to work, adjusting the tone and pitch of my voice, choosing alternative words, and practicing how I would tilt my head to the right as I spoke. I knew I was drawn to the Iraqis and their shop because there I could catch my breath before leaping into the jungle of the outside world. The old dusty rules of the East still had a hold there, keeping me safe and unharmed. I knew I had to get outside eventually, but weeks would pass, and the outside world remained a cold, foreign place, like a magic mirror shining a light on all your imperfections.

When I got to the optical shop that afternoon, I didn't want to wait any longer and told Ashur about the appointment immediately. The prep work paid off, as Ashur, sitting in his usual position with his back pressed against the chair and his legs crossed, blurted out, "No p-p-problemo, Mariski!" without even turning his head. I sighed with relief, pride and guilt mixing strangely inside my inflamed conscience. Then, suddenly:

"What d-d-doctor you going to?" he said.

No matter how simple, I hadn't expected a follow-up, so his question caught me off guard.

"D-dentist," I stuttered.

"Ha!" he replied, suddenly turning around with his whole body, lowering his voice and looking straight into my eyes. He always made that impression before he was going to say something important.

"Listen, you need m-m-money?" he asked.

"Oh no, Ashur, but thank you!" I said. "Thank you so much—I am okay."

It was obvious that he mistook my anxiety for a fear of the dentist. He got up from his chair and walked slowly towards my desk, his shiny shoes producing a pleasant tapping. Ashur placed his right palm on my shoulder, lowered his face so that his reading glasses didn't obstruct his view, and said in his cigarette-coarse voice:

"Mariski, if you need anything, you c-c-come to me, okay?" he said. "You need money, you need a ride, you need to b-b-buy something. Okay? Okay? You come to Ashur! I don't want shy, I don't want you t-t-talk like this, in this voice like that. You know what I mean? Speak up!" He laughed a laugh that turned into a cough. "What happened, Mariski? A cat ate your voice or something? Ha!" He burst into a roaring laugh. "I know you g-g-go through a lot. You c-c-come here. You so young! How old are you?"

"I am nineteen."

"Ooh! Too young! Too young! What am I going to do with you? Ha, ha, ha. Mariski, you listening to me? You need help, what you do? You c-c-come to me!"

"Thank you, Ashur. Thank you," I said.

"Of course! Of course, Mariski! We are f-f-family. Not *like! Family!*"

After Ashur's heartfelt monologue was over, he went to the back of the shop, poured himself another cup of coffee, spilling some on his shoes and spitting out his usual "*Pieceashit!*" Then he took his seat by the coffee table.

The sun slowly disappeared behind the clouds, erasing the subtle signs of spring and thrusting us back into unwelcoming cold. I sat in my chair, my elbow pressed on the desk and my palm supporting my chin, and inspected the bitten nails on my left hand—a nasty result of all the worrying for the past two days. Then I looked at Ashur. His body formed a straight line supported by the chair at exactly two points. He straightened his legs and placed one on top of the other, quivering them right and left nonstop. His hair was carefully combed back and covered with glistening gel, and a double chin had come out as a result of his strange sitting position. Ashur drove me home that evening. I sat in his car and looked out, feeling both relieved and a little guilty for not being discovered. *How strange it is that you can live side by side with so many other people, pass by all these buildings, see the clouds move about their head, and yet be entirely consumed by thoughts that are inside of you,* I thought.

Now that the dreaded conversation was behind us, I suddenly noticed the rushing pedestrians, heard the tweeting of the birds, and observed how the leaves swayed with the wind. I was not at ease, yet the burden of a necessary lie had been lifted.

. . . .

CHAPTER 35

THE BEAUTIFUL EYES
OF DR. SHAFAEI

That Wednesday, I showed up at Vision Express Optical earlier than usual to finish all the paperwork in advance. At eleven, Arash picked me up from the store to drive me to Lincoln Park. I dropped my heavy bag into the back seat and felt relieved that I wouldn't have to endure the long commute of two buses and a train to Lincoln Park. Youel and Shammoun stepped out to the shop front, their hands on their waist, their eyes scanning Arash and his car. We waved at them and drove off.

On our way, I found myself marveling at Arash's attention to detail when it came to his looks. His black curly hair was spiked up in a fashionable manner and his cleanly shaven face had a satin shine. I enjoyed watching him when he was preoccupied with something other than me, almost wishing I could be invisible, only so I could study the way he shuffled the songs on his old CD player, took a sip of water, and tapped the steering wheel with his fingers.

A light rain began to drizzle outside, leaving elaborate traces on the car window. I looked outside and noticed the row of colorful clusters of two-story houses lined up in the distance. We were in Park West, a neighborhood just north of Lincoln Park. The street crowd was peppered with familiar rebellious fashion statements of green and purple hair, colorful beanies, fingerless gloves, and vintage saddlebags. Bunches of plump pigeons crowded the sidewalks, occasionally fighting over yesterday's muffin.

Dr. Shafaei's office was in a six-story gray building with a semicircular glass entrance. The words "Resurrection Healthcare: St. Joseph Hospital" were plastered on the facade that faced the intersection. Leaving Arash and his car behind with a quick goodbye, I entered the revolving glass door and inhaled the smell that filled all hospitals in the world—a strange mix of ointments and disinfectants and pills. The lobby was filled with incoming and outgoing patients, some on foot and others in wheelchairs, and nurses who lurked in between the sliding doors of the offices. Despite the natural light pouring into the lobby through the glass entrance, the fancy couches in the waiting area, and the light blue suspended ceiling, this place still had an unwelcoming atmosphere, as if illnesses of all sorts still peeked their ugly heads out from every corner of the lovely decor. Still, compared to medical offices that I had unfortunately needed to visit back home, this place looked like a fancy hotel glistening with freshness. I felt slightly overwhelmed with the intoxicating, charming hygiene of this place, so much so that I threw myself a quick glance in the first reflective surface I passed, wondering if I was clean enough to be here.

When I walked in, there was no one at the front desk, so I had a moment to look around. The waiting area was small, with four armchairs, a slim coffee table in the middle, and a large window with blinds. The walls were painted a pale yellow that gave a summery hue to the light that poured in. There was a tall magazine rack on the wall. Just when I was done inspecting the place, a short receptionist with shiny hair and small eyes approached the reception window.

"Good afternoon, can I help you?" she asked.

"Yes, I am here to see Dr. Shafaei and Amina."

"Do you have an appointment?" she asked, glancing at the computer.

"No, I came to talk to her about a—" I stuttered, "—a job."

"Oh, I see. Let me get Amina."

Amina showed up a moment later. Somehow, she was able to maintain that same serious look in her eyes while her lips formed a smile—two personalities living side-by-side in one person.

"Hey, did you get here all right?" she asked, without waiting for the answer. "Let's go to the back office and I'll give you a pair of scrubs and shoes. You wear size eight shoe, right?"

"It's actually nine," I said, always a little embarrassed by my man-sized feet. "Why do I need scrubs today? Didn't you say she will talk to me first?" I asked.

"We need help today—if you start working right away, she'll see that you are eager to help! Makes sense?"

"Yes, kind of . . ." I said and followed Amina to the back.

"These are my old scrubs—I washed them yesterday. There is a little stain on the pants from bleach, but this will do for now. We'll get you new ones soon!" she said.

I changed into the scrubs and wanted to put on the shoes Amina got for me, but they were one size too small, so I stayed in my sneakers. When I passed by one of the dental rooms, I saw Dr. Shafaei hunching over an elderly patient with graying hair and wrinkly skin. The doctor had shiny brown hair with red highlights.

Her face was young and beautiful, nothing like I had imagined. She had light hazel, almost orange-colored eyes that were accentuated with eyeliner that she must have applied every day because it was done to perfection. Her desk was covered with unopened mail, dental brochures, supply catalogues, magazines, stapled sheets of paper, and patient files. I took a seat in the visitor chair and looked outside the window into the sea of commercial buildings, high-rises, and scattered greenery.

There was nothing else to do in those moments awaiting my future employer, other than to take a moment and enjoy the vacuum between the past and the future. I was back at my game of images—the midnight drive to the airport in my uncle's car, the wet cloth on my mother's hypertonic forehead, the dusty optical with three arguing, elderly Assyrians, the sudden appearance of Eric, which started a feverish crush in my misery-stricken, depressed soul, the cold verdict of the registrar's "we cannot accept you at this time," the cardamom smell of Persian tea served by a tall, dark Persian with contagious happiness, the silhouette of Mother sitting by the window and looking out with millions of worries going through her head, and now the piercing honey-hazel, almost orange stare of Dr. Shafaei's captivating eyes.

"Here we go," the doctor said, breaking the silence. "Very nice to meet you. My name is Farah Shafaei. You can call me Dr. Shafaei."

"Hi, Dr. Shafaei," I almost murmured.

I don't quite remember what else she told me during our five-minute conversation, because the whole time I was marveling at the lines on her face—the elegant arch of her eyebrows, the black swoop of her eyeliner, her thin but feminine lips with light brown lipstick, and the attractive curvature of her chin. Hers wasn't just a beautiful face. It spoke of an elegance and strength that was worthy of admiration. She wore a wide-sleeved doctor's robe, but I could see that she was quite slim. She suggested I follow Amina today and watch her closely.

"Do you have a Social Security number?"

"No, but I do have a tax ID." I had learned to say this when asked about a Social Security card, which just wouldn't come in the mail.

"Good, that makes things easier. Let me talk to my accountant, and I'll let you know through Amina. If it all works out, we'll need your help on Wednesdays. We have Dr. Goodman on Wednesdays, and you will be assisting her and maybe helping out with the front desk."

"Sure," I replied, wondering what else I could say to her. "Do you have a book that I can read on dentistry?"

She seemed impressed with my question and turned to look at the tall bookshelf to her right. "This should be a good start. If you have questions, you can ask me or Amina. She said you are very smart!"

Of course, Amina just keeps saying that! I thought to myself. The dentist stepped out of the office without saying anything else. I got up and went searching for Amina, two conflicting feelings grabbing at my throat—my instant infatuation with the radiating beauty of the doctor and an overwhelming feeling of being a foreigner in this place. The rooms were full of curious medical objects, paper cups, strips of inked paper, strange plastic x-ray holders of different colors, gauze pads, Q-tips, and impression guns.

The patients who frequented this establishment looked as sanitized as the place itself, in their custom-cut suits with leather briefcases, rolled newspaper under their arms, and paper cups of coffee in their hands. The women wore clothes in pastel colors. And just like their outfits, I noticed an unfamiliar subtlety in their emotions, or lack thereof. Their greetings and smiles were exaggerated, yet devoid of the unspoken warmth and familiarity that I could recognize so well. I nodded in response and uttered the absolute minimum to hide my anxiety, disappearing from their sight as fast as I could.

Suddenly, I became aware of my long black hair, braided and reaching down to my waist, somehow announcing to the world how foreign I was here. My skin suddenly appeared much darker than theirs, my body not slender enough for the light-blue scrubs that I borrowed from Amina, and my bulky sneakers adding a final touch to how ridiculous and out of place I felt at Blue Dental. This sense of not fitting in eventually morphed into almost physical discomfort, which my body tried to get rid of through cold sweat and heart palpitations.

I spent the day watching Amina as she opened the drawers, grabbed tubes with composite material, squeezed out a little of the creamy substance, mixed it with a spatula, and then handed it to Shafaei at the right moment. It seemed as if her body and mind were perfectly tuned to receive unspoken messages from Farah. Their two sets of hands seemed to be locked in a mysterious whirling dance, bound by an unbreakable magic spell with no room for error. They effortlessly exchanged objects, rinsed and suctioned the patient's mouth, and used up three pouches of sterilized instruments.

What a world, I thought. I felt both mesmerized and discouraged, convinced that I could never learn *that*. I could never pass on instruments like a card dealer and predict Dr. Shafaei's steps like Amina did. Yet she hired me. Closer to the end of the day, she asked Amina if nine dollars an hour would be a suitable hourly rate for me. That meant almost ninety dollars each Wednesday, almost as much as I made in a week at the optical. Amina didn't ask what my decision was. She knew I wasn't in a position to turn down money like that. When all the rooms were cleaned with disinfectant wipes, the chairs raised with their water and suction cups and lamps, and instruments carefully placed into the dental autoclave, I walked into Dr. Shafaei's office to say goodbye.

"Dr. Shafaei, I am leaving for today," I said.

"Oh Maryam, come take a sit for a few moments," she said. "Or do you have to go? Is someone waiting downstairs?"

"I have a few minutes," I said.

"Sit down, we didn't get to talk much," she said, her face now relaxed. "Wednesdays are so crazy, as you can see. So, you're here with your mom and brother, right?"

"Correct. We moved in June of last year. We live in Skokie," I said.

"And what do you do? Do you go to school? Your English is so good! You don't even have that much of an accent." She extended me a handful of almonds.

"Yes, I go to Oakton Community College. Taking general course-work. I go on Tuesdays and Thursdays."

"Good! Very good! Any definite plans for future education?" she asked. "Or you haven't decided yet?"

"Back home, I wanted to become a doctor. Now, I haven't decided yet. I like all the classes that I take," I said and then thought it was probably a silly thing to say.

"And you've worked at an optical store and now here. Hardworking and driven!" she said. "And a little shy! Well, what can I say, Maryam? This is what it takes to make it here. It's difficult in the beginning, but you can rest assured, the hard work will pay off in the long run."

Frankly, I was getting tired of getting this line from everyone. The hardest part for me was not working or studying. It was patch-ing up the hole inside, the hole made up of lost family, relatives, uncles, aunts, neighbors, and the million sounds of the city that had apparently inhabited my soul for years. I suddenly felt tired and ready to go home.

"I don't think any of this is difficult. I learn fast," I said, somehow feeling brave enough to.

All this time Farah had been writing something hastily in a large black book. She raised her eyes and smiled.

"Well, how do you spell your first name and last name, Maryam?"

Farah copied my name and then carefully ripped off a piece of paper from the black leather book.

"You earned this today," she said, handing me a check.

"Oh, thank you, Doctor. I didn't expect a paycheck today. I didn't really do much work."

"I value the time you spent here," she said. "And besides, training is also work. Have a good evening."

I took the yellow check with my name on it and said goodbye. Even though I had no idea how to cash the check, a childish contentment took over me. I wanted to hop and dance and showcase my check to everyone around me. As I was leaving the office, the short receptionist, whose name turned out to be Olivia, finally smiled at me, perhaps sensing the positive air that filled my lungs. As I waited for the elevator, I marveled at the emerging Chicago skyline from the tall window. It seemed as if the whole city was celebrating my victory tonight. My fears and doubts disappeared even if for one evening, leaving me hopeful and proud.

. . . .

CHAPTER 36

A THIN WHITE ENVELOPE

I found Mother and Rufat in a cheerful mood that evening, all because of a thin white envelope with a greenish paper inside, which turned out to be an invitation for a fingerprint appointment. Our application had been received by United States Citizenship and Immigration Services and was being processed. Mother's eyes glistened with hope that our family was slowly moving in the right direction. She scrambled beef frankfurters with eggs in a rich butter and we munched on them with yesterday's bread, taking turns looking over the light green paper with our date, time, and the address of our appointment.

After we finished our dinner, Mother brewed a fresh pot of tea. The sweet smell of cinnamon filled our pink kitchen and mixed with the overwhelming aroma of cardamom. Rufat kept dipping pieces of bread into the buttery remains in the pan.

"Think we can get there by bus?" Mother asked. "I don't want to bother Teymour with this stuff all the time."

"You can get anywhere by bus in this city," Rufat interrupted. "You both should know that by now." He was still dipping the bread into the pan.

"Rufat, are you still hungry?" Mother asked. "Stop beating that dead horse. Nothing left in that pan. If you're still hungry, I can make you a sandwich with cheese."

"That is factually not true," he said. "But I won't say no to a sandwich!"

"Mother, you know, I am sure Arash will be happy to give us a ride, too," I said.

In fact, I realized that Arash would insist on taking us until we all agreed to it. He had somehow managed to become my mother's favorite in such a short time. His gallantry and manners had their charm and Mother's aristocratic roots took over. She thought the world of Arash, and in all honesty, he was truly a gentleman. When we went somewhere together, he'd phone Mother and tell her when he would bring me back home, and then he'd come get me from the door instead of calling or just honking. He would speak slowly with her, making sure she understood his every word, and patiently waited while she answered in her basic English.

"If your mother spoke English fluently," he would say, "she'd run for president of this country and, trust me, she'd win."

"Sweet talker!" I'd say, but deep inside I knew he was right. Just like him, Mother was a world-class diplomat, infatuating those around her with her melodic voice, her wit, and her green eyes. She must have put something in the food she'd cooked because anyone who sat in our small, crowded kitchen, eating Mother's stews, *menemens*, or even eggs with frankfurters, drinking her cardamom-infused tea, had joined a tight-knit circle of supporters who stood by us in those early days of our immigration journey.

"Who's coming over?" I asked, noticing another glass and saucer on the table.

"Teymour is on his way," Mother answered. "I told him about the fingerprints notice."

"Well, guess what," I began. Rufat raised his eyes from the pan. "I got the dental assistant job," I said.

"No way!" Rufat said.

"And that's not all of it," I went on. "I got my first paycheck too!"

"Oh darling, I am so happy to hear it," Mother said. "A nice, clean job and you'll have Amina with you there. I wish we had come here with enough money to avoid all this, but it is what it is. Maybe it's not so bad."

"Mama, it is not bad," Rufat replied. "I wouldn't have it any other way."

Mother smiled, her face wide open and clear of any doubts, like a cloudless sky. There was an untarnished hope glowing in her eyes tonight. No doubts or worries tainted it. Her happiness appeared almost complete. She wrapped her arms around me and Rufat, and for a moment we stayed still, a triangle of heads, a clumsy but sincere embrace that, I realized, was a first for us.

I gulped down my tea, picked up the three empty glasses from the kitchen table, and opened the faucet to wash them, just as someone knocked on the door. Mother opened the door and I heard Teymour's voice in the background.

"The wind picked up," he announced. "So, you got the fingerprint appointment? That is a very good sign." He took the slip of paper from Mother and pored over it.

"You hungry?" Mother asked. "Should I warm up some food?"

"What food? It's nine p.m., Leyla!" he answered. Then, "Well, what do you have?"

Then why do you ask? I thought to myself and smiled. By now, I welcomed his random appearances at our house, his dry, hit-and-miss humor, the way he couldn't pronounce the letter "R," and how he butchered the Russian language after years of not using it.

"Maryam got a job," Mother said, wiping her hands with a kitchen towel.

"What kind of job?" Teymour asked, without lifting his eyes from the paper.

"A dental assistant job!" Rufat answered.

"Oh, so you're leaving the old Assyrian sweatshop?" Teymour joked.

"No, I am not. This is only a once-a-week job," I answered. "I'll work part time at the dental place. The place is in Park West. Remember Amina?"

"Mm-hmm," Teymour mumbled.

"Well, she got me the job," I explained. "She introduced me to the dentist today. It must not be too far from your apartment."

"Seven train stops away on the Red Line," Rufat added. "Did you pass by the Wrigley Field on the way there?"

"Well, not today. Arash took me, but we drove by a large baseball field. Is that what you're talking about? What's special about it?"

"Well, it's the home of the Chicago Cubs," Rufat said. "Baseball, Maryam," he added to clarify. "Stuff you don't get. Never mind!"

"No regrets there, brother," I said.

"Wow, he is right," Teymour said. "It *is* exactly seven train stops away from my place! Nice job, Rufat!" he added. "Maryam, congrats on the job! Impress that lady and land a full-time job there, I'm telling you. Get out of that stinky place."

No matter how much I tried, I could not convey why I felt so at ease in that "stinky place." It was true that the place was out of order, full of smoke, and did not offer much future prospects. On top of that, the smoke was ruining my health. Somehow, the optical store had helped me catch my breath in this leap over the ocean. It had helped me regain balance, because I turned out to not be as brave and ready for this new, unknown world as I would have hoped. I held my thoughts in my heart and nodded in agreement.

Mother poured tea into the one remaining glass on the table, added a spoonful of sugar, and handed it to Teymour. He took the glass and paced around the room, asking random questions and offering the answers on his own. Through his slight sarcasm, I could see that Teymour was both excited and relieved that we received the fingerprint appointment and were progressing, even with baby steps, on our path to independence in this country.

I spent the rest of the evening aimlessly flipping through my psychology textbook. I couldn't help but compare these neat, colorful books to those I'd had back home—black and white, printed on thin, cheap paper, with long, boring texts full of names and dates, illustrations that were impossible to make out, and peppered with historical errors and typos. These books resembled a tabloid magazine with colorful boxes of relevant trivia, pictures of celebrities with interesting facts from their biographies, and quizzes that helped you seal in the newly learned information. These books made studying feel like a pleasant pastime as you traced your finger from page to page, reading each chapter with interest and highlighting the most important sections with a marker. These books inspired me to keep reading on and on, while back home I'd felt driven by the pure fear of getting anything less than an A. It was fear of being anything less than the best that had kept me up all night, working through the same math problems to speed up my pace and reading through boring passages of history books in the hopes of retaining something.

Each time I entered Oakton Community College, I was taken aback by a good feeling. This place, treated so normally and without any excitement by the rest of the students, stood in such stark contrast to all the other places I'd visit during the day—the train stations, the buses, the dust-filled optical with its rundown carpets, rows of brown boxes, and faded posters on the walls. Weeks passed, but I still felt as if I were unwrapping a Christmas present every time

I walked in. The coffee tasted better, the pastries were out of this world, or perhaps, that's how they were to me. I found an indescribable luxury in buying a chocolate cream-cheese muffin and eating it with a cup of coffee in the morning.

"You want the regular? Coffee and a muffin?" the guy at the register would say, and I'd nod.

I'd pick a table by the window, with sunlight coming through, cut the muffin into eight pieces, and savor each one. While I ate, Arash sat across the table, watched me contentedly, whistling a tune, tapping a melody with the tip of his fingers, and leaning back in his chair.

That evening, I thought of all the people back home I would have called to give them the news of the dental assistant job. People who were missing. My grandma and dad would be first on the list, followed by my always grumpy uncle who would spring out of his indifferent mood as fast as he'd succumb to it. All three of them would interrupt me nonstop, asking about some irrelevant details and later incorporating their own half made-up elements into their version of the truth. Yet I would give anything for the ability to pick up the phone and dial them now. While it wasn't impossible, there were more than ten hours of time difference between us. And then, I couldn't properly describe what getting a job meant to me, no matter how hard I tried, because I was not able to put that feeling into words yet. You had to sleep through the cold winter nights, looking out at the wild shadows from the naked branches of trees in a foreign country, miles away from your home, without any idea what the future will bring. You had to hang on to a temporary job that pays for your weekly groceries, hoping for a day when things will come more easily, yet partially understanding that, while things might come in time, they will never come effortlessly again, the way they once did. That is the context you had to understand to feel the same joy we felt over a formal letter and a ninety-dollar weekly paycheck.

. . . .

CHAPTER 37

FIRST TIME FOR EVERYTHING

My job at Blue Dental revolved entirely around assisting Dr. Katie Goodman, a short woman in her thirties with intelligent eyes, a pointy nose, light brown, shoulder-length hair, and infinite patience. Her amusement with how I managed to drop things even when I was just turning around seemed to be stronger than her frustration. Every time I'd drop an instrument on the floor or squeeze out more of the expensive composite material than needed, her lips would form a silent smile and the crow's feet around her eyes became more pronounced. In my hours assisting her, I found out Goodman was the last name of her first husband, whom she had divorced a few years ago but still remained friends with.

I also found out that she was born on January twenty-fourth, which meant her astrological sign was Aquarius, like mine. I clung to this fact as it was, in my mind, the only thing we had in common. Once in a while, I'd bring up random facts about Aquarius to engage her in a conversation, but she always found astrology trivial, which astounded me because I'd spent all my teenage years obsessing over the Chinese horoscope to the point that I could predict a person's sign after speaking to them a little (I was wrong most of the time).

Dr. Goodman came to the office clutching the paperback she was reading. She must have been an avid reader, as the books changed almost every week. There was an air of ease and lightness about her that was contagious. Looking at her, I wondered if one day I could simply wake up and be as cheerful and light as she was. I also wanted to hop into the office with a light paperback in my bag, my hair smelling of shampoo, and my eyes as blue as hers.

Those first few months of spring working at Blue Dental were difficult. I was constantly afraid of making a mistake and angering Dr. Goodman, worrying that I looked out of place with my long braid, thick eyebrows, and accented English. The pace of work never slowed down. There was no time for coffee breaks and even the radio that we turned on in the morning was tuned to a channel supposedly chosen to put the patients at ease. Since Wednesdays were packed with patients who favored the evening hours both doctors offered, there wasn't much time to chat, so I barely had a chance to speak with Amina.

On days when I couldn't concentrate and fell into the clutches of my anxiety, I'd take a few Advil and find refuge in the eyes of our patients. The long periods of idleness afforded by root-canal procedures allowed me to study the eyes of our largely white patients and get lost in their green- and blue- and hazel-colored irises, some adorned with brown dots. Most of them were unaware of my silent gaze and stared straight ahead, flustered by all the drilling and the unpleasant anticipation of sharp pain that would paralyze them any moment now. I found a strange serenity in exploring their eyes. Somehow it did the trick of blotting out the string of mistakes I'd made in the past few months, but most of all it helped me forget where I was. Somewhere in the depth of their eyes, I could hear the long-lost, familiar music of morning teahouses in Baku's Old City. I could smell the morning aromas coming from my grandmother's kitchen, announcing the start of a weekend. I could see the faded sunlight seeping into the large bedroom of our summer house with its thick green carpet and wooden walls. This sweet escape usually ended abruptly with Dr. Goodman's "Maryam, I need the curing light," signaling I had to quickly jump back to reality. Yet I felt grateful for those few moments of solitude.

Before long, I realized that I could not remain in this role of a bad dental assistant forever. I was lucky not to work with Dr. Shafaei on a regular basis, but my endless mistakes, clumsiness, and inability to master the art of assistantship bothered me. I noticed that Olivia, the front desk receptionist, was the only one out of us three who managed to escape regular scolding from both doctors, so I watched her as much as my duties allowed. I wanted to figure out how she did it—how she managed to get on equal footing with Dr. Goodman and Dr. Shafaei. She handed me the answer once, which was much simpler than I expected, as she was developing a set of full-mouth x-rays in the back office. The room was dark, and I could only see the silhouette of her face, long shiny hair, and white teeth.

"If you want to be good, Maryam, you will do everything quickly. You understand?" Olivia said. She picked up the pace with which she unwrapped the film and placed the negatives into the developer. "Even when you don't have to be quick, you get it?" she said. "With these doctors, you have to be two steps ahead and the only way to do that is by being very fast."

And indeed, I noticed how quickly her hands moved as her mouth uttered the words. Her advice kept ringing in my ears for days until I intentionally began to do things quickly, turning it into a contest of some sort. I taught myself to do everything as if I were in a hurry and, contrary to my concerns, none of the quality was lost as a result. I applied this strategy to everything that I did and soon I started seeing incredible results. I got better at handling instruments and dropped fewer and fewer things. During the gaps in assisting, I cleaned the rooms, washed instruments, organized the counters, and prepared the instrument trays for the rest of the day, timing myself with a watch. In my free time, I'd go back to Olivia, watching her speak to the patients, call up insurance companies, and schedule follow-up appointments, soaking up everything that she did, hoping that one day I'd acquire the same polished vocabulary and professional tone that patients appreciated. Dr. Goodman noticed this change soon and even mentioned it to Dr. Shafaei, who'd already been losing hope that I'd live up to Amina's infamous "she's smart and a fast learner" promises.

Olivia lived very far away, in a Hispanic neighborhood south of Park West, and she had to travel for an hour to get to the office. She had a three-year-old daughter named Camilla who looked just like her boyfriend, Oscar. He would show up at the office to drop Olivia off if the weather was bad or to pick her up if we stayed late on Wednesdays. Olivia was always nice and friendly, but she had an air of mistrust about her. Somehow, I could sense that Olivia knew better than to get attached to people. She sounded polished and refined when she spoke with Blue Dental patients, leaving no trace of doubt that she couldn't care less about them. This was her job, a source of income and nothing else.

One Wednesday in May, I came to work earlier than usual. I had just finished changing into my scrubs and was putting together trays with instruments, gauze pads, and floss strings when Olivia and Oscar walked in. It was an hour before the office opened, so she didn't expect me to be there. I wanted to come out and say hi but hung back when I realized they were having a fight. Oscar was holding Olivia by her elbows and hissed something at her in Spanish. Her hair, still slightly wet from the rain, covered her shoulders and her face turned red. She barely raised her voice, but I could sense her anger from afar. They looked like two angry dogs in a fight. Then he suddenly let her elbows go. For a second, it seemed like the whole thing was over. Oscar's hands fell to his sides, and he turned his face away. But then, he made a 180-degree turn and slapped her. *Slap!* For a moment I stood there, watching her hair fly all around as she stumbled back against the entrance door. I stood there in silence. I'd never seen a man hit a woman before. They were both staring at each other. Then Oscar saw me and stormed out of the office. Olivia did not move.

"Let's go to the back," I said, putting my arm around her shoulder.

She didn't acknowledge my presence for a few moments. There were no tears, no despair in her eyes. She rushed to the back office, examining her reddened cheek, checking to see if he'd slapped her hard enough to leave a mark, I guessed. I felt helpless and unsure of what to do so I simply followed her from one room to another, holding her bag and keeping quiet. When heavy makeup was carefully applied to both cheeks and shiny gloss covered her lips, she finally poured herself a fresh cup of coffee—that she'd managed to brew while fixing up her face—and sat down in Dr. Shafaei's chair.

"Well, there is a first time for everything, they say," she said.

I tried to come up with something supportive to say, but the shock had left me speechless. I could still hear the slap. I kept picturing her hair flying around her face like a scarf. I could still see the way she'd taken a step back, her back supported by the door. Finally, I put both my hands on her knees and looked at her, trying to say something with my eyes. She smiled. It was a different kind of smile. I could tell that she knew how clueless I was about the reason for today's fight and about her life in general, but, for the first time, I could see the reflection of my own sympathy and tenderness in Olivia's eyes.

"Maryam, Maryam," she sighed. "What do you know about this world, little Maryam?"

I held her gaze for a moment, but soon the tenderness in her eyes was gone and Olivia Lopez was back at her game of being fast and furious. She quickly scanned today's schedule, flipping through the files of patients.

"Two new patients and four root canals for you, Maryam."

"Yes, another root canal marathon. Don't you just love them?" I tried to joke.

"I don't, but the doctors do. They're nine hundred apiece," she said.

At this moment, Dr. Shafaei stormed into the office and the race against time was officially on. *Do things fast*, I kept repeating, *even if you don't need to*. Amina showed up in a cheerful mood and we went on with our day as usual, greeting and seating patients in comfortable chairs that reclined into almost-horizontal positions. We'd offer them tea or coffee and bring them a variety of magazines so they could busy themselves reading the tabloids while we sterilized a new batch of instruments, developed full-mouth x-rays, and prepared the impression guns.

A few times that afternoon I tried to catch a glimpse of some emotion in Olivia's eyes. Lost in the pace of the crazy day, she did not give herself away. She went on appearing calm and collected as always, but when the sun descended behind the horizon and the office filled with a gentle pink light, I caught a few troubled looks on her face. I could not tell if it was sadness or pain. I could never forget the look of despair in her eyes that afternoon, like a wounded beast, no longer able to maintain her strength, forced to show a sign of weakness. "First time for everything," I could hear in my ears.

CHAPTER 38

. . . .

DOCTORS CAN'T
AFFORD MISTAKES

Arash never said he loved me. In fact, he carefully avoided the topic at all times. But his gentle feelings manifested themselves again and again. They were clear in the corners of his eyes when he watched me eat. They were present when he breathed in and out around me, and when he carried my backpack so carefully, and every time he lowered his voice when pronouncing my name. When it became difficult for him to keep this knowledge to himself, Arash found a way out. He arranged his entire life to shield me from the world, no longer hiding his opinion that the more of me he stole from the world, the better. The world could get by without me, but he could not.

"It's my personal, selfish desire, Maryam," he said. "I need to see you happy."

When he spoke of me, his words and phrases all suggested one thing: He was determined. He was obsessed with coming up with arrangements that would shield me from an endless list of things—rush hour traffic, time spent on hold on the phone inquiring about scholarships, long lines at the bookstore, rude customers at work, Youel and Shammoun and Ashur, and so the list went on and on.

This creation of his, this world stripped of stress and the pitfalls of ordinary life, was a cozy place. It felt familiar and warm and deserved, and I settled in it gladly. He smoothed the rough edges of my existence and convinced me that the world was, again, devoid of any evil.

In this imaginary world, though it did not exist, I did bloom into a version of myself that perhaps I would not have become had it not been for Arash. He seldom paid attention to how I dressed, if I had any makeup on, if I gave any thought to the jewelry that I had on that day. One evening in June, Arash picked me up from the Red Line station, exhausted and still in scrubs, while he wore a tux.

"I had to help out with the catalogue shots," he explained. "So, I thought I'd come pick you up like this!"

"We are quite a match, Arash," I joked. "What do you say?"

"Yeah, I should have grabbed something from the women's section," he joked.

I leaned back in the passenger seat of his impeccably clean Ford, patted down my blue scrubs, and ran my fingers through my hair. My body was tired from nine hours of hunching over patients, handing off instruments, shuffling between rooms to get them ready for the next patient, and occasionally answering the phone in the hallway. I smiled the way you smile when you turn on the light in your house after a long trip. Arash was *home* to me. I felt good at home.

"You look tired, Maryam," he said looking at me. "I wish you knew how tired and how beautiful you look."

In those moments of physical exhaustion, I also recognized a subtle internal change, a different kind of look, when you completely surrender to work because it must be done for reasons that are vague and stretch out into the future. In those moments, I stopped caring if my eyeliner was smudged and if small pink patches of ChapStick remained on my lips. Looking into the mirror, I also saw serenity that softened the lines on my face, as if beauty had finally settled in now that I no longer cared to keep up with it. Those evenings Arash would trace my face with his index finger, brush the tips of my fingers with his lips. Our friendship had long since become romantic, but we both kept quiet about it.

On Fridays, after work, we'd drive to Wilmette beach, park the car across from the water, and listen to music. Sometimes, we sat and looked into the abyss where water and sky became one. I'd think about the parallel life in which I'd never come here, I'd never had to work so hard, I'd never broken out of the protective shell that my father created for us, and I'd never become addicted to those little green pills. Arash sat opposite me and did not utter a word, with the same reassuring look in his eyes. The rolling waves of the water unbuckled the hinges in my soul. Some days I cried quiet, silent tears about a vague feeling of missing something that I could no longer remember, but also could not forget. Other days I smiled and joked, tucking away anything nostalgic. No matter what came in these moments of solitude by the lake, Arash welcomed them, the way only he could.

One warm evening at the end of spring, Arash proposed going to the movies to watch *Alexander the Great*. He showed up in front of my house in his old Ford Taurus, wearing jeans, a pullover, and a leather jacket, his hair shiny and his face matte from a fresh shave. By now, I was accustomed to how much attention he paid to his looks and so I wore a pleated skirt with a blouse and a jacket. It was the only jacket I had, and it didn't really match the rest of my outfit, but there was nothing else to wear.

A light breeze ruffled the leaves on the trees and spread a sweet scent of the approaching summer and with it the assurance that life was good. I greeted Arash with a kiss on the cheek and off we went to the Old Orchard Mall with the windows down and the wind in our hair. The ticket line was long. We took a spot and went on exchanging silly jokes and soaking up the sun when his phone rang. It was a colleague from Carson Pirie Scott.

"Hey man, how are you?" Arash said. "Oh, those suits came in on Tuesday. They're not on the floor yet." The guy on the phone went on, saying something about the new batch of suits that had just arrived, and while he was at it, Arash snatched the moment in time. He pulled me closer with his left arm and kissed the top of my head. A swift and gentle kiss. It was a kiss of claiming, a sure and confident kiss. I leaned in and nestled my head between his chin and his throat. This was the place where I felt most welcome. Now, years later, when I look back at our time together, I always find myself in that moment. So unplanned, so sincere, so timeless.

We drove to Wilmette beach after the movie, took off our shoes, and walked on the beach, our feet touching the cool water of Lake Michigan.

"I get it that they're not fans of history in Hollywood, but to get an Ethiopian guy to play Cyrus the Great?" Arash asked, indignant.

"You're right. It was kind of ridiculous," I agreed.

"There are three million Persians living in Los Angeles and they couldn't even get the language right!" he went on. "I mean, you know you can take the driver's license exam in Persian in L.A.? That's how widespread the language is over there. Idiots!"

"Screw it! I'm sure they got Alexander the Great wrong too." I tried to cheer him up.

"But you saw it, right?" he said. "The audience was having a blast. They loved it!"

"Well, it was quite entertaining! I mean, the fights," I explained.

"Maryam!" he said and laughed.

"All right, all right!" I said and laughed too. "It was dumb."

Frankly, I didn't care much about the movie. I was taken up by the summer warmth finally taking over the city and the humid air of the lakeside and the happiness that spills out everywhere inside of you during the beginning stages of a love affair, when every word and gesture is drenched in magic. Arash, on the other side, was pre-occupied by deconstructing all the historical errors of the movie. I noticed that these inconsistencies truly hurt his feelings, so I put a grave expression on my face and held his hands as he spoke. When he was finally done, he smiled again and got up from the sand. We continued our walk hand-in-hand, in silence.

When I think back to the time we spent together, I am surprised by how much of it we spent in silence, looking around or into each other's eyes, and by how little we spoke of our feelings, how we found ways of expressing them through unrelated comments and glances. I wonder if anyone will ever love me in a way that makes words unnecessary as Arash once did. That evening, right before we made one last circle around the shore, he suddenly broke the silence and spoke about his feelings.

He walked a few steps ahead and turned towards me.

"I cannot tell where these emotions are taking me, Maryam," he said. "The only thing I know is I am going a hundred miles an hour on an empty highway, and I am unable to slow down." He paused. "Do you know what I mean?"

"I think so," I answered.

A veil of worry came over his face. Back then I couldn't under-stand the reason for the heaviness in his voice or that veil over his eyes.

"Surgeons," he added suddenly

"What about them?" I asked. I had no idea where he was going with this.

"They cut you open to save you, to operate on your wound or take out a tumor. Then when they're done with their thing, they close up the wound. They suture you up and off you go." He looked at the waves. The evening was falling, and the air was humid.

"We can make mistakes in life, but surgeons can't afford them," he said. "Because if they do, nobody is there to correct them."

I knew what he was talking about. Hadn't Mother bet on a surgeon to amputate her heartbreak, so she could come to this country and seek a life free from painful memories? The surgery was done, but the wound kept hurting and there was no way to fix that mistake. I knew what Arash meant. All of this could end, like many good things end prematurely, falling victim to jealousies or simply going wrong. However, on that beautiful day when the sky had an indigo hue and the waves broke out in pure white by the shore, it was hard to picture how anything could go wrong. We both felt happy, but I could see a crack in his heart, a fear that this could end, that the doctor might make a mistake when operating on his heart, a mistake that no one, not even me, could correct.

CHAPTER 39

WILL YOU BE
MY PREY TONIGHT?

It was a sunny afternoon. I finished filling out the public aid forms and picked up the green box with names of patients who called about their glasses. Ashur would write their names on a Post-It and leave it in the box. I would then go through a printed report that we received along with the glasses and check if the name was in there. Ashur numbered the boxes and so I'd go through it, checking each individually wrapped frame to find the name of the caller. It was amazing how many of them never showed up for their glasses. Since the glasses were free and you could always reorder another pair, our patients were not really careful with them, but then, many of our patients were kids, and kids are not careful with anything. Piles of brown boxes with glasses that had never been picked up by their owners stood to the left of the front shop counter, like a leaning tower of Pisa. I went on with my task.

Sanjay Gothana
Preety Gupta
Sandeep Kaur

I read the name and realized I recognized Sandeep. I remembered her subtle beauty, her thin wrists, and the hint of green in her eyes, a familiar shyness. She barely needed the glasses, her vision was almost 20/20. She came in with her mother, a tall woman of similar beauty, same olive oil skin and the green Kashmiri eyes. The glasses were free as long as you needed them, and inhabitants of the Devon neighborhood seemed to be deeply drawn to that word. If it was free, it must be acquired. It must become theirs. I was no different in that sense, hunting for free stuff, but soon I resented this impatience with the world and the desire to own everything there was to claim. I picked out the frame, wrapped it in a slip with her name on it, checked the birthday to confirm it was hers, and placed the pair into the pick-up box. I tried to think of another task to pass the time, but decided I was too lazy. So, I sat at my desk and took out my sketch book and started on another rose in a glass. In those moments of idleness, I'd developed a habit of drawing a single rose in a glass of water. There were several of them now taped to the wall in front of me.

It was just me and Ashur at the shop. Shammoun and Youel were out somewhere. I enjoyed the silence, the hum of the city, the occasional siren sweeping through town. I liked registering the calm inside, then contrasting it with the anxiety I felt in those early days when I had just started working. For a moment, sitting at my desk, my rose drawing in front of me, a workday about to finish, life felt good.

Then it all ended abruptly. My memory blocked some details, but not all. Those that were not destroyed by it still haunt me. I can still feel the touch of Ashur's square hands on my bare back and my blood runs cold. I recall the few seconds it took me to understand what was happening, as I tried to look for answers and found none. I felt his weight against my body, his right hand grabbing my jaw, and his lips pressed on my cheek, then my lips. That stupid shock, like that of caught prey, paralyzed me, which he might have interpreted as a sign to go on.

I tried to scream, but my mouth was mute, my strength leaving my body. He pushed himself closer and pressed his lips to mine. I felt the cold and humiliating touch of his lips—his wet and mine dry, dead. My arms were dangling loose. My mind, in a submissive way, chose to focus on the texture of his lips, their revolting pressure on mine, the repulsing heat emanating from his body. I attempted to push back, but my arms and limbs were devoid of strength. *Why? Why do my arms feel so loose, my legs powerless, my consciousness arrested?*

Then, something revolted inside me. Suddenly, I turned into a wild animal, shrieking and screaming, fighting to survive. I managed to push him away and saw a strange surprise in his puzzled face. Something like a shriek of a wounded animal escaped my mouth, but all I was able to say was "Don't!"

I had taken a few steps back towards the back office, but I stumbled and fell. My legs were somehow too weak to get back up, so I crawled my way to the back door, when I felt his grip in my hair. As I felt the burning in my scalp, my nails dug deeper into the surface of the tile. For a second, he let go of my hair and I tried to get up and run. There were only a few steps to the door. It was locked, I knew, but I kept crawling. He grabbed me with both hands and picked me up from the floor. I spat in his face and saw a spark of anger light up in his eyes. I felt a passing victory, but it took only a second for him to slap me and I collapsed in the corner. He fixed his rimless glasses and wiped the spit away. He began to take steps towards the corner where I crouched. His steps were slow, determined.

Then, suddenly, I heard sounds behind the door, on the street— the slam of a car door and the jingling of the keys. I managed to let out a loud scream, a jumble of words, before Ashur wrapped his palm around my mouth, forcing himself on me to keep me still. His eyes were mad, his palm was preventing me from breathing, I could feel some iron object on the wall cutting into the flesh of my back. It must have been the door hinge. The metallic taste of blood was in my mouth, my cheek hurt, and my eyes burned. I felt helpless and trapped in this corner of the world, at the edge of humanity, at a point where all things end. Then suddenly someone pulled him away. I saw Eric. Immediately, my hand reached up my back and my fingers came away with blood on them. I remained in the corner and watched how Eric pushed Ashur into a far corner behind the coffee nook.

"You sick man!" Eric yelled. I heard no replies, strangely. Ashur wiped his forehead, fixed his hair, and patted his palms on his pants. He appeared to be in a stupor, unmoving, watching me.

My fingers traced my lips, and the same dark red covered them. I stared at my hands through the loose strands of my hair.

"Are you all right?" Eric asked. Then, "Get up, let's go!" He reached out a hand and I shuddered, afraid.

"Oh God, Maryam," he said. "Don't be afraid! I will help you, but we need to get out of this place now." He spoke softly. "Okay?"

Eric picked me up and took me to his car. I cried and refused to buckle up, but he managed to do it, and we drove away. He stopped at a pharmacy and bought some gauze pads and alcohol, some ointment and water. He sat with me in his car as I stared into nowhere. He drove me home in silence.

I managed to thank Eric for the help and convinced him to leave me a few blocks away from the house.

"Who is at home?" he asked.

"I don't know," I replied. "Maybe no one. Hopefully no one," I added.

"I am sorry this happened, Maryam," Eric said. "And I am so glad I . . ." his voice trembled. "God, if I hadn't shown up."

At this thought, I began to cry and rock back and forth. The thought hadn't occurred to me until now. Things appeared as bad as they could be, but now that he said it, my mind was painting the picture of what could have happened, had he not shown up and intervened. These images were frightening, much more frightening than what happened. They were more than I could process. I forced the tears to die down and left his car.

"You should never go back there," he said as I stepped out of the car.

My hairband must have slipped off at some point and my hair was now covering my face. I caught the strange glances of the passersby. I floated inside my grief like a boat, moving farther and farther away from the shore, disappearing into the blue. Occasionally, the urge to cry would come over me, yet I choked on it. I bit deep into the flesh under my nails, getting a strange pleasure from feeling physical pain. If I relaxed my jaw, the pain in my fingers stopped. That was pain that had an end, unlike this new pain that didn't.

I found myself in front of our two-story building on Bronx Street. I stood on the other side of the street and looked inside the window, hiding behind a tree. The lights were on, and I noticed the silhouette of my mother by the window. I looked at our small apartment, with its cozy light and Mother by the window, and I cried silent tears of mourning. Years later now, I have become accustomed to the loneliness that harassment of this sort imposes on you, how it plants a deep fear in your soul that keeps you hostage until the end of your days. That night, I cried because the incident with Ashur had, suddenly and immediately, split my world into two kinds of people: Those who go on living their lives without knowing this kind of pain, and *us*, those who have lived through it. It is true that part of each of us survived what happened to us, but there are parts that did not make it. We carry these dead, lifeless parts around with us from that point on, because regardless of the death of these parts, we cannot shed them.

I slowly crossed the street, gathering whatever sanity I had left in me to appear normal in front of my family. If I didn't talk about it, maybe I could convince myself it had never happened.

I spent the night in apathy, disturbed by occasional waves of anxiety filled with shades of tree branches hovering like demons. They surrounded me. I pressed my knees to my chin. A few times I dissolved into light sleep and woke up sweating. The wind howled, the branches did their monstrous dance, and the night took forever. When the first rays of the sun illuminated the cars and the trees outside, I felt exhausted, frail, and, surprisingly, hungry. I felt a stinging pain every time I moved my back. The loud voice of a Russian radio host came from the kitchen. Mother was awake and at her morning ritual of a cigarette by the window.

I waited for half an hour until I heard the door close behind her and slowly stepped out of my bedroom as if it were a prison cell. Rufat had gone to school and so had Mother. I entered the kitchen and turned on the teapot, opened the fridge, and took out the containers of butter, cheese, and kielbasa, but realized I was too nauseated to eat anything. I noticed the pack of cigarettes Mother had left on the table. I took one out, rummaged through the drawers for her lighter, and found one eventually. I lit up the cigarette and took a few drags. I'd seen Mother pick up her pack with trembling hands and by the time there was only the butt of her cigarette left, she seemed relaxed, her composure intact again. *It must do the trick for me, too,* I thought. I hoped.

Contrary to my expectations, I felt nothing but the bitter taste of the smoke filling my mouth. It irritated my throat and worsened my nausea. I coughed and I cried. A strange coarse cough mixed with the tears that leaked into my mouth. A broken cry. I threw away the cigarette, took a sip of my tea, and curled into a ball on a kitchen chair. It was Wednesday and I needed to get ready for work at the dental office. I washed my face but found my own movements so rough, almost scrubbing. I was angry that the feeling of dirt still lingered, covered my body and my face. It wouldn't fade no matter how much soap I lathered onto my cheeks. The fingerprints of his hungry, square palms were still on my jaw, on the side of my nose and my chin and my lips. After a while, the urge for violence died down. I no longer had the strength to keep scrubbing. *Scrub, scrub, scrub. What's the use?* I said to myself. "There's a first time for everything," echoed in my head.

· · · · · · · · · · · · ·

CHAPTER 40

UGLY LITTLE THINGS

I sat at the back of the express train, leaned my head against the window, and looked outside. I still felt nauseated. Once in a while a painful snapshot of yesterday's events would come to me unbidden and send a tear down my swollen face. The scratch on my back had dried up a bit, but I still felt a dull pain that intensified whenever I leaned. *I shouldn't have bothered with the Band-Aid,* I thought. Buildings, parks, cemeteries, and rows of trees rushed past me in the window. I caught myself thinking that it was unfair that none of yesterday's horrors found reflection in the pristine beauty of the morning. People went about their day, trains ran on schedule, and summer advanced upon the city.

With disturbing calmness, I registered that I had woken up a different person this morning. It was as if someone had shifted me to a parallel universe devoid of colors and emotions, a life where no bad thing was off the table. A life where safety, kindness, and goodness were nonexistent, people were not to be trusted, and fairness was not to be expected.

What a peculiar verb, I thought. *"Forcing yourself"* on someone. *The moment is gone but some stuff has been forced on you. You walk around with bits and pieces of humiliation, a large hole inside of you stuffed with ugly little things that someone* forces *on you, and you take years to then* force *them off your consciousness. Only you fail each time and continue carrying them around. These ugly little things.*

I walked into the office and found Olivia and Amina drinking coffee and munching on a cherry cheesecake Dr. Shafaei had brought in.

"Is she here?" I asked.

"No and good morning to you too, Maryam," Amina said.

"I'll go change," I said, marching on past them.

"You all right?" I heard Amina say.

Soon the crazy pace picked up and we shuffled from one room to another with trays full of instruments, gauze pads, and Q-tips. Lost in work, I seemed to have regained my old self, dropping instruments and expensive composite materials and not reacting as quickly to Dr. Goodman's instructions. Luckily, some of her patients had cancelled so I retreated to the back office to develop x-rays while everyone else had lunch in Dr. Shafaei's office. I turned on the bright red light and inserted the films into the x-ray solution, inhaling its strange scent with pleasure.

Now that I had gained Olivia's trust, she would share things with me once in a while. Out of all the days, today she decided to have a girl talk.

"I've had it with Oscar already. Now that I think of it, he is not so good for Camilla either. He moved out a week ago and I did nothing to stop him," she said, arranging the patient charts in the scheduled order. "This might be too premature, but I've been talking to someone too, Maryam." She smiled.

"Talking to someone?" I said.

"Are you all right?" she suddenly asked. "You look kind of shaken up."

I couldn't bear the thought of having to explain myself, so I tried to stick to the topic.

"I am fine, just a little tired. So, who is it you're talking to?" I asked. "Somebody new?"

"Actually, no," she answered. "This guy is a friend from school. I've known him since childhood. We've always lived in different cities, but he did have a crush on me years ago. Anyways, we've always been in touch, all these years, but now that he found out about the break-up, the tone of his voice changed, you know?" she said and winked. "It's all different now, he keeps insisting on planning a trip to Florida where he is stationed. He keeps asking about Camilla and I can't help it. Sometimes I picture all of us together as one big family."

I did my best to force a smile, but I must have been doing a pretty bad job, because Olivia squinted her narrow eyes and said "Are you listening to me? Maybe you're all dreamy about that devout boyfriend of yours. I swear, if I had a boy like that driving all the way from Wilmette to bring me a cookie and a peach tea, I'd move anywhere for him."

At the thought of Arash, everything inside began to hurt, but I blocked the feeling. I nodded.

"Anyways, so I asked him 'How about Camilla?' and you know what he said? He said, 'She's part of you, Olivia. I love her just as much because she is part of you.'" Her eyes took on an unusual, dreamy expression and I forced a smile.

"Why don't you do it? What's bad about moving to Florida and trying it out? There are dental offices there too, you know," I said. "Go there and try it out."

"Well, I'd need to go for a week to see how I get along with him," she said, clearly seriously giving this idea some thought.

"I'd need someone to cover for me here though and I can't think of anyone," Olivia said.

There, there it is, my ticket out of that horrible place, away from Ashur, away from all those men and their cigarettes and their "family" kindness, I thought.

"I'll do it," I said, and then I began to beg. "I'll do it. You'll train me, I'll learn it all quickly, I swear!"

"Wow," she made a full stop. "Maryam, I love you, girl, but you barely learned how to not drop all those instruments and answer the phone!"

"You're right, but I promise I will learn. I'm much better with the papers," I said. "That is all I do at the optical, remember? I fill out forms and answer the phone. Come on, Olivia!"

She stared at the computer, and I saw her mulling things over. It was time for me to go back into the exam room, but I felt that the seed had been planted. I knew that without a darn Social Security card or an employment authorization paper, I would stand no chance to get any other job. It was a cash job or nothing at this point, but here at the dental practice, I was already on the payroll and extending my hours wouldn't be a problem. This was my ticket out and I was ready to muster whatever strength I had left to fight for it. I took a deep breath and walked back into Dr. Goodman's room.

"So, Mr. Clark, how have you been doing? Can I get you a glass of water?" I asked.

Mr. Clark was in his thirties and had a strange habit of staring into your eyes. During his root canal, he'd fix his eyes on mine and wouldn't turn away. He hardly blinked, too, so you'd sit there covered with a mask, protective glasses, feeling completely exposed in front of his piercing, poisonous green eyes. During the five-minute pause when Dr. Goodman inserted medicated strips inside the canals, I caught my own face in the mirror and noticed that a dry indifference had replaced my childish look, but then the moment was gone and I was hunched over Mr. Clark's face with a white suction device in my hands, picking up the chips of his tooth, remnants of the temporary crown materials, and his saliva. We finished the root canal and came to the front to schedule a follow-up.

"We need thirty minutes a week from now," Dr. Goodman said. "Michael, don't worry, no more drilling like today. Now that the nerve is out—"

"There is nothing to hurt," Mr. Clark finished her sentence. "I've had three of these," he added.

"Somebody's eating too much candy, I guess!" she said with a laugh.

"You keep refusing to go out with me, so I got no choice," he said.

Dr. Goodman blushed a little but didn't lose her composure, but I felt that his comment had taken her by surprise. *I always knew he was a creep*, I noted. I thought of Arash again and felt a sting of pain inside, somewhere around my throat. I wondered why all feelings concentrated in my throat. They bunched up there, blocking the air and sucking the life out of me. Mr. Clark finally paid, picked up the card with his next appointment scribbled on the back, and left the office.

"I've thought about it," Olivia said. "I do want to go, and I am grateful that you want to help, Maryam. I don't know if she will agree, but I will try."

"You're welcome. I only want to help," I said. Before I could say anything else, I heard the phone ringing and retreated to the back to answer it.

"Blue Dental. How may I help you?" I asked.

"Hi, Maryam," Arash said.

Hearing Arash's gentle voice made me recall the life that had ended yesterday, its carefreeness and privilege of unconditional love. All the pampering I had enjoyed in the past few months since we had started going out seemed so far away now. I held the receiver in my hands, thinking of what to say while scratching off the remainder of my nail polish from my fingernails.

"I'll be downstairs in an hour. That's when you're done, right?"

Clutching the receiver, I suddenly realized that I couldn't tell him any of what had taken place yesterday, so I gathered whatever strength I had and made up a story about Mother visiting family friends in the city. "I won't need a ride," I told him, and he quietly agreed, a hint of mistrust in his voice.

I popped another Advil and looked outside the window. The rush hour had passed, and the city donned its usual evening glow. I sucked on the sweet coating of the pill and swallowed it, feeling momentary relief. If only I could prolong the unwinding that came with it or find another drug, an even better and stronger one, that would make me feel less tortured. It had been some time since I'd started taking the round orange pills not just for headaches, but to lessen the anxiety that I felt at moments. I blamed it all on headaches and was careful not to give myself away with too many empty containers in the trash can.

I wiped the chair and replaced the plastic covers and thought of Mr. Clark, wondering if he led a secret life. I pictured his abandoned apartment with an unmade bed, boxes of leftover pizza and Chinese food, all the way at the end of another silent hallway with identical doors and faded carpet, just like the building where Amina lived. My imagination was running wild in dark places.

After all the patients were gone, we collected the instrument trays and took them to the back office, while Olivia printed out insurance claims, attached x-rays to those with crown and root canals, and put them into individual envelopes for the insurance companies. All rooms, except for one, were cleaned, the dental chairs freshly wiped and elevated so that the cleaning lady could wipe the floors in the morning. The radio played "Stuck on You" by Lionel Richie.

Dr. Shafaei was still working on her last patient, a young investment banker named Gary Schneider, who could only make it to the office at seven p.m. I thought of my family back home. After yesterday's events, I felt even more disconnected from them, convinced that after what happened, they could no longer understand or accept me. I took out two more Advil and gulped them down with left-over tea. I'd had six in the last twenty-four hours. Moments after I swallowed them, I felt relief, but it was short-lived and evaporated quickly. I knew I was on a path to addiction, but I lacked the strength to resist. *The damage done by the pills cannot outdo the ugliness that still lingers on my body*, I assured myself.

I closed my eyes and for some reason recalled my grandfather's face the day before he died. I had woken up one night to find him pacing about the living room, rubbing his stomach, frowning with pain. He'd gone to the doctor several times that week and had come back with a cocktail of medicine that was supposed to ease his pain, along with a white pharmacy pouch full of digestion-aid pills. His stomach wasn't the issue, we had found out after his death. His heart was twice the size of a normal heart, and so the digestive aid cocktail did not do much. He was gone the next morning.

Back in Skokie, I got home late and found Mother fixing the bedspread on the sofa, getting ready to sleep. She appeared tired and didn't pay much attention to me. Rufat must have been in his room watching a movie. I went into my room, changed the Band-Aid on my back, and collapsed on the bed. My vision focused on the uneven surface of the pink walls of the room. I thought about the kind of troubles I used to lose sleep over back home, unaware that one day it would be put in perspective rather cruelly. My father's drinking, my mother's tower of loneliness that made us, her children, almost invisible, the late-night parties of our household filled with alcohol, cigarettes, loud music, and my father's friends. Then I thought of frightening images of police beating up the protesters in the '90s that I feared so much as a child. I used to roll in my bed thinking about the unfairness of the world and wondering if I could somehow make all those around me happy again. Now, it seemed as if I had joined their ranks. Exhausted and out of tears, I fell asleep.

CHAPTER 41

. . . .

TO CARRY ON

In the following weeks, my state deteriorated. I refused to talk about the incident with anyone, afraid of inviting more hurt into my life. I convinced myself that I would only invite more evil if I spoke of it, that it would spread like an infectious disease and stain everything and everyone around me. Arash would lose that shine in his eyes forever. Mother could recover from a heartbreak, but she would not recover from this. Along with that, I felt raw shame at the idea of ever having to admit those hands had been on my body, how dirty I had felt all over. So, I kept quiet.

My decision to keep it to myself eventually seeped into all good things in my life. A long, dark corridor led into unknown, unwelcome places and I followed blindly, stumbling upon the uneven surface, one basic step after another.

My days were bearable, but at nights I suffered from night-mares. I'd see Ashur pushing me into the corner and hear my own mumbled voice calling for help. In some of these dreams, I was saved by Eric again, but in others I would shrink in size, my body diminishing from the foul-smelling sweat that was emanating from it. I'd feel my nails dig into the wall by the door and the metallic hinge would cut deeper into my body, the scent of iron from my blood mixing with the sweat. In some of my nightmares, Ashur sat on a chair and looked at me while I crouched on the floor, looking as if he'd done what he had wanted to and was finished with me. I'd wake up sobbing, my body covered in cold sweat and with a shooting pain in my stomach. And with each nightmare, my determination to keep it all to myself grew stronger and stronger. I could not bear the thought of exposing this ugliness to anyone. The thought of it did not offer any relief.

I never told Arash or anybody else what happened to me. His several attempts to shake it out of me failed. My reaction was so bizarre and alarming that he finally backed off and waited for things to make sense.

One evening, he came over unannounced and found me sitting on a table in our neighborhood park, smoking a cigarette. I had noticed him following me around a few times already. I'd spotted his car in the parking lot of the train station, empty and locked. He must have watched me from afar, maybe from inside the Starbucks next to it. I'd see it parked on the street by the dental office. He was inside this time, sitting, tapping the wheel with his hands, thinking. *If only he'd leave me alone*, I thought. It was just a matter of time until he found out I no longer took the bus to Devon.

Arash approached me with a sad look of a person who is being pushed out of someone's life against his will. There was no careful approach to the subject this time, no subtle questions. I drew in the cigarette and glanced at my nails, bitten down to pink. I was a mess standing next to him in his ironed clothes and his shoes, inhaling his fancy aftershave. Me, with my unwashed hair in a messy bun, my eyes red with insomnia and nightmares, and, of course, the ugly record that couldn't be washed clean.

"Will you tell me what's wrong," he tried one last time.

"I don't want to talk," I said.

"Then tell me why can't you say it, Maryam? Explain it to me and I'll leave you alone."

"What do you think? I just woke up and decided to pick up smoking and started gulping down pills? Something did happen, but I cannot bring myself to talk about it. I'm afraid." I tugged at my throat.

"Afraid . . ."

"Afraid it will multiply. Afraid it will grow and become bigger and then I won't be able to handle it. I've only got this much strength in me now, and I have to protect it. Maybe then . . ."

"You think you'll get your strength back and then you'll be able to face it, right?" he asked.

"Maybe." The tears began. Round, heavy tears rolling down my cheeks, blurring my vision.

"It doesn't work that way, Maryam. You'll just learn how to live with it. And then it'll be cemented deep down."

"Then let it be, Arash!" I screamed. "Let it be that way. Why do you keep pushing? Why can't you just go away? Don't you see it's better when you don't bother me with your kindness, with your endless attempts to fix things! You can't, you get it?"

"I am trying to help." He was running out of things to say. I knew I had to hurt him deeper to make him go away. Ruthlessly, just the way we sometimes hurt the most loyal people in our life, I went on.

"Don't help! Don't come, don't try, stop being so careful around me, treating me like I'm made out of some fragile china. I'm gone, that girl that you obsessed over, she's gone. What's left is this. You see it?" I grabbed his hands and made him touch my messy hair. "This messy hair, this cigarette smelling mouth, these nails, these ugly bitten nails, this is all that is left. And you won't leave me alone. You stand here with your good, open heart, your perfect face, your perfect hair. I can't stand it!" I covered my head with my hands and wept. "Please leave!"

"Look, what's so scary about saying it? Did somebody do something to you? Say it, trust me, Maryam, I'll help. I'll try to help. Where have you been these past weeks? You don't let me give you a ride, you don't call . . . I don't know what to think."

"I wish I could, Arash, but I can't. I've decided not to. Now go."

That evening Arash left and didn't insist on things anymore. He stopped following me around. Only at nights, I'd see his car parked on the other side of the street, his gaze fixed on my window, a new painful expression in his eyes.

I never went back to the optical store or Devon, and no one ever called, except Eric. He left a few voicemails with halting messages with "I hope you are doing fine, Maryam" at the end. I never called back. At home everyone still thought I worked in Devon, and I dutifully brought in my hundred dollars a week to Mother, using up whatever savings I had accumulated in the past year. I was careful to show up at the right time, but, of course, Mother noticed that I was irritable and low on energy, and spent more time in my room. I blamed it all on the training at the dental office, Dr. Shafaei's perfectionism and other things—traffic, humidity, construction crews in the city, and all sorts of other things. These excuses worked in the meantime, but I knew it was only a matter of time until she figured me out.

Mother came home late these days. She'd be too exhausted by the commute, a full day's schedule, and all the pacing in between the patients.

"A funny, but actually not-so-funny thing happened this afternoon," Mother said, hanging her brown leather bag on the kitchen chair.

"Make up your mind, Mama," Rufat said. I took one of the kitchen chairs and listened in.

"I take the 34A bus. It goes straight to Des Plaines and from there, it's a five-minute walk to the office. Anyways, Teymour was right, most people in this area drive and those I see on the bus are people who just can't get a driver's license, and me. In other words, they're not there because they can't afford a car. They're there because they cannot drive. You know, people with mental health issues and all, disabled people, and people like us."

"Illegal people," Rufat added.

"We're not illegal, Rufat," Mother corrected him. "I wouldn't do that to you guys." She sounded hurt.

"I was joking," he explained, only it wasn't funny. "All right, so what happened?" he asked.

"I take the seat by the window, always. And there is this middle-aged man, gray hair, round glasses, tall but with a childish smile. His schedule is fully synced with mine, so I see him every single day, no exceptions. He has a kind smile and I always return it. I figured he likes me, so I smile back. I think he does have some mental health issue; he is a bit like a child. Anyways, he smiles, I smile back, it's all part of the routine, really. Today, I don't know what's gotten into me, I pulled on the rope to signal I wanted to get off at the next station, but the driver kept driving."

"What did you do then?" Rufat asked.

"I wanted to stay 'stop it.' But that is not what came out of my mouth," Mother went on.

"Come on, I'm on the edge of my seat here. What came out of your mouth?"

"Instead of 'stop it,' I said, 'stupid,'" Mother said, opening her right palm and resting her left on her waist.

"Noooooooooo," Rufat said.

"Oh yes!" Mother confirmed.

The story was too funny to leave me neutral. A laugh escaped my mouth, especially when I saw Rufat clutching his stomach and laughing so hard.

"Mama, you made up for all your lack of humor just now! This story is a gem!" Rufat says.

"Lack of humor? Listen, I'm not even done yet," she goes on. "You can imagine, or rather, you *can't* imagine, the face of the bus driver after I call him stupid. He is mad and fuming. At this point, my not-so-secret admirer gets up from his seat. He is visibly mad, angry with the driver for missing my stop, and walks towards him, yelling 'she said stop it, so you stop it if she says so.' Oh goodness, can you imagine all this? I'm blushing and trying to explain that English is my second language as best as I can, but the guy is confronting the driver. What a commotion instead of my usual quiet, peaceful commute when nobody speaks, besides the driver announcing the stops." Mother poured hot water over the tea leaves in the kettle. Something inside lightened up and I allowed myself to be taken over by a brief, sincere laugh, like an oasis in a desert of gloom. At first, I did it not to attract any suspicions, but then I pictured the whole scene and couldn't help but laugh.

"I suggest you find another bus route to work, Mother," Rufat said, wiping the tears from his eyes.

"There isn't one. What I need is a car," Mother said.

"Car would be nice, but we ain't got money like that yet."

"Not just the money, we don't have a driver's license either, but once we get it, a friend of mine at the office may give me her old Acura. Something about a tax write-off," she explained.

"Who's that?" Rufat asked.

"Simona, a young dentist who just started at our place three weeks ago. I fixed one of her drills," Mother added.

"You know how to fix dental drills?" Rufat asked, pouring tea for himself.

"I didn't, but now I do. Easier than all that physics stuff I did in the lab at the Academy of Sciences."

"You guys used all that equipment to fry potatoes for lunch, if I remember correctly," Rufat joked.

"We actually did, I can't believe you remember that," Mother said and laughed.

"After Dad's basement office, your lab was our favorite place to go," Rufat said. "The computers were old, nothing but that boring Prince of Persia game to play, and he kept slipping and falling into a trap of swords and dying. That was the one game that came with those old computers you guys had, but it still was better than nothing. The jokes of your colleagues were funny, there was always something to munch on."

I recalled that Rufat was right. My mother's physicist friends, a group of them who worked in that old lab, were quite fun. They all had different backgrounds—a rich kid who was into science, a genius physicist in his mid-forties with a thick provincial accent, curly hair, and sneaky eyes, a balding professor who mostly tutored students and stopped by the lab to eat and gossip. There wasn't much entertainment there, I figured, so our rare appearances must have made quite a splash. We'd get spoiled with bowls of fruit, chocolates, lemonade, or some lab-made fries.

Mother had always looked happy with this bunch and that was one of the reasons why we liked hanging out there. Some of these guys knew Teymour as well, Mother had said. *A bunch of undecided physicists stuck in a half-operating lab, making it through the day*, I thought. The episode lightened me up a bit and I clung to this good feeling as much as I could. I poured myself a glass of freshly brewed tea and retreated to my bedroom. Since that dreadful day, all good memories became vague and distant. It was hard to believe that I truly lived through them at some point. The shadow that hung over me was too wide and too heavy, such that I now thought of these as things that happened to another person, a person who no longer existed. They still made me smile, but no warmth spread from them. That light was cold and bright, like a full moon on a February night.

Weeks passed and my decision to hold it all inside did not falter. Dr. Shafaei agreed to let me fill in for Olivia while she visited her boyfriend in Florida. I started going to Park West every day now and finally told Mother, Rufat, and Arash that I no longer worked at the optical store. I relived the experience in my head every evening in a silly attempt to learn how to "live with it," and in some sick way, it started working.

With the help of pills and cigarettes, I got through my days, but I was back in a glass box, watching the world go on as if nothing had happened—and on it went. The heat advanced on the city, the cars lined up in the evening traffic, the enormous sun descended upon the suspended train station, painting everything orange and the train cars pitch black. I traded my front seat in my classes for one in the back, occasionally chatting with a girl named Maggie Doyle, who seemed determined to befriend me.

Everything about Maggie—her deep brown eyes, her light curls falling on her shoulders, the tip of her snub nose—screamed that she was from another time, another era. She spoke differently. She moved differently. She had a forgiving, humble smile that quickly grew on me. I refused to be picked up by Arash from then on, but we still met up at the cafeteria to study calculus, although I could no longer concentrate and bit my nails instead. No matter how useless our study sessions became, Arash kept coming, but he had given up on trying to figure out what my issue was for the time being and that gave me some relief.

Now that Mother was working late and Rufat had a crowd of friends from his high school in the area, I'd end up home alone quite often, which meant one thing—panic attacks. One evening, I called

Arash and asked him to take me to Wilmette beach. His white Ford pulled up on our street half an hour later and I saw him rub his temples as I walked towards the car.

"Hello, Maryam," he said.

"Hello," I replied. "Thank you for coming. I really wanted to go to the beach," I said.

"And so, you called me," he said. I wasn't sure if it was bitterness I heard in his voice. I looked straight to avoid his gaze. We drove in silence, both staring at the rolling hills, framed by the greenery, some wildflowers adorning the sides of the road, announcing the coming of summer. There were lots of cars in the parking lot, the beach full of families after some sunlight and fun in the sand.

Arash parked the car and stared at the wheel. I figured he didn't want to leave the car just yet. Then, suddenly, he smacked the wheel with full force. He smacked it hard several times as his eyes glistened with anger. I covered my ears with my hands, still hearing the loud thumps. Next, I felt him pressing me against his chest, kissing my hair. He did it in fast, nervous movements as his arms locked me hard in an embrace. We stayed like that for a while and time was still, my body shaking and Arash trying to keep me together with his arms.

"It's going to be okay," he repeated, stroking my hair. "I promise you. It's going to be okay. I don't understand why you're doing this, but, I promise, it will be okay in the end."

. . . .

CHAPTER 42

STILL STANDING

I spent the whole summer alone, licking my wounds, using up whatever energy I had left to learn Olivia's job at Blue Dental. It was hard to concentrate, so I gulped the pills and smoked cigarettes to get me through the day. One morning, when washing my face at the sink, I noticed a small bald spot on my scalp, a little souvenir of my newly developed insomnia. My nightmares had diminished, but if I ended up having one it'd always surpass the previous one in how graphic it was. Some nights, afraid of another nightmare, I would spend the evening hanging out in my brother's room, pretending to watch him play computer games or volunteering to organize his closet. He sure never turned down that offer. Other nights, he'd kick me out and I'd sit on my bed, fighting the desire to collapse and rocking back and forth, back and forth like one of those roly-poly dolls my dad got me for Women's Day.

Olivia came back from Florida ready to move in with the guy, so the tough task now was to convince Dr. Shafaei to hire me full time. Olivia did her best, and so did Amina, even though her reasons were impractical and not very convincing, the same old "she's very smart, you know," but Amina was truly beside herself at the thought of having me there every day. We failed at convincing Dr. Shafaei to promote me to office manager, but she said I could take care of things while she looked for someone. This meant I was there until my first big screw-up. We had until Christmas before Olivia left, which was plenty of time, but I had to focus, which was hard. Everything was so hard.

Olivia took the training so seriously, as if the happy end to her story depended on it.

"First of all, we'll need to get you a nice set of new scrubs because you'll now spend most of your time at the front desk." She pointed at the bleached spot on my top. "I'll ask Amina to order you a new pair of white sneakers. These one won't do," she said and pointed at my gym shoes.

"When you pick up the phone, stand straight and speak up! You must smile when you talk to people—they'll feel it on the other side of the wire. You see how Amina talks on the phone with that grumpy expression on her face? Never do that. She sounds sleepy because of it." She said this even though Amina was standing right next to us.

"Hey, that is not true!" Amina protested. "Well, maybe a little! The problem is we start the day too early and also—" she paused, scratched her head. "Also, I can't help it. They ask dumb questions. You know, 'my tooth hurts when I touch it' stuff. Well, then stop touching it!" All three of us laughed. "Maryam, she's right, though. Listen well and make sure you take notes, I want you to hang around as long as possible." Amina winked and disappeared in the hallway.

Olivia went on with her training for another thirty minutes as I frantically took notes in a green notebook I'd found in one of the drawers. She was a direct and demanding teacher, expecting undivided attention and effort. She split our training into several sections and covered each thoroughly in the weeks leading up to Christmas. The notebook was all used up by the time we were done.

"It's not rocket science, girls," Dr. Shafaei would say passing by. "I took fewer notes in four years of dental school." She was, of course, pleased with how seriously Olivia took the whole thing. As for me, I was in desperate need of a job because my savings were dwindling and the thought of not being able to put in my share for the weekly grocery bill troubled me. I looked over the notes while eating my mushroom sandwich at lunch and then again while I rode the train to Skokie.

I was good with theory, but when it came to applying the knowledge, my progress was slow. Olivia would leave me at the front desk to practice checking out a patient and inevitably would have to jump in at some point to cover up some out-of-place comment I made or to collect a payment I had almost missed. I did much better with insurance claims though. I'd had some practice filling out forms and that helped, only here I had to do all of this on a computer. I quickly learned the rules of insurance policies, which procedures were covered at what percentage, and how to look up the special rates that we had to honor to those patients who came in through the insurance website referral.

"Olivia, you're still sure she can do this?" Dr. Shafaei asked after another big screw-up at the front desk. I had forgotten to collect a payment and schedule the follow-up appointment for a patient who was difficult to get hold of. That meant, almost certainly, that we had lost him.

"She's learning, Dr. Shafaei. Yeah, she does make mistakes, but I see progress. I wouldn't write her off yet. Besides, she's good with the insurance claims. Never forgets to attach additional exhibits when needed, remembers the codes well, and even found a way to download some info online, instead of waiting on hold for hours."

Dr. Shafaei nodded, looking somewhere in the distance.

"I guess we'll give her some more time," she said.

Amina would pace about the office, offering me tea or coffee several times a day to cheer me up after another failure, occasionally caressing my hair or offering a friendly hug. She appeared to be smiling more often since I started my training. The somber frown in her eyebrows cleared up and the sad expression in her eyes was gone. Ours was more of a sisterhood than a friendship, with all the misunderstandings, fights, and hasty make-ups that came with it. It was not a mature friendship between two grown-ups, more like two children feeling close even though they had little in common. Still, the feeling was mutual, and her presence was soothing.

On the weekends, I would copy all my notes neatly into a new notebook I picked up at the college bookstore. I would practice polished office behaviors in front of the mirror in my bedroom with Rufat making fun of me the whole time. Then, I made him and Mother play the part of the picky customers, rehearsing my pre-written phrases, adjusting my tone, and maintaining that sterile smile of a front-desk person. By the end of the weekend, they were both sick of it, but looked content that I had gotten some of my old self back even though it was through this strange, obsessive studying and role-playing.

Finally, the week of Olivia's departure arrived. It was the week before Christmas, and she wanted to arrive in time to spend the holidays with Camilla and her boyfriend. With her departure upon us, there was a strange nostalgic mood in the office. That last day, I saw her standing by the window, gazing at the city, trying to take in the last bits to carry with her, but I knew well that you cannot pack up a city, cannot suck it in with air and tie it to yourself forever. I knew that firsthand. Olivia grew up in Cali, Colombia, and it was not her first move, yet beautiful cities capture your heart, no matter what your head tells you. She'd glance at the stunning Chicago sky-line, like those million-dollar smiles that Dr. Shafaei polished day in, day out. The branches of the trees were bare, covered with the twin-kling lights that shone bright and announced the festivities that were about to begin. Her daydream was cut short by the tall and hand-some Brady Davidson stepping out of the room after his cleaning.

"Have a happy Christmas, Brady!" Dr. Shafaei said to him as Brady licked his white teeth, which looked almost bluish in contrast to his tanned skin. *Doesn't he live in the same city we do?!* I thought.

"Bye, Farah!" he said in a dreamy voice. "I'll see you in six months! Happy holidays, ladies," he said and waved to me and Olivia.

When the last patient left, and the rooms were wiped clean and the last packs of instruments were slid into the autoclave machine in the back, we gathered in the front office to give our hugs and well wishes to Olivia.

"Here's the recommendation letter I wrote for you," Dr. Shafaei said, handing her an envelope. "Whoever gets you there in Florida is super lucky, Olivia. Kiss Camilla for me."

"Thank you for everything that you've done for me and Camilla," Olivia said. "Thank you for your patience."

"Can't survive without patience with these two," Dr. Shafaei said giving a gentle nudge to me and Amina.

I stood last in line to get my hug, opened my arms, and embraced Olivia, staying like that for a moment longer. I felt deep gratitude because I realized that replacing her was a big stretch for me, but thanks to her, I made it. I was still sometimes broken and unable to focus, with bitten nails and greasy hair, taking lunch breaks to smoke and cry, but I was still standing.

When I unlocked my embrace, I noticed the slight tremble in her eyebrows, the subtle worry about her future. I noticed the flut-tering of her tired eyelids. She'd built a fence to protect herself and

Camilla and the fence had worked, but behind it, she remained just a girl who longed for a happy ending. The hope of a new life bloomed into a spring in her pragmatic soul. Now, it was as if she had passed her usual steely, stern look on to me. I had taken on the same determination to crush everything in my way. Her heart had softened to receive love while mine had hardened and cooled, ready to get on with a solitary uphill battle.

. . . .

CHAPTER 43

SAVE YOUR TEARS

My first week on the job, Dr. Shafaei watched my every move, picking up on the slightest errors and dissecting them like a neurosurgeon. She tried to be nice, but it didn't take long to realize that business came first here. Naturally, the situation got tense quickly and I found myself buckling under the pressure. Soon, all I aimed for was to finish the day's work without bursting into tears, to close up the office and leave with dignity. *Keep your tears for the train ride,* I thought. It wasn't just the pressure to be flawless in my job. I had developed a strange paranoia that I was simply unfit for this place, a foreigner, a stranger who would never learn the ways of things. My daily interactions with patients kept cementing that thought deep down into my consciousness. Some of them commented on my accent, others couldn't pronounce Azerbaijan or locate it on the map, some asked if it was a province in India. One of the patients, after I seated her and offered a magazine, chuckled and asked if she could have a foot massage too. Unfortunately, I didn't realize that was a joke and went to check with Dr. Shafaei, who shook her head.

"Of course it's a joke, Maryam," she said without raising her head from the patient's chart. "A bad one though," she added.

I went back to the front, my shoulders slumped and spirits down.

"I really want to do better," I said to Dr. Shafaei that evening.

She realized I had come into her office for a serious conversation and looked up from her chart. She rubbed her eyelids and tucked a few strands of loose hair behind her ear.

"Sit down, Maryam," she said. "And, please, no tears." She touched my knee before she went on. "I was twenty when I came here. I was working at this tea place, serving tea, washing dishes, whatever they needed me to do in the back. I had some girlfriends who came to Chicago around the same time. They came from families with money, connections, possibilities. They studied well and did a lot of fun things, but it was different for me. My dad died when I was a teenager. My mother brought us up alone. Five children. Four of us girls and one boy. That woman, I don't know how she did it, really. Anyways, by the time I was done washing the tea glasses and keeping up with coursework, I didn't have much time for fun. Up until then, I don't think I had realized what *tough* really meant. Feeling foreign, not belonging, doing things that you must and not what your heart wants. This is *tough*. Life here is *tough*. And I know very well that I," she paused, "that *I* am tough. But I demand so much because I see it in your eyes, that you are capable of getting better, learning, rising to it. Forget Abby's stupid joke today. These things happen, they happen a lot. They make you stumble and doubt yourself. That's okay, Maryam. Take your time, stumbling is a part of growing, but then— then you get up and fight on. Keep going and remember: There is no looking back. You're in this country to make it."

"I will do my best, Dr. Shafaei," I said. "Dr. Shafaei, may I ask you a question?"

"Go ahead."

"When does it get better?"

"When it *does* get better you never notice it," she said. "What you notice is the rock bottom."

I knew if I kept going, there would be tears, so I wrapped up our conversation.

"Thank you," I said. "Thank you for your patience. For talking to me."

"You are welcome, Maryam," she said and began to arrange the charts on her desk.

"I'll finish writing this tomorrow morning. Let's get out of here. I'll give you a ride to the train station."

That night I didn't cry. I felt a pleasant emptiness, carelessness, detachment from this world. I did not want to run or hide. I looked at the shining lights of the city from the train window. I looked at the dark gray skies and the airplanes cutting through like enormous metal birds. I peeked into the living rooms of an apartment building that ran parallel to the train line, where dinners were cooked, tables were set for evening meals, and television sets were turned on to report the evening news. For the first time, I realized, with bitterness, I did not miss Baku. The emptiness inside made me feel hollow, like one of those thin Japanese vases my grandmother brought from India. Up until that evening, I did not realize that hollowness could be liberating.

CHAPTER 44

. . . .

AS BEST AS I COULD

Mondays and Fridays at the office were often quiet, but the rest of the week the office was on fire. We'd see somewhere around sixteen patients a day between the two doctors, which meant that between me and Amina we'd have to clean the rooms, sterilize instruments, and develop x-rays seventeen times, in addition to seating, entertaining, and checking out each patient with smiles on our faces. "Do things fast even if you don't need to," I kept repeating in my head, imagining Olivia enjoying the sun somewhere by a pool in Florida. The truth is, I enjoyed the crazy pace of the office. The busier we got, the more focused I was, and the fainter were the demons in my head who brought with them painful snapshots of that day. I stayed away from the window, I stopped looking deep into the patients' eyes when assisting, and I avoided seeing my own reflection in the mirror. Amina sensed the changes, but because she didn't like being questioned herself, she let me "figure things out on my own" as she put it. I was grateful for that.

Besides the crazy pace, office life had some unexpected adventures that would take over the day. In just three months, I had witnessed so many curious cases with patients. Some were hilarious and some plain sad. A gentleman named Richard Hart showed up one day, wearing construction worker's clothing. He had mud on his knees. His hair was greasy and his hands covered in callouses.

"My wife says she refuses to kiss me until I get all my teeth fixed," he announced without a hello.

I seated him in one of the rooms, put a bib on his chest, and took a full mouth x-ray, wondering if I'd be able to get this guy to pay the hundred bucks for x-rays, let alone any other dental work. You didn't need to be a doctor to figure out he'd need thousands to get all his teeth fixed. It seemed this guy hadn't been to a dentist in years, but as Dr. Shafaei explained, we could not refuse service to anyone, not based on looks, certainly. She entered the room with his x-ray in one hand and a smile on her face and charmed the guy with her beautiful eyes. The treatment would take six visits, she explained, a few months in total, and fifteen thousand dollars in cash, since he had no insurance.

"Money is no problem. See all that construction on Diversey Parkway, over by the museum?" He pointed at the massive scaffolding across the street. "I own the damn thing!" Richard said.

Richard became one of our favorite patients, never showing up without a box of chocolates and an old joke. As promised, he walked out of the office three months later with a dazzling smile, and from then on, he even came in regularly for his periodic cleanings.

Then there was Edward Beard, a famous lawyer, a grandfather of seven children, a philanthropist, and a big patriot. Despite his borderline-diabetic blood sugar, the man would not stay away from sweets, which landed him in our building quite often. He'd come to see the endocrinologist to get another lecture about his sugar levels and to get his cavities filled by Dr. Goodman. Edward kept bringing me books on American politics that I could barely understand, but I thanked him each time, so the books kept coming. I accumulated a whole shelf of them that I kept in the back office. "Romeo is here," Amina would joke, and I'd rush to the front to get another present.

The patient I remembered the most was an acclaimed sculptor who never took off his aviator sunglasses. He was diagnosed with cancer and things were not looking good, but he kept coming to get his implants. I heard him tell Dr. Shafaei once that he was sick and tired of all these appointments, but he had to keep going, had to act like he'd live a long life and these implants would pay off. Some days, he'd shrivel with pain, unable to sit through his visit, and leave before the work was done. I still remember him calling out, "Farah, Farah, come on and finish up the work. I can't stand the pain any longer. I need to go!"

Some evenings, I sat by the window and thought of the optical store. Just like the rest of the world, I bet life went on there with the usual pace. Youel, Shammoun, and Ashur opened up the place in the mornings, turned on *Cops, Married with Children,* or *CNN News* to check on the war in Iraq, complained about the headache after the weekend in the restaurant, drank bad-tasting coffee, and burned bissma. The picture of Mariski standing next to a gigantic cross in some church was still there on the wall, along with the others. I bet the patients still came in bunches on Tuesdays, asking for freebies, ordering glasses they didn't need as the public aid tax dollars rolled into Ashur's bank account. Now that time had passed, I felt somewhat responsible for what happened. After all, Ashur had held my hand that one evening in the car and I'd done nothing to stop him. He must have noticed that I had feelings for Eric, who was many years my senior. "If she could like Eric, then why not me?" he probably thought. As I pieced the story together, I was left with an utterly broken heart in my hands. I was left with no faith in the world. All my dreams seemed stupid and foolish now, but, contrary to my belief, life did not end. I woke up each day, forced myself out of the bed, and faced it as best as I could.

CHAPTER 45

. . . .

LIKE AN ASHTRAY

One night in November, I woke up to my mother's voice coming from the living room. She sounded alarmed. I looked around the dark room until I made out the table lamp on the nightstand and turned it on. I slipped on my wool socks, wrapped the green fleece blanket around my shoulders, and stepped into the hallway. For a moment, I considered eavesdropping on Mother, afraid that she'd hide who was calling at this hour and why, but by the time I reached the kitchen, she had hung up. I walked into the living room and found her slumped on the edge of the sofa, staring out the window.

"Come, Maryam," she whispered gently. "Did I wake you up?"

"No, I wasn't sleeping," I replied.

"Eldar called," she explained.

Nobody ever called us from back home unless it was an emergency. It was too expensive so all of our relatives, even Nana, had learned to write emails, which was how we communicated, through emails and messengers.

"Eldar the Elephant?" I asked.

I knew Mother and her cousin were close. Eldar was one of the most prominent soccer referees in the country, and quite a celebrity in her family. He traveled to different countries, attending tournaments, coming back with trinkets and fun stories to tell. Unfortunately, I was rarely present in these gatherings, so I mostly knew him from my mother's stories. She said he had a red mark on his forehead, like her, and had the same loud and contagious laughter like my grandfather.

Mother said that he called to simply chat with her, but she sensed an alarming tremor in his voice, as if he'd been keeping something from her.

"Perhaps, he just wanted to see how we're doing?" she asked me with a hopeful look in her eyes.

I nodded in response, unable to say anything else. However, I knew from the past that midnight calls usually meant bad news was on the way.

We found out about Eldar's death a few days later in a sad and unexpected way. Rufat read on a popular sports portal that a famous Azeri referee had passed away from a fast-spreading form of cancer. He hadn't really seen Eldar as much as I had, so he didn't recognize him in the photo in the article. But Mother's last name was unique, and he came into the living room after reading the article to check if she knew him.

"I thought he'd turn out to be a distant relative or something," Rufat explained to me later. "Man, I wish I had checked with you first."

"So that's why he called," Mother said, looking away, tears welling up in the corners of her eyes.

I got up from my chair and took a seat next to her. I wanted to hold her but sitting next to her was all I dared to do. She fell silent and looked outside the window. The street looked deserted. Leaves fell from swaying branches. Her eyes fell over the rows of cars parked on our street. She had that familiar absent look of grief, as she bit into her lips and rubbed her palms. This was all the emotion Mother would allow herself to show. Everything else she was to keep to herself. She got up from the couch and headed to the kitchen. For the next hour Mother poured herself into preparing halva, a rich buttery sweetmeat made of flour, sugar, and saffron, usually prepared during the forty-day mourning period according to Azeri tradition. I sat at the table but did not speak, hoping that my presence would ease the load of the news. When it was ready, she brewed a fresh pot of tea and poured it into tall crystal glasses. We ate halva and drank tea as she recounted a handful of stories about Eldar. There weren't many, but they always produced the same reaction—a mourning smile. After the tea cooled off and the halva was finished, the evening went as usual and Mother returned to her usual self, planning what she would cook throughout the week and busying herself with house chores.

I went back to my room. My mind kept drifting to what was going on at Eldar's house, to the mourning procession that must have taken place a few days ago, to the crowds of friends and relatives who flocked to Eldar's home, perhaps causing traffic, to all the food that was cooked and laid on the long tables covered with white tablecloths, to the loud *mullah* invited to recite passages from the Qur'an, to all the plates and pans that had to be rented for the funeral, to all the women of the family gathering in the kitchen to wash the dishes, brew fresh tea, and distribute decorated plates of halva through the rooms.

Mourning miles away from those who passed left you one-on-one with the grief. It attacked you unexpectedly. It lived alongside you, rearing its ugly head to sting you without warning and then lingered for days. Mourning away from your loved ones meant sorrow that never expired. You just learned how to live with it. It seemed as if by immigrating we silently accepted the loss of all of our relatives. We didn't lose them to death, but to the distance that severed the connection. Death only furthered the damage. You'd miss a person and then suddenly realize they were no longer there to miss. This way, you relived their death multiple times until you got used to the thought. And sometimes, you never got used to it.

Somewhere under the rubble, I still had feelings for Arash, but the damage was permanent, and we slowly drifted apart. The moment to open up and tell him what had happened had expired, and I was stuck with whatever became of me as a result of that decision. It felt safe to stay bitter and skeptical, accepting the kindness that life showed sometimes, but not expecting it anymore.

With time, acting normal got easier and I learned the painful spots in my consciousness that better remained untouched. I avoided them like you avoid rooms where unpleasant things have happened. There was no hand on my throat this time, no silent torturer, just a numb, hollow feeling somewhere in my gut. Arash made me a CD with Chopin's nocturnes and I made it a habit to walk along Lake Shore Drive with Chopin in my ears. I was glad to rediscover the pleasure of listening to music and watching the white of the seagulls across the blue of the lake. Cars sped by and Chicagoans still biked with their children bundled up, sitting comfortably on the back, despite the fierce December windchill. Arash never joined me on these walks, but he was present in the sound of the piano and in the gentle flicker of the evening lights.

I found myself thinking about him when I settled in the warm seat of the train, my body surrendering into the tiredness of an eight-hour day and a good two-hour walk on Lake Shore Drive. I remembered the trembling and the dampness of his hands when he spoke of things that mattered to him. I smiled at the thought of the two moles on his left cheek, right below his eye, the ones I'd touch with my fingertips and blush. When alone, I allowed myself to think of him freely, as you might think of a thing in the past, a thing that is beautiful and no longer possible.

Arash's obsession with my eyes and hands and everything else remained puzzling to me, but by now I fully grasped how deep the feeling ran in his veins. Whatever ran through my veins was muddied, with the imprint of pain and humiliation, with the absence of courage to face my fears, with the numbness that could only afford attending to my wounds, covering them with patches of pills or cigarettes. I would suffer from a strange feeling of disgust when I thought of how pure his feelings were. I wanted to tell him how broken I was, so that we could be broken together, so that he would help me untangle the dried-up bloody knots in my inflamed mind. Maybe if we cried together, I could let him in and maybe if I let him in, we could stand a chance. But I didn't, and the feeling rotted away day after day.

No matter how hard I tried, my heart remained empty and closed. In my solitude, I welcomed thoughts of him, but I could not find any affection to share with him. I felt like an ashtray, full of things that once were.

Arash gave up questioning me, but we still saw each other. We ended up in the same American Government class taught by a pedantic gray-haired Alexander Van Gaal, a former Capitol Hill aide who was now the mayor of Skokie. Once, chatting with him after class, I found out Van Gaal did Russian studies in grad school and belonged to the category of scholarly men who were infatuated with that subject. Even though I explained I was ethnically a Turk and spoke Russian only because we'd been a part of the Soviet Union for seventy years, he singled me out as a living, talking dissertation thesis, a sort of personification of Russia, a country that had swallowed up a good year of his grad-school life. He'd talk about the Cold War, the perestroika years, and mostly about the psychology of a Soviet man. I thought I didn't know much about these subjects. After all, I was only a child, not even a teenager, when the Soviet empire had crumbled. But a few minutes into the subject, I'd say something, and he would draw an eloquent, logical parallel tying it to some social theory.

"You see, it makes perfect sense why your father insisted you study in Azeri school, my dear," he'd say. "All of the fifteen republics had their language, culture, and music suppressed and altered to be in line with the Communist ideology. And when the bubble burst, all the patriotic feelings and identity surfaced again."

Van Gaal managed to add academic elegance and sophistication to what I always regarded as the routine of life back home. He carefully picked moments to use his scarce Russian and I could see a subtle, content smile on his face that signaled that he'd been awaiting this opportunity for years. Arash would patiently wait for us to finish our conversations, but I could tell that he was jealous not only of the time I spent with Van Gaal, but also of how much I enjoyed the company of this old, gray-haired man.

"Why do you like to spend time with Van Gaal?" he asked once. "I'm not jealous, I just want to know. You change into a different person almost. You appear excited. I don't know, you look as if you've been promised some kind of a gift."

I pondered on the answer for few moments, trying to dig deeper into my consciousness to put it all into the right words. His description was spot-on. The mere presence of Professor Van Gaal opened a window into some parallel reality populated by men and women with polished manners, eloquent language, and a taste for higher things in life. The part of me that admired all that was, apparently, still alive.

"There are things that are basic knowledge to me about the way I grew up, the way things were back then. To him, it's a period of history that he pored over, studied, and tried to understand. I, on the other hand, never tried to understand any of these things and, frankly, never thought I'd meet someone who would care about all this. He puts this basic knowledge into an interesting perspective, a new way to explain things. And I like it that he listens so carefully," I explained. "He is a good listener."

Arash smiled and nodded, and despite what he had said, I did see a trace of jealousy in the corners of that smile.

With time, I carved out a role for myself in these discussions. I would draw parallels between life back home and here, to demystify his often dry academic concepts by explaining the real reasons behind people's behavior. His theories were good and all, but sometimes he overlooked simpler explanations, and I'd show him things as they were in real life and not in his thick books on Russia.

I became a worthy partner in these discussions, someone who could offer a different view, and these exchanges got me hooked. The thought of being able to offer an opinion that is much simpler and crisper than his theoretical musings excited me. With time, I honed my skills of putting it all into words, sometimes trying to mimic his elegant way of speaking, using phrases I'd heard in his class or read in the books that Edward Beard brought for me. Soon he started speaking of "my future," as he put it, and that future seemed much brighter than I could ever have imagined it. In his vision, I was either a diplomat, a politician, or "someone who could build bridges across the oceans," Van Gaal would say, and suggest yet another book for me to read, or another play to attend. I read the books, even though I did not understand most of them, and attended the plays. Perhaps the future that he dreamed up for me was possible out there somewhere.

CHAPTER 46

THE ART OF NOT GIVING UP

The number of wrongs I committed at the office barely went down, but Dr. Shafaei still did not fire me. At first, I told myself that she pitied me, but I soon realized that it was something else. Farah rarely gave up on things, in general—goals, plans, or people. She didn't mind that it took forever. She patiently went through the same frustration with Amina, correcting her every mishap, showing her the right way of doing things, despite the absent expression on Amina's face. So, the fact that I still wasn't fired had more to do with her persistence than my progress. I'd come in the office twenty minutes early, print out the schedule, tape it on the wall in each of the rooms, and prepare patient charts for our morning huddle, while Amina brewed a fresh pot of Folgers coffee while mumbling under her nose.

It was precisely due to her direct and unsparing nature, her perfectionism that somehow comingled with genuine care, that I came to love Dr. Shafaei. No matter how rough she could be in her language throughout the day, she always ended it with a warm, forgiving smile, which meant that all was not lost for me and Amina. I'd watch her chat leisurely with her sisters and friends in Persian, amazed how the same person could be so feminine and appear so fragile, yet run her business with so much zeal and always be on guard. With time, I noticed that she also used rehearsed lines with the patients. The gap between her and her American patients in their pastel suits, Kate Spade bags, and coffee tumblers was smaller than mine, but it existed. Who knows—she, too, probably stood in front of them at some point, feeling foreign, lonely, and *unfit*. She had just mastered the game better than me and the gap had lessened thanks to her persistent character and the sheer magic of time. Maybe she was right, and I could do it too. Maybe I "had it in me," like she'd said.

Every day, I boarded the train and then the bus at exactly the same time, greeted the cheerful bus drivers in their dark blue CTA uniform, and proceeded to my seat at the very back. There, I'd sit next to a tall, gray-haired, beautiful woman with piercing blue eyes, dark cherry lipstick, and clothes that were always in pastel colors. She had a regal air about her, with her head slightly tilted up and her palms royally clasped on her lap. Her hair was cut into a perfect bob and while she maintained the tranquility of a queen, she managed to notice everything about everyone in the bus. I soon started nodding shyly in her direction to "say" hello. She welcomed my nod and was quick to strike up a conversation with me. That is when I realized that she was a patient of Dr. Shafaei and even remembered seeing me there on one of the Wednesdays.

I admired Anne Holland. I marveled at the depth of her confessions, the philosophical weight of her stories, the elegance and eloquence of her speech, and the royal air that filled the room whenever she spoke. I admired her choice of words, later trying to use them in my conversations with Van Gaal and blushing a couple of times when he chuckled and explained that I used a phrase in an incorrect way. The fact that I looked so different from Anne made me wonder: Did that silent strength, that eloquence and sophistication, come along with sharp angular features like Anne's, or was it something that could be refined through years? I found these thoughts silly and sporadic, but they'd visit me every time I saw her. Occasionally, we'd be joined by a tall Black security guard, Michael, who worked at a bank close by and whose schedule happened to coincide with ours.

This random comradery lightened up my mood and made mornings less stressful, for no matter what the day had in store, it would begin with me sipping a hot cup of Dunkin' Donuts coffee, talking to Michael about a recent baseball game (even though I knew nothing about it), and enjoying the wonderful company of Anne Holland.

One day, around this time, as I sat by the window in the large, warm auditorium of Oakton College, my thoughts were consumed by the delicate snowflakes that were weaving a blanket over the college grounds. It was February again. The trees swayed with a gentle wind, sometimes dropping a heap of snow on the ground as I sat behind a desk, propping my chin with my right hand. There were more than ten minutes left for the class to begin, so I let my daydreaming take me away from the snow, from the buzz of the incoming students, and from the worries of another day at the office. My mind never faltered when it chose a mental escape. I was back at our summer house in Mardakan, recreating the grape vines and the two ancient mulberry trees with their generous branches reaching the ground under the weight of berries. I thought of the chores that my grandparents made us do on a daily basis—pulling the weeds, raking the ground, watering the flowers, and picking figs, the tender and yellow ones, from the trees along the fences. The stillness of white snow against the heat of the classroom made me dreamy. I closed my eyes and savored the details of the place, like a painter savoring the startling beauty of a piece that he just finished.

Then, suddenly, I heard a clap, something light dropping onto my desk. I turned around, still half-asleep in my daydreaming, and noticed a thin paper pamphlet in front of me. I raised my eyes and saw Van Gaal looking at me with a curious grin.

"I nominated you for this program, Maryam," he said, taking off his round, rimless spectacles. "I think that it should be good for you. Read up on it and schedule an appointment at the mayor's office when you're ready. It's not far from here. I wrote the address on the back."

When I came out of my stupor and looked up, Van Gaal was already at the front, arranging his notes on the table and clearing his throat to silence the students. I picked up the glossy pamphlet and read it. It was an application to a semester-long program to intern in Washington, D.C., and take classes at Georgetown University. The pamphlet invited students to apply for the program but also mentioned that professors could nominate outstanding students in their classes. The front page had a group of participants dressed in suits and dresses standing against the backdrop of the U.S. Capitol with a huge American flag waving over the marble steps of the building. These students looked different from the ones at Oakton. Their eyes shone with a certain poise. They appeared so confident, like they were ready to take on the world's toughest challenges. Their bright heads were probably full of brilliant ideas, ambitions, and, surely, it would all work out for them. I hardly had the courage to face what was inside of mine—a dark hallway, full of rooms I avoided, shadows of a city lurking around, and nothing but a small wooden house in a seaside village to keep up the flickering flame of hope. I could never stand so erect. I would never be able to shine like that.

Still, I kept flipping through it, reading into the text, and giving into this dream, as Van Gaal slowly walked from right to left, covering the famous Watergate scandal. The program was only for one semester, but, somehow, I was convinced that if I moved, it would be for good. There would be no coming back. Still, I heard my inner voice loud and clear, there was no denying it. If it was possible, I would choose to go. However, was it possible to just go there and not worry about utilities and grocery bills, and focus only on reading textbooks, chatting with professors, and exploring what Van Gaal gracefully called the "political landscape of the United States"?

After the class, I approached Van Gaal and asked how, in his opinion, was this a realistic prospect for me? He looked at me with his clear blue eyes and his lips formed another smile that suggested that he knew something I didn't.

"My dear Maryam," he began, "why don't you take care of the application and let God take care of the rest? Do you think you're the first student in the United States who got accepted to a scholarship program without a penny? Besides, D.C. has the highest number of law firms per-capita." He paused. "I am confident I can pull some strings to get you a well-paid internship in one of them. You're one of my best students, Maryam. You are well-versed in English. You have a depth of knowledge in international politics. You are *the* kind of young lady these guys are looking for. If they don't take you, then I don't know what business they're in."

I feared that if I intervened with my pragmatic thoughts, the magic spell would be broken and Van Gaal, too, would recognize that it was a silly idea, so I instead nodded and promised to call the mayor's office for an appointment.

CHAPTER 47

A WHITER SHADE OF PAIN

I spent the coming weekends at Skokie Public Library, working on my application and gathering the rest of the documents. Finally, both my personal statement and the required recommendation letters from my professors were ready. I scheduled a meeting with Van Gaal in his office only to find out my personal statement was "too simple" and did not "emphasize my potential." Those were the words he used.

"Don't get me wrong, Maryam, it's good! But I need you to work on the items that I underlined."

"Professor, every sentence here is underlined," I objected.

"I may be old, but I am not blind. Now get on with it," he said and saw me out of his office.

And so I did. I went back to the library, annoyed with all his remarks and not entirely sure of what he meant by "potential." The more I worked on the statement, the more meaningless and pompous and pretentious it seemed. I soon realized I needed some other thing to fill time between studying and working on the application or

I would lose my mind. On my way home from the library, I stopped by a local arts and crafts store and picked up acrylic paints and a canvas to work on a painting for Arash. His birthday was coming up in a few weeks.

I worked on the painting each evening, pouring into it the feelings that I could no longer show, words that I could not utter. I ended up with an abstract flower with petals of irregular shapes. Every evening I drew silhouettes of men and women in each petal, deepened the shades and added more intricate details—musical instruments, figs and mulberries, scattered ornaments, and silhouettes of lovers. I was consumed by the painting for weeks, spending hours in my bedroom, working under candlelight, confessing it all to him in this strange, secret way. My most coveted feelings, dreams, hopes, and disappointments I poured into this painting. I knew well that this might be my last chance to leave a piece of my soul with him, with all its dreams and ruins. I finished it on the eve of his birthday, and just as I had sensed, with it came our final goodbye.

I told him I wanted to give him a present and asked if he could come to our house. It was a windy Saturday. Mother and Rufat went to pick up groceries with our neighbors and I stayed at home. He showed up in an hour, a false hope in his eyes. *This is going to be hard,* I thought.

"I made this for your birthday. I didn't want to tell you anything about it until it was done. I've never painted with acrylic paints. It was mostly watercolors for me in school, but they fade quickly and, besides, I wanted to try something new," I said. He smiled all the while I was talking, until I added, "I hope it reminds you of me."

The smile disappeared. He looked at the painting for a long time, and to my surprise, did not ask any questions. I was relieved.

"It's beautiful," he said and then added, "It's all in there, isn't it?"

I smiled. There was nothing else for me to add.

"That and some more," I answered. "Happy birthday."

"Thank you," he answered.

He put down the painting, leaning it against the wall, and approached me without a word. He wanted one last embrace, I read from his face, but the weight of his hands on my shoulders felt like an electric shock. Sensitivity to touch and awareness of other people's proximity to my body became a thing for me after the incident. I guarded the space around me as if my life depended on it. I was careful not to let any strangers brush shoulders with me on the train or lean on me on the bus. When Arash tried to hug me that morning, I jerked away, and he interpreted my reaction as a full-blown rejection. I had neither the composure nor the energy to explain anything, so I stood there like an accused person refusing to say anything in her own defense. Arash was deeply hurt, and I did nothing.

"I'm sorry," I mumbled.

He stepped away, raised his hands as if promising he wouldn't move any further, and sighed. Then he picked up the painting, turned around, and left without a word. I stepped outside into the February cold and watched him leave, my arms wrapped around my chest. I stood there for few minutes, hoping the cold would calm my racing heart, and it did. Then I walked back into the house and made tea only to watch it go cold on the coffee table. I wrapped myself in a shawl and curled up on my bed facing the window. My room was full of things that he'd gifted me—a wool sweater, a sketchbook with charcoal pencil, a turquoise thermos that came with its own cup, some shells he picked up at the beach.

I watched the swaying of branches on naked trees, like a pendulum of an ancient clock. *What will he do with the painting?* I wondered. Would he hide it in a closet and never take it out, or even worse, throw it away? Did he turn to it in my absence just like I found refuge in sweaters, coffee cups, pencil boxes, and seashells?

The pain was real, but it could not be spoken about. Leaving Arash was the only way to preserve the good feelings we'd had, so I did not have any regrets. I was slowly recovering, but some things were beyond repair. I might have had the energy to learn a new job, keep up with classes, and even make out some future for myself, but sharing affection was out of question. My love was mute, my soul was barren. Here in my solitude, in this room full of still objects, this love could survive, away from spoken words and blinding lights, so I held on to it by letting Arash go.

After that last meeting, I barely saw Arash. He still attended the classes with me at Oakton, but he'd sit away from me now. Our conversations were limited to greetings and some small talk about the tests. There was no bitterness in his voice, no reproach in his eyes, but he was careful not to cross the line again. His pride was hurt, and he would not step over it, not even for me. Still, he'd casually say something about a winter advisory, warning me to dress warm or stay in. He would ask if we'd heard anything from our lawyer, going an extra mile not to give away that he worried about it as much as we did. I answered all the questions, keeping my answers to a minimum, and would disappear as fast as I could. It was painful to sense that hint of defeat in his body language, a sign of rejection on his face. I struggled not to blame myself for it but failed. This, too, was my doing, like the mistake of a surgeon that could no longer be undone.

CHAPTER 48

NOT BEING ABLE
TO DREAM

"We've provided all the additional evidence that USCIS requested," our green-eyed lawyer said, rubbing her freckled nose with her long, manicured fingernails. "Now we wait and keep our fingers crossed."

"No way to speed up this waiting process, Irina? We've been here for almost two years now. We still don't have the official permit to work. We're all working for cash and having to ask friends for anything that involves papers. Isn't there anything you can do?" Mother asked.

"I hear you loud and clear, but I can't do anything. These things take time," she said. "Take this number and call them occasionally." She circled the USCIS 800 phone number and our case number on the receipt. "Your case number is on all of the receipts. You can enter it and check the status," she said. "Have a little patience. You've waited for so long, we're almost there."

She arranged our papers in a neat pile, put it inside the folder, and handed it back to Mother. We left her office in low spirits, preparing ourselves for the long wait, not excited at the prospect of calling an 800-number to hear the same message over and over. Nevertheless, Mother clipped the receipt with the circled number on the fridge and we took turns calling to check the status. We all had cell phones by then, and I estimate USCIS received at least one call a day about our case from one of us. The whole thing was handled by an automated system, so it's not like we sped anything up, but we kept calling to hear "Your case is being processed. Once a final decision has been made, you will receive a notification by mail." Soon Rufat learned the message by heart and would recite it, mimicking the voice and the intonation of the recording while it played. Mother laughed and we'd go on with our evening.

Another life, unknown yet desirable, was waiting for us on the other side of the phone when the automatic machine would utter the word "approved," and while we knew nothing about it, we dreamt of it. For each one of us, that message meant opportunities that would be fulfilled, plans that would materialize. Rufat would quit his busboy job at Zhivago and have the weekends back to himself again. Mother would stop counting cash on Fridays and could get a higher hourly wage, like all the other dental assistants who had papers. I could get reimbursed for the tuition that I paid out of pocket at college, and who knows, maybe get accepted to that Washington program on full scholarship.

In the meantime, I rewrote my personal statement almost entirely, fixing sentences Van Gaal underlined in the original copy, and after seven or eight reiterations, he finally said it was good. Now it was full of lofty phrases about my "rich cultural background," "multilingual abilities," "interest in foreign service and diplomacy," and desire to be "exposed to all that Washington had to offer." "My dream is to build bridges across the nations," he would dictate. I'd type it up obediently and think that, really, my dream was to once get through the day without making a mistake at the front desk. By the time my personal statement was finished, I hardly believed a word of it, but Van Gaal was finally satisfied and that was all that mattered. Besides nominating me and supervising the entire application process, he also set up several interviews with his friends from Washington who now lived in Chicago, so I could chat with them and learn from their experience. William Rozman, a Harvard law grad and a big-shot trial lawyer in Chicago, was one of them. He lived in Evanston, not far from Northwestern University, where he taught part time. William agreed to meet me at the Starbucks by the train station on a Saturday morning. He ordered black coffee and asked the barista to serve it in a ceramic mug since he was going to enjoy it on the terrace. I got my tall mint tea and mixed in some sugar. He spoke to me of Washington as if I were a native Chicagoan who was moving to the capital, comparing the opportunities that were simply not available in Chicago, even if you had all the prerequisites.

"You probably know, the law school here in Chicago is very good," he said. Of course, I had no clue. "But the city where you live determines half the opportunities. You simply don't have the Embassy Row here, the breadth of knowledge of all those diplomats who live and work in Washington. There, you never know if your next job opportunity waits for you somewhere on a train ride or at some free embassy event around the holidays. Plus, it's a beautiful, small, compact city, full of museums, theatres, shows, and free events. I was at Harvard Law, but we came down to Washington quite often. The advantage of the Northeast is that everything is close, you know? You hop on a train and you're in New York in a few hours."

I listened and said just enough to keep the conversation going, but not enough to give away that I lacked the background to understand most of the things he mentioned. I barely knew Chicago outside of Skokie and a few intersections in Park West, not nearly enough to compare it with D.C. Even though my lack of knowledge made these conversations a little awkward, I never turned them down and each one left me a little more optimistic about my future. I'd mention that I spoke four languages and these successful demigods who spoke in a polished, literary English raised their eyebrows. I'd go on to explain that the only language I truly learned was English, that, Azerbaijan being a former Soviet country, Russian was a native language for us and that we picked up Turkish to be able to watch cartoons and shows on the few Turkish channels that were broadcast in those early years of independence.

"Imagine it this way," I explained, "I had to know Russian to study at school. I had to know Azeri to speak to my grandparents. There were no more than two local channels back then, plus two Russian ones that were state controlled and boring. If you wanted to watch cartoons or shows, you had to watch Turkish television, so little by little, we picked it up. And then, of course, English was the lingua franca, so we learned that in school as a foreign language. You needed four languages to get through the day. Nobody just decided to become a polyglot and pick up four languages by age twelve. The number of languages was, in a way, proof of the twists and turns of history of our region, as our country was handed over from one empire to another, ending up as an independent state almost by accident."

It was pleasant to see that something I grew up with and regarded as a normal thing impressed such educated men and women. After four or five of these appointments I learned an important skill, something that Van Gaal called "holding yourself." I now felt comfortable with the fact that there would be gaps in my knowledge and that it was not shameful to ask questions. I practiced and learned how to introduce myself without telling a twenty-minute-long life story that sounded like a Mexican telenovela. I realized most people came from somewhere, and even though those last few days in Baku habitually rose in front of my eyes, I'd keep all that to myself and focus on other aspects of my biography—the languages, my education, my career interests, the books I read, and the classes I took. I "tailored things to the audience," and "kept it short and sweet," as Van Gaal put it.

I have to admit that this newly found confidence was rooted completely in things I heard from others. If stripped of the opinions, hopes, and well-wishes of Van Gaal and his colleagues, I did not think myself capable of moving to another city, away from Mother and Rufat. Nevertheless, the confidence that I borrowed from other men and women served as fuel, and with it, I carried on. *I think they're crazy, but what do I know?* I thought. *They must know what they're talking about.*

Mother was excited for me, but her joy was mixed with endless doubts. Her questions did not cease: How are we going to afford all this? Where would we find the money? Since I had no answers to these, I'd get mad at her for "not being able to dream." However, the truth was we didn't have money to cover even one-third of the tuition, and the prospect of landing a job in D.C. was only a possibility at this stage. None of these things were certain. I ploughed through these uncertainties hoping that in time things would work out on their own. Magically.

Slowly I got better at my job. I practiced *holding myself* and *tailoring things to the audience* with our patients and it was working. I'd spent enough time with our frequent patients to learn their backgrounds, tastes, and habits. Some enjoyed a nice long conversation about recent news, some liked to hear about what it was like on the other side of the world, and some wanted nothing but a glass of water and to be left alone. I finally read a few of the books that Edward Beard brought me and would spend some time chatting with him during his visits, after which he left beaming and came back with more books.

Amina came up with a way to remind me about the follow-up appointments, my number one most frequent screw-up. She took the entire thing upon herself. When the patient was done, she checked his chart to see when he needed to come back and did not leave my side until I scheduled it. That was a real lifesaver, and forgotten appointments, which lead to lost clients, were no longer an issue.

I did some research and figured out a way to submit claims electronically, which meant we'd get paid quicker and save on paper and ink. Dr. Shafaei was skeptical in the beginning, but soon the checks rolled in, and she was amazed that the whole thing worked. Occasionally, the program would break, and I would call customer support somewhere in India or bother an IT guy whom I'd met in the building, but eventually these issues would be sorted out. Soon, Dr. Shafaei came to rely on me. She'd leave the office with a smile on her face, allowing herself to relax and pay little attention to my insurance-related tasks. I insisted on reviewing the accounts receivable report with her on a monthly basis, and while she half-listened, I could see that she trusted me now.

"Can I go home, Maryam?" she'd ask from her office.

"Just sign these two papers and I'll take care of the rest," I'd respond.

I never thought the feeling of accomplishment could be so delicious. Once I got the hang of things at the office, life changed. On my train ride home, when I glanced at Chicago's beautiful skyline, I no longer felt squashed by its size. Quite the opposite—its grandeur and beauty sharpened my appetite to jump into a new battle, to try myself out in another jungle. I kept imagining Washington, D.C., with its government buildings, museums, art galleries, theatres, and diplomatic missions, its people filling up metro stations and buses, always reading the latest papers, and rushing to some important meeting. Maybe there was a place for me in that city.

CHAPTER 49

OF MONSTERS AND MEN

By the end of April, we were convinced that the harsh winds and snow of the winter had finally retreated and given way to a blossoming spring. Then one day the snowstorm was back in all its glory. Dr. Shafaei closed down the office and told us to get home before the blizzard paralyzed the city. When I made it back to Skokie, both Mother and Rufat were already home. We sat by the window in silence and marveled at the size of the snowflakes falling from the sky. It was our second winter in Chicago, but we still hadn't gotten used to the sight of so much snow and such low temperatures. Waiting for public transportation in a blizzard was no fun, but watching the show from the warmth of a heated apartment with a hot tea warming your fingers was another story. The deserted trees, the heaps of snow falling from the sky, the white ground that blurred with everything else looked like a fairy tale.

Mother went to make dinner and soon I heard the usual clanking and jingling of pots and silverware in the kitchen. That evening, the house smelled like a proper buttery Azeri pilaf infused with a generous portion of saffron. It brought back memories of my grandma's kitchen, the loud family parties that would take place in her crowded living room, the sound of the out-of-tune piano played by my father's cousin, and the myriad of voices that spoke over each other during the whole thing.

The contrast between the aroma of homemade Azeri pilaf and winter's last revolt against spring left me dreamy. I sat on my bed and looked outside, lost in thought, feeling both nostalgic and hopeful. The streets were empty. I imagined families that rushed home to avoid getting caught in the snowstorm. The mute serenity of falling snowflakes awakened long forgotten sentiments inside of me. If not for the sound of the television coming from the living room, I'd be convinced that my room was in the middle of some enchanted deserted forest, held hostage to snow. I imagined the crowded living rooms of our families back home, tables covered with too much food, delicious scents rising to the ceiling, grandparents and children playing checkers, chess, or perhaps backgammon while listening to some folk music on the radio. In those moments of daydreaming, I'd start doubting if coming to the United States was worth the sacrifices that we made and all the loved ones we left behind. Now that we were stripped of the simple pleasures of our imperfect yet close-knit family, they seemed so much more important than imaginary victories that lurked on the horizon. What was the use of a personal victory if you had no one to share it with?

I remained consumed by my dreamy nostalgia for life back home as the evening slowly turned into night. It was one of those rare nights when I took my time to prepare for the next day. I washed my face with the scrub that I convinced Mother to buy on one of our aimless wanderings in Walgreens, then patted it with a round cotton pad dipped in bluish, bitter-tasting liquid called "toner," and applied a bit of Mother's night cream. I felt enveloped by a strange contented feeling that one feels after pampering. Until now, the only "pampering" that I allowed myself was monthly trips to Natasha, an Indian salon on Devon Avenue, where a plump lady in a colorful sari with an absent look on her face would thread my eyebrows as I wept from pain. This, in contrast, truly felt like pampering. I changed into pink flannel pajamas, a present from Amina for Christmas, and hopped into bed.

All three of us were awakened at around two a.m. by a loud growl of machinery, similar to the prehistoric sounds of the garbage truck that would patrol our neighborhood on Thursday mornings. Only this was louder. We rushed to the living room, looked outside, and saw a large car with an oversized metal shovel attached to its front. Dmitry, the tall, grumpy husband of Barbara, our Bulgarian landlady, was in the front seat. At first, we could not understand what he was trying to accomplish, but soon we realized he was trying to clear out the snow from the front of the building, only it wasn't working. It wasn't working at all. He kept backing up and approaching the front again and again, but since the machine was not cooperating (or he simply didn't know how to operate the damn thing), he got frustrated and lost his cool, which was not hard since he was always a little mad. He decided to try one last time, so he backed out and approached the house again. Only this time, he must have pressed the gas pedal too far, and the car rammed into the front of our building with a roar. This scene was both frightening and hilarious at the same time.

"Hey Dmitry! Leave the building alone. We'll shovel it ourselves, eh!" screamed someone from the top floor.

Finally, Dmitry gave up and directed the machine away from the building. Some of the tenants peeked out of their windows to thank the guy from upstairs. All of the neighbors stayed by their windows until Dmitry left. Now that the spectacle was over, we could all go back to bed. *Good luck trying to sleep after this,* I thought. We were wide awake, but there was nothing else to do at this hour. Before I went back to my room, I dialed the USCIS 800 number, waited for the end of the disclaimer, and entered our case number. I yawned, prepared to hear the usual message and go back to bed, when I suddenly heard:

"Your case has been approved."

CHAPTER 50

ON THE EDGE OF WINTER

The hours after that fateful midnight call will stay etched in my memory as some of the happiest. Years have scrubbed the details of how we celebrated that night, yet from time to time I find myself recounting the story to someone just so I can relive that blissful feeling of victory that ignited the night. I clearly remember walking back to the living room, my cell phone in hand, both joy and confusion on my face. I recall Mother's clueless expression when I broke the news to her. At first, she thought it was a mistake, a glitch in the system.

"But I called recently," she said. "Rufat called yesterday. Let's call again!"

We called again and again, but the message did not change. We took turns listening to it. We danced and sang songs, unafraid of waking up the neighbors. Approval meant we would no longer be held hostage to our jobs and meager wages. It meant we were free to choose another job. We were free to put our first and last names on all official documents. We could apply for driver's licenses and buy a car. It meant we no longer had to hold our breath, praying that the documents we scrambled and produced for some application or other would be sufficient to grant the simplest of privileges.

After the first wave of euphoria was gone, we all fell silent for a bit, reminiscing about both happy and sad moments that we collected as souvenirs in those first two years in America, bathing in a sweet vindication for all the times when we had to bite our lip and live on. Yet there was no bitterness about the struggles that came as a package deal with immigration. We grew closer, got to know each other better, learned how to be patient, how to get up after a fall, and how to fight for things that we wanted. Here in the U.S., no matter how good or bad life got, we always knew that there was no one else to rely on except the three of us. That snowy night on the edge of dying winter brought our family our first common victory. And it felt incredibly good.

CHAPTER 51

. . . .

THE RETURN TO YOURSELF

I sat alone by the gate, waiting for the tall, slender brunette with dark red lipstick to begin the boarding of our flight to D.C. I had checked in a large suitcase with clothes and books that I decided to take with me and a photo album with whatever photos I found of our summer house. By now, looking at those pictures was a weekly ritual, a way to stay connected to my past, to remember the place where I'd felt the happiest, to hold on to its serenity and peace in turbulent times.

I wore a black cotton top with front pockets, faded jeans, and a leather belt. My backpack was heavy, filled with items I couldn't fit into my suitcase. I left it on a chair to make sure no one sat next to me. That habit had stuck with me for good. There were some wounds that never healed. I saw the plane that I was about to board from the window. It was much smaller than the Airbus that had brought us to America two years ago. In a week the internship program would begin.

I looked outside and thought of Mother. This morning when I was still packing, I caught a rare sight of her in my bedroom. She looked lost, unable to deal with the fact that I was leaving. Wrapped in her purple robe, she watched my rushed movements, bit her lower lip, and rubbed her palms. For once, she didn't say anything about the mess in my room, the clothes lying around everywhere, my notebooks, binders, and textbooks and several cups of unfinished tea on my desk. I noticed the sudden unpreparedness in her eyes, an unfamiliar anguish, as if she were hoping all of this was a joke and I'd be back before dinner. She tried to repack my suitcase, then suddenly offered me tea and food, and then walked in aimless circles around my crammed bedroom. She was afraid of letting me go. We hugged outside the security line, a long, silent, knowing hug. Somehow, we both knew I was leaving for more than a semester.

I held a yellow paper cup with coffee in my hands, feeling the last few drops of its warmth in my palms. My thoughts drifted to the day when I received the acceptance letter from The Fund for American Studies. It happened on a cloudy Monday morning as I was getting ready for work. I decided to check my email before heading out and saw a letter from Patty Gentry, the admissions officer at TFAS. She congratulated me on acceptance to the program and wrote that the fund would cover half of my tuition, which left me with five thousand dollars that had to be paid before classes began. A week after the email, when I was frantically searching for some magical solution and slowly losing hope, we finally received our green cards. They arrived in a plain white envelope just a week after our USCIS interview. We finally held the tiny green laminated cards in our hands and couldn't believe our fortune. The feeling of victory was intoxicating, but I still didn't know how I would finance the out-of-pocket portion of my tuition.

One afternoon, while I was chatting with Taney from the admissions office, I found out that the financial aid office at Oakton could reimburse me for a FAFSA scholarship for the whole year now that I was a lawful permanent resident. It turned out that the money that I needed was patiently waiting for me at the financial aid office. I remember staring at the light-green check with my first and last name carefully made out in pointy script next to an amount we considered a fortune at the time, and not believing my eyes. The lucky chain of events crowned me with a particular aura of youthful invincibility, a dumb luck that follows those who don't think of failure as an option not because it is not possible, but because they are too caught up in the romance of their success. Dr. Shafaei was quick to catch this vibe. I felt how excited she was for the prospect of education and a bright career in law for her "talented but unorganized" office manager. She even bought me the ticket to D.C. and threw me a farewell get-together at her house.

Along with the highs, there were some lows, too. Some days I would stare at my reflection in the train window, feeling unsure and hesitant, unprepared for life outside of what had become normal for me—a steady job, small community college, house chores, weekly meetings with Van Gaal, and the slow rhythm of life in the village of Skokie. In those moments, I'd close my eyes and envision a class full of students, charismatic professors, policy briefings by members of the House or Senate, the heated debates that would unfold in an apartment I'd share with others, late night studies, and cramming before exams. These images were both vivid and inspiring, yet with them came the realization that I was taking another step away from everything that was dear to me. I desperately wanted to be a part of these pictures, but my heart would tremble when I realized that I wouldn't wake up under the same roof with Mother and Rufat, wouldn't hear the annoying sound of that Russian radio, and wouldn't smell the welcoming aroma of Mother's Saturday breakfast. The world seemed too big and chaotic in those moments, and I felt unprepared to swim in it.

As I continued to sit by the window, I thought of that night in the Baku airport when friends and family came to say goodbye and wish us good luck on our journey. How things were different back then. How clueless and ecstatic we were about moving across the ocean, completely unaware of the rollercoaster ride that life in the U.S. had in store for us. It seemed as if that night still went on and on in some parallel reality filled with loud music, bittersweet tears, and tight embraces.

Unlike that evening, today I was left alone in this huge airport. No one here knew me or cared where I was going. I still missed Baku, but my memories were vague, like a pastel watercolor painting, lacking firm lines and bright colors. Strangely, it wasn't just Baku that I was going to miss. I carried nostalgia for both the city where I was born and raised, as well as this new city that I still hadn't fully explored. Now, from the window of O'Hare Airport, Chicago no longer looked foreign to me. No matter how painful, memories of Devon flooded my consciousness. I saw those colorful streets come alive in front of my eyes. I saw the heavy traffic during rush hour, the crowds of girls in saris accompanied by their mothers, the cheerful vendors of street food and owners of convenience stores lounging by the entrance of their tiny shops, playing backgammon or smoking hookah. The tall Georgian baker next door had probably just taken out the last batch of pastries and was dreamily looking outside, lost in his thoughts.

Mother and Rufat had probably made it back to our little apartment on Bronx Street, among the tall oak trees and bushes. The evening tea was brewing, and the television was on. The distant sound of Azeri rap could barely be heard from my brother's room. I tried to imagine Mother in her purple robe, wandering in the long hallway and entering my empty bedroom, where my clothes were still lying around my bed, some on the floor.

I closed my eyes and saw her. I tried hard to hold on to the image because I knew that it would eventually escape me. Here she is, sinking onto my bed and looking at the picture collage on the wall, realizing that she never really studied it in detail. Her gaze stops at a picture of me and her standing shoulder to shoulder in our kitchen on the day of our departure from Baku. She has a faint smile on her face. Her hair is shorter than usual and there is very little makeup on her face. At first, she notices how different we are. My body frame is athletic, while hers is petite and feminine. Her blonde hair shines, while mine is darker and straight. But there are similarities, too. We share the same round face, and the snub nose, the same pursed lips and arched eyebrows. I suddenly appear as a black-and-white reflection of her youth, just a bit taller, with wider shoulders and longer hair. She wonders how she never noticed how similar we are. She throws one last look at the bulky nightstand with my lamp, the unmade bed, and the boombox on the floor, and sighs. As the airplanes takes off, as it steals me forever, a bittersweet smile lights up her face.

AKNOWLEDGMENTS

Writing acknowledgments for a novel that took six years to complete is a tough task, but I'll give it a try. I'd like to start by thanking Betty Blair, whose fateful email sent on a fine December day made me do it. "Dear Mary," she wrote, "I think you are ready to write a book." There it was: permission to chase my dream granted. Thank you, Betty, for your faith in my writing and your love of literature.

I'd like to thank Kamran, my husband, who took care of our beautiful, rowdy boys on those Saturday afternoons when I retreated to Agora to finish another chapter. Thank you for being my first fan and critic. Without you, this book would have been a victim of my perfectionism, a mere Word file on an old laptop. Thank you for being there on the bad days when my doubts were stronger than my hopes.

I'd like to thank my grandmother, Saida, for teaching me that despite all the problems, this world is a beautiful place, and we're all lucky to be here. I love you, Nanulia. A big thanks goes to my brother Ray and his wife Ksenia and my big Azeri family for supporting me along the way.

A huge thank-you goes to the Greenleaf team—Sally Garland, Jen Glynn, Jared Dorsey, Ava Coibion, Amanda Hughes, David Endris, Scott James, Chelsea Richards, Valerie Howard, and

Kayleigh Lovvorn—for guiding me through this yearlong journey towards publication.

Lastly, I'd like to thank my friends who read the first drafts, sent me long voice messages with their feedback, and offered their input during the whole process—Murad Aliyev, Aysel Isayeva, Hanum Aziz, Aiten Cemal, Nazrin Guliyeva, Minai Massimova, Adila Canete, and Rebecca Wittrock. I am one lucky girl to know you.

ABOUT THE AUTHOR

MARY EFENDI was born in Baku, Azerbaijan, and moved to the United States in 2003. After almost two decades in the US, life took Mary back to Baku. When she is not reading fiction or drinking cortado in a coffee shop, she can be found painting on large canvases in her studio in Baku's Old City.